Kate Sawyer

THE STRANDING

CORONET

First published in Great Britain in 2021 by Coronet[new line]An Imprint of Hodder & Stoughton
An Hachette UK company

This paperback edition published in 2022

1

A CIP catalogue record for this title is available from the British Library

Paperback ISBN 978 1 529 34068 6
Trade Paperback ISBN 978 1 529 34067 9
eBook ISBN 978 1 529 34069 3

Typeset in Adobe Garamond by Hewer Text UK Ltd, Edinburgh
Printed and bound in Great Britain by Clays Ltd, Elocraf S.p.A.

Hodder & Stoughton policy is to use papers that are natural, renewable and recyclable products and made from wood grown in sustainable forests. The logging and manufacturing processes are expected to conform to the environmental regulations of the country of origin.

Hodder & Stoughton Ltd
Carmelite House
50 Victoria Embankment
London EC4Y 0DZ

www.hodder.co.uk

THE STRANDING

For Ruby

Prologue

'Tell me something you miss, from Before.'

'Toast.'

'Yes, bread. Fresh, crusty bread.'

They both lie quiet.

Remembering.

She can feel the water on her body, drying where it pooled in her navel.

Today there is no trace of saline coating her with fine white powder but she can still feel her skin tightening, puckering in the sun.

Her breathing is measured now, her heart returning to its habitual rhythm. The staccato beat and shuddering breath of their love is evaporating into the noises of the surrounding forest, just as the water they brought from the lake evaporates from the smooth rocks they lie on.

'Glitter.'

'Glitter?' He snorts.

She nudges him, her bare skin against his, and he turns his head, dipping his cheek, kissing her shoulder: a fleeting apology for a fleeting slight.

'Would you go back, though? If you could? You know, for the glitter.' His voice dances, navigating a difficult question by lacing it with levity.

It's a question she asks herself daily, to which she still has no answer.

'I think it'd depend on whether you could come with me.'

She slides her hand along the sliver of rock between them, searching out his. Their fingers easily entwine, their palms flat, one against the other. She feels a flush of heat course through her body, a heat that warms her from the inside, as the sun heats her from without.

Opening her eyes, she tips her chin back so she can see the trees behind them, their branches spread wide, splayed like a ribcage. The lungs of the world, she thinks, and closes her eyes once more.

Through the thin skin of her eyelids, the world seems pink, magenta, fuchsia, orange at the edges where the sun shines through.

She pulses his hand in hers, reminding them both: we're together, we're safe.

The warmth of the day and the physical exertion of the morning are taking their toll: she can feel sleep nibbling at her, consciousness ebbing.

She retraces their day. The walk through the forest. The cackle of the bird-calls from the trees above – some sounding like shouting human voices, jeering at them. Freedom as they plunged into the clear, deep water.

His hand encircling her wrist.

Her mouth against his skull, behind his ear.

Her thoughts swim, losing lucidity. Dreams pull at her, waves receding against sand.

A tail: wide, curved, black.

No, not black, teal. Teal flukes breaking water?

No, land. Hitting land.

Teal flukes slamming wet sand.

*   *   *

The sun is sinking now as the day pushes on. It is sliding down the sky, casting the shadow of the branches over her face.

She lets herself fall back into the freedom of her dreams just as the water of the lake had suspended her as she swam.

She is reading a book, lying on a blanket in the dappled light of an apple tree. She is hungry for new worlds. It's a novel she's never read before. The words swim on the page, but she can feel the potential of a new story in her hand.

She wiggles her bare feet against the wool of the blanket; it's itchy.

She laces her fingers into those of the hand she is holding against that scratchy wool. A hand that makes her feel safe.

A bright pink sky. Magenta, fuchsia, orange.

She is holding a baby, wet with new life.

She can hear the radio, a woman's voice, her mother's knife against the plastic cutting board.

Someone is calling her name.

Her daughter?

Mama?

A lilting voice calls to her from across the sand.

A small head tilted up to a giant skeleton that hangs above them.

A little hand pointing to a writhing form in the sea.

That teal colour again. The teal of deep water.

Singing.

Laughter.

Pouring more wine into a glass, a jealous cat looking on.

The light through the tree playing on the pages of the precious book.

She closes her eyes. Is it possible to dream of dreaming?

Her name again. His voice.

Time to go, it's getting late. A hand stroking her damp hair.

She turns the page of the book. Let the calling voices go unanswered. She'll delay just long enough to finish this chapter.

A rush of air, a groan so forlorn it hurts her heart.

A noise that cannot be unheard.

A white frame above her, a spine, the ribs splayed wide, the jaws like pincers, brackets.

The bones of the whale glow slightly in the dark.

She closes her eyes. My old friend, she thinks, my home, my sanctuary.

'Thank you.'

One

Among the masses of driftwood, the creature lies sprawled on black-flecked sand.

From far away, it had looked like a giant slug, bloated on the shore, but now, nearing it, Ruth can see it is a mammal. A warm-blooded, air-breathing mammal with a belly button, just like her.

The size is overwhelming, too much for her exhausted brain to take in, her eyes too. For a second she wonders if she might be hallucinating but, no, there is the smell – she can almost taste it.

She has come so far to be here, to see this animal. It is a moment she has envisaged ever since she was a little girl, but it was never like this, never in these circumstances.

It is so big that as she gets closer – her muscles aching, her breathing ragged – she realises her eyes are tracking back and forth, past the elegant fin splayed among the trailing seaweed, from muzzle to flukes and back again, just to take in the whole animal.

'As big as at least two double-decker buses.'

How many times has she read that?

The skin is not blue, as she'd always imagined, but black. It's not a glossy black like hot tar, but a deep green-blue black, teal almost.

Like the hallway tiles in Fran's flat, she thinks.

The hide of the animal looks like cracked, varnished wood. Like an old piano. A giant grand piano from the ballroom of a wrecked ocean liner, washed up on the shore. The long white underside of its belly is ridged, like bricks of pale plasticine. The shell-like white, beige, cream skin is flecked with grey, black, coral-orange markings. Around its mouth and eyes the same orange spreads like rust: clumsy make-up that has smudged in the water.

Ruth feels a pulse of awareness: she is being watched.

She notices now that the creature's eye is open. Lashless yet, somehow familiar, the black pupil, surrounded by a ring of colour, a white-yellow edging.

So human.

It seems to be watching, seeing.

She wants to kneel and place her hands on it in . . . in what? Reverence? Devotion? Worship? The urge to lay her hands on it is irresistible.

She is struggling to catch her breath, her chest heaving. Her muscles are screaming – lactic-acid accumulation stiffening them – her foot turns slightly in the sand and pain shoots through her ankle: she can feel where she fell earlier. Her throat is burning, raw, her mouth dry, her thirst intense: she has not drunk enough water for days.

Ruth unclips her bags and lets them drop onto the sand heavily next to the creature.

She has never seen anything more beautiful.

Next to where the creek pushes its way out of the rushes towards the sea, a truck is parked on the sand. The pink sky looming over the ocean is reflected in the windscreen, obscuring the occupant.

Nik turns off the radio and sits, watching the woman through the pink-tinted glass.

Where she let the giant rucksack slide from her back, the skin on each shoulder is peeling: too much time exposed to the sun.

He leans forward against the steering wheel, watching as she bends and riffles through her bags, strewing items on the sand. She pulls out a container, a plastic box: the type you'd pack sarnies in, with the clip-on lid. He watches as she pulls off the lid and discards it, then tips out the contents and takes off towards the sea at a run.

She makes it to the water quickly.

Her legs must be long, though her height is impossible to gauge – next to the whale, everything looks small.

Where has she run here from?

Her clothes are visibly damp with sweat, her hair, with its inconsistent gold flecks, looks wet. It is pulled to the crown of her head, several tendrils making their escape and sticking to her forehead and neck with perspiration.

He watches her bend her knees with difficulty at the water's edge, dipping the container into the surf, filling it. He grasps what she is doing: attempting to ferry water to the beast that lies on its flank so unusually far inland. Definitely not a pro, then.

Only an animal lover, a tourist, witnessing an ending.

He watches as she runs back to the beast, salt-water sloshing from the tiny container as she moves. Then, when she is level with the animal's eye, she raises her arm to throw the water at it. He notes, with surprise, another patch of hair, like that on her head, beneath it.

One of those women.

He raises his eyebrows, looks at the increasingly pink sky and, inhaling deeply, gets out of the ute.

Ruth stops in her tracks, her back to the sea, as she registers the man. 'Please! Help me!'

She runs again to the sea and fills the plastic box. It is too small for the job: maybe he has something more useful in the back of his truck.

A pain slices through her abdominals as she turns to run back towards the whale.

Throwing the contents over its drying flank, she stops, her breath laboured, and places her hand reassuringly on the rough skin next to the whale's eye. She whispers to it. 'Hold on.'

She raises her head to look at the man. He is leaning against the truck, his arms folded. 'Don't just stand there. Help. Have you got something to carry water?'

He is squinting, as if he can't understand what she is saying.

She shakes her head, then, staggering slightly, heads back to the shore to fill her makeshift bucket, running to return to the whale.

Nik leans back against the bonnet of the ute, his head cocked watching her run towards the water. He eases himself to standing and moves towards where she has strewn her belongings, watching her trying to balance the tiny pot of briny water between both hands but spilling it everywhere.

Behind her the sky burns pink, reminding him that any exchange he makes with this woman is completely pointless. So utterly, painfully pointless. 'It's no good, eh?'

She snaps round to face him. They stand eye to eye – not something he's used to, particularly from a woman. So she's tall. Tall and angry.

'Well? Have you got a bucket?'

An accent. He hadn't heard that before.

'Have you come here to help me? Or not?'

A Pom? Great.

The woman's breath is warm in his face. It smells slightly stale: it is some time since she last ate.

'Have you seen the news?' he asks gently, as if approaching an angry cat.

8

She looks at him, jutting her chin, but she doesn't answer his question.

'You're British, aren't you?' He sees a flicker of something cross her face. 'I'm sorry,' he says.

Struggling for breath, she turns again and jogs towards the sea.

He looks down at her possessions lying on the sand, around him. A small backpack, a net of oranges spilling out of it; the contents of a first-aid kit strewn where she upturned the box she is dipping into the surf. There is a large rucksack too, the straps straining, stuffed full to bursting. Things hang from straps: a metal water canteen, a torch. A tent is strapped to one side, a bundled sleeping bag to the other, a towel, wrapped in a plastic bag, tied beneath it.

'You travelling on your own?'

Ruth's head flicks round to assess him, this stranger. She matches him in height and, she doesn't doubt, speed, but he is considerably wider than her, likely much stronger.

'Yes.' She pauses to catch her breath, feeling as if her lungs are on fire.

There is a movement in the whale, a full-body muscular heaving as it struggles to pull its flukes into the air. Then, with a crash, it slams them down against the wet sand. It is an almighty slap, like a crack of lightning. The motion sends sand particles flying high into the air and is accompanied by a heaving sigh.

It hurts her heart to hear it.

'Oh, no!' Ruth's voice has a high-pitched edge, a betrayal of her panic. She can hear it herself. She looks to the man, imploring him for instruction. 'What do we do?'

*   *   *

Nik meets her gaze more softly now. 'There's not much we can do.'

He notices her eyes are slightly swollen. The rims where her long eyelashes sprout and curve outwards, then back towards her skin, are rubbed raw – they look tender.

'I wish we could do something, believe me. All we can do is wait, be with it.'

She is still staring at him fiercely.

It's as if he can feel the grief radiating from her – it's almost too much to bear.

He looks down at his feet. Slowly he draws a figure of eight with the toe of his boot in the sand. How can he possibly find the right words? Better to say something and get it wrong than not do anything at all. 'I am sorry for your loss.'

She will not cry – there isn't time for crying. Biting her lip Ruth lowers her eyes, then closes them and inhales slowly, her nostrils flaring slightly. 'I don't need your sympathy. I need your help.'

The man smiles. It's a half-smile, really: his lips are crooked. It looks almost as if he can't be bothered, like he tried to smile, but gave up halfway. 'Even if we both had big ol' buckets, nah, even if we had a big ol' boat – five boats – it wouldn't make any difference. What's coming is coming.'

Ruth feels her legs softening beneath her and she sits with a thud on the sand. 'Why is this happening? It's so . . . unfair.'

In echo of her tone, the whale emits a groan. A high-pitched but hollow creak, like the sound of a boat's hull as it scrapes upon a rock. A gentle but certain death rattle.

'No.'

Ruth leaps to the side of the whale, crouching beside its visible eye. 'Stay with me, please. Please don't leave me.'

The whale makes a final halting exhalation. Air escapes through its blowhole in a rush, like a boiling kettle. Its eye, only marginally smaller than Ruth's head, stills. Like a blind being drawn across a window against the summer sun, the life disappears.

Ruth watches, holding her breath, then falls to her knees, her forehead against the whale's desiccated skin.

Two

The bar has become crowded since Ruth first found her seat. She looks towards the door, but it is obscured by baying City traders dressed in shades of grey. A suited young man, his tie askew, has his buttocks against her left arm causing the right to touch the damp brickwork beside her. She leans into him lightly to give herself more space and angles her book so it catches the minimal light, allowing her to read on.

Someone grasps the back of the chair on the opposite side of the table.

'Sorry, waiting for my boyfriend.' Only a slight stretch of the truth. Not her boyfriend, as much as she would like to be able to use that term. Her lover, perhaps. I'm waiting for my lover? No, awful.

Ruth smiles politely at the girl, who throws her a tight smile in return and totters into the throng of bodies, vainly hoping to find a chair that will take the burn out of the balls of her feet.

Ruth lifts her wine and takes a sip. She went for a glass, hoping that Alex would choose something by the bottle that she wouldn't have considered, something that tastes like 'licking a stone' or 'eating a peach' or 'smelling a newly tilled field'. Her discovery of wine is somehow inextricably linked with her physical longing for him.

Ruth sees him now, moving through the sea of grey and charcoal, his curls flattened where his cycle helmet has depressed them. He is looking for her, slight concern in his brow. He rubs his palm against his chest as he cranes his neck to seek her out. She loves the few seconds before he sees her: she can observe him, remember his face, let herself savour her body's response to his presence.

'Alex.' She calls to him, rising slightly from her chair and articulating the fingers of her right hand into a greeting.

He sees her and his face brightens. She sits back and watches him push through the crowd, beaming.

'What a palaver!' Alex collapses into the seat opposite her. He turns his wrist to look at his watch. 'I'm so sorry, my darling, couldn't get away.' He picks up Ruth's glass and takes a generous gulp, humming approval. 'Nice. Soave?'

She nods, watching him pull up his beige jumper to reveal a grey T-shirt. It is slightly damp beneath each arm and she takes in a breath of him as he struggles with it over his head. He smells of washing powder, clean and warm. 'I just got a glass. I wasn't sure if you'd want to stay.'

He pulls the menu across the table towards him and starts leafing, studying the options as he speaks. 'A bottle here, then back to yours? I can't be late-late, but I don't need to hurry. She's well ensconced with her sister.'

Ruth looks over her shoulder. She can't quite get used to being out in public, just a mile or so from his wife and sleeping children.

When they first started seeing each other it was all in absolute secrecy. A chance meeting in the street, an urgently locked toilet at a party, a luxuriously leisurely hotel room, her hurriedly tidied flat, a restaurant where they were surrounded by foreign voices. But recently they have allowed themselves the danger of meeting in public locally, aware they could always write it off as a chance meeting.

Some mornings she wakes up appalled at the adolescence of it, the grubbiness of sneaking around, but she wasn't so stupefied by lust that she didn't know that was also a part of the thrill. She hadn't told anyone. It was so unlike her. Even the people to whom she would ordinarily tell the most sordid details of her love life were in the dark. She felt protective of what she and Alex had. She didn't want the usual eye-rolls and seemingly benign little digs, didn't want his faults pointed out to her, even if it was 'for your own good', and she really didn't want anyone getting up on their high horse about his marital status. She wanted to preserve the enchantment of their attraction. Outside judgement would ruin everything.

'I haven't got anything in for dinner.'

He nods decisively. 'A bottle, then back to yours. I don't want you for your cooking.'

Later, they will lie together in her bed until the last moment possible and he will pop into a local supermarket on his cycle home, the factory-made sandwich a poor understudy for the three-course meal his wife will believe him to have enjoyed with 'a visiting Norwegian'.

'Where are you supposed to be tonight?'

'Does it matter? I'm here. Let's talk about you, far more interesting.'

He places the menu on the table and, without breaking eye contact with her, raises his hand to attract the waitress's attention. He orders an orange wine. 'Not made of oranges, but so-called because of the hue. See?' He holds his glass above the candle, letting the light permeate the amber liquid. 'It's from the oxidation of the grape juice as it ferments on the skins.'

She is not immediately impressed by it. It is both sweet and tart and has a slight effervescence on her tongue that reminds

15

her of fruit salad that has been sitting in its bloated plastic packaging for too long. But as he talks, asks her about her work, laughs as she tells him about her train journey earlier that day – an elderly couple had opted to share her table in an otherwise empty carriage and her resolute pig-headedness had prevented her moving, even though her right leg cramped an hour into the journey – she realises that the strange fermented juice is working on her affections and her sobriety.

He doesn't kiss her until they and his bike are in the back of a black cab, heading south for her flat in Deptford. Every time they kiss there are three distinct phases for Ruth: disbelief (Why would this *man*, want to kiss a *girl* like her?), growing disorientation (Is that her hand or his? Are they in a car? What year is it?) and, finally, pure animal desire. She has rarely let herself get so lost in feeling before him. She doesn't care who sees or what the ramifications may be. All she wants is him, as soon as she can, as violently as she can. She is surprised by the force of the feeling, every time they meet, every time his lips first touch hers.

Back at hers, he sits on the edge of her bed pulling his T-shirt over his head. She lies back, sated, the damp sheet coiled between her legs.

'When will I see you next?' She traces her finger along the edge of his belted jeans, where his elasticated boxers show.

He sighs and lies down on the pillow next to her, his hand on her cheek, taking in every part of her face. 'I'm going to leave Sara,' he states matter-of-factly. 'It's no good for anyone. I have to leave her.'

He's never said this before. Ruth is motionless, holding her breath, careful not to disturb the air that lies so still between them.

'Will you have me?' he asks her.

She weaves her fingers among the curls on the crown of his head, bringing her face to the side of his, and softly bites the top of his left ear, then moves her lips slightly lower. 'Yes,' she whispers into his ear. 'Yes.'

Three

Ruth sits with her back against the whale. She is bone-tired. When she closes her eyes, she can feel her body sliding into sleep, but then – a pulse – she remembers: it's unlikely she'll ever sleep again.

How sad. She has always loved sleep.

She opens her eyes and is immediately aware of the man, his boots in the sand close to her feet. She had forgotten he was there. She looks up at him, her eyes still stinging with tears.

He is tall, broad, with wide cheekbones and a shaved head. She can see tattoos creeping across his chest and arms, just visible at the edges of his T-shirt.

Nik looks down at the woman, the pile of limbs heaped on the sand before him. Her upper lip is wet with mucus. She wipes at it with the hem of her vest, revealing a soft, curving stomach. There is a mark in her belly button where once there was a piercing.

He averts his gaze, stepping beyond her and towards the whale, and places his hands on its skin. It feels warm under his palm, the last vestiges of life still present. It makes him feel sad.

'It's been days, you know.' Nik takes his hand off the whale and wipes it on his jeans. 'Not a nice way to go. They're designed to be in water.'

'I just wanted to try and do something.' She sighs. 'I feel so helpless.'

'Everyone does.'

Ruth feels a surge of anger. 'How was this allowed to happen? Why weren't more people helping? I thought everyone here loved whales. I thought they were supposed to be sacred!'

The man snorts, a sound that could almost pass as laughter if his face wasn't set as it is.

'Ah, yeah? Nah, yeah, guess folks were watching the news, had a quick check-in with the ancestors and decided the impending apocalypse was the priority.'

She feels her cheeks warm with embarrassment. She's offended him. 'I'm sorry.' She looks him squarely in the eyes.

He nods and breaks eye contact. 'How long you been in New Zealand?'

'Boxing Day.'

'Ah.' He rubs a hand over his shorn head. 'I'm sorry.'

Ruth looks up at the man. He isn't much older than her, early forties at a push. He seems tired too, and sad. 'What does the news say? You mentioned the news.'

'Just a matter of time they reckon.'

Nik takes a seat on the sand next to the girl. He can smell her sweat over the scent of the whale. It's not unpleasant.

He takes out a pouch of tobacco, removes some papers and a shrivelled bud of marijuana, then starts to roll a joint. 'Don't mind, d'you?' He raises the pouch towards her.

'Knock yourself out.' She smiles. She hasn't done that before. It suits her. 'In fact, feel free to hand it this way and knock me out too. What the hell? Might as well go out high.'

Nik rolls carefully, making a T with two skins and an impro-vised filter, rolled from the side of the cardboard packet.

They sit in silence, watching the sky grow pinker and pinker.

She gestures to the reddening sky. 'It'd be beautiful, if it wasn't, you know, The End.'

He lights the joint. 'Fuckin' weird.'

'Very.'

He offers her the joint and she takes it from between his fingers. She draws on it hard, holds it, then exhales.

'In England there's this saying: "Red sky at night, shepherd's delight."' She starts to giggle.

Nik takes the joint from her. 'Well, at least the fuckin' shepherds are happy.'

Her giggles turn to throaty laughter and, before he knows it, Nik is laughing too.

Ruth's muscles have relaxed; her grief feels less present. For the last few days she has worn her pain like a mantle. The joint has lifted it slightly: she feels the pull of gravity on her bones marginally less.

Her energy no longer concentrated on keeping hopelessness at bay, she can allow herself a flirtation with curiosity. 'You don't want to be with your family?'

Nik runs his hand over the stubble on his head and blows smoke in a direct stream through his pursed lips. 'Haven't got much family left. Not alone in that, though, am I?'

'No.'

He hands her the last of the spliff, but she declines. They sit, listening to the waves.

'I'm Nik, by the way.'

'Ruth.'

She looks up at the great mound of the whale next to them. It's like a huge rock, as if it had grown out of the beach, through the sand as the plates of the planet realigned in some earthquake long ago. Or like a meteor, one of many that rained to earth as dinosaurs ran for cover, embedded in the sand from its fall.

'Do you think the whale knew she was going to die?'

'Who knows, eh?'

Nik buries the end of the joint in the sand and peers at the sky. 'Are you scared?'

'Of course. Aren't you?'

'I think I'm in denial, it feels so surreal. Thought people would come to the whale too. That's why I'm here, photos. Tryna drum up a bit of freelance stuff. No one coming, that's what's brought it home. This is it. Thought it was gonna be just me and the whale.'

'And now you're stuck with me, too.'

'Yeah, looks that way.'

He makes a series of short snorts through his nostrils: he's giggling again.

'What?'

'Just thinking about you running back and forth with that little Tupperware, sloshing water all over the place. Don't know why I talked to you – anyone else would've gapped it.'

Ruth covers her face with her hands and groans. If someone had told her it would be possible to feel silly in these circumstances she'd have laughed in their face, but there is no escaping it: she is embarrassed.

'Nah, you're right. I get it. Just looked pretty funny, that's all.'

Nik stands and places his hand on the animal's skin. 'Still warm.'

He steps around Ruth to the head of the whale. Gently, with both of his hands he slides the lid of the animal's eye closed. 'Majestic beast.'

'Bigger than two double-decker buses.'

Nik turns and walks towards his truck. He opens the door and reaches in to grab something. When he slams the door, she sees he has slung a camera around his neck. He brings it up to his face and points it directly at Ruth. She can feel his gaze on her as he focuses it. Her stomach clenches, though she knows it is almost impossible that the photo will ever be seen. Her cheeks burn as she hears the click of the shutter. 'Are you taking a picture of me?'

Nik lowers the camera, so she can see his eyes.

'I am. You and the whale. It's . . .'

He has never been able to articulate why he takes the photos he does. He just knows he needs to. He doesn't 'see' something. He can feel it. It is something about the quality of the air, the conversation, the light. He can be doing anything, even something mundane, and he will reach for his camera. That instinct has been the basis of his entire career.

Nik walks across the sand to Ruth and crouches to show her the viewing screen of his DSLR. 'See?'

She blinks, focusing her tired eyes on the screen.

He has framed it so that only the whale's head is visible. The whole image is bathed in pink light. She is where she is now, next to the whale's giant fin, staring directly into the camera. She looks exhausted but, though she is surprised to admit it, interesting.

The picture is beautiful.

'You're good.'

'I do okay.'

He brings the camera up to his face again. The shutter clicks as it closes, capturing her face in close-up. He stands and walks to the front of the whale, the shutter rhythmically clicking as he documents it, then turns to photograph the darkening sky.

Ruth realises she is shivering. Now the sun has almost gone, it is chilly. She stands, acknowledging the ache in her back and her legs from the exertion of the day. The skin on her shoulders is tight and burns hot despite her chilled limbs. She takes a thin jumper from the top of her backpack and pulls it on. As her head emerges, she sees that Nik has the camera trained on her once more and raises her hands to shield her face.

'Sorry, you've got an interesting face.' He lowers the camera.

'I've got a tired face.'

He sits down heavily on the sand beside her as she repacks her bag.

'That's why it's interesting. Will you sleep?'

'I don't think so – you?'

'Nah, wouldn't mind another smoke, though. Join me?'

She smiles at him and he pulls the pouch from his pocket. He sits cross-legged, looking at the whale, the sea to their right.

He freezes as he feels her skin on his shoulder.

She leans on him, groaning softly as she finds her way to the ground. 'My legs ache, from running.'

He can feel the imprint of her cold hand on his shoulder for the entire time it takes to make the joint.

Four

Ruth's hands are sweating into her gloves from the exertion of dragging her bag up the hill. She spots Fran ahead, leaning against her car bonnet. Her head is bowed, too concentrated on her phone to notice Ruth's approach, despite the rattle of the suitcase wheels on the uneven pavement. Ruth watches as she tilts her head in appraisal then, with either a pout or a grimace, swipes in one direction or the other. Her arms are bare, the T-shirt sleeves rolled up at the shoulder.

'Put a coat on, you madwoman!'

The winter air carries Ruth's voice clearly. Fran looks up from her phone and pushes her sunglasses onto her head.

'You're the madwoman. I've only had three hours' sleep.'

Ruth laughs and lugs her suitcase the final six metres. 'Good party, then?' She comes to a standstill alongside the convertible.

'Mate. No idea!'

They indulge in a brief hug to greet one another. Ruth detects a distinct whiff of stale alcohol beneath the layers of toothpaste and perfume, a heavy scent that she can never smell without looking around, expecting to see Fran.

Fran inspects Ruth's luggage. 'I see you're travelling light.' She heaves the bag into the boot. 'What's in here? Your ex-boyfriend?'

For the last few years, the journey home has been as much of an event as Christmas itself.

They have a playlist to which they both contribute – Mariah Carey, Chris Rea, Eartha Kitt – and they are singing along by the time they merge onto the A406. When they hit the M11, the stereo has been turned down and they are in deep debate about Ruth's inclusion of The Pogues.

'Really? I can't keep up.'

'Do better!'

Fran winks at her and sips the coffee Ruth bought her at the services.

Ruth has been questioning her judgement on getting into this car for the last twenty miles: Fran barely has her hands on the wheel, drinking coffee with one hand and gesticulating with the other. She is trying to keep her friend's attention on the heavy goods vehicles she is weaving the small car around at speed, but Fran is intent on sharing the horrors of the previous evening.

'The sit-down bit was particularly excruciating. They mixed departments, so I didn't know anyone at the table. The girl next to me kept her eyes closed as she talked. So annoying.'

'There's a bloke at work who laughs when he talks. I'm like "All right, Ben?" and he's like "Ha, yes, ha, I'm, ha, good, ha, ha." He'd drive you nuts.'

'I bet he wears pastel shirts and does rock-climbing.'

Ruth doesn't answer but smiles, keeping her eyes on the road, hoping Fran will follow suit.

'You fancy him!' Fran inspects Ruth over the rim of her sunglasses.

'No, I'm still giving all that a rest.'

Ruth knows the time is approaching when she's going to have to tell Fran about her relationship with Alex. The growing myth of a now six-month period of self-imposed celibacy is feeling increasingly unwieldy. Since their early teens, Fran has told her it isn't a requirement to go from one partner directly to another, but Ruth has historically secured the next object of her affections before disposing of the current one. She sees now that the hastily blurted lie was subconsciously designed to gain Fran's approval. It would have been far more convincing to tell Fran about every date but pretend each was with a different guy. The wholesale man-drought she'd invented was the biggest stress of the whole affair. Why was she so bad at lying? Everyone knows the best lies are when you stick to the truth, changing only a few minor plot points to hide your wrong doing.

Ruth looks to her right to see Fran scrutinising her.

'Really?'

Her stomach flips. 'Road!'

Her heart thumps and blood rushes to her cheeks as Fran rights the car. Yes, she would like to avoid being a pre-Christmas travel statistic, but the true cause of the spike in her adrenalin is nothing other than her having avoided yet another opportunity to tell her best friend about Alex.

Why is she so scared to say it? *I've met someone and this time it's different.*

After the speed of the motorway, back on an A-road, the buildings around them grow denser as they approach the town of their childhood. It is late afternoon and the wide grey skies of East Anglia are darkening, the orange lights at the roadside flicking on. The signposts are populated with the names of familiar places.

Ruth and Fran make plans to meet at one of their old haunts tomorrow, on Christmas Eve-eve: the tradition of drinking an anaesthetising bottle of wine each in preparation for three days with no escape from their families.

'Anne and Jim on good form?' Fran guides the car to the side of the road outside Ruth's parents' festively decorated Georgian house.

'Come in and ask them yourself.'

'Ha! I've got my own parents to deal with. And the brothers and all the screaming offspring.'

'You love those kids.'

'And the sisters-in-law.' Fran cringes.

'Sweet-sweet small talk.'

'Next year I'm spending Christmas at home, in London. You'll have to find another mug to drive you.'

'Sure.'

'I mean it. We're getting too old for this nonsense. Say hi from me, okay?'

As Ruth waves to the tail lights receding into the dark, she promises herself that she will tell Fran when they meet tomorrow. By then she'll have had practice.

She looks up at the house and smiles broadly as the door is flung open to reveal her mum, red reindeer pinny covered with flour.

Although she's lived in her London flat for the best part of ten years now, Ruth has never managed to replicate the atmosphere of 'home' that exists at her parents'. For some reason her lounge always feels a bit cold, as if it's been staged for a photo shoot. She's tried adding rugs, more cushions, putting up art. But it just feels a bit empty. She's wondered if it was the smell, and purchased a candle in black glass to emulate the effect of an open fire, but discovered she could never quite match the lived-in scent of her parents'.

She drops her bags at the bottom of the stairs and breathes it in.

Her dad is at the kitchen table, his glasses lit blue from the tablet he's scrolling on. 'She's home! How was the traffic, kid?' He doesn't rise but turns off the screen and sets it on the table. He removes his reading glasses and leans back in the chair.

'Pretty busy.'

'The Annual Exodus,' Jim pronounces. 'Now, girls, tea or G and T?'

Her mum has repainted the walls of her childhood bedroom a tasteful mustard yellow since she was last at home. It covers the Blu-tack stains of the posters she carefully arranged when she still lived here, images of young men in checked shirts and some with no shirt at all bearing down on her as she lay in her bed at night. Only one of her posters from her childhood remains, a giant anatomical drawing of a blue whale, an animal Ruth was obsessed with as a child. She had spent hours poring over books about the creatures, reeling off facts about them to her parents at every mealtime. Did they know a whale's plunge into the sea was called a 'sounding'? Did they know that whale oil was what first burnt in the lamps of shops to allow for opening beyond daylight hours? Did they know that whale blubber was used to make bombs in the First World War? Did they know that lipstick was made of whale fat? Margarine too?

She had made herself unpopular at school for her relentless circulation of petitions and requests for sponsorship to stop whaling. Her impromptu lectures in the canteen didn't gain her any friends, but Fran had stood by her, had even joined her in saving a year's pocket money to send to Greenpeace for the Save the Whales campaign. Not long after that Ruth discovered boys and her interest in whales abated somewhat.

Anne has had the poster framed and it hangs on the wall above her chest of drawers. This and the wardrobe have been altered too, reclaimed by Anne, painted to match the new decor. But beneath, is the dented oak furniture of Ruth's youth, still holding relics of her past.

She lies on the freshly washed duvet and checks her phone.

No texts, as usual, but an email in her inbox, titled 'Tonight'. Alex will call her at 10 p.m., he says. He will take his parents-in-law's dog for its final walk of the day and they will have a chance to talk without being overheard. She has five hours to wait to hear his voice.

The sky outside her window is completely black but for a few stars blinking – she sometimes forgets they exist when she's in London. Turning off her bedside light, she plunges the whole room into darkness.

Closing her eyes, she listens to the sounds of the house: the pipes creaking as the central heating switches on, the sound of a male voice on the radio following the beeps that mark the start of the news, her parents pottering in the kitchen below her. Her mum is icing the cake, her dad disagreeing with her about something the silky-toned news-reader is reporting.

'I despair of you, I really do. It's not "sticking our noses into other people's business", Annie. They are flagrantly breaking the rules of the Geneva Convention.'

'Jim, it's Christmas. Can we just leave the politics to the side for three days, please?'

'It's worrying, Annie.'

Ruth hears the door of the fridge open and close, the hiss of a can as her dad opens a beer.

'Worrying.'

'Can you see if your daughter wants a mince pie? There's a Christmas quiz on the box at half past. I thought we could watch it together before the others arrive.'

Ruth hears her dad grumbling to himself, then making his way up the stairs to tap at her door. She keeps her eyes closed, feigning sleep.

'Ruthie?'

The door creaks as he pushes it open.

'I'm just having a little rest, Dad.'

'Okay, but come and wrap those presents downstairs. Be like old times having you singing to yourself in the corner while we tuck into the sloe gin.'

'Five minutes.'

He pulls the door behind him, and the catch softly clicks.

Ruth opens her eyes.

This is the moment to tell them about Alex. Her aunt and her cousin's family will be here in just over an hour, so they won't be able to debate it for any longer than forty-five minutes.

Five

Ruth lies with her back on a rug that Nik pulled from his truck. She rolls her head from side to side, watching the stars leave a trail behind them, the sand squeaking beneath the rug as she does so. 'I'm pretty stoned.'

'Same.'

They begin to giggle again.

His hand brushes hers and, in a moment of reflex, she takes it, her fingers interlinking with his. The intimacy of it silences their laughter.

The fibres of the rug scratch against the side of her hand. She feels her palm moisten against his. They lie gazing up at the full moon above them. It has a faint edge of pink, the stars surrounding it bleached out by its rose-coloured glare.

'I'm thinking—' Ruth cuts herself off.

'You're thinking?'

'Yes, seeing as we've probably only got, well, hours, minutes left alive. You know what everyone says? What people say when you ask them, "What would you do if it was the end of the world?"' She doesn't turn to him.

He is silent beside her.

Still.

He doesn't move, but continues to hold her hand.

'Well, lots of people would say, "Have sex with the nearest person."' She continues to look up at the pink-rimmed moon.

She hears his breathing become deeper.

She can feel his palm, warm and still, against her own.

Ruth keeps hold of his hand but turns onto her side to look at him. His profile is lit by the moon. His eyes are closed. His tongue darts out between his lips and wets them, making them shine in the light.

'Are you one of those people?'

She reaches out her left hand to stroke his face. She traces the outline of his features with her forefinger, starting at the stubble above his forehead, bringing her finger across the ridges of his frown to rest between his dark eyebrows, before scaling his nose and dropping to bring her finger across the soft crease of his lips and finally over his chin, down his neck to the dent above his clavicle where she can feel his pulse beating wildly.

'I want to have sex with you.'

He turns his head and opens his eyes to regard her. 'You're stoned.'

'I am.'

'Tell me about your family.'

She takes her hand from his throat and releases his palm, rolling over onto her back again. She feels a stab of pain through the haze of her intoxication.

Mum.

Dad.

Fran.

Everyone.

Her eyes fill with tears. She feels them leak onto her cheeks, rolling down her skin and into her ears.

It is his turn to touch her face. He wipes away the tears, but they keep coming despite his efforts.

He reaches out and rolls her into his chest, holding her tightly, allowing her to sob until she catches her breath.

'Sorry, I was being . . .'

He watches her blow her nose on the sleeve of the fleece he gave her to cover her pointless summer jumper. 'You're pretty full-on, eh?'

She covers her face with her hands.

'Ah, come on. No harm done. But honestly? I'm not sure if I could. Don't take it personally.'

She smiles at him. The snot shines on her upper lip. 'Trust me to see out the end of the world with the only guy who doesn't want his last moment on earth to be having sex.'

'I reckon there are more of us than you'd imagine. And not to be funny, you seem nice now, but it's not so long since you were running around, chucking water at that poor beast.'

He winks at her and warmth washes over her, relaxation.

He's funny, kind.

And it's a relief that he didn't call her bluff. She lightly taps the back of his hand to thank him for not making her feel too much of a fool.

A barrier has been crossed. They lie quietly, listening to each other's breathing and the sound of the sea on the shore.

'Is it real, do you think? Is it the end of the world?'

'I don't know.'

Ruth pushes herself to sit, looking out at the ocean before her. At the edge of the sea there is a pink line of light. 'Look.'

Nik sits too and looks where her finger directs. The horizon appears to be glowing; the colour is starting to spread.

'Is it dawn?'

'I don't think so.'

Ruth gets to her feet, stumbling slightly under the effects of the drug, her eyes glued to the horizon. 'Is this it?'

The pink is rising up the sky, a warm breeze caressing her face from across the water. She watches the light growing as if she is enchanted, unable to take her eyes away.

Then it is as though she is being repelled: something is telling her to pull herself away from the light. She clutches Nik's hand, pulling him to standing.

'Grab the stuff. Bring it to the whale. Quick!'

Nik does as she says, watching her run towards the whale. He yanks up the old rug and swiftly shoulders Ruth's bags. He runs to join her, dumping everything beside them at the mouth of the whale.

She is pulling at the orange-speckled lips of the great beast.

He understands then: leverage. They need a lever.

He is running towards his ute, fumbling in the back, behind the spare tyre.

Please let it be here.

He is beside her again, wielding a crowbar.

His face is lit by the moon on one side and the burning pink on the other.

She hears him grunt as he uses his upper-body strength to lift the lip of the whale, revealing its wall of long interlinked teeth.

'Hold this.'

Ruth bends and takes the weight of the whale's top lip.

It is heavy but not impossible for her to bear. It brings to mind the lifting of a heavy curtain, like you'd find on the stage in a theatre. Drapes? She thinks that's what they're called.

Beneath her arms, Nik forces the crowbar under the baleen plate – the sieving teeth – standing guard at the whale's mouth.

She's starting to sweat. The wind across the sea is becoming warmer and she can feel the skin on her face prickling in the growing heat of the pink light.

Nik is now fully illuminated. He puts pressure on the crowbar and manages to open the whale's teeth wide enough to get both of his hands inside. He places them on either side of the creature's mouth and begins to wrench its jaws apart.

She is aware of warmth emanating from the darkness inside the mouth, a putrid smell. Surely they'll suffocate – they'll be smothered to death.

'Throw the stuff in.'

'What?'

She has let go of the lips and is helping him pull apart the jaws.

'Get in!'

He is shouting at her, screaming above the howl of the wind, his face slick with sweat.

She wants to say it's madness, but she can't look at him now: the light is so bright.

Her skin is stinging from the heat of the wind. It's burning.

So she does it.

She throws her bags into the darkness of the mouth and crawls in against the soft wetness of the creature's enormous tongue. It is like lying on a hot, sodden mattress. The smell is horrendous, an overpowering stench of a warm, salty rubbish dump. Above her the whale's mouth arches; there is room enough to sit, possibly stand.

She turns to Nik.

His mouth is moving but she can't hear him, she clamps her hands over her ears vainly trying to muffle the piercing shriek.

He is crawling into the mouth towards her, pulling at the inside of the whale's mouth as he does, closing out the pink light to darkness.

The warm moisture of the beast's tongue is soaking into her clothes.

It is hot, dangerously so.

They will cook, she thinks. Suffocate, then cook.

They need to get out. This was a stupid idea.

And then, in the dark, he is on top of her, the pressure of his weight winding her.

She snatches for breath, then feels she might vomit, such is the taste in her mouth.

He has his arms around her, holding her, his head above hers.

She thinks her eardrums might burst, the noise is so loud.

'Close your eyes.'

His voice, right next to her ear is raised to a shout now to make himself heard above the uncanny howling outside.

She closes her eyes, squeezes them tight.

All at once it is silent. Dark, still and wet.

Nik's warm, solid form weighs down against her.

Then, in a soundless moment, with her eyes pressed closed, she can see him above her.

She sees his skull, the outline of his jaw. And beyond him, backlit by the whitest light she has ever witnessed, she sees the bones of the whale forming an arch above them, the frame of the spine and ribs in relief above their prone, entwined forms.

Six

'If you eat all of those too, you won't have any room for spuds!'

Her mum is barely audible over the cacophony of voices in the lounge.

Ruth is singing quietly to herself as she works, humming the carols from the service they watched earlier, but she stops as Anne approaches. Even with her back to her mother, Ruth feels the air change as she enters the kitchen from the hall. Anne pauses briefly on the threshold, then makes her way to the sink behind Ruth. She deposits in it the wooden bowls that the children have emptied of crisps.

'Gannets!'

It's the first word that has passed between them in over twenty-four hours. Sensing the potential for reconciliation, Ruth turns to face her mum. 'More roast parsnips for us if they're full of crisps.'

Anne raises her eyebrows and lifts white wine in a cut-crystal glass to her lips, drinking deeply. Her eyes focus beyond Ruth to the freshly peeled carrots her daughter has been cutting into perfect discs and piling into the steamer. 'Oh, I was going to do batons.'

Ruth looks down at the chopping board on the tiled surface in her mother's kitchen. There are only two carrots left for her to prepare. 'Sorry. I was just trying to help.'

'Yes.'

Anne puts on her oven gloves. As she bends to open the door, the already-warm room is filled with the delicious scent of roasting fat and flesh. 'Right on time.' She closes the door with a snap and takes the steamed-up glasses from her forehead to buff them on the hem of her apron. She fires up the gas on the hob and places the last of the carrots from Ruth's chopping board in the steamer, lifting the lid to check there is enough water before putting it to boil.

'I'll go and help Dad.' Ruth wipes her hands on her apron and turns to leave but Anne raises her hand, a motion that asks her daughter to pause.

She leans back against the counter. 'I don't want to argue with you, Ruth, not at Christmas.' Anne reaches for her glass again and drains it.

'Neither do I, Mum.'

'I just wish you could understand why your father and I are upset.'

Ruth sighs and grabs the wine bottle, refilling their glasses.

They both stand for a while, their backs resting against opposite counters. From down the hall, the noise of four young boys battling their father, mother, grandmother and great-uncle at a word-play game fills the silence between them.

'All we want is for you to be happy, Ruthie.'

'I am, Mum. For the first time in ages, I can honestly say I'm happy.'

'It's a surprise to us too, Ruth. Of course we hoped you'd met someone. We aren't totally oblivious, you know. We knew there was someone on the go. You haven't called so often. "There's a spring in her step," your dad said, when you were down here last. But it all seems so accelerated. He'll be moving into the flat before we've met him. That's unusual even for tenants. We'd ordinarily at least have references.'

'Alex isn't going to be your tenant, Mum.'

'Well, no. That's another point. Why should this man we've never met benefit from living rent-free in the flat?'

'He'll be paying his way, Mum. And, anyway, that's between me and him.'

'Surely he already has a mortgage. And then there'll be his child care obligations. Why should we be subsidising his mistakes?'

'Mum.'

'Darling, you have to understand. This grown man, this adult, he's onto an absolute winner. I don't doubt he loves you – who couldn't? You're wonderful. But you must admit he has rather fallen on his feet. What would be happening if he'd fallen for a young woman whose parents hadn't helped her buy a flat close to central London? He'd have to find his own place. That's what. He'd have to take some responsibility. And instead he's going to be ligging off us, taking advantage of you, and we haven't even met him. I'm suspicious of him. And you should be too.'

'You'd like him. You really would.'

'Darling, I think I'd find it difficult. Maybe if I didn't know of his nefarious dealings . . .'

'Mum, there's nothing nefarious about his "dealings". He works for a bloody NGO!'

'Good men do not leave their wife and children for a younger woman. That is not the action of a good man. It's grubby.'

'He's only forty-three, Mum – he's hardly cradle-snatching. My *Lolita* days are a couple of decades behind me.'

A sudden sizzle from the hob interrupts them.

The water from the steamer has made its way between the sandwiched metal, a white foam cascading onto the flames. It hisses violently and spits at Ruth as she slides the pan to the side. The noise ceases as she turns off the gas and the room is quiet again. The starch in the water from the overflowing pan has burnt, adding an unpleasant lingering base note to the delicious scents of their imminent feast.

Anne smiles tightly: reconciliation, of sorts. 'Let's not spoil dinner. I'd like it if we could be friends again. Tell your father to come in here and help me. Can you make sure everyone washes their hands and help them find their seats?'

At dinner, Ruth applies herself to drinking. She finishes the white wine from the kitchen, happily accepts a glass of champagne to toast, and refills her glass with the Rioja that her cousin has supplied for the occasion. It's a brand she's seen in the supermarket: drinkable but nothing to write home about.

'Enjoying the wine, Ruth?'

Ollie is watching her inspect the bottle, smirking at her. She sticks her tongue out at him.

Ruth's cousin is only a year older than her. They used to be great friends when they were kids; she'd take pride in being mistaken for his sister on holidays and would get teased by Fran for returning back to school with a lilt to her accent that came from hanging around with him all summer long. But then he'd met Andrea and they'd got married and had kids. And now, whenever they see each other at these family occasions, it feels as though they're from different generations. She might work with kids, but she can't begin to understand why anyone would have four of their own. She's only had to endure being sandwiched between the seven-year-old and the five-year-old for the last half-hour but, even numbed with the best part of two bottles of wine, she can't promise that she isn't going to plunge the prongs of her fork into their constantly moving hands to try to stop their ceaseless chatter.

Her dad, noticing her discomfort, winks at her across the table. 'Get used to it, Ruthie. You'll have a ready-made family of your own to deal with soon!'

The table falls quiet.

How everyone can have heard this one sentence when they have all been engaged in their own conversation at such a decibel level is unfathomable.

'A ready-made family?' Her aunt, her father's sister, breaks the silence.

'You've met someone? At last!' Andrea raises her glass toasting her.

'It's a bit complicated.' Ruth can feel herself blushing. She pours herself more wine.

In the dark of the night, she is woken by her phone vibrating insistently.

Snatched from her dreams, she struggles to identify where she is. The phone is filling her room with blue light, just like the water-filtered sunlight in her dream. Slowly she realises she is awake. Her head banging from dehydration, her mouth dry, her eyes are unable to focus on the screen to see who is calling.

'Hello?'

'It's done. I'm in the car. I'm coming to you.' Alex's voice is strangely high-pitched with giddiness. 'Ruth?'

'I'm here. Sorry, I was asleep.'

'I'm on my way. Send me the postcode.'

She hears the car door slam, the engine starting. 'You're coming now? It's Christmas.'

'I'm not proud of myself but I couldn't stand it a second longer.'

She takes her phone from her ear and squints at the time: 4.08 a.m. Four in the morning on Boxing Day. If Alex is coming from his in-laws in the Cotswolds, he will be at her parents' house by breakfast time.

Her stomach makes a leaping motion: she thinks she might be sick.

'Ruth?'

'Yes?'

'I love you.'

She listens to the sound of his car rushing along the tarmac, heading towards her, and tastes the last of yesterday's wine rising up her oesophagus, burning her throat.

'Well? Don't you love me too?' He laughs, his bright bellowing laugh, so sure of her response.

'Of course I do,' she says. 'Of course.'

Once Alex is off the phone, sleep evades her.

She rises and tiptoes down to the kitchen, past the closed rooms containing her softly snoring family.

In the kitchen, she takes a glass from the cupboard, filling it with tap water and gulping it down three times before she feels her thirst subside.

She takes a shower. She sings to herself softly: Stevie Wonder.

As she is shaving her legs she is grinning broadly. She laughs at herself, her giddiness, and shaves her armpits and, after some deliberation, uses the slightly blunt razor to remove most of the curled hair that covers her pubis.

She turns off the light in the bathroom and creeps across the landing to her room where she plaits her hair, then moisturises her body and her face.

She puts on her nicest bra and fresh knickers, then her pyjamas, and gets into bed to wait.

She watches as dawn creeps above the row of houses behind her parents'. Opposite, the reflection of the sun rising is caught by the glass of the framed whale diagram. It throws the light across the room in glowing beams.

Her awareness moves to her heart. It is thumping: he'll be here anytime now. She looks at the clock on her bedside table: the hands, barely visible in the dim light, read 8.12 a.m.

Outside, her alert ears locate an engine making a turn into their street. It pulls up outside, puttering as the car is parked, then coming to a hush.

Seven

There isn't a noise. But there is sound. It is as if she is underwater: her ears aren't ringing but there is a vibration, like rushing liquid.

Her body is wet, her clothes stuck to her skin.

There is a weight on top of her. She feels crushed.

She opens her eyes, but they cannot adjust to her surroundings.

It is dark.

She feels nauseous and disoriented.

Has she been asleep?

Has she been in an accident?

Where is she?

The weight above her shifts and she feels two hands take her face. With the little strength she has, she struggles against them.

Then she remembers.

Nik.

His body is moving above her, his weight shifting as he lies down beside her. He too is now on his back in the dark, next to her.

The air is thick, animal, putrid.

Her breathing is laboured. She exhales slowly, trying not to panic.

There is a warmth around her crotch and Ruth realises, with shame, she has contributed to the wetness of her garments, the urine between her legs mingling with the moisture of the whale's tongue.

She inhales deeply, filling her lungs; the air is full of odours.

She coughs, retches, bile burning her throat.

She is alive.

Next to her Nik shifts. She can feel the vibrations of his voice, but she can't hear him.

'I can't hear!' Ruth's voice pierces the rushing in her ears, like a foghorn, so loud.

Nik's response rumbles next to her.

What is he saying?

He shifts again. He is sitting.

She tries to do the same, but as she moves her limbs hold her down. Her clothes seem heavy with more than sweat, urine and whatever whale saliva is called. She feels as if she is wearing chainmail: her bones are weighing her down.

At her feet she can feel Nik moving. How does he have the energy to do so?

She inhales the foetid air deeply once more.

She is alive.

Nik traces his hand along the animal's flesh below Ruth's feet.

His muscles ache. His skin feels taut, restricting his movement. He reaches out his hands and manages to trace the puckered membranes of the interior of the whale's mouth, searching for his crowbar.

He is unsure how many hours he has been unconscious, but he knows they can't have much oxygen left in this damp cavern. Though he doesn't know what he will find beyond the flesh walls of their bunker, the only possible route to survival now exists beyond it.

His searching hands happen upon a metal object beside Ruth's wet leg.

She still isn't moving and his ears are ringing so loudly that he can't hear what she is saying.

Is she in pain?

He needs to see her, to know if she is all right. He needs to see himself, his burning skin.

They are alive. But for how long?

Using the crowbar, he opens the jaws of the beast to the world beyond.

The cool air rushes in, and with it, a strange light. It is the green-tinged light of snowy landscapes reminiscent of hazy ski trips as a child.

He looks back into the whale and tugs on Ruth's leg. 'Ruth?'

No response.

Using his back, he levers the jaws of the beast open further and drags Ruth towards him. Her face comes into the light: her eyes are closed, her face blistered and raw.

'Ruth?'

Her eyes open slightly, focusing on his face. Her mouth opens to speak but he cannot hear her words.

'I can't hear you.'

She grimaces as she raises her hand to her ear, pointing, then wagging a finger. She can't hear him either.

He nods in understanding.

Looking back out into the world beyond, he can see his ute through the gloom. The paint from its body has been stripped entirely. The tyres deflated, it sits on its uppers, the engine glowing where the last of its petrol is burning away.

He looks towards the sea. It is wild.

From above, a kind of snow is falling. It covers the sand and rests lightly on the water of the creek, still flowing towards the sea.

He becomes aware of how dry his mouth is.

He braces the jaw of the whale with his crowbar, leaving a slim window open onto the rapidly lightening day beyond.

His body cries out in agony as he crawls back along Ruth, reaching for her backpack beyond her. Locating the water canteen, he opens it and pours water into his parched mouth, then falls back to Ruth and, using his fingers, opens her mouth gently. Her eyes widen with concern but, on feeling the cool of the metal against her lips, she puckers them to accept the water greedily.

Ruth rolls her head to see beyond the bulk of his body. Her eyes widen on noticing the dust falling. She looks back at him for an answer.

He shakes his head.

He doesn't know what to do next either.

He lies down again next to Ruth. He feels damp from his sodden clothes, but still warm.

She turns her face to his. 'We're alive.'

He nods. He can read her lips, though her voice is only a distant murmur.

'How?'

He shakes his head. He has no idea.

She raises her hand to touch his face. He feels a stinging pain. It must be blistered just as hers is. Her forehead creases. She brings her hand to her own skin. She recoils sharply from her touch.

Ruth's face feels as if it's on fire. In the bubble of her deafness, Nik's is barely illuminated by the light from outside.

She feels like she's dreaming.

She lets her hand fall to her side and searches beside her for Nik's. Though it stings her raw skin to do so, she takes it and looks at him.

Her heart surges with gratitude for this man she barely knows. His eyes are closing. She allows hers to close too. She squeezes his hand and, in reply, he wraps his arm over her, enclosing her body against his. She listens to the rushing of her blood, the noise in her ears like a waterfall hitting rocks. She feels his limbs relax.

His consciousness ebbs and his thoughts shift to dreams.

Outside, a heavy dust covers the scorched hide of the whale, the whole beach glowing white in the gloom.

The sky is heavy with dust that now belches forth, the ash of humanity's crematoria.

Soon the whale becomes part of the beach, as does Nik's truck.

Dust covers all.

The sky lightens as the sun fights its way through the billowing particles.

But it does not wake these survivors who sleep pillowed on the tongue of a dead whale. Their arms around each other, their bodies beginning to knit the damage that stress and heat has wrought, they dream of a world that no longer exists.

Eight

Ruth is woken by the warmth of Alex's naked body against her back. She is uncomfortably slick with sweat, but she doesn't move for fear of waking him. She feels the vibration of his light snores against her, his sparse chest hair stuck to her shoulder blades and his penis limp beside her left buttock.

She moves her hand to stroke the length of his thigh along her own, feeling the muscles taut beneath the fine hairs; her stomach clenches slightly with desire. It's like being a teenager, living with Alex. She feels she is discovering her sexuality all over again.

Carefully she slides the duvet back to allow at least her front to cool, her breasts feeling the chill of the new January air from the window. It is still open from last night when they noisily wished the locals of Deptford joy for the coming year, gleefully banging saucepans with wooden spoons into the still midnight air until they fell laughing into bed. Her nipples harden in response to the chill and the memory of their celebratory love-making only hours earlier.

Behind her, she senses a change in Alex's breathing pattern. He starts to harden against her as his consciousness creeps back. 'Happy New Year, my little radiator.'

She is pulled by the waist so her buttocks grind into his groin. His hands run in opposite directions along her body. He bites her ear and finds his way inside her once more.

*   *   *

Alex has been living in her flat for a week now. Ruth would like to say that it is pure bliss but, in truth, she is struggling with the lack of sleep. His energy is endless. Alex is always moving, talking, thinking. He claims to be 'obsessed' with her and his obsession seems to manifest itself largely sexually: on waking, before sleeping and often on his return to his new home. It's not that she is tiring of the sex, of the muffled transcendence it provides, but her body is crying out for rest. When she had the flat to herself, any break from the weekday routine meant discarding the alarm clock, rising when her body desired and allowing herself as many late nights as she wished. But this Christmas break, since returning from her parents' with a new flatmate in tow, she's found herself desperate for sleep. Alex's work is predominantly abroad and does not recognise any more than official bank holidays. His calls and online meetings have been daily, starting an hour earlier than British office hours. He seems intent on rousing her to arouse her at the crack of dawn when they went to sleep just a few hours earlier.

Other than the sleep deprivation, their cohabitation is everything she hoped for. He is fully domesticated, unlike her previous boyfriends. In fact, he is tidier than her. Other than his presence, the changes are subtle. In a week there have been a few noticeable adjustments in the kitchen: the supermarket own-brand produce replaced with recognisable labels, the recycling now being thoroughly washed and sorted, not just rammed into an overflowing bag that wasn't taken out until it got a bit smelly.

On his second day in the flat she noticed a new loo brush beside the toilet. She reddened to realise that Alex had felt the necessity to purchase such an item, and her cheeks burnt even more when she wondered whether it was her or him who had made that requirement apparent. It wasn't the only scatological matter that raised the colour in Ruth's cheeks. Alex was opposed to the use of any chemical or aerosol-propelled household products. Over the past week, on several occasions, Ruth had found herself wafting pungent air out of the window and running the tap to foam soap in the hope of masking the smell of her natural functions. Though it was worse when she had walked in and been greeted with air almost warm with the memory of Alex's recent visit. But the long hours of conversation and laughter more than made up for the downside: the faint grey bags beneath her eyes and the inevitable recognition that her lover has a full range of bodily functions.

He has, over the last week, transported boxes from his old life. When he returns from those trips, his eyes are glassy and he looks drawn. They don't shy away from it, though. She opens them both a beer and lights a candle on the kitchen table, where they sit and talk. How he misses his kids, how he fears for his soon-to-be ex-wife's mental wellbeing. It feels as though there is nothing they keep secret from each other.

'You drive me insane.'

He exhales with a shudder, collapsing on top of her.

She kisses his ear. 'Your avocado on toast drives me insane.'

Alex laughs and rolls off her. 'Didn't know I'd signed up to be your lover *and* cook and cleaner.'

'Always read the small print.' She flips the duvet so it lands over his head and jumps out of bed to beat him to the shower.

As the hot water cascades about her, Ruth hums the song she and Alex danced to at midnight last night. As she sings, she soaps her hair and congratulates herself on a New Year's Day with barely a hangover. She hopes to have a positive start every year: a long walk, followed by an afternoon watching classic films and an early night. But it is usually scuppered by some unplanned antics with Fran, leaving her hung-over and bedridden for the majority of the first day of January. Yes, the party was usually worth the pain, but it was nice to wake up with a sense of hope rather than in a fug of guilt, doom and paranoia. As she raises her arms to rinse her hair a stab of pain shoots through her shoulder. She rolls her arm in the socket to relieve the tension.

Last night she had excused herself from any revels. She messaged when it was too late for Fran to talk her out of it, feigning 'swollen glands'. Another rubbish lie, yes, but she didn't feel too guilty about it. She wasn't exactly abandoning Fran to seeing in the New Year alone: her friend had already been in Soho for hours celebrating and, from the ebullience of her messages, was unlikely to miss Ruth's presence when the bongs struck.

The residue of guilt that she couldn't wash away was that Fran was still unaware of Alex's existence. She didn't even know Ruth had a boyfriend, never mind that he'd moved into her flat. Was it true that she still hadn't had an opportunity to tell Fran about Alex? She could have told her over their pre-Christmas drink, but she was exhausted from arguing with her parents. Fran was in such a good mood that delivering news revealing Ruth had been less than truthful for the last six months didn't feel like an option. It was so rare that they had the time to hang out, just the two of them. She missed it and didn't want to curtail it. Ruth knew that, once she started to tell the truth, the full details of the situation would tumble out and, knowing Fran as she did, that would really put a dampener on things. So she held her tongue once again and they huddled in the corner of the pub where they had first used their fake IDs, drank terrible wine and laughed until their stomachs hurt.

Rinsing the conditioner from her hair, her thoughts turn away from Fran to last night with Alex. The candlelight, music playing on vinyl, that special bottle of Chianti, both of them dressed up, dancing – just the two of them – in the lounge, the coffee table pushed up against the sofa. Untarnished memories like that were worth the weight of a few little fibs.

She hears voices, then the slam of the door. I hope he ordered pizza, she thinks. Wrapped in towels, she pads into the kitchen to investigate.

'Feeling better?' Fran, her face blank, is sitting at her kitchen table.

'I didn't know you were poorly yesterday, my love.' Alex's face is awash with concern. He turns back to the kettle and tips steaming water into the cafetière waiting on the counter.

'My glands were up, that's all. No big deal!'

Ruth's cheeks are burning as Fran observes her.

Alex hands a black coffee to Fran. 'Are you sure I can't get you something stronger? Hair of the dog?'

'No, thanks.'

Next to Fran, a bag full of shopping from the corner shop. Through the plastic Ruth can make out Lucozade, paracetamol and a frozen pizza. I'm a terrible friend, she thinks.

'Well, Happy New Year, Fran. I've heard so much about you!' Alex raises his mug towards Fran.

Ruth looks down. Her bare feet are cold, a slight numbness creeping into her toes, the water running off her legs pooling on the kitchen tiles. She looks up. Fran's eyes, hard, staring directly at her. In the background, Alex is jabbering on, but all Ruth can hear is the whooshing of the blood pulsing in her ears. She reaches out for the table to steady herself, her knees weakening.

'Darling! You do look a little peaky, you know.' Alex pulls out a chair, ushering Ruth to the table.

'I'll grab your dressing gown.'

Ruth dares to look up from the kitchen table to face her friend.

'Well?'

Ruth looks back at the knotted wood beneath her sweating palms. She'd known it was only a matter of time before her secret caught up with her, but she hadn't understood until this moment the damage it could potentially do to a carefully cultivated lifetime of trust. She'd shared nearly everything with this woman for as long as either of them had understood the concept of sharing.

'I didn't realise it was serious until it was.'

'Have you completely lost it? You don't move someone in after a few good dates.'

Can she possibly get away with telling Fran she's just met Alex? That she'd been swept off her feet? Plead temporary insanity? She can't bear the idea of it. All the lies she'd have to engineer to cover her tracks. It makes her feel exhausted just thinking about it.

'We've been seeing each other for a while.'

'A while?'

'July.'

From the other side of the table, there is a steely silence. Her eyes still lowered, she sees drops of water hit the table. Fran has tears freely flowing down her face. She is shaking her head in disbelief.

'Sorry, got waylaid by the news.' Alex raises his hands in surrender. It's one of his little foibles: a news addiction. Then he wraps the dressing gown around Ruth's bare shoulders. The warmth of the towelling against her skin makes her aware of just how cold she is and she shudders.

*　　*　　*

58

The walk is not the New Year's Day stroll she'd anticipated. Ruth knows that Fran only accepted Alex's offer as an opportunity to continue their interrupted conversation. She feels as though she is waiting outside the headmistress's office. Fran is biding her time. As they walk, she chats away to Alex, probing him on his work. Alex happily expounds on seeds and the technology cryogenics is offering to agriculture; he talks animatedly about the new plan to grow crops in old mattresses in refugee camps. Fran has always befriended Ruth's boyfriends. It's a win-win situation for her: she either makes a new friend or can highlight to Ruth just how unsuitable this man is. Watching Fran and Alex deep in conversation ahead of her, she tries to read Fran's body language: is Alex going to pass the test?

At the top of the hill, they join the mass of bodies reaching for their smartphones to capture the bravery of their New Year's Day outing. Fran offers to take a photo of Alex and Ruth together, the skyline of London behind them, then Alex returns the favour and the two women stand close, arms around each other. Fran leans into Ruth and whispers to her, 'You idiot.'

There is a softening in her admonishment: Alex has charmed her. Of course he has. Who could resist him?

At the bottom of the hill, they find a pub and order a pint of the local pale ale each and two packets of crisps, which they tear open to create a sharing platter for them all. When Alex goes to the loo, Ruth braces herself for Fran's verdict. But the critique she was expecting doesn't come.

'I just don't understand why you kept him to yourself. He seems into you. It must have been killing you, keeping it quiet.'

Ruth shrugs. 'Maybe I've finally grown up.'

She leans into Fran, feeling the warmth of her arm against her. Now would be a good moment to tell her how the relationship with Alex started. It'd be pretty difficult for Fran to change her opinion just because he's married, wouldn't it?

Out of the corner of her eye, she spots Alex as he returns from the Gents. He heads to the bar, miming drinking a pint, to check that they want another round.

'I like him.'

Ruth can't easily recall the last time Fran had said that about anyone she was seeing. She beams back at Alex, who is smiling at them from the bar, reaches for another handful of crisps and jams them into her mouth.

Nine

It is her own shivering that pulls Ruth from sleep. She is cold. Her wet clothes stick to her and her skin burns.

She feels Nik's breath against her face. Smells its sour tang.

Ruth opens her eyes.

His face is so close to hers she cannot focus on it; she pulls back and sees that the blisters on his skin have popped. They are weeping. The stickiness on her own face must have been caused by the same condition.

Her body aches as she shifts to look outside. The brightness hurts her eyes.

She frees herself of Nik's sleeping form, pulls herself to the front of the whale's mouth and straightens, standing to witness the landscape around her. The sun is bright in a clear blue sky and all around her is reflected in the crisp white dust that covers everything as far as her eye can see.

She imagines for a second her mother emerging from a safe place – under the stairs? A newly discovered cellar? An improvised bunker like her own? – and making her way into the garden, the buddleia and mimosa covered with white ash, a new world of white.

Ruth shakes her head to dispel the image, and with it the hope of possibility.

Gingerly she removes Nik's fleece, avoiding her sore face. Free of the sodden material, she finds the skin of her arms clear and pulls off her trousers to find the same of her legs. She strides towards the sea, removing her vest and underwear, and walks naked into the waves.

Her skin stings as she holds her head under the water, but as she comes up for air she can feel that, beneath the pain where the salt meets each blister, it is soothing the heat of her damaged skin.

She falls back, dipping below the waves again and feels the sand against her spine as she lies full-length in the shallows. She lets herself float on the surface and opens her eyes to the sun, her ears below the water. As she floats, she observes her empty stomach contracting and her mind turns to food. There is a little in her backpack, enough for tonight for her and Nik. But they'll need more – and soon. They'll need something anti-biotic for their skin: the whale's saliva, which has covered them for the last several hours, will surely accelerate infection.

She feels a pulse of adrenalin.

She has survived this far, but if she wants to stay alive she needs to move.

Nik watches Ruth emerge from the waves, completely naked. He focuses on her hands and face, how sore they look, raw from the burns they have sustained. Studiously he keeps his eyes away from the weight of her breasts and from the generous hair that sits below the curve of her belly. She smiles as she walks towards him, bending to retrieve her underwear from the dust of the beach.

'Can you hear me?'

It is distant, as if she is talking to him through an insulated wall, but he can hear her voice more clearly than he could before they slept – how long had they slept? – although the rushing sound in his ears persists.

Ruth nods in understanding. 'You stink. Get in the sea.'

She is over-articulating, exaggerating the movements of her mouth to aid his understanding. She is holding her nose with one hand, pointing towards the waves with the other.

Nik removes his jeans and his T-shirt, but stops at his pants. He follows Ruth's footprints in the ash towards the lapping waves.

He doesn't look back to see that he need not feel self-conscious: he is not under Ruth's gaze.

Ruth has already gone into the whale's mouth to retrieve her backpack. She pulls out her ground sheet and lays it on the ash-covered sand before unpacking the contents of her bag. When she comes upon some clean pants she puts them on, but otherwise continues to work semi-naked.

She piles the resources she has onto it:

Clothes, towel
Tent, roll-mat, sleeping bag
Toiletries, Swiss Army knife, first-aid kit
A little food

She retrieves the elements of the first-aid kit that she'd shoved into her bag, her heart sinking to see so few disinfectant wipes left. Carefully she arranges the little tubes and blister packs of pills, the plasters and plastic-wrapped bandages in the small plastic box.

For a second, she sees her mother, just days earlier, packing the box as Ruth is now.

Her lovely mum.

She is laughing at something she's heard on the radio, standing at the kitchen counter, her reading glasses pushing her hair back from her face, fitting each carefully selected item into the box, like a jigsaw puzzle.

Ruth brings a hand to her throat, as if the image is choking her and she is trying to dislodge it. She closes her eyes and brings her teeth together tightly. She cannot dwell. She needs to move.

She opens one of the small packets and draws a citrus-scented wipe across her raw skin, first her face, then her palms and the back of her hands. She grimaces as the antiseptic burns the open wounds.

She pulls a sports bra over her head as Nik approaches her, his body dripping. He pulls his boxer shorts away from his body to prevent the outline of his form being visible to her. She shakes her head at his prudishness and throws him her damp towel. 'Food?' She mimes eating with a spoon.

'Do you have something?'

She pulls three tins, a vacuum pack of dry-looking rolls, some salted pretzels and a net of oranges from her bag. 'Here.' She throws him an orange and moves towards him, tearing open another antiseptic-wipe sachet with her teeth. 'This is going to hurt.'

He flinches as she dabs his face, then swears as a blister pops under the pressure.

After disposing of the soiled wipe and its packaging, Ruth uses the can opener from the Swiss Army knife on a tin of baked beans. She flicks to the spoon attachment and takes a mouthful, then hands the can to Nik. 'This is all I have.' Ruth stretches out her arms to show the items laid out on the ground sheet of her one-man tent. 'We need to get supplies. Find help. Others.'

Nik nods in agreement, handing the can back to Ruth.

He wrings out his jeans and T-shirt then lays them in the sun to dry on the spare section of ground sheet next to Ruth's worldly goods. 'Ute's munted, eh?'

Ruth crinkles her nose, her face awash with confusion. She either can't hear him or hasn't understood what he's said.

He points towards where the truck stands in the ash.

The landscape beyond it looks alien, like that of an alternative planet from a blockbuster movie. It reminds Nik of the salt-flats in South America he'd seen pictures of on social media. Poor digital images, playing with perspective. Like Christ the Redeemer in Rio, the salt-flats in Bolivia seemed to be somewhere tourists felt the need to prove they'd visited by littering the internet with these virtual passport stamps. When the internet existed.

How about that? he thinks. There isn't any internet.

Maybe there aren't any salt-flats either.

Will he never get the opportunity to take some decent photographs of them himself?

'We should go and see what the damage is. See who else has made it.' He looks up at the sun's position in the sky. It's past midday, slipping into the afternoon. 'We should go now, while it's still light. Can you manage it?'

Ruth still can't hear him clearly, but she can make out a little by watching his lips.

She nods, chewing another mouthful of beans.

She picks up a pot of moisturising cream from her washbag and smears it generously over her skin, wincing as she does so. Nik is watching so she offers it to him, but he declines.

She repacks her things, splitting them between the rucksack and the smaller backpack. She loads the latter with a few essentials: a torch, the Swiss Army knife and water canteen, the first-aid kit. She hands Nik an empty canvas tote bag from a pocket of her backpack and he accepts it dazedly.

'Can I put this in your van?'

She points between the packed bag and his stripped automobile. The fire is long burnt out, the engine no more than a shell. It is now a cupboard on wheels.

He nods in assent and watches her heave the bag onto her shoulder, wincing, then wrangle with the door of the ute. Finally, she manages to open it. She turns back to him and raises her thumbs: the cab is intact. She throws her bag into the truck and slams the door. 'Should we lock it, do you think?'

He looks at her blankly, so she mimes locking the door, but still he doesn't understand so she returns to him.

'Key?' Ruth shouts, performing an exaggerated mime of the turning of a key in a lock.

Nik smiles. What point is there in locking the door? 'Pretty sure she'll be right, eh.'

Ruth's face is blank, she hasn't understood him. The energy involved in explaining himself is more than it'd take to lock up. So he nods, jumps up and jogs over to the ute. He locks the door, then screws up the canvas bag to put it into his still-damp jeans pocket, along with the key.

'Let's go have a look-see.'

Ruth watches him walking away from her, squinting. The dust is almost blindingly white in the glare of the mid-afternoon sun.

He turns and beckons to her, a silhouette encouraging her to walk away from the whale, the water, the beach, to what lies, unknown, through the ash.

She slings the bag of supplies over her shoulder and follows him.

Ten

Ruth smoothes her hair; it is starting to frizz in the mild January drizzle. There are now only three people ahead of her. She calculates that, since Fran is always late, she has time to purchase a flat white with a pastry treat on the side for each of them and make it down to the river by their agreed meeting time. She hopes the gift of a coffee will start their day off on the right foot. She's aware she's still on friendship probation and is looking for any opportunity to improve her plea.

In front of her, a young American couple are bickering under their breath about eating in or taking away. Beyond them, a woman asks about the cakes. 'Are any gluten-free?'

'The almond and blueberry is.'

'It doesn't have gluten?'

'Yes. I mean, no, it doesn't. It's gluten-free.'

'Does it have fruit?'

'Yes, blueberries.'

'Oh, I can't have fruit. I'll have a croissant.'

'Ah, that has gluten.'

The young barista pauses his tongs above the pastry as the woman considers.

'That's fine.'

Ruth checks the time on her phone. She's cutting it fine.

*   *   *

Fran is waiting with her arms crossed over her chest. Her hands are tucked into her armpits and she's impatiently bouncing on her heels. She stands with her back to the river, the water running grey and brown behind her. From where she is, Ruth knows she won't see her approaching. She seizes the opportunity for an ice-breaker. Standing as close as she can behind Fran without revealing herself, she brings her face right up next to her ear and whispers, 'Coffee?'

Fran flings out her arm in fright, knocking a tenner's worth of hot coffee all over the uneven pavement. They look down at the milky puddle between them. Ruth holds out the grease-stained paper bag towards her. 'Just the croissant, then?'

They walk along the river, the drizzle creating a haze across the undulating expanse of the Thames. Covent Garden seems much further than it did when they'd made this plan.

'How's work?'

'I don't go back till Monday.'

'Part-timer.'

Ruth doesn't rise to the bait. It's easy to get into a minor skirmish over Fran being flippant about her job – they've done it enough – but she doesn't want to rock the boat. Anyway, as she's the first to admit, she's hardly teaching in the school of hard knocks.

They pass the brutalist concrete blocks of the National Theatre and the imposing, glass-fronted bulk of the Southbank Centre, then cross the river via the footbridge. A screech of metal against metal occasionally interrupts their conversation as trains arrive and depart from Charing Cross.

It is the sort of London day that makes you feel as though you were perpetually damp. As they pass the halfway mark of the bridge, though, the sun makes an effort to force its way through the clouds. Fierce strands of light break through the blanket of cloud above, blinding them for a second. Ruth curses herself for not bringing sunglasses with her. Fran, of course, has hers on the bridge of her nose – she is rarely without them.

Behind them, a couple from somewhere northern – Leeds? York? – are discussing the bridge.

'I don't think it's this one, Michael.'

'It is. It's the Millennium Footbridge.'

'No, that was the wobbly one. They had to close it.'

'Well, what's this bloody bridge called, then?'

Fran looks over her sunglasses and catches Ruth's eye. It was a discussion they'd had many times themselves, but they were proper Londoners now. They could name all the bridges and tunnels from Kew to Woolwich.

They pass over the top of Heaven nightclub, the destination of one of their first secret trips to London. Ruth vaguely remembers dancing among welcoming semi-naked men beneath the arches until dawn while Fran spent face-to-face time with girls she'd been corresponding with from the personal ads at the back of the *NME*. Come sunrise, they'd boarded the first coach back and arrived at school halfway through Tuesday registration.

They walk through Charing Cross station, with its distinct scent of hot pasties and the expensive sandalwood perfume that Ruth rather likes, but Fran describes as 'basic'. Ruth loves railway stations at the weekend: without the jangled energy of commuters elbowing their way between tube and train they are full of potential. She considers, for a second, suggesting to Fran that they jump on the next train to Hastings. It's so long since she saw the sea. She'd love to sit and stare at the horizon, watching a murmuration of starlings above the white crests of the waves, then return home with the smell of ozone still in her hair.

There is a demonstration in Trafalgar Square. There always is on a Saturday, these days.

'We should probably be there.'

Placards and candles are held in vigil among the crowd huddled on the steps of the National Gallery.

'Probably, but if we're fucked, we're fucked. I'm hungry and I want to get at the bargains.'

They walk along Charing Cross Road and cut up towards Oxford Street through Soho.

'How's Alex?'

Ruth had told her the truth of how they'd met when she and Fran had gone to the theatre last week. She had booked the tickets on the strength of the cast, a treat for them both: two actors she'd always fancied and a woman who was a favourite of Fran's. As soon as the curtain went up it was evident that the play was about an affair so finally coming clean in the bar afterwards had felt like good timing. She wasn't surprised at Fran's annoyance when she revealed another layer of her lies about Alex, but she *was* upset by her continued coldness over the course of the week. Ruth wanted to avoid the subject of Alex and just try to get things back to normal.

'He's great. What do you fancy for lunch?'

By the time they are on Old Compton Street, the thaw between them is distinct. Fran puts her arm through Ruth's. 'Will you let me go make-up shopping?'

Fran is looking up at her with her eyes wide and her bottom lip thrust out, begging like a puppy. It is the last thing Ruth wants to spend her day doing but, aware they're still on shaky ground, she agrees.

They wander around the cosmetics displays in the ancient

department store. The scents of multiple hairsprays, perfumes and candles are intense, making Ruth – now hungry – feel slightly nauseous. Fran tries various lipsticks on the back of her hand, before looking around to check the proximity of the nearest assistant. Checking that they are all engaged with other customers, she carefully but swiftly applies it to her lips and turns to Ruth, pouting. 'What do you think? Too much for a third date?'

'You're seeing someone?'

She feels Fran's sardonic glare hit her.

'That's what we do now, right? Keep our love lives to ourselves?'

They have lunch in Soho, Ruth managing to manoeuvre them towards one of their favourite restaurants rather than the pricier option of Fran's members' club. They share three plates of pasta, all different shapes: wide, velvety sheets, slippery with butter and sage; fine metre-long spaghetti, musty with shavings of fresh truffle; fat rolls of *pici*, speckled with pepper, the Parmesan dissolving before them. The ice cubes in their Negronis jangle against the glass.

'Jenny. She's funny and we seem to have stuff in common. Been single for ages. Bit grumpy about the world in general and, as a bonus, the sex is fantastic.'

It's good to hear Fran talk about her new love interest. It's normal. It makes Ruth feel like she's been forgiven.

'Does she want kids?'

'We didn't pick out nursery colours on our second date or anything but, yeah, she wants a family.'

'Exciting! Where are you taking her for date three?'

'She's taking me.'

'Good luck, Jenny!'

'I'm doing my best to make my peace with surprises.'

Ruth looks down at her drink. She fishes the orange slice from the glass and eats the flesh. 'I'm sorry. I don't know why I didn't tell you about Alex.' She twirls the orange peel around her finger. 'I think . . .'

'Go on.' Fran is nodding encouragement but Ruth shakes her head. It's not that she's withholding something this time; it's that she can't quite articulate what she's feeling. Is she ashamed? Ashamed of finding someone like him attractive? His loud voice, his posh vowels, his handsome face: they make her feel so obvious, so predictable. She's ashamed of wanting something so classically desirable.

'I think part of it was that I knew what you'd say.'

'Really? And what is that?'

Does she want to seed more doubts in Fran? 'You'd ask if I met him through Camille.'

Fran's look of concern evolves gradually into a smile. 'And where did you meet him?'

'Shut up.'

They both laugh and Fran cuts the final sheet of pasta in half for them to share.

'What does Camille make of you being a homewrecker?'

'We are not currently in communication.'

'So, there are some benefits to your being a scarlet woman, then. I do hope she holds a grudge.'

They spend the rest of the day working their way around the axis of Oxford Circus, gradually adding bag upon bag to their forearms until the skin stings in complaint. Fran has, for the most part, made purchases of clothes that are full price, striking and, in Ruth's eyes, somewhat indulgent. Ruth hasn't gone as mad, just a few bits that caught her eye. Even Alex couldn't baulk at her returning with additions to her wardrobe that are mostly neutrals for wearing to work, could he?

They walk to the tube, the rain falling lightly again. There is a queue, a mass of people waiting to descend into the station at Oxford Circus. Ruth and Fran wait patiently to get to the steps. It serves them right for going to the West End on a Saturday during the sales.

As they get closer to the stairs, the reason for the hold-up becomes clear. A woman, about their age, with a pushchair, a crying baby strapped into it and several shopping bags hanging from its handles, is bending over and talking softly to a small girl in a blue mackintosh. The child's curls are dishevelled and fat tears are rolling down her cheeks.

'Can we help?' Fran asks the woman.

Ruth is frozen.

She has recognised the children.

The little girl with curly hair squints up at her quizzically. 'Hello!'

The child's reedy voice seems to ring out above all the noise that surrounds them: the huffing commuters, the honking traffic, the man with the loudhailer proclaiming that the end is nigh.

In what feels like slow motion, the woman bending over turns and straightens to stand opposite Ruth. Her face blanches on seeing Ruth's features; her eyes harden as she grips her daughter's hand and the handle of the pushchair that holds her infant son. 'You.'

Fran hasn't noticed the exchange. She is down the steps below the pushchair, lifting it by the footrest.

'You get the top, Ruth. Let the lady take her daughter down.'

Given the opportunity to avoid Sara's eyes, she takes the handles of the buggy.

'No! Don't you dare touch my son.'

Ruth immediately steps back. The rain is falling heavily now. Her hair is sticking to her forehead.

'"Rain, rain, go away."' The little girl in blue intones the nursery rhyme as she looks up towards the heaving sky, eyes squinted at the rapidly falling drops. She has Alex's eyes. And his scowl.

Lily, Ruth remembers her name, Lily and Jake.

'We'll help get you down these stairs,' says Fran. 'Come on, we're all going to get soaked.'

But Sara is immobile. She grips Lily's hand and stares.

Ruth feels acutely aware of the way the rain is forcing the wild mass of her hair into a wet helmet, flat against her head.

'Ow, Mummy, my hand!'

Lily wriggles her hand from her mother's grasp to be free, turns and grips the grimy banister above her head with both hands, starting to take each step down into the station with dogged determination. The second her daughter is free of her hand, Sara turns away from Ruth, and looks towards Fran. 'Thank you.'

Slowly they descend the stairs at the same speed as Lily. Sara stays by her side for every step, Fran's arms straining to hold the double buggy, heavy with the weight of sleeping Jake, the bags of nappies and reduced-price children's clothes that hang from the handles. Ruth descends behind them, the rain still falling on her. She feels a pain in her palm. Her nails are digging into the flesh: she is clenching her hands into fists.

At the bottom, Lily falls into another screaming fit because there are no stairs left for her to descend. Sara bends over and negotiates with her. Once Lily is calm, she stands and looks at the two women before her squarely. She shakes her head, smiling. 'You know what?' Sara deftly lifts Lily onto her left hip. 'Good luck. You're going to bloody well need it.'

Ruth watches the woman guide the pushchair towards the barrier, which she opens with ease while talking to Lily, balanced on her hip. The little girl stares back at Ruth curiously as she disappears over the edge of the escalator heading down to the Central Line.

'You know her?'

Ruth nods. 'She's Alex's wife.'

Beside her, Fran becomes very still. In the harsh glare of the fluorescent lighting, the sunglasses still on top of her head are flecked with raindrops. Ruth can see her doing the arithmetic.

'You got together when his wife was pregnant?'

'It was already over between them. It's not as bad as it seems.'

But it is, and she knows it.

She knew from the moment Alex had sat next to her at Camille's dinner party that he was married. After all, she'd been Camille's bridesmaid with his wife. She knew that Sara wasn't there because, at her age, this pregnancy was proving trickier than her first. She knew he must be a bit lonely, coming there on his own, just as she was always lonely as the only unmarried one – the only 'single gal' – at all of Camille and Charlie's get-togethers. She knew that he'd always laughed at her jokes a little longer than necessary, that he'd always made time to talk to her at parties, that he'd always commented on her outfits, asked her about her work. She'd known all of this before she'd leant towards him during the hubbub of the meal and quietly asked him if he'd be willing to teach her about wine. He had smiled and told her to close her eyes, then hunt for the flavours of blackberries and manure.

'Oh, Ruth,' says Fran, 'no wonder you didn't tell me.'

Eleven

It looks like the aerial images Ruth had seen of flattened towns after hurricanes but her current view is not from above.

They stand in silence, taking in the scene before them.

Piles of rubble and tiles lie where the yacht club had stood.

When had she run past? Just hours ago? Yesterday?

Ruth has no idea how long they were inside the whale.

They walk through the ash to what was evidently a car park. Burnt-out cars, some on their sides, are pushed into a pile against a row of trees that stand naked, burnt, stripped of their leaves. The singed branches line the perimeter of the forecourt, like black cardboard cut-outs, the dust upon them like a covering of fake snow.

'I feel like we should cover our mouths and noses. This stuff is probably radioactive.'

She reaches across to Nik and tugs the screwed-up canvas bag from his pocket. Using her teeth, she creates enough of a tear to gain purchase and rip the material into two long strips. She hands one piece to Nik, who takes it, watching her wrap it around her face and tie it at the back of her head.

'We probably need gloves too.'

Nik watches Ruth shake her hands, like she's performing the end of a big musical number.

What is she on about?

Communication is going to be even harder with their faces covered. His hearing hasn't entirely returned and the cotton covering not only prevents him from reading her lips, it also muffles her voice. Whatever she's trying to say, the priority is finding food. Everything else can wait.

'Food first.' Nik mimes eating, then wraps the material around his face in the same way, tying it tightly at the back of his shaven skull, and wincing as he bursts several more blisters. He turns to go but Ruth puts her hand on his forearm to still him. She pulls the makeshift mask away from her mouth.

'Hello? Can anybody hear me?'

He heard that.

They watch carefully for any movement among the mounds of rubble. They hold their breath, trying to listen, straining to hear beyond the high-pitched ringing in their ears.

A few minutes pass and there is no response.

No movement.

No noise. Or, at least, none they can hear.

Ruth pulls up her mask and walks closer to the rubble, but Nik softly touches her upper arm. She turns back to him. He is shaking his head. She nods, and they turn from the rubble and start to walk into the town.

All the buildings along the way are the same. The public washrooms that he used just yesterday: a scattered pile of brown bricks, half the end wall still standing, a ceramic basin pointlessly attached to it. Water mixes with the ash causing a great sludgy river in their path. They step over it carefully. A pipe has burst within the rubble. It spurts forth, washing away the ash, leading it down the hill towards the sea.

They walk on.

There is nothing but destruction.

The small town in which he'd spent the last few days is reduced to nothing more than a neat grid system of bricks and rubble. Cremated trees and bushes poke out on the edges of the road, the odd car with its paint scorched and engine burnt out. The entire scene is criss-crossed with semi-fallen electrical and phone wires.

Is it the same everywhere?

For once he is pleased that he doesn't have a place to call home. At least something that doesn't exist can't be destroyed.

It occurs to Ruth that one of these ruined buildings might be where Nik lives. Or did he say he was from out of town? That he'd come here just for the whale? She remembers him saying he didn't have any family left, but surely he's got friends, colleagues. Surely he has people he needs to get to. People he needs to know are okay.

She drops back to walk a few paces behind him, trying to assess his emotions, but she cannot read him. She knows so little about him.

His name is Nik.

He has a pick-up truck.

He's a photographer.

How strange that she only knows these few facts about him, yet her fate feels inextricably bound to his.

They come to a crossroads. There is still an X where one road passes over the other, but nothing lies on either side, other than broken bricks, concrete and protruding metal poles.

In the distance, Ruth can see some structures that are higher than the rubble surrounding them. She taps Nik's shoulder, leaning forward and pointing them out to him.

He follows the line of her finger and nods. They walk faster towards the raised forms. Ruth can piece together the scene before her. She is slightly out of breath. Their pace has increased – Nik, ahead of her, is almost running. He is striding through the rubble and glass.

Many of the caravans still stand but with the paint removed from their surfaces, as if they had been sandblasted to nothing but their original metal. Nearly all the glass in their windows is blown out. Some lie on their sides, their tyre-less wheels in the air giving them the appearance of dead insects.

Ruth follows, panting now. She bends forward, her hands on her knees, trying to catch her breath. She watches as Nik stops and spins on the spot, orienting himself, before heading to one of the caravans. It sits alone, one of only a few that haven't been burnt out, the curtains flapping lightly in the windows that have shattered.

Nik pulls down his mask. He is smiling. 'I never connected the gas.'

Is this his home? Ruth hurries to catch him up.

Nik pulls at the door, once, twice, and then, using his foot on the metal as a lever, he finally manages to force it open.

The room looks as though it has been burgled. Papers and pictures are strewn everywhere, a light film of dust over all.

'I'm not sure we should touch anything.'

Ruth is behind him, her mask pulled down beneath her chin, her eyes searching the mess. Little does she know it doesn't look that much altered from when he left it.

He puts his face into the crook of his elbow, to cover his nose and mouth and opens a cupboard. It is filled with clothes, none folded. He grabs his beanie and pulls it over his head.

Better. He feels immediately less naked.

He retrieves a pair of gloves and his old snap-back cap and tosses them to Ruth. She catches them and puts them on, tucking her dust covered hair up into the cap and covering her blistered hands with the woolly gloves. He sees her forehead crease as she wonders why he's got winter clothes with him at the height of summer. Ah, well. Let her wonder.

He opens the drawer beneath the wardrobe and takes out a small but dangerous-looking knife, which he unsheathes. The blade is pretty sharp, could be handy.

Ruth draws back a little.

'It's my old fishing knife. Relax.'

'Is this your place?' She is turning, looking at the photographs strewn around the room, covered with a fine layer of dust.

'Kinda. I don't . . .' He stops himself. Is it really any of her business?

'Yeah, while I'm here it is . . . was.'

Nik turns to the shelf above the sink, which contains several cans of food, a packet of cereal and biscuits lying on their side, covered with a thin layer of dust. He reaches out to pick one up, then pauses.

He can feel her watching him. He turns back to her. 'You know, my gut is just telling me to get back to the beach.'

'It is?'

'I mean, I'm no scientist, but I'm pretty sure that this place is humming on a Geiger counter.'

'I thought there was some dispute over whether it was nuclear.' Ruth had watched more news in her few days in Auckland than she had in the last year. Newsreaders with panic in their eyes trying their best to present information that they simply didn't have. Not one report from Europe had been clear. There had been complete annihilation but no one was sure exactly what had happened. All they knew was that when it had happened everything was obliterated. It was destruction on a scale never witnessed in recorded history.

Nik is lit by the afternoon sun filtering through the window. He waves his blistered hand up and down, disturbing the motes of dust floating in the air. 'Look at all this shit we're breathing in. Whether it was nuclear, dirty bombs or some chemical shit, we don't know what all this crap is.'

He grabs a hoodie from the cupboard and pulls it over his head.

'I reckon we let the dust settle, get back to the beach, make a fire, pitch your tent, make a plan. It seems pretty obvious there isn't any human life to speak of here, but we can't be the only ones who have survived. That doesn't make sense. We just need to wait it out, see what happens next.'

Ruth nods. There is nothing Nik has said that doesn't ring true. Her stomach rumbles. 'What about food?'

'You've got more beans, right?'

'Yeah. They won't last long, though.'

'Hopefully they won't have to last us long. And we should eat seaweed.'

'Seaweed?'

'Yeah, roast it on sticks like I used to with Pops on fishing trips. For the iodine?'

Ruth shakes her head.

'After Hiroshima, Nagasaki, Chernobyl, they took iodine tablets. And iodine is in seaweed, yeah? I don't know exactly how it works. Just that it stops you dying immediately. You probably die of some hideous cancer later on, but we'll cross that bridge when we get there.'

'Seaweed and beans for dinner, then.'

He smiles at her and indicates the door. 'Ladies first.' He looks at Ruth: her jaw is set as it was when he first met her on the beach. He nods, contrite, and extends his arm. 'Sorry, what I mean is, lead the way.'

Twelve

'Pack your bags!'

Alex bursts through the door with his bike on his shoulder. Ruth looks up from her book. She can feel her stomach fizz. This is why she decided to share her life with this handsome, dynamic man.

'I'm whisking you away. Don't forget to pack some proper walking shoes and a waterproof!'

A waterproof? Her heart drops. She doesn't own anything that could be classed as a raincoat. She was hoping to escape the relentless dirge of February for a few days – sitting on a veranda, sipping cold drinks with the sun on her face – not heading somewhere that required weatherproof clothing.

She knew in her heart of hearts that leaving the UK was highly unlikely: Alex's New Year resolution was to use air travel only for work. She was destined to holiday via road or train. They could still be going to Paris, though, couldn't they? It wouldn't be warm, but it would be Paris.

She lets herself feel excited again: a little half-term adventure, just what they need.

She knows the trip has been engineered so Alex can distance himself from Sara taking the kids to her parents'. To Ruth the news that Lily and Jake weren't coming to stay was a blessed reprieve from having to play stepmother, but Alex had been bitching all week about his ex-wife making arrangements without consulting him. The change in his mood is a relief, and even if this mini-break is as much an opportunity for him to stick it to Sara as it is a surprise for her, she's delighted to be in receipt of a treat. One of the things Ruth first fell for in Alex was how absurdly romantic he is – the flowers, the grand gestures. He's like a character from a novel: her own Mr Rochester or Rhett Butler.

As they head towards King's Cross, Ruth feels giddy and light. She loves travelling by Eurostar. She is hoping for a rerun of their first weekend away: a hotel in the Marais, twisted in white sheets. Sunday spent walking through Beaumarchais, selecting oozy cheese in the market, oysters and wine on the street while a band plays on the corner. Then weaving their way back to the Gare du Nord, drunk on each other's company, her sleeping on his shoulder as they speed home under the expanse of the Channel.

The furrowed mud of the barren tilled fields flashes by as Ruth stares out of the rain-spattered window. It is a decidedly English panorama: wet, muddy, grim.

At King's Cross they didn't make the short transfer to the beautiful bricked building of St Pancras to enjoy a quick glass of champagne before boarding the train to Paris.

Instead Alex led her to a table on the 9.52 a.m. train to Leeds and her heart became distinctly weightier in her chest. She's not on her way to a late lunch in Montmartre, Alex has chosen her a sandwich from M&S that she doesn't like, and there is no room for her legs. He keeps opening his newspaper so it crosses her vision and distracts her from her book. Ruth is ready to scream when he reaches around her face and removes her headphones from her ears. 'How are you doing, Grumpy Guts? Forgiven me for the Wensleydale sandwich yet?'

Ruth sticks her tongue out at him and he catches it between his thumb and forefinger making her squeal. She feels her resolve melt and she laughs as he tickles her while they speed past Doncaster.

In Leeds, to her relief, they change trains and he allows her to choose her own coffee before they board, making a show that he would hate to be thought of as 'one of those men who always makes choices for his woman'. You do, though, she thinks, and orders a flavoured latte with whipped cream, just to get his goat, but he surprises her and orders the same. They both giggle like schoolchildren as they run for the next train, trying not to spill their drinks. They just make it. Alex holds the door open for her with his foot as she races along the platform. She jumps in just in time, and they fall into the carriage, laughing, as the conductor tells Alex off for obstructing the doors.

'Trouble seems to follow you wherever you go, Ms Lancaster.'

Alex's face is right next to hers as he whispers. She grabs him by the collar of his polo shirt. When she kisses him she can taste whipped cream and chocolate on his lips.

A woman on the table opposite tuts at their public display of affection. Ruth turns, her hackles raised, but the woman is now smiling broadly: Alex has already put her under his spell with a winning apologetic grin. A little flutter rises in Ruth's stomach. She knows it's shallow, but she can't help feeling smug that her boyfriend is so handsome.

At Settle, they're met by a ruddy-cheeked woman in her fifties who hoists their bags into her Range Rover and they wind across the Dales until they draw up in front of a little stone house with the lights on.

'Here we are!'

Their driver dismounts and lugs their cases into the house. She shows Alex how to work the heating, the fire and the stove while Ruth looks out of the window and wonders where on earth she'll be able to purchase the tampons she'll require before this week is through. Last month she had discovered to her dismay that the practicalities of menstruation was one of Alex's sensitive subjects and she was keen to avoid any bullshit surrounding it.

Their landlady, Rose, waves over her shoulder as she pulls out onto the narrow road and speeds up the hill towards who knows where.

'Alone at last.' Alex slides her shirt from her shoulder and places his lips against the skin of her neck.

In the kitchen, she slices the cherry tomatoes as instructed.

Alex is cooking tonight. She is the sous-chef.

Ruth sings to herself as she cuts each tomato into two. It's a song that an author she's fond of chose on the edition of *Desert Island Discs* she listened to earlier in the bath. She becomes aware that her singing is somehow discordant: while Alex chars peppers over the flames of the gas ring he, too, is humming to himself. He must have started quietly, but it's become more and more noticeable. She stops singing and listens to his humming. She recognises the bloody theme tune of that TV programme, the news quiz show he'd insisted on watching last night.

She'd begged him not to put on the telly, asked that they keep anything depressing at bay for their few days of holiday.

'You can't completely cut yourself off from what's going on in the world, my darling girl.'

'Watch me!'

She'd read in the bedroom as Alex had chortled along with the studio audience, laughter filling the lounge.

Ruth shakes her head to rid herself of the irritation and lets Alex's humming wash over her, mutely focusing on the tomatoes under her knife.

They eat their dinner at the dining table, with a single candle and the surprising silver cutlery that comes with the cottage.

Once they finish the meal, Alex pushes his chair back and gestures for Ruth to sit on his lap. She laughs but obliges.

'So, my love, let's talk about you. How are you feeling?'

'Full.'

'Ah, do I need to be a little more precise in my questioning?'

'I'm good. I'm happy to be here with you. And I'm a little anxious.'

'Anxious? Why?'

'Anxious that you're going to make me walk for miles tomorrow.'

'My lazybones.' He laughs. Softly he pokes the expanse of her belly. 'A nice long walk is just what you need, you pudgy piglet.'

His fingers moving on her stomach are ticklish and she catches her breath, giggling.

Alex leans back, smiling at her. The light hits his face from the right, casting shadows across the side nearest to her. Her stomach flips, recognising his tired beauty.

Does she love this man?

Her chest tightens.

'I love you, Alex.'

Her voice sounds rough, as if she needs to clear her throat.

'Oh, my darling, I know you do and I love you too.'

She feels a pricking at her eyes and, quickly, they fill with tears.

She kisses him hungrily, aggressively. Her tears continue to fall as he kisses her back. She stifles a sob and stands. She extends her fingers and pulls at his belt then unzips his trousers. Once he is inside her, his eyes closed, she continues to weep silently. Now they have started the tears won't stop.

She wipes at them with the heel of her hand.

She is getting breathless from the exertion, sweat blooming on her forehead. She raises herself and lowers herself again.

Again.

The oblivion that climax brings will turn off the voices in her head.

It will quell the hollow feeling in the pit of her stomach that lingers despite their recent meal.

It will dissolve the shadow of the newspaper on the train, the headline she averted her eyes from.

She knows that if she loses herself in him, if she blunts her thoughts with orgasm, she can avoid it all for a few seconds and the tears will stop.

'Careful.'

She is hurting him.

She is hurting herself a bit too, but that is the quickest route to escape.

In the morning, she agrees to his walk. She is keen to please him – in her mind it goes some way to making amends for her equivocating thoughts.

Alex straps on his hiking boots but assures her that her trainers will suffice. She holds his hand and follows his directions. It is easier, she finds, to agree to his instruction. She likes not having to make decisions: there's less responsibility if things go wrong.

'Up here.'

'Faster.'

'Come on!'

It makes her feel safe, cared for.

The drizzle has made his hair frizz a little and he looks younger with his cheeks flushed. It is a relief to take his large hand as he helps her over a stile and through a field full of sheep. She is thinking of nothing but what they are doing.

He makes her laugh. Playfully he gives the sheep voices and opinions as they pass through their pasture.

For lunch, they stop at a pub he has been to before. He orders them both a pint and a ploughman's without asking her what she'd like: it's as if he can read her mind.

She watches him at the bar, his long, straight back damp where the rucksack has pressed his T-shirt against the perspiring skin under his waterproof. As they eat, he tells her about the last time he walked these moors. She nods and smiles where appropriate while she chews. She doesn't say it, because she is enjoying his story, but it does make her feel a bit odd hearing about a trip, remarkably similar to the one they are on now, he took with his ex-wife.

As they pull their coats on to head back out into the grey afternoon, Alex diverts to the toilet and she takes the opportunity to hide the untouched pickled onion from her meal beneath a scrunched-up paper napkin on her plate. She doesn't want to risk the possibility of onion breath scuppering an impromptu snog on the walk back.

On Saturday night they read, sitting at each end of the settee, their legs entangled in the middle, feet on each other's belly, chest, under an armpit. Alex occasionally leans over and places a kiss on Ruth's foot while still reading through his thin-rimmed glasses.

She looks up and watches him.

He is deep in some history thing while she is engrossed in a new novel, a web of words about tangled lives. She wonders if they would be as absorbed in their reading if they swapped books. She feels a dull ache in her chest that comes from knowing that they would likely be asleep if they did. She tosses that thought aside as she is distracted by Alex peeling off her sock and kissing her ankle.

On the way back to London, Alex holds her hand and continues to read.

Having finished her book, Ruth watches the world pass by through the train window. Her mood is lighter than just four days ago, and the momentum of the train makes her feel as though she is achieving something despite sitting still. She has always wanted to experience long-distance travel by train, to cross continents overland, to see landscapes evolve as she slides along the rails from one country to the next. She has had a lifelong dream to travel on the Trans-Siberian Railway. She remembers using the dial-up internet on the family computer as a teenager, researching and putting together a budget for a journey that would take her from St Petersburg across the Gobi Desert all the way to Beijing. It was a project to which she gave more energy than she did to her revision. She wonders what happened to the spreadsheets she'd so carefully worked on. The spreadsheets that had never been used, cast aside for a summer spent experimenting with drugs at festivals with Fran and too much time waiting for that idiot Sam to call her back.

She's never got around to travelling as much as she hoped. Yes, she's been to bits and bobs of Europe but she's always wanted to see more of the world, to go on safari in Africa, to see penguins in Patagonia, whales off the coast of New Zealand.

She imagines taking a boat across the Atlantic to America

with Alex, how they would have to take buses and trains for weeks to get somewhere she's always wanted to explore, like Brazil.

Her hand grows sweaty in Alex's palm, thinking of how his ban on flying means she will never see the earth from above the clouds again. She will never again marvel at the surprising number of outdoor pools in southern England.

By the time the train pulls into King's Cross, Ruth has removed her hand from Alex's and has her fingers tightly interlaced in her lap.

Thirteen

They set up Ruth's tiny tent on a patch of sand where they have cleared the dust. They gather driftwood from along the ash-covered beach as the night closes in, building the driest sticks into a small fire in a pit they dig with their bare hands in the sand. To their mutual relief it catches from Nik's lighter. Once it is burning, they admit to each other that neither of them knows how to light a fire by rubbing sticks together. Then Nik burns his blistered hands trying to warm the can of beans in the flames. 'I'm a city kid, eh. Never really gone bush.' Nik flinches as he applies the antiseptic cream Ruth has forced upon him.

'I've only been camping in the South of France,' says Ruth.

When they wake the next morning, aching, and hollow at the remembrance of their reality, it is starkly apparent that the odour emanating from the dead beast has become stronger. It smells burnt with a lingering whiff of rot.

They collapse the tent and pitch it again, further away from the corpse of the whale on the other side of Nik's truck.

Nik cautiously runs a hand across the charred surface of the animal's skin. 'It's like it's been on the barbie. Just not done all the way through.'

A gruesome thought.

What would have happened to them if it had cooked?

Why hadn't they, anyway?

'It's really gonna start to reek soon. We need to find a way to puncture the belly too – they can explode, eh?'

'Wouldn't that be the icing on the cake!'

Despite its complete transformation from live, elegant beast to petrified bulk, Ruth still can't help but stare at the creature. Its size is entrancing, even if it now looks more like a mound of coal.

She looks at the mouth, now frozen open where they squeezed their bodies under the baleen plate to be born anew into this scorched world.

Already she is questioning that they were inside the whale when it happened. That they survived.

The memory of being curled beneath Nik, the stench, the darkness, the bright light, the sinister echo of the screaming wind. It seems distant already, like a half-forgotten dream.

She wants to ask Nik, 'Did it happen? How did it happen? How are we alive?'

But she doesn't dare. It is frightening somehow, to ask. As if by doing so she will break the spell and they, too, will disintegrate, become nothing but white dust, floating aimlessly before settling, a handful more ash upon the layer that now covers their world.

Nik suggests they fashion large letters spelling 'SOS' on the beach with rocks, in case there should be a rescue mission from above. They should keep the fire burning throughout the day should a ship pass and see survivors on the shore.

After these basic measures are in place, he finds there is little left to do but sit and think.

The questions start to percolate.

How many others have survived?

How is it they survived when it seems no others in the town had?

Will there be a rescue mission? How far does this desolation extend? How much longer do they have to live? Has anyone he knows survived?

It is too much to contemplate.

As they eat the rubbery seaweed they had toasted in their fire for the second night running, Ruth broaches the one question she feels safe to ask.

'What are we going to do about food?' She is starving. But, also, she needs something to do. An activity to keep the incessant questions to the margins of her mind.

She watches Nik in the firelight as he picks at his seaweed, its puckered, rubbery surface wrapped around the charred stick held before him.

'Nik?'

'Yeah, I'm thinking.' He rubs his hand across his forehead, then winces. 'I dunno if we should stay put or get out there. How do we know if anything we find'll be safe to eat?' He has left a charcoal smear across his skin and inflamed his angry blisters further. 'It could all be radioactive, or contaminated, or . . .'

Ruth nods for him to continue. It's good to hear that he doesn't know what to think either. It makes her feel less panicked to know that they're floundering together.

'We're probably already fucked anyway.' He indicates the blistered skin of his face.

Ruth brings her fingers to her neck and withdraws them quickly: it still burns at the slightest touch.

'I mean the water from the creek. It's bound to be poisonous, even though it tastes right.'

He pauses and turns to Ruth, a slight pink colouring his cheeks. 'Cos, not to be indelicate, I've got a proper case of the squits. Don't know about you?'

'Yes, my tummy is a bit upset.'

Going to the toilet has been the most physically distressing aspect of this new situation. Crouching in the dark at a distance from Nik, far enough so he couldn't hear her groans – but not so far that he was out of earshot altogether: she could call him for help or warn him of friend or foe approaching. In the water of the creek, she had washed the widest, softest reeds she could find to rid them of dust so that she could wipe herself, but still their grassy texture stung and cut as she did so. This evening she had tried shitting by the bank on the creek before burying it, like a cat, then washing her arse in the cold water. Later, when she watched Nik filling a can with water from the creek she blushed, feeling guilty for the part she might have played in contaminating the water he was about to consume.

'But beneath all that rubble out there, there must be enough packaged and canned food to keep us going for, well, months, if not years.'

Ruth considers all the houses and farms she had passed when she first arrived in the town. She can envisage the contents of their cupboards beneath the fallen bricks and concrete. The thought makes her stomach rumble.

Nik sighs. 'Fact is, if we don't eat . . . well, we're guaranteed to die and pretty soon. So, on balance, finding some food – even if it's glow-in-the-dark – is probably our best chance of survival. We'll keep up the seaweed, though.'

She watches as he places another charred rubbery shard of the once-green matter into his mouth. 'Oh, absolutely,' Ruth replies. 'Just try to make me give it up.'

*   *   *

As soon as the navy of night gives way to morning grey, they begin to sweat. The heat of the summer sun is working its way through the thick covering of clouds above them, although the day is murky.

They agree to head back to the caravan park to take what they can find from the caravans as a first port of call. Then they will investigate the viability of moving the rubble of what was once the village shop, see what they can scavenge.

'Worst case with the dairy will be that we'll find that lady from the campsite under the rubble.'

'Dairy?'

'Shop. Store. Whatever you Brits call it.'

Ruth has never seen a dead body in real life, only on television.

She fights off a shudder at the thought of finding the woman she'd met when she made her last purchases of food on arrival at the village. She has no idea what a body might look like in these circumstances.

She tries to ready herself by thinking of the most gruesome possibilities.

Would it be charred, petrified, like the skin of the whale since the blast?

Or would it be desiccated? Just bones?

Would the flesh still be on a body? Would she be able to see an expression on its burnt, stone-like face?

Ruth shakes her head, trying to dispel the images that flood her imagination.

She feels her empty stomach clench at the thought of Fran's familiar face, caught for ever in a grimace of fear and pain.

Maybe there won't be bodies, just shadows on the walls, like in Hiroshima. X-rays of the humans that were once there.

Please let it have been quick. Painless. A lightning-fast dispatch.

Who she is asking that of? She's never believed in a Higher Power and she certainly doesn't now. But it's less painful to imagine atoms scattered. To think that what remained was like a shadow on the road on a late summer afternoon.

Silhouettes of her mum, her dad, Fran, all those she would recognise in a heartbeat.

Is there still something elegant about a shadow if it arrived by such horrific means?

The caravan park is exactly as they left it.

Nik stops in his tracks and looks up to the burnt trees on the perimeter of the park, listening. 'No birds.' There is triumph in identifying the absence that has been bothering him for the duration of their walk. It is so still, so quiet. 'If we see anything sus, I reckon we both just gap it.'

Ruth looks at him blankly.

He's going to have to be careful to use less slang. She doesn't seem to understand half of what he's saying.

'Make a run for it, if anything seems dodgy. We meet back at the whale. Yeah?'

Ruth nods at him in agreement.

'Best to expect the worst until proven otherwise, I reckon.'

Nik hopes his anxiety about people turning feral is just a hangover from watching too many films about zombie apocalypses. He'd like to be more positive, more hopeful about the human spirit, but he doesn't want to have survived this far to lose it all by trusting someone he shouldn't.

Then: he doesn't know this woman from Adam and here he is putting his life in her hands. What choice does he have? Surely their best option is to stick together.

He puts up his hand, indicating for Ruth to pause and look around, his eyes scanning the dusty landscape for movement, then cautiously opens the door to his caravan.

Immediately he sets to work: he pulls the blankets and sheets off the bed, rolling them into a tight bundle and forcing them to the bottom of the bag – he's been freezing the last two nights. It seemed off to ask Ruth to share her sleeping bag, but a hoodie and a fleece just weren't cutting it. His neck is stiff too. He grabs the two pillows from the bed and straps them to each side.

Ruth watches Nik as he packs things, his every move disrupting the dust and filling the air with ash. She pulls her mask tighter, then starts picking up the papers and photographs that are strewn about. She tries not to look at the printed letters – it feels invasive – but she can't ignore the photographs. They are beautiful. The black, whites and greys of the images make the subjects seem as though they are from another time. The people in them seem not to know they're being photographed, absorbed in their own world. This one, a woman, her face obscured by long hair, sitting on a kerb, smoking: the cars on the road in the background are blurred, out of focus.

'Sweet as, bro!'

Nik's voice makes her jump and drop the photograph.

She turns to see him laughing, a package of toilet rolls held aloft like a trophy. Only one of the six has been removed from the plastic packaging. His voice echoes around the caravan and he tosses the package to Ruth. He has opened another door to reveal a small toilet, a basin with a mirror above it and a shower cubicle so small it seems unlikely that his frame could fit inside it.

He pulls on the mirror and it opens to reveal a cabinet. He drags all the fallen items off the shelves: a toothbrush, a tube of toothpaste, a small bottle of bright green mouthwash, a large bottle of shower gel, shampoo, and then a small glass bottle in the shape of a man's torso. He sprays himself.

'Are we here to get you ready for a date or on the hunt for food?'

Nik shrugs, then sprays her too. She protests and waves her hand to disperse the strong scent. 'Sorry, mate, but you could do with it.'

Ruth turns her back on him. Her cheeks are burning. Washing just hasn't seemed a priority since they first dipped into the sea and somehow, though she has been doing little other than gathering wood, time seems to have been contracting and expanding so she has lost all sense of sequence. She has no idea when she last had a good wash.

They set to work scavenging from the main room.

Opening the cupboards, Ruth finds little in the way of food: some crackers, cereal, a jar of peanut butter. Nik can't have been here long. Did he really just come for the whale? Doesn't he want to get back to his home?

What will she do if he does that?

Go with him?

Or stay here? Stay here alone?

Ruth shakes her head: less thinking, more action.

She opens a drawer and finds a scant amount of cutlery, which she empties into her rucksack. She keeps one spoon in her hand, though: she pulls down her mask, twists the plastic lid off the peanut-butter jar, plunges the spoon into the smooth paste and lifts it to her lips.

'Oh, yeah, that's what I'm talking about!' Her words are muffled, the peanut butter sticking her tongue to the roof of her mouth.

'Hit me up!' Nik, his hands full, opens his mouth with the request. Ruth refills the spoon and feeds it to him. He closes his lips and the spoon reappears, clean, in less than a second.

Nik closes his eyes and groans in pleasure.

It becomes apparent to Ruth that they are in extremely close proximity.

She can smell the aftershave he sprayed on himself just minutes before, but also the smell of him, a scent that has become more familiar over the past few days as it has increased in strength. Ruth is the closest she has been to Nik since they lay on the rug that night, Before.

His eyes are still closed.

She looks at the width of his mouth, his lips ridged from dehydration, the hairs on his face and chin forcing their way through the grimy surface of his angry skin. She looks at his eyelids, the lashes curled at the edge of each almond-shaped crescent.

Nik's eyes open and look directly into hers.

She is holding her breath.

There is a tingling in her palms starting at the base of her thumbs.

'We should try the tap.'

Ruth turns away.

She reaches out to the tap and turns it. It doesn't even splutter.

'It's connected to the main tank. Probably evaporated with the heat.'

Ruth picks up a bottle of washing-up liquid, closes the lid firmly and drops it into her bag. She wants to wash her clothes.

Nik stretches over her and takes the radio from the window-sill where it lies on its side. He turns the dial. Nothing happens. 'Munted.'

That unfamiliar word again, the meaning now clear.

Nik registers Ruth watching eagerly as he takes off the back of the radio to inspect it. They'd discussed how a radio might be a possible way of making contact. With others? With a rescue mission? It seems a little hopeful. 'Don't fret, just needs batteries. Hopefully some in the dairy. Under all the rubble.'

How useful it'll be with batteries is questionable. He's good with cameras but he doesn't know where to start with long-wave radio stuff.

He's getting ahead of himself.

Some batteries'll be a good start.

Nik flings it into his bag with a few final things: the last of his clothes, his paperwork and photos that Ruth has piled on the desk.

'Okay. Let's try the next one.' He indicates for Ruth to exit the caravan by the open door.

He watches as she readjusts her mask and pulls her cap down to step outside. He waits for her to move away from the door, then turns back into the bedroom and opens the drawer beside the bed. He picks up the notebook that lies inside it and slides an envelope out from between the leaves.

A faded colour photograph of a smiling woman wearing shorts and a vest. Her long black hair is flecked with grey in a plait that hangs over her shoulder. She is sitting on the steps of a wooden porch, looking directly at the camera. A scruffy black and white mongrel sits at her knee, its head cocked, also looking into the lens.

Nik holds the photograph carefully between his forefinger and thumb, brings it up to his lips and closes his eyes, then puts it back in the envelope and slides it carefully into the back pocket of his jeans.

The mobile homes that aren't burnt out haven't been occupied recently. There is little to be scavenged, though Ruth suggests the padding from the built-in seats, the material from the curtains and possibly even piping and wires might be useful, in time.

'We won't be around long enough to have to think about that.'

'Cheery,' says Ruth.

'I mean, hopefully we'll be rescued.'

Ruth suspects he meant exactly what she had originally understood.

They are at the corner where the shop once stood. The dust coats everything. The metal sign that stood on top of the building just days ago protrudes from the fallen bricks and tiles. The 'dairy' is nothing more than a pile of debris.

'Okay, I guess we just start.'

Nik takes the half-filled rucksack off his shoulders and drops it in the middle of the road.

They move the bricks slowly and carefully. Two piles grow: bricks and rubble on one side, anything they consider 'useful' on the other. One pile is growing much faster than the other. It is hard, heavy work. Ruth is sweating profusely. She wants to take her hat and mask off, but she knows they afford her a little protection from the dust that swirls around them.

'Sweet as!'

Nik is some distance away from her, rapidly moving pieces of rubble. He picks something up and raises it to show her, wiping the dust off it with his glove. He extends his arm, holding out a dented brown can towards Ruth. 'Take it.' He hands it to her, then returns to the same spot and lifts another can from the rubble. He rubs the dust onto the leg of his jeans and wipes around the lip. The can hisses to life.

Nik pours the liquid from the can into his open mouth. 'Stoked! First thing we find and it's my favourite soda!' Ridiculous to be so happy about lemonade, considering the circumstances. But he's loved this stuff since he was a kid. It's always been a treat.

Guilt prods at him. He shouldn't be enjoying himself.

As if in response to his thoughts, the light starts to fade. The sky is turning a darker shade of grey.

'Bit early to be getting dark, isn't it?' Ruth sounds nervous. Does she, like him, find it hard to believe that the worst has passed?

He looks up at the descending gloom above them, then down at the scant pile of cans, tins and packets that sits at his feet. 'We've not done badly, eh? Enough to keep us going for a bit. Better pack up and make a move.'

They load the goods into their bags, trying to shake and wipe as much dust as possible from each item as they do.

Pulling the heavy bags onto his shoulder, Nik's head is drawn to a noise behind him. A soft thudding. He turns. Rain is falling, slowly revealing the red of the shop's sign.

He looks up at the sky and a drop hits him directly in the eye. He pulls down his mask and opens his mouth, letting the raindrops fall into his mouth.

Ruth is struggling to see. The rain is heavy now, torrential. The weight of the bag on her back hampers her speed and makes the muscles of her legs burn, just as it did when she'd run towards the whale, Before.

Nik is running behind her – she can hear him panting, and the splash every time his feet make contact with the ground.

The road has become a black river as the grey ash runs off the rubble into the street. The rain removes the ash and it becomes more obvious where one material ends and another starts. At the beach the black-flecked gold of the sand is visible once more, and the soft green of the reeds along the bank of the river.

Ruth takes the heavy bag from her shoulders and pushes it under the truck to protect it. She grabs the few empty vessels they have – the baked beans tins, her water canteen, the plastic bottle – and places them on the vehicle's paint-stripped bonnet. Quickly, they start to fill with water.

She removes her hat, her gloves and then each item of her sodden clothing, slinging each piece over the side of the truck's flatbed. They begin to show their true colours as the rain washes white dust from their fibres.

Nik stands motionless.

She laughs at him and opens the door to the truck.

Retrieving what she was looking for, she turns to Nik, the bar of soap in her hands. 'You said I needed a wash!' And begins to lather her naked body.

Nik can feel the heavy rain starting to soak through his filthy clothes.

Ruth is laughing wildly. Her voice reaches him even over the cacophony of the rain. It looks like she's having fun.

'Fuck it!' He removes his shirt, his boots and socks, his vest, his jeans and finally, his pants, chucking them all into the ute. Naked, he moves closer to her and holds out his hand for the soap.

When the rain stops, they realise they can't build a fire: the driftwood is too wet.

They shiver next to each other, eating peas, cold, from a tin.

They share the last orange, the sweet juice running down the sides of their chins, and agree to store the wood beneath the truck from now on.

With no fire, they head into the tent as soon as it is dark. They each have a pillow now and Nick spreads the additional blankets he took from the caravan over them both.

'You have them. I have a sleeping bag.'

'Nah, we're in this together. Share whatever we find. Deal?'

The air inside the tent smells of soap. They have fresh clothes on. It feels almost normal, like they're on some sort of outward-bound course and Ruth's sharing a tent with a colleague she doesn't know particularly well.

She reaches up over her shoulder and tugs at the zip of her sleeping bag, pulling it down from top to bottom, and pushes the covers off them both.

'Hey! What are you doing?'

She pulls the sleeping bag from underneath her and arranges it over them like a double quilt, then the blankets.

'Deal,' she says, into the dark.

She tries to stay very still; without the sleeping bag, she is aware of the proximity of Nik's body next to hers, the heat emanating from him. She has an overwhelming urge to shuffle back into him, to feel the warmth of his chest against her.

Unbidden, an image of Alex's sleeping face comes to her.

Alex.

She feels a pressure across her chest.

She scrunches her eyes closed, trying to dispel the image, push away the questions that are forming in her head.

Where would he have been when it happened? Did he know it was coming? Was he scared?

She'd been so angry with him when she'd left.

Her breath is shallow. She feels as though she can't fill her lungs, as if the air is getting stuck in her throat.

Nik places a hand on her back, his palm flat and firm between her shoulder blades. 'Just concentrate on exhaling.'

She breathes out through her mouth, then in through her nose for eight counts, just as she had always told the children at school to do when they were upset.

She feels calmer.

Exhale.

Inhale.

Exhale.

Beneath the clean, soapy scent of the man behind her, she can smell the burnt, rotting whale carcass festering outside in the dark.

Fourteen

There is a distant promise of spring as Ruth opens the door of her mobile classroom. Works are taking place in the main building and this has forced Year Two out of their usual space into mobile classrooms, dotted along the perimeter of the playing field.

Ruth prefers these caravan-style rooms. They have been cold since November, but she enjoys the way sunlight streams in from both sides, big golden shafts that light the little faces concentrating on forming the alphabet with their newly sharpened pencils.

When it rains, the percussion on the roof reminds her of camping trips as a small child. Dinners of baguette, unsalted butter, cheese and ham directly from the *supermarché* carrier bag; warm, set yogurt eaten using the lid for dessert as the sun set and the midges nibbled at her bare ankles.

It feels as though her class is cocooned with her inside the rectangular Portakabin shell. They aren't connected to any other classrooms, so when the children are quiet, reading or taking 'rest-time', with their heads on their folded arms, she can't hear the shrill voices of other lessons taking place next door. Just the planes passing overhead at regular four-minute intervals and the occasional siren beyond the school gates.

For most of the afternoon she has mistakenly thought it was Friday. She had even given little Marcy the care package for the class hamster she was taking home for the weekend. Then she'd remembered, with a drop in the pit of her stomach, that it was Thursday and a full school day lay between her and the freedom of her weekend. Her heart sank.

It is still almost light, but it will be evening before long, though it is not yet five o'clock. She is longing for the clocks to go forward so that she can leave school in daylight. The imminent change of season means it will soon seem that she finishes teaching in the middle of the day again, and she smiles to herself, locking the door behind her and placing the classroom key in the front of her leather satchel.

'Fancy a drink, Ms Lancaster?'

Ben. He has his bag slung over his shoulder.

'I should probably go home. My boyfriend gets back tonight.'

'Just the one? I could do with one after today's news, couldn't you?'

Ruth has been studiously avoiding the news. It's too depressing. She has disabled the alerts on her phone and is watching only streaming services, limiting her listening to podcasts without any current-affairs discussion. It has been particularly easy to avoid this week, with Alex away for work. But she is prepared to go back to her old routine of reading in bed, listening to classical music through her headphones as he shouts at the political pundits on the late-night news. He has been away only five days, but she is delighted to find that she has missed him. He won't be home for a bit, though – she's got time for a quick pint.

They opt for the 'Monty', the Montego Arms, the pub closest to the school and the teachers' regular. Ruth dislikes its purposely peeling flock wallpaper and broken furniture, but there are several corners in which to hide, in case other members of the faculty have decided to drown their sorrows too – and a particularly good pie-and-a-pint deal for teachers that keeps her and the rest of the staff at Ladywell Academy loyal.

Ben places her drink before her. 'American pale ale. Was your choice influenced by today's events?'

'No. One word about the news and I'm off.'

'Sure. If you want to stick your head in the sand, I'm happy to join you.'

He mimes zipping his mouth shut and locking it, then sits down next to her with a thud. 'Ugh, what a day.'

'Those ten-year-olds been running rings around you again?'

'Yeah, all right, Professor. Some of us are prepping for the eleven plus, while you waft around teaching the ABC and one plus one is two.'

Ruth is fond of Ben. She thought him a bit wet when he started in September, but as she's got to know him, over microwaved soup in the staffroom and the odd pint after work when Alex is running late, she's begun to like him.

He's not immediately handsome, but there is something sweet about his slightly upturned nose and broad cheeks. He dresses like a child's drawing of a teacher in the 1970s: corduroys, flannel shirts and a satchel that used to be his dad's, which Ruth finds particularly endearing – she has the leather bag her mother started university with at eighteen.

'So, where's your boyfriend?'

'Norway. Some conference to do with the charity he works for.'

'Is he religious?'

'What?'

'Working for a charity, doing God's work.' Ben takes a sip of his pint.

He's flirting with her. Their conversations have a distinct arc that she has become used to. He will start by enquiring into her welfare, expressing an interest in her partner, asking how she and Alex's cohabitation is progressing. Then he will be laughing at Alex, finding something risible in whatever she has disclosed to him and undermining Alex ever so slightly to try to worm his way into her affections. The thing is, just because she's noticed the pattern, it doesn't mean it's ineffective. On occasion she has left the pub with Ben to return home to Alex. Later, seeing Alex's bike carefully chained up to the railing outside her building, she has been rattled to find she's smiling to herself at Alex's meticulousness. She has noticed him at the kitchen sink on a Saturday morning, scrubbing a plastic yogurt pot thoroughly before he places it in the recycling and giggled, remembering a pointed question from Ben the night before about Alex's recycling habits. She has watched Alex teasing his curls with his fingers to give them volume and blushed, recalling Ben's request for insight into Alex's hair-care regimen.

'I'm not sure you're going to be able to find too many jokes about my boyfriend helping to feed refugees. Sorry to disappoint!' Ruth smiles and picks up her pint.

'I'm just interested!' Ben raises the pitch of his voice in mock outrage. 'Honestly, I mean there's not much to say about the guy, but we can all agree he's got an interesting job.'

Ruth laughs, and hits Ben on the arm. It is surprisingly firm under her open palm. 'Bloody hell, welcome to the gun show! Have you been pumping iron or something?'

Ben flexes his biceps. 'Just a little light working out.'

She brings the back of her hand to her neck and notices it feels hot to the touch.

She looks at her watch: it is nearly 6 p.m., the sky outside is dark, the lights of the cars whizzing past the pub causing streaks on the windows. She drains her pint. 'I'd better go.' She wipes the corners of her mouth with her forefinger and thumb.

'Oh, come on, just one more. What time does his flight get in?'

Ruth puts her bag on the kitchen table. She looks at the clock. It is nearly nine.

Her phone vibrates, making her jump.

Just landed at City. Will die if I don't have you the moment I get home. A x

Ruth puts the tips of her fingers to her lips. She goes to the bathroom without hitting the light and scrubs her teeth with her electric brush, then rinses with Alex's herbal mouthwash.

She looks at herself in the bathroom mirror.

She wants to shower too. She turns the tap, increasing the temperature until it is almost scalding. She steps under the flow of water, letting the heat cascade over her.

She lathers her hair, the scent making her stomach turn. She can still feel Ben's hot breath against her ear telling her how good she smells. She rinses the conditioner out of her hair and turns off the shower.

She stands in the dark, naked, dripping into the bath.

The sound of the front door brings her back to the present. The hallway floods into the dark bathroom through the glass panel above the door as Alex turns on the light.

'Is there a gorgeous woman in the house?'

'In here!'

Ruth steps out of the bath, still wet, and reaches for a towel to wrap herself in. She quickly wipes between her legs as she hears Alex approach down the hall, and notes how sensitive she is.

'Saving electricity?' Alex laughs, turning on the light as he enters the bathroom. 'Showering in the dark? Now that's commitment.' He steps towards her and snakes his arm around her back, pulling her towards him. 'I see you've relieved me of the effort of undressing you.' He pulls the towel, exposing her skin to the cooling air of the bathroom. He drops his head and takes her nipple into his mouth.

For the second time that evening, Ruth feels her palms tingle and the back of her knees soften and she leans into his touch.

She can feel the water from her freshly washed hair soaking into the sheets as Alex's body moves above her. She doesn't like the idea of sleeping in a damp bed. She should have just let him get on with it in the bathroom, as he'd seemed so keen to do.

Ruth looks over his shoulder at the uneven plaster of the ceiling. There is a darkening patch on the paintwork by the window where the growth she covered with anti-mould paint last summer is fighting its way through.

With a grunt, Alex collapses on her, out of breath, and kisses her neck. As his muscles soften, he becomes heavier, crushing the air out of her. She doesn't complain, though. She lies, her breathing constricted under the weight of his bulk, staring at the ceiling, wondering how long it will be before she needs to get out her ladder to scrub at the mould, then paint over it once again.

Fifteen

The sun hasn't broken through the covering of thick grey cloud since the rain set in. The complete blackness of the night turns slowly to navy, sliding into a soft grey. That lasts several hours, until it fades over the horizon; the navy returns, then gives way to black again.

The initial adrenalin of their situation has abated.

Their sleep is no longer the dreamless coma that their bodies first employed to protect them, allowing their minds to process what had happened, to preserve energy for the stress of the next day.

Now they dream vividly. Images of their former lives haunt them in lurid distortion.

Ruth dreams of home: an England where her parents morph into celebrities from glossy magazines as she tries to embrace them.

She dreams of eating writhing insects from a dirty tin while at a table in a fancy restaurant with Fran, who morphs to Camille, then Alex and back again. They sit on chairs made of the spines of creatures she cannot identify, a chandelier glitters overhead, and through wall-length windows she can see red Routemaster buses flying through fuchsia-pink skies.

Waking each day, she feels disoriented and disbelieving.

Is she still dreaming?

Is this a nightmare?

How can this new reality be as strange as her dreams?

The relentless gloom of the days since the sun was occluded, in which day is barely separated from night, do not help. Her only company being a man of whom she knows next to nothing makes matters worse.

It is not the first time in her life she has woken up beside someone she barely knows.

Before, waking up beside a snoring stranger had come with the joy of quietly sliding back into her jeans and exiting an unfamiliar flat with a careful click of the front door. So clear is that feeling of emerging onto a morning street with bird's-nest hair, the mild embarrassment at the curious glances on the early half-empty tube, the gleeful joy in texting Fran news of her latest conquest. What she would give to be able to text Fran.

Now, waking to see the ruched bedding where Nik has spent the night sleeping beside her serves only as a reminder of the desperate grief that is pursuing her. She can feel sadness lapping at her heels. She is running from it, turning from it, pushing it away; she is trying to focus on what she needs to do to survive.

But surviving is painful too.

What they need to do to survive seems as nightmarish as the grief she is avoiding.

Ruth exits the tent.

It's a scene that she's not sure even her subconscious could have conjured in such gruesome detail: Nik, stripped to the waist, covered with a fine pink spray of blood and fat.

A portion of the hide of the whale spread out on the sand, like a trophy rug. The flayed entrails of the most majestic creature she has encountered.

Nik is slowly dismantling the whale piece by piece.

They haven't spoken for days but exist like an old married couple after an argument.

The shock of it, when she had returned from collecting driftwood yesterday, had propelled her into a fit of anger she hadn't seen coming. Before she knew it, she had dropped the wood she was carrying and was upon Nik, grabbing at his arms pulling him away from the creature.

Now, they silently keep their agreement to share, but they haven't done so with good grace.

Ruth has abstained from assisting him in taking apart the whale, and he has responded by ceasing communication other than to share food and shelter.

She has watched him uncover the horrifying loot of the whale's belly: a giant fishing net with multi-coloured floats; a tarpaulin, barely ripped; glass jars – some even with lids; a red plastic chair, their only furniture, not damaged and strong enough to hold Nik's weight; and, most horrifying of all, a giant, tumescent twisted mass of multiple plastic bags. To see him discover these items and more within the guts of the beast was to feel the guilt of her own survival topped with a new layer on each discovery. A testament to the waste, greed and disregard her species has shown to the sanctity of all life, as if the scorched land that surrounds them doesn't speak loudly enough to her of that already.

Nik looks round from his crouched position near the growing flames to see if she is watching. She isn't. Her focus is on her knees. She is frowning.

With a grunt, Nik heaves a chunk of the gelatinous white material onto the fire. The small flames catch and it is immediately ablaze. He stands and throws another two large pieces of driftwood onto the flames. He is shirtless still, though it is now dark: the heat of the fire means he can dry his body and clothes quickly after washing them in the creek.

He turns to where she sits at the mouth of the tent and, as if feeling his gaze upon her, she looks up.

'Join me?'

'It stinks.'

Progress!

He has tried to get her to talk for days now, to no avail. He feels a wash of hope to hear her voice over the roar of the flames. He's still raging at her – the spoilt little princess – but keeping this up is not helping either of them.

'Yeah, it's shocker, but it will keep us warm.'

She walks towards him and takes a seat on the sand near the blaze, studiously avoiding Nik's eyes.

'Still packing a sad?'

Ruth is jutting her chin.

'Jeez. You're like a three-year-old.' Nik shakes his head and turns towards the ute. He returns with two cans, opens them and places them in the glowing wood with a gloved hand. Ruth is studying the map she'd found in the glovebox of the ute.

'Planning a trip?'

Ruth purses her lips in response.

'I reckon we should stay put. The set-up here is pretty sweet. Start moving, you'll get lost in the debris. You'd have to carry food, set up camp. And you might bump into others, eh? Others who might not be as friendly as me.'

He smiles widely, performing. If he could just break the ice with a laugh, maybe they could untangle this sorry mess of an argument.

Ruth scowls and folds up the map, laying it on the sand beside her. She stares into the flames; her eyes shine red.

Nik pulls the two cans from the fire, swearing as he burns himself through the gloves. He's not made for this outdoors lark. He empties half of each can onto the two enamel plates they took from the caravan and hands one to Ruth. 'Dinner is served, madame.'

His eyes glint with good humour in the glow of the fire. 'Far out, you're really gonna keep this up?'

He leaves a gap to allow Ruth to reply but she remains mute, her chin pushed out in defiance.

'Give me strength.'

Ruth pushes the canned spinach around her plate, the four unnaturally coloured frankfurters now surrounded by a bed of vivid green. 'It just seems . . .' She stops talking abruptly but Nik waits expectantly.

He is hungry for more words, any words. Even another argument would be better than being alone with his thoughts.

'. . . brutal,' she says flatly.

Nik nods in agreement. 'Yup, it is brutal all right.'

They sit, eating the salty sausage and spinach. After a while Nik breaks the silence. 'It's brutal and it's bloody hard yakka.'

He pauses. Reframes the sentence. 'It's hard work and I could do with some help.'

Ruth nods.

'It's not something I want to do, eh? It's about surviving.'

'I know. It's just so horrible.'

'True.'

'We could have moved further away.'

'I don't know much, but I know that Survival 101 is to stay put. If there *are* rescue parties, it's best to stay right here. A moving target is much harder to find.'

'Okay, but we could have gone just a little further down the beach.'

'Do you have any idea how far the smell of one of these things rotting would spread?'

'No.'

'Far, plus it's a waste. It'd be a waste of good materials. Of fire lighters. Of skin. Of bones. Of food.'

'You're expecting me to eat that?'

Ruth points to where Nik has set up what looks like a rudimentary washing line that criss-crosses the sand next to the truck. But it isn't clean, fresh laundry that hangs on it, flapping slightly in the wind: it is long strips of meat, flecked with fat.

'The cans won't last for ever.'

Ruth sits in silence.

'The temperature is dropping, Ruth. We need to think beyond pulling the odd can out of the rubble. Plus, like I said before, it's a waste.'

The fire crackles as the fat hisses and burns, turning the flames white and purple.

'I'm sorry.'

Ruth's words hang in the air, like the stench of the burning whale fat.

At last, an apology.

That was what he was after, wasn't it?

But now he's got it he's not sure he wants to accept it. He's stuck with this woman, yes, but that doesn't mean he has to like her. It irks him that he feels a responsibility towards her. Why doesn't he just let her go?

Let the stupid Pom go bush and fend for herself. What does he care?

Does he care?

'I know you're right, about the waste. About making stores. But our whale. She saved us. I don't know how, but it would seem that we're alive, when no one else in the vicinity is, because of this creature. Cutting her up? It feels wrong.'

Her?

Of course she's identified the creature as female.

Nik sighs and runs his hand over his head. Best to pick his battles. He really could do with help to dispose of the rest of the whale. And, anyway, it's surely best to stick together, even if you're with a Pom princess whose mental stability you aren't entirely convinced of.

'If the purpose of this beast here was to save us, I figure, by leaving it to rot, we're saying a big old "fuck you" to whatever it is that has allowed us to survive this far. You've seen what I have. It's bleak. This could be the difference between us surviving the winter and not.'

Ruth nods. She knows he's right. She knows her outrage is a vestige of a set of beliefs she can no longer afford to have. She knows little about the new world they're living in, but she does know that fighting with Nik when he is only trying to keep them alive is a very stupid thing to do. 'Tomorrow I'll help.'

He smiles at her, a real smile, not the tight one that barely covers his blatant dislike of her. It is a smile that betrays his relief. A smile that extends peace between them.

She returns it.

It feels good. It feels good to let her anger capitulate to his kindness.

The spark of an idea.

She's not sure if it's possible, but it feels as though it might go some way to paying tribute to the animal, while also fulfilling Nik's desire that it be put to use.

'How strong do you reckon the bones are?'

'Pretty strong.'

She blushes. Will he laugh at her for the suggestion?
Maybe she shouldn't have mentioned it.

But he's smiling at her, nodding, encouraging her to speak.
So she does.

Sixteen

'Darling!' Anne waves at them with both arms from her kneeling position on the front lawn as the car pulls up. 'Jim! They're here!' she calls, into the house, as she carefully gets to her feet.

Ruth's mother has on a floral dress, much more formal than she ordinarily wears for gardening, and a full face of make-up. Although she is also wearing gardening gloves and is holding a trowel, there is little evidence of her altering the state of the border along the side of the lawn.

'Just thought I'd pull a few weeds out before our horticulturalist guest arrived.'

'Mum, you make it sound like he's a judge for the Chelsea Flower Show.'

'Well, darling, agriculture and horticulture do go hand in hand. Anne! You look radiant.' Alex steps in front of Ruth and grabs Anne to kiss her on both cheeks. To Ruth's horror, she witnesses a touch of pink spread across her mother's face. 'Thanks so much for having us for Easter, Anne. The wine is covered, as requested!'

Alex heads into the house, his neatly packed bag slung over his shoulder and a box of wine under his arm. Ruth hears his voice raised in greeting to her father.

'Do make yourself at home, Alex!'

Anne eagerly follows his large strides into the house.

Ruth is left alone by the car, wrangling with her overstuffed suitcase, considering how it seems he already has.

It's Good Friday and tonight the four of them will enjoy a barbecue before her aunt, cousin and the boys arrive.

Alex is helping Anne in the kitchen, cutting the salad ingredients to specification. 'Is this how you like them sliced, Annie?'

'Perfect, thank you, Alex.'

'Call me Al.'

'Like the Paul Simon song?'

Through the floorboards, Ruth can hear the trill of her mother's laugh as she flirts with him.

She can hear her dad outside, busy at the barbecue, scrubbing the spokes of the grill with his trusty metal brush, changing the gas, generally fiddling more than is required to cook a few slabs of beef.

Ruth slides the neatly folded blanket from the top of the airing cupboard and goes downstairs silently, then slips out of the side door. Cautiously, she walks over the loose shale of the path along the side-return of the house in her bare feet. She ducks under the kitchen window so she is not seen by her mother and boyfriend. The hard edges of the stones are hurting the soles of her feet without puncturing them, on the edge of pain and pleasure. She crosses the smooth paving stones behind the house. Her father's back is to her, but still she tiptoes on the cool stone so she is not heard. On the grass she picks up her pace and goes to the end of the garden.

Beneath the apple tree she lays out the rug and sits on it. She looks up at the sky, still visible through the branches above her, the leaves of the tree only partially unfurled. Then, with a satisfying sigh, she lies down and raises her book above her.

Opening to the title page, Ruth finds an inscription, a poem in a hand that resembles her mother's. It's quite sexy – she feels her neck prickle with embarrassment. Was this written to her father? Another lover of her mother's who existed before him? A university fling? An unrequited crush? It makes absolute sense that Anne is a sexual being – Ruth is her daughter after all – but it still feels slightly strange to come across evidence of it in verse in the front of a dog-eared old novel. It's a book she's never read before, though she's meant to. She pulled it off the shelf, slim and smaller in size than the books surrounding it, its cracked green spine calling to her. She flicks past the poem to the first page of print. The words swim on the page, but she can feel the potential of a new story in her hand. She reads on as the sunlight dances through the leaves of the apple tree. Ruth rolls over to lie on her belly and wiggles her bare feet against the wool of the blanket; it scratches, a comforting sensation she loves.

She can hear the radio in the kitchen. The programme her mother is listening to has the cadence of *Woman's Hour*, but it's too late in the day, surely. Maybe it's a repeat. The dulcet tones of the female presenter mix with the sound of a knife against a plastic cutting board. She hears her mother's voice calling her, then asking Alex to look for her. She hears his voice upstairs seeking her out and returning to the kitchen to tell Anne she is nowhere to be found. Her mother knows her hiding places, though, and soon the vivid images of the New England restaurant are punctuated by Anne calling to her from the patio. She asks her to lay the table.

'Coming! I'll just finish this paragraph.'

A few more pages. She'll delay just long enough to finish the chapter.

* * *

After dinner, they sit outside in the fading light. Anne rolls a cigarette – her weekly indulgence – and smokes it. She is slightly drunk, gesticulating, as she tells them about the disagreements in her book club this week.

'Do you ever like the same books, Mum?'

'Rarely. But we all enjoyed this year's Booker winner.'

They ask Alex about his work, about the process. Jim refers to the latest breakthrough in famine aid that Alex is so proud of as a 'Franken-crop', an expression Ruth knows he is likely to use for as long as Alex is part of her life.

That thought shocks her. *As long as he is part of my life* – is she considering a part when he won't be?

She thinks of the words she read earlier, of the paralysing fear the character in the book experienced. A panic, a strange sort of alienation and distance from her surroundings as though she was dizzy or underwater.

Ruth realises she is holding her breath.

'You're uncharacteristically quiet, Ruthie.'

Of course her father would notice that she's not quite herself. He is less in thrall to Alex than her mother.

'Oh, just thinking about life.'

She reaches out from under the woollen rug she brought over from the apple tree as the sun lost its warmth. Her hand finds her father's and clutches it tightly.

'Strange times we live in,' he says, gripping hers in return. 'There'd be something wrong with us all if we didn't need a quiet moment every now and again to think about everything that's going on in this confused old world of ours.'

'Please no politics, Jim.'

'Annie, life is politics, and while it might not be affecting our day-to-day at the moment these issues aren't abstract, you know. Your mother thinks that if we all pretend it's not happening it'll go away of its own accord.'

'Like mother, like daughter! Ruth puts any newspaper I bring into the house straight into the recycling.' Alex leans forward, spying his opportunity for a debate: his favourite pastime.

'Can I help you clear the table, Mum?'

In the kitchen, they work in silence, moving around each other with ease. They can hear the men's voices outside, discussing the refugee 'situation', so Anne closes the window.

'Your dad and Alex seem to be getting on well.'

'Yes. Unexpected.'

'We've both been looking forward to getting to know Alex properly.'

Ruth raises her eyebrows in disbelief and bends down to put the rinsed plates into the dishwasher.

'We have, Ruth.'

'I didn't say you haven't, Mum.'

'I know we didn't start off on the right foot at Christmas, but Daddy and I are happy if you're happy. You know that.'

Ruth nods and puts the glasses into the sink. She squirts washing-up liquid onto a sponge and starts washing them by hand.

'You are happy, aren't you, Ruthie?'

Ruth pauses with her back to her mother, then turns, soapy sponge in hand. 'What makes you say that, Mum?'

'It's just I haven't heard you sing at all since you arrived.'

That's what it is, Ruth thinks. That's what's different. I'm not singing.

It is not until the early hours of the morning that Alex creeps into the bedroom. Earlier, while Ruth and Anne chortled through a classic rom-com on the TV, he'd sat with her father on the patio, debating and discussing. The two women had raised eyebrows at each other hearing the voices echoing in accord and dispute on the patio, another bottle having made its way to the outdoor table, lit only by a guttering candle. In bed, reading her book, now set in a vividly drawn Manhattan apartment, Ruth could still hear them talking without being able to make out the content of their conversation. She fell asleep with the light on, expecting Alex's imminent return, but was woken by him turning it off. Looking at the clock on her bedside table, she sees it is now closer to dawn than sunset.

'Were you talking all this time?'

'Setting the world to rights.'

'Come to any conclusions?'

'Just that we'd definitely be okay if your dad and I were in charge.'

'And as you aren't?'

'Well,' Alex purrs, nuzzling her neck, his hand finding its way past the elastic of her pyjama bottoms, 'as we aren't, it's best we make hay while the sun shines.'

Alex's body presses her into the mattress. For a second she imagines what it might feel like if he were to push and push, if the mattress would give way, like quicksand, and slowly her body would slip beneath the surface, engulfed, swallowed, and Alex would be left on the surface, humping away at nothing but a twisted pile of sheets.

'We'll have to be quiet.' His voice rasps in her ear. It isn't whispering, it's something more guttural.

He places his hand over her mouth, his fingers clasping her cheek. Ruth thinks about when he first did it, the novelty, the thrill at being so under his power. It doesn't feel so exciting now that it has become an integral part of their love-making.

She has thought to mention it, but during sex, she doesn't feel she can, and afterwards, she's worried it might start a fight.

She'd like to ask Fran how to deal with it, but she knows that will result in a lecture.

Alex lifts her then and turns her onto her front.

She feels a bit floppy, still half asleep.

She turns her head so her ear is against the pillow.

She can hear his breath, heavy, and she can smell alcohol. It makes her stomach turn.

Her eyes are adjusting to the dark, and they focus on the portrait of the whale. She remembers when she bought it. It was a wet Saturday and she had purposefully marched Anne into the poster shop, dragging her by her hand. She had flipped the plastic frames full of images until she found the one she wanted.

'Are you sure? This one is so much nicer.'

But Ruth didn't want the photograph of the whale breaching, jumping into the air. She wanted the one that looked like an old-fashioned scientific drawing, the one with a section removed, revealing the interior of the whale. She wanted the one with the carefully labelled parts she could study for hours. A whale's heart is the size of a small car and weighs approximately half a tonne.

As Alex moves on top of her, she watches how the light from the streetlamp outside reflects on the picture, obscuring the image. Then when she shifts back, the whale is visible again.

There.

Gone.

There.

Gone.

The image is distorted now: she can see neither the whale nor the reflection of the room in the frame. Her eyes are filled with tears. The reflection is smeared as if someone had taken a paintbrush and feathered the edges of the light.

Alex's breathing becomes more rapid in her ear and she feels a surge of relief as her body relaxes, responding to his rhythm. She turns her head into the pillow and lets it swallow the noise that comes from her mouth.

Seventeen

Together, they build a hut.

They bind the wide bones of the whale's ribcage to create a structure, planting the jaw bones into the earth to create an entrance. Tight over it, they pull Ruth's ground sheet, the tarpaulin that was in the belly of the whale and other items they've found. They lay Nik's rug over the sand and build a bed from the seats of the ute and a mattress that they lug all the way from the caravan park.

They have a hut. A place to sleep. It is waterproof and windproof but the elements are still around them: they can hear the sea from their bed, see the light of the moon and the sun shining through the tarpaulin, little though it is through the constant cloud. It is not warm unless they are under their piles of blankets, but it is somewhere they can rest after the toil of the day.

They work now to dismantle the rubble of the small town, just as they had the carcass of the whale. They labour silently and swiftly, listening out for danger, concentrating on their work, processing their loss.

They find the cart in the second farm they explore. It is evident it had originally been meant for attachment to a truck so they are astonished to find that the wheels turn despite the heat it had endured. With a bit of improvisation they create a harness to pull it. The spread of the weight and the use of the harness means they can load it heavily and still pull it.

Pulling the cart becomes Ruth's job. They have a tacit agreement that it is the best division of labour for her to use the length of her legs to pull their haul, while Nik carries the rucksack, and whatever else he can manage in his increasingly strong arms.

The mobility of the cart opens up new worlds of scavenging. They clean out not only the contents of the farmhouse kitchens but the outhouses and fields too. They bring back bales of hay to insulate their ever-growing hut, padding beneath and between the whale bones that arch above them.

The roads are relatively clear, other than the odd tree that has fallen – scorched by its entanglement in a now dead electric wire – or, on the frequent rainy days, a slew of dirty water running across and along the buckled tarmac.

They sift through the rubble and dust.

They pile scavenged food to one side and objects to the other. Then at the end of the day they pack their bags, negotiating with each other as to what should take precedence to be carried back to the camp.

There is also the land: potatoes and beets buried in the ground; grain, not only stored in sacks, but also flattened in the fields – corn, wheat, barley.

They collect and store more than they could possibly eat in a single winter.

The flatbed of Nik's ute becomes their storehouse, metal panels from fallen sheds and fences creating further covered space.

Nik builds and stores.

Planning absorbs him, a happy distraction.

He covets any metal, wood or plastic they discover, any item that might be put to use in their camp. He finds solace in every acquisition. Strange. He'd had so few possessions, Before. I've become a hoarder like Ma, he thinks. Must've been in the genes after all. Does he have green fingers like his pa, too?

'We need to think ahead. I know bugger-all about farming, but we should be thinking about it, shouldn't we? There might be crops this year – but next?'

They separate and dry seed, ready to sow in the spring.

He suggests they try burying potatoes in boxes of sand and hay. He is hopeful that they will last for as long as the weather is cold. He keeps one box of the tubers above ground but still covered with darkness. He hopes they will go to seed, and bring them future crops.

He remembers the process, vaguely, from his childhood. He remembers his pa, mud in the cracks in his thumbs, pushing a delicate seedling gently into a red plastic pot, sprinkling fresh compost over the searching white roots. He remembers the tang of the vines hanging in the heavy air of the greenhouse, the back of his leg being smacked, his ma telling him to keep his bloody hands to himself. How, when he was finally allowed to take a bite of the flame-red fruit and the sweet seed of the tomato flooded his mouth, he saw she was right: it was worth every second of the wait.

He considers the storage and propagation of every edible plant they come across, saving the seeds they find in cans.

'Will they grow if they've been cooked?' Ruth asks.

'We can only try,' he replies.

And they do: they try everything.

He hopes that by trial and error they will land upon the means of survival.

*   *   *

Ruth has never done such physical work. She is aware that her clothes, the only clothes she has, are becoming loose. She examines the jut of her hip bones, traces the hair that grows untamed up to her navel and feels a throb of sorrow for the loss of her belly – she had always loved it. She ties her jeans at the waist with a piece of plastic cord.

The toil of existing is relentless. Each day they rise and wordlessly set about the tasks they had decided on the previous night.

The days slide by in a blur of lifting, carrying, cutting, planting, cooking and sorting.

Soon the days grow longer and Ruth realises that summer is approaching again.

A year has passed. It seems like only yesterday that she stepped off the plane into that strangely quiet airport, yet it feels as though she has lived out an entirely new life in just the last four seasons.

And all that time, next to her was Nik. She still knows so little about him.

And him? What does he know of her?

She begins to encourage him to talk a little as they walk back to camp after their day's toil and in the evenings around the fire. Though they still share only glimpses of their past, slowly it feels easier to indulge in conjecture about what may still lie beyond the small sphere of their knowledge.

Some nights they jointly imagine that their situation is a reality that doesn't stretch any further than them. 'Maybe, just beyond here, life is continuing as normal. It can't only be us left, can it? What are the odds?'

She looks across the fire, at Nik lying on his side. Today was hard: they walked far and found little. She can see he is tired, grumpy.

'Wouldn't we have seen planes? Boats? Wouldn't we have heard something on the radio, rather than just white noise?'

Tonight they will not revel in the idea that any day now, someone, from the places that were untouched by disaster, will arrive to collect them and take them back to real life.

Each day, as she works, Ruth tries to piece together how it might have happened, but it is all conjecture. Without facts she finds the bigger picture impossible to comprehend. Would it have been any different had she watched the news as avidly as many of her friends and family had? It hadn't helped them to know what was coming, had it?

Would knowing what had happened mean she could understand *why*?

Even though she's living through the aftermath of what appears to be the complete annihilation of humankind, she can't believe it's true.

It doesn't add up that everyone is gone, yet she is still alive.

Her?

Why her?

And as for how she is alive, she finds herself questioning that even more.

Is she remembering it right?

Did she really escape the end of the world by hiding in the mouth of a whale?

The more time that passes, the more preposterous it seems. It's like something from a fairytale, a myth, a parable constructed to illustrate a moral lesson to a child.

Were there a child to tell, they would never believe her.

If it weren't for Nik, she would think she'd made it up herself.

When the nights have turned cold again, the scent of woodsmoke in their hut, she is reminded of a time when she camped with her parents. In the dark, she tells Nik the story of how Jim had sat too close to the fire and melted the soles of his shoes.

'Who is Jim?' he asks, when her giggles have ceased.

'My dad.'

It is the first time she has talked about her parents to him. She has been scared to do so for fear of missing them even more. But, it seems, the more she talks about them, about all the people she loves, the more a part of them still exists.

She begins to tell him stories so he knows by name the people who live in her heart.

They look up at the soft smudge of light that suggests the moon is at her fullest behind the constant layer of smog.

'I wish we could see the stars,' she says.

'Or the sun,' Nik adds.

Nik uses the cart to bring a boat they find to the shore. It is a rowing boat, an escape vessel from one of the larger boats upturned in the marina of the yacht club. He puts it into the water and pushes it out, expecting it to sink.

It floats!

That evening, they eat fresh fish hot from the coals. More fillets scent the air, drying on the newly fashioned racks nearby.

He can still feel the motion of the waves. A trick of his inner ear. He feels off balance, not himself. And this is why, when Ruth asks him where he learnt to fish, he finds himself telling her about the trips with his pa. He tells her how he learnt to thread a piece of bread, to pierce a wiggling worm onto a hook under his pa's watchful eye. He tells her he can remember it so clearly, his father's hand guiding his own small one, the blood on his fingers from the punctured worm, yet he can barely remember his father's face. He tells her how his ma never found another man after his pa. How she never got over him, only ever loved him. How he'd never understood it. Until Eva.

He hears his voice ringing in the air.

'Eva.' He hasn't said her name in so long. He had almost forgotten the sound of it.

The fire crackles.

He looks at Ruth, silently begging her not to push him to say any more than he already has. She smiles at him. Does she understand?

'Teach me to fish?' Ruth asks.

He smiles back. Gratitude. 'Of course.'

As the days lengthen once more, fishing becomes Ruth's preferred contribution. She discovers she has a talent for it. She discovers she loves it.

The perspective of the shore from the boat.

Waiting for the lines to begin dancing as a helpless fish begins to tug.

The solitude.

She lies in the bottom of the boat and watches the clouds swirl under the grey.

What is the grey? Ash? More clouds?

She watches the horizon, always hoping to see a boat, an ocean liner.

She remembers reading *Life of Pi*. She wonders if she and Nik could make it to Australia in the tiny craft, just as Pi traversed the ocean with his imaginary tiger. She wonders if they would find anything different in Australia from what is here.

One day in the boat she looks back to shore.

She can see Nik absorbed in his work, unaware that she is observing him. His torso is bare. Even from this distance, she can see that his muscles are more pronounced: the heavy work is making them both stronger, leaner. She cannot help but admire his form – he seems almost Grecian as he labours in the sun. She looks away, feeling that she is overstepping an unspoken agreement between them and gazes towards the horizon instead. Then, without considering what she is doing, she involuntarily fills her lungs and begins to sing to herself. She feels her voice ripple through her body, vibrate the bones in her face. It tickles her nose.

She sneezes, then laughs and continues to sing.

She feels lighter than she has in a long, long time. It is as if the cadence of her voice is lifting the weight of her sorrow, like removing wet clothing, layer by layer.

She sings.

She sings songs she loves at the top of her lungs, trying not to think about the fact that she may never hear their rhythm again: the strum of a guitar, the crash of a drum.

She sings instead with the rhythm of the sea.

On the shore, as Nik tends his seedlings, the breeze carries the lilt of Ruth's voice to him. He stops working and stares out to where the boat dances in the water. He closes his eyes and listens to her harmonising with the wash of the waves on the shore.

A warmth spreads across his chest: she sounds so free.

Eighteen

'Back in five, ladies and gents, back in five!' the host calls, over the Monty's PA, rattling the windows. Ben and Ruth stand on the patio at the side of the pub, the heat lamp above lighting them. It casts strange shadows across their faces, their foreheads lit orange by the element. Ben inhales from the cigarette a final time and hands it back to Ruth. She brings the filter between her lips, still damp from Ben's mouth.

He winks at her as he exhales a plume of smoke. 'I fancy our chances, you know.'

Ruth lets the smoke escape between her pursed lips, her throat burning slightly from the unfamiliar sensation. She isn't a smoker, well, not any more, but when Ben asked her if she wanted a 'crafty', the opportunity to be alone with him, to talk about what happened, what they'd been dancing around, beckoned. But all she had dared to do so far was share a strong cigarette and talk about their progress in the Monty's quiz. Banter. She hated it, yet she found herself engaged in it so often. Why was that? It would be quite possible, she thinks, to spend your entire adult life avoiding any deep discussion, as long as you chose to talk to people who showed a fondness for banter.

'I don't know. I killed it on the picture round, obviously. But Amrit let us down on the music and now it's just politics and that tube map round to go. I suck at both of those.'

'I'm all over politics.' Ben is leant against the wall, radiating smugness.

'Really? You never talk about it.'

Sarcasm: banter's closest ally.

'You comfortable sitting there on your fence? Watch you don't get a splinter in your bum.' Ben smiles at her lopsidedly, so she can see the chip on his front tooth. Her stomach clenches. He glances at his watch. 'We'd better resume our seats, Lancaster. Pint?'

She knows another drink will tip her over the edge into drunkenness. She hasn't eaten, other than the chips with which Sheila always provided the Ladywell Quizzers on arrival ('Something to line our stomachs').

'I'm not sure I should. I'll be drunk.'

Ben cocks his head. 'I rather like you drunk.'

'Do you?'

'I did last time.'

He holds her gaze and she feels the pulse in her palms throb.

'Okay, then. Yes. I'll have another.'

Ben heads inside.

Ruth brings the cigarette to her lips again, even though she is now alone. She inhales deeply, feeling the smoke rasp against the delicate lining of her throat.

'How can a team called We've Got A Smartphone win? It's just not fair!'

They have the top deck of the bus to themselves and Ben is filling the space with his booming voice. His volume seems to correlate exactly to how many units of alcohol he has consumed.

'I didn't know you had such a strong sense of justice.'

'Of course I have a strong sense of justice! I'm a teacher. I lead the future generation in being able to discern right from wrong.'

'I didn't realise Year Six had such a focus on ethics.'

'It's not part of the syllabus, but there's no doubt I play my part in moulding the young minds of the nation.'

They are sitting on two seats opposite each other at the front. 'I'm driving,' Ben announced, as he scrambled to take the seat on the right when they got on. Since then he'd sat with his legs stretched out along it, the soles of his leather brogues pointing towards hers.

'Where do you get off?'

'Same as you,' Ben replies. 'I'm coming back to yours.'

In the flat Ben picks things up, inspects them, puts them down. He might have been at a car-boot sale.

Ruth makes them a gin and tonic and pours a pint of tap water for each of them.

'Big reader. You or him?' Ben is at her bookshelf, pulling out books, briefly inspecting and returning them. He doesn't know that she reads, or indeed that Alex doesn't. He doesn't know her at all.

'Me.' Ruth hands him the two glasses.

He puts down the book he is inspecting and takes them from her, downing half the pint of water in one go. As he does she can see his open mouth through the glass. It is both disgusting and oddly fascinating to be able to see his molars magnified as he gulps.

'A regular bookworm, aren't you.'

It's a statement rather than a question. He wipes the water from his lips onto his shirt sleeve and moves across to the pictures on the wall. He cocks his head, studying a photo of her cousin and his family leaning over a balcony. 'Whose are the rug-rats? His?'

'My cousin's. Auntie Ruth. Though I'm their second cousin, I think. Bit confusing.'

She sips her G and T, the ice rattling in the glass as she does so.

'Cute kids.'

'They're annoying, but I love them.' She stands from her seat on the arm of the sofa and joins him next to the photos. Ben has now moved on to a photo of her with Camille, Charlie and some other people from Bristol.

'Is one of these fine chaps him, then?'

'Oh, is that what you're looking for? A picture of Alex?'

Ben shrugs and moves to a picture of her and Fran at a festival. They are lying on the grass, their heads close together, their arms outstretched towards the camera. 'How long were you blonde for?'

Ben examines the photograph, placing his now empty water glass on the sideboard.

'Most of sixth form, I gave it up at uni. A pricy habit, bleach. Plus my hair used to snap off in handfuls.'

'I much prefer the current do.' Ben turns and touches her hair. Their proximity means it doesn't take much to pull her to him. He only kisses her very softly, but she can feel where his lips were as he moves away from her to the couch and sits down.

'So, you don't have any photos of him and I can't really see much sign of a bloke living here. Are you sure you haven't made up this boyfriend of yours to play hard to get?' Ben doesn't look at her as he says this: his attention is on the gin in his right hand, in which he is circulating the ice cubes. Ruth takes her phone from her bag and comes to sit next to him on the sofa, her leg touching his. Opening her photos, she finds a picture of Alex from their trip to Paris. He is sitting opposite her in a busy brasserie, his linen shirt open at the collar. He smiles into the camera, a piece of bread in his right hand.

'This is Al. Not imaginary.'

Ben takes the phone from her hand gently and zooms in on the picture. 'Handsome bloke.'

'Yeah, he is.'

Ben locks the phone and returns it to Ruth. He shuffles on the sofa to turn towards her. 'So, I don't want to do myself out of a promise here, or anything—'

'You're not on a promise.' Ruth cuts him off.

'Of course, but I just mean . . . Why am I here? Why did you let me through the door? Especially after last time . . . if you've got this Al coming home to you, what, tomorrow?'

Ruth stops Ben's questions by leaning forward and placing her palm flat on his chest. He leans into it and she brings her mouth to his. In a jumble of arms and grasping hands she pulls herself up to straddle his legs.

'I think there's a bit of a mess.'

Ruth hears Ben's voice reverberate through his chest where her head rests. They are lying on the sofa, softly slick with sweat.

'What?'

Ben shuffles from beneath her. 'Sorry, not sure how long these have been in my wallet.'

Ruth watches as Ben grapples with the split latex. He reaches for a tissue from the box that Alex recently installed on the coffee-table and wraps the rubber mound in his hand before wiping his palm with another. She is aware of the flood of endorphins that engulfed her body seconds ago being replaced by a wave of anxiety.

'I mean, you're on the pill, yeah? I assume you and whatya-macallit don't use these bloody things.' Ben pulls another tissue from the box and hands it to Ruth. 'Ruth?'

She takes the tissue and wipes herself, horrified at how wet it is as it comes away.

'Ruth?'

'Don't worry. I'll sort it.'

Ruth rises, pulling a blanket from the back of the couch to wrap herself in. In the kitchen she stands at the tap with her hand underneath the flow of water, waiting for it to go cold.

She returns from the kitchen with the two refilled glasses of water. Ben is pulling on his shoes, otherwise fully dressed.

'Thought I'd better make a move. Actual school night and everything.'

'Alex isn't coming back until the weekend, you know.'

'Yeah.' He shrugs, tying his laces, his right foot across his left knee. 'I just prefer to sleep in my own bed, y'know?'

She stands, holding the two glasses, as he locates his jacket and his bag where he dropped them by the door. He slings the bag over his shoulder, adjusts the strap over his chest and runs his hand through his hair. 'Thanks for a fun evening. Better get going – it's late.'

He doesn't make eye contact: he is checking his phone.

'Do you know the best way to get back to yours?'

'I'll call a cab.'

He's already at the door, twisting the lock open. 'See you tomorrow.' He pauses. 'Sorry.'

Ruth stands on the threshold of the kitchen, naked – but for the blanket, tucked beneath her armpits – listening as his footsteps descend the stairs. The door to her flat faintly rattles as he slams the one to the street. She drinks as much of the water in her right hand as quickly as her throat will allow, then sits, still wrapped in the blanket, on the sofa.

Just minutes ago she and Ben were lying entwined in this exact spot. Then – in a moment – something shifted and everything changed. She feels a sharp stab of grief. Sometimes things are lost before you're even aware they exist.

Ruth shakes her head and reaches for the remote. She navigates to the planner, searching. It is actually not so late, she notes, from the time in the corner of the screen. Though Ben had made his hasty exit using the time as excuse, it has only just turned ten o'clock. She presses the button and the screen fills with a newsroom. A ticker-tape of information scrolls. She turns up the volume, so she can hear every word the reporter is saying. It is months since she watched the news. She lets each word hit her. She can feel her adrenalin spiking as she listens to what the pristine woman says. She lays her head on the arm of the sofa and continues to watch the images flash across the screen. Tears pool in her eyes but she makes no movement to wipe them, just lets them roll down her cheek into the upholstery.

Ruth wakes, cold, on the sofa. The blanket is wrapped around her, her body still naked.

She has been dreaming.

In her dreams she was naked, too, but her skin was not her own: it was different, something animal, marine. She was swimming, and as she swam, images flashed before her, the images she had seen on the news. Every time she was confronted by a flashing screen filled with cruelty, she tried to swim in another direction. But the images were coming faster and faster, the water felt thicker and thicker, until she felt as though she were swimming in treacle, unable to move her naked limbs. Hateful images of suffering people blocked her escape, no matter which way she turned.

The TV flashes blue light onto her face as she tries to slow her breathing. A documentary about the sea is on, a repeat with audio-description. In the corner, a woman translates to sign-language the information that David Attenborough is imparting about the animals that glide across the screen: 'The bond between mother and calf is particularly strong in cetaceans. Calves may remain with their mothers for up to ten years, depending on the species, and travel thousands of kilometres across the ocean with her. Almost half of the eighty species of cetaceans can be found in the Pacific Ocean . . .'

She finds the remote control that has been wedged uncomfortably beneath her ribs and silences the narration, turning off the television.

The early morning is creeping in through the curtains. Ruth looks at the clock on the wall above the television. There are only two hours until she needs to leave for work. Picking up her phone, she retreats to the bedroom and slides under the duvet. Setting her alarm for one and a half hours' time, she closes her mascara-streaked eyes and falls into a dreamless sleep.

Nineteen

Sitting in the boat, Ruth feels the texture of the air alter. The relentless grey does not betray the season, but the way the warm breeze quickly turns to a cold, sharp wind is typical of what she has come to expect from autumn.

She pulls at the oars, turning the boat, and begins to head for shore. Four large silver-coloured fish lie in a box at the bottom of the boat – a meagre catch.

The wind whips her hair into her face, but she dare not tie it up for fear of losing control of the oars or her direction. The rain is falling in droplets so large that she can feel each one as it breaks on her skin. Soon her hair is no longer in her face: it lies slick across her scalp.

As she gets closer to the shore she can see Nik, in her worn-out yellow raincoat, looking out to sea. It is too small for him – when he waves his arms as he spots her through the driving rain, he cannot lift them above his head.

She aims the boat towards him on the shore, as he runs to where the sea foam gathers on the sand.

The waves are fierce.

Ruth angles the oars to bring the boat in, just as Nik has taught her, but she doesn't seem to be making any gains. She fights through the foam, getting wetter and wetter as the boat takes on more water. She grips the box of fish between her feet for fear of them being thrown overboard and rendering the day fruitless.

Eventually, she is close enough to the shore for Nik to guide her in. The bow of the boat stutters on a wave and bolts upwards into Nik's chin. Ruth watches in horror as his teeth are forced through his lip, breaking the delicate skin.

With the boat safely ashore and the fish by the truck, they both run for the opening of the hut, stripping off their wet clothes. They wrap themselves in blankets, rubbing their hair dry on the towel Ruth brought with her all the way from Deptford.

'Let me see.'

She tilts Nik's face backwards towards the little light afforded by the rain-filled skies. His bottom lip is badly split, blood spilling onto the patchwork of scavenged rugs that make up the floor of their home. 'It's bad,' she says.

Nik sits on the floor, holding the now blood-soaked rag against his lip to stem the flow.

Ruth returns with a small black pouch and a bottle of the whisky they found in one of the farm's metal sheds.

'Is that for me or for my lip?'

'Both.'

Ruth sits opposite Nik and looks him directly in the eyes. 'Listen, my only knowledge of medicine comes from watching *Grey's Anatomy*. But that cut on your lip is serious – I think it needs a stitch if it's going to heal.'

Ruth opens the little pouch on her lap. It is a travel sewing kit her mum gave her. It contains several needles, little scissors, a small contraption for threading and a piece of cardboard wrapped in strands of colourful cotton. 'Do you have a colour preference?'

Ruth holds up the cotton over her forearm, like a sommelier proffering a bottle of wine. Nik smiles grimly, but in doing so he opens the wound on his lip further. Ruth pours a little of the whisky onto his lip.

'Fuck!'

'It's only going to get worse, I'm afraid.'

Ruth notes her hand is shaking slightly as she attempts to thread the thinnest needle in the sewing kit.

'You'd better drink deep.'

Nik tips his head back and pours the whisky directly down his throat.

In the hut that night, Ruth rolls towards Nik as he sleeps.

She can smell the whisky on his breath.

She shifts towards him, close enough to feel the heat radiating from his face against her cheek.

Slowly, trying not to make a noise, she raises her hand above the cover and in the dark she cautiously moves it towards where she believes his forehead must be.

She finds the top of his head. The bristles that sprouted from it when she first touched it have gone. In the time that has passed she has barely noticed it happening, but his hair is now long: it hangs in curls about his ears. She feels his hair under the tips of her fingers. It is softer than she expected and feels cleaner than her own.

Holding her breath, she allows her forefinger to trace the silhouette of his face, just as she did on the night they first met: his forehead, his nose – the way it softly arches away from his face. As her finger reaches his upper lip, his hand grips hers and prevents it from moving any further.

'I thought you were asleep.'

She can hear her own pulse, feel the heat of shame spreading across her face. She is thankful for the dark of the hut for hiding it, though the lack of light won't let her escape the fact she has crossed a line.

'Nah.'

She can feel his whisky-scented breath against her face. Her finger is trapped in his vice-like grip. Ruth tries to pull away her hand, but he won't let her.

Then she has a presentiment of what is going to happen, feels her breath catch in her throat. He grips her finger tighter and slowly pulls it towards him, taking it into his mouth.

She breathes in sharply, desire taking hold of her. 'Nik?' She whispers into the dark, her finger clamped between his teeth in his mouth.

She feels his arm encircling her, pulling her towards him.

Through the multiple layers of clothes, she can feel the heat of his chest and, lower, the warmth of his groin against her own.

He releases her finger from the grip of his teeth and moves his mouth to her ear. 'Is this a good idea?' His voice rasps in her ear.

Ruth takes either side of his face in her hands. Gently, careful of the stitches she administered just hours earlier, she draws his bruised lips towards her own.

Before, Ruth had often felt the need to talk during sex, to ask for what she wanted, to tell whoever was upon her to stop doing something or try something else, and sometimes – she cringes to remember it now – she even talked dirty. It was a performance, asking lovers to reveal their secret desires, pretending to divulge desires she knew would turn them on, occasionally, in moments of unexpected abandon, revealing her true kinks.

But there is no need for words.

Words are replaced by his searching mouth upon her skin.

Her discovery of his every scent.

His exploration of every curve, every hollow.

No words are required when he looks directly into her eyes as she shudders to climax with his hand, wet, between her legs.

There might not be words, but there is breath.

Her breath as it lengthens again, her orgasm fading, like the last rays of the sun at the end of the day.

His breath in response to a finger trailed, almost without touching, down the length of his spine.

Her sigh as his lips hover at the top of her thighs.

His breath that momentarily disappears as he explores her wetness with his lips, his tongue and so, so softly, his teeth and she surrenders, the taste of salt on her tongue, heat engulfing her senses so it seems, for a second, life is suspended.

Then, their shuddering breath as they discover a new rhythm together. As they configure their limbs, their bodies getting closer, clamping on to one another.

The rush of his breath in her ear, his head so close behind her own, as he wraps one arm around her ribcage and his stomach muscles contract.

Their protracted breaths as they lie, half asleep, coiled around each other.

The days shorten into the cold, wet dirge of winter.

They don't leave the safety of their hut for days other than to attend to nature's call, eating only what they had stored, dried and preserved.

At times, it is frighteningly cold. Much colder than last winter. For several days the rain becomes sleet; Ruth fears snow, but Nik assures her that snow at sea level on North Island is pretty much unheard of.

'The world has changed, though, Nik. "The chiding autumn, angry winter, change their wonted liveries, and the mazed world, by their increase, now knows not which is which . . ."'

'Poetry?'

'Shakespeare.'

The cold reaches into Ruth's bones and chills her. She breaks a fever. She fights nausea after every mouthful of food. She is so tired that one day she sleeps from when Nik leaves the hut at dawn to when he returns as the sun sets.

Before, Ruth would use the internet to diagnose even the smallest ailment. There are many things about the internet Ruth misses, but online health forums are not one of them. She knows in her aching bones that this unshakeable lethargy, this unquenchable thirst and the constant seasickness, is just the beginning of the illness that will kill her.

Yes, they survived the initial blast, but surely the diseases that radiation causes in the human body must be imminent for them both.

They still regularly question the miracle of their survival.

They think now that it must have been the whale's flesh that protected them. Nik says he remembers reading something about whales never having tumours. He thinks he saw it in a documentary. Could that account for why the whale protected them?

Ruth argues that it is too perfect that Nature had engineered a creature that could withstand the most destructive invention of man. More likely, she thinks, that the body of the whale was almost plasticised before it had even died: it was so full of the chemicals and microplastics humankind had pumped into the ocean that its body was like some toxic shell that even nuclear fission couldn't tear apart.

*   *   *

Nik strokes Ruth's back as she vomits onto the rug that covers the floor of their hut.

It reminds him of rubbing Eva's back as she heaved into that little cardboard bowl as he sat next to her, careful to give room to the tangle of tubes that were attached to the cannula in the back of her hand.

He remembers how she pressed her forehead to the metal bars on the side of the hospital bed, cooling herself as she listened to him read to her from the newspaper.

Cleaning up Ruth's sick, he longs for bleach and thinks of the antiseptic smell of that last private room, which stuck to his clothes even after he returned to their apartment, alone.

He'd promised himself he'd never let that happen again. That he'd take a leaf out of his ma's book.

And now look at him: he watches Ruth's every move.

He had left all the photos of Eva in Auckland when he'd left. Only kept the one of her smoking, where he couldn't see her face. He'd told himself that looking at her face, which he'd never see again, was only making the hurt worse, stronger. But now he wishes he'd kept them.

He'd like to show Ruth who Eva was. Let her put a face to the stories.

He wants to be able to photograph Ruth. Every day he catches himself reaching for his camera, then remembering. He knows it wouldn't keep her with him, but what he would give to have a record of her form, her face . . .

But he can't.

So instead he takes every opportunity he has to drink in the sight of her, the smell of her, every detail of her.

Nik watches Ruth wipe her mouth on her palm, shivering.

'I just can't get warm.'

He pulls her to him and rubs her arms. He can feel the goose-bumps on her skin through the shirt that is draped over her increasingly angular frame.

'What I'd give for a bath, a hot bath with bubbles. I used to have some bubbles, smelt of geranium. A bottle cost more than a three-course meal. I used to feel so guilty buying it, but when I used it, heaven.' Ruth's eyes shine as she talks.

He can't tell if it's the sickness or the remembering that is making them appear so glassy, but it is scaring him. 'Go back to bed.' He covers her with blankets and stokes the fire.

He boils water to ensure it is clean and warm, then mashes some tinned peaches. As always, he checks the tin carefully for perforation before using it for fear of contamination. Though he fears what ails Ruth is more serious than food poisoning, he doesn't want to risk making her sicker.

Bringing the food into the hut, he can hear Ruth snoring gently. 'Ruth?'

She wakes and smiles at him, smelling the sweet juice of the peaches.

He helps her to sit. He kisses her forehead as she chews. It is a relief for him to see her eat, even though it is a meagre amount.

'I feel a little better, I think.'

'Are you sure? I'd like to go and check the nets, but I'm reluctant to leave you.'

'Check the nets.'

Ruth reaches out to steady herself as the earth seems to tip on its axis. The dizziness is intense but she continues to stand, using the central pole of the hut as a support.

The whole hut smells of her sickness, Nik's perspiration and woodsmoke.

Everything smells of woodsmoke.

Feeling a little less off balance, she peels open the flap of tarpaulin that forms their door. Outside, the sea air hits her immediately. The day is dry: one of the first without rain in months. She breathes in deeply, hungrily taking in the oxygen. She takes off her trousers – tracksuit bottoms of Nik's, in desperate need of a wash – and walks towards the ocean in her underwear and jumper. She stands calf-deep in the gentle surf, wiggling her toes, feeling the grains of sand between each one.

Something makes her look up – although, when she tells Nik later, she can't say what it was. There is a gap in the grey. A sliver of blue peeking through.

Blue sky.

The gap widens and her face is bathed in light.

She pulls off the shirt she has been wearing for days and throws it behind her onto the sand. She stands, arms extended, eyes closed, and exposes her translucent skin to the sun, laughing. She reaches down to the water and splashes the surf onto her naked body, washing off the weeks of sleep and semi-consciousness. She rubs the brine along the length of her arms, luxuriating in the sensation of the sun warming her moments after the water falls in droplets from her skin. She cups it in her palms and brings it up to her chest, letting it fall in cascades over her breasts, her nipples.

Ruth pulls her hands away, as if she had touched hot metal.

A pain sears through her chest where her fingers made contact with the delicate puckered skin at the peak of her breasts. Curious, she touches her nipples once more: it feels like an electric shock.

She lowers her hands to her abdomen as she silently counts. She has lost days in the hut, maybe weeks and it has been many weeks since she last tore rags from a scavenged sheet to line her underwear and catch the blood that pooled there.

Ruth's hands explore her belly. A softly curving bowl has returned. Despite eating so little there is a marked width to her abdomen.

She has never been completely attuned to her menstrual cycle. In her teens and twenties, it often took her by surprise. Any bout of tearful anger twenty-five days after her last period failed to ring any alarm bells, and nearly every time she found blood when she wiped herself she was astonished, despite it being a monthly occurrence. Then in her thirties she started to make use of technology to track it. Camille had used an app to get pregnant and suggested it to Ruth, who was delighted to find she could use it for the opposite purpose. When it became apparent that it wasn't as accurate as she might have hoped she still found it useful – it meant she was rarely in a cubicle without a tampon. Of course, there are no apps now, her phone mute and lifeless among her most treasured belongings in the biscuit tin she keeps beneath the bed, waiting for the possibility of electricity so she can open the portals to her real life once more.

She looks out towards the horizon, the sun glinting on the water, and sees Nik, in the boat, returning to shore. He stands when he sees her, gesturing to the sun, to the blue that is beginning to stretch across the sky.

She can hear his whoops of joy being carried on the wind.

Her heart flutters to hear his voice raised in happiness.

Deep inside her another heart, beating much faster than her own, responds.

Twenty

North London has always felt completely foreign to Ruth. Though she's been living in the capital for more than ten years, any further north than Euston feels like a different city. At Highgate she gets off the now half-empty tube. The recorded message on the platform pronounces, 'This station is *Hy-gut*.' Is that how you're supposed to say it? She doesn't know the area very well and instinctively dislikes it.

She walks up the hill from the station with her hood up, shielding her made-up face from the elements. As she gets over the peak of the hill she raises her eyes. Through the drizzle she sees Alex pull up outside the house.

She can always spot him at a distance – something about his physicality draws her eye. The length of him.

When they first started seeing each other Ruth wondered whether she was developing a sixth sense, so sure she was that Alex was approaching before she saw him in the most unexpected places. Once, she bought a coffee by the roundabout at Old Street and glanced up from entering her PIN into the card machine to see Alex whizz past on his bike. If she had looked up at any other second, she wouldn't have seen him. It was things like this – like him standing behind her in the queue for the coffee festival just days after the dinner party, like him being on the same Overground train as her on that late-August afternoon – that made her feel they were 'meant to be'. Now she questions how much of this response was influenced by hormones: the adrenalin of their clandestine meetings and messages, the oxytocin induced by their physical touch. At the time she'd felt like an addict, constantly thinking about him, desiring him and in retrospect – the hormonal fug having somewhat lifted – she had been.

She watches him now dismounting his bike. He chains it to the lamppost in front of Camille and Charlie's house. Unaware of her surveillance, he takes his time to add padlock and chain before turning to the house. Someone inside must be watching because he looks up and places his unclipped saddlebag by his feet, using both hands to wave at the onlooker. She hears a child's voice call to him and he lollops, long-legged, towards the house, easily unlocking and reclosing the wrought-iron gate as he moves towards the hidden greeting. The kids will be there today, of course, and Sara will be constantly disappearing into whichever room Ruth is not, the baby on her hip. Ruth stands for a minute in the rain to gather herself, then walks towards the house.

The house is full of the screaming voices of numerous five-year-olds.

'We've got an entertainer. She's supposed to be that princess from the cartoon they're all obsessed with, but she looks hung-over and rather disillusioned with what promised to be a glittering career when she left drama school.'

Charlie swiftly helps Ruth out of her wet yellow coat.

'Milla is wisely hiding in the kitchen with the other gals. Head on through and grab yourself a glass.' He shakes her coat over the doormat before hanging it among the many hues of wax jacket beneath the stairs. 'You know where the loo is if you want to tidy yourself up. Poor thing, looking like the proverbial drowned rat. This bloody weather. It's supposed to be spring!'

In the downstairs toilet, Ruth sees that she does, indeed, look rather the worse for wear and she grudgingly forgives Charlie for what she immediately assumed was his habitual misogyny. He's always felt free to comment on women's appearances, convinced his point of view was either important or relevant. To Ruth's knowledge the only person who has ever directly challenged this habit is Fran, and that long night of raised voices and tears wasn't something she was in a hurry to live through again. Inspecting herself in the mirror, Ruth sees her mascara is running in rivulets down her cheeks; the foundation and blusher she so carefully applied with sponge and brush have all but disappeared to give way to the streams of black. She reaches for some toilet paper to try to repair the damage, and is reminded of Camille admonishing her at university: 'Oh, my God! What are you doing? Never use tissue on your skin, cotton wool only.' It seems something about this memory stirs her stomach: she turns to the toilet, lifts the lid and promptly vomits.

'Bubbles or white?' Camille is balancing seven-month-old Zadie on her hip.

'Have you got any fizzy water? I'm feeling a bit delicate.'

Camille turns from the fridge to face her, raising one eyebrow. 'What sort of delicate? Too-much-wine delicate, or baby-growing-in-your-uterus delicate?'

'Milla!'

'Oh, my God! How exciting!'

'Milla, I am not pregnant. Can you keep your voice down?'

'Don't worry, Sara's moved on . . . Oh, right, yes, of course, early days! Hush, hush, we won't tell anyone, will we, Zades?' Camille presses her nose against that of the wide-eyed infant in her arms and pulls a bottle of sparkling water from the fridge. 'I drank so much of this stuff when I was carrying Alfie, couldn't stomach it with Zades, though – maybe you're having a boy! Xander will be so delighted.'

'Camille, stop, I'm not pregnant.'

Camille loads a tall glass with lime slices and ice from the bowls on the table, then hands Zadie to the latest German teenager employed to help with the children. She pours the sparkling water into the glass and hands it to Ruth. 'Sorry, I'll stop. But let me just impart this little gem: if you're going to keep it under wraps, always make sure you have lemon or lime in your glass. That way people just assume you're drinking G and T and no one bothers you until you start turning down steak tartare and oysters.'

Camille raises her own glass of wine to Ruth. 'Cheers, darling. I hope it sticks.'

Ruth shakes her head but clinks her glass with Camille's all the same.

'Mummy! We're opening presents!'

The birthday boy, Alfie, skids onto the tiled kitchen floor in his stockinged feet. He wears formal dress trousers, a shirt and a waistcoat with a pale blue bow tie – he looks like a page boy for a member of the royal family.

'Alfie, darling, say hello to your godmother,' Camille instructs.

'Hi, Ruth. Have you got me a present?'

'Alfie, that is not polite.'

'I think Uncle Xander brought it, Alf.' Ruth smiles down at Alfie's red-cheeked face, his pupils dilated with sugar and adrenalin.

'Uncle Xaaandeeer?' Alfie runs back to the other room, his feet sliding as he goes.

'We'd better go in, I suppose. Poor you, not drinking, no anaesthetic to the squealing. I'll warn you now, there are sixteen under-fives in there.'

Camille grimaces and nods to the au pair to take the baby into the lounge. When they have vanished she turns to Ruth conspiratorially.

'So, Sara is in there, but don't worry, she's all loved up with this chap she met on some single-parent app. I've yet to meet him, but hopefully he's coming this afternoon and then everyone can just relax and get pissed.'

Camille links her arm with Ruth's and draws her towards the cacophony of screaming voices. In the hall, before they enter the lounge she pauses and places her hand on Ruth's abdomen. 'So exciting!' she whispers and then slips into the room.

Ruth stands on the threshold of the room for a second, watching Camille enter the fray. The floor is covered with small children wearing dishevelled party outfits, grubbied by two hours' wear, the dust of the crisps and the purple stains of the halved blueberries they have been consuming all over their hands and faces. Camille's cream carpet has several marks where food has been trodden in.

Among the floor-level mayhem, she spots Lily's head bobbing as she negotiates swapping the wooden toy she has won for the foil balloon another child is gripping to his chest. Ruth carefully lowers herself into the sofa in the corner, hoping Lily doesn't notice her. She's become rather fond of the stubborn little girl, even though she looks so like her mother – a constant reminder of her guilt. Her personality, though, is like Alex's: she is forthright and opinionated and constantly instructing others in what to do.

Alex moves towards Ruth, holding his son. Jake has only recently been relinquished into Alex's care by Sara, who now stands by the fireplace chatting animatedly to some well-groomed women, a large glass of wine in her hand. She must feel Ruth's gaze on her because she turns, almost immediately, to meet Ruth's eyes. Her face is hard momentarily. Then she quickly rearranges her features to form a fixed smile. The women with Sara peer around her to see who she is smiling at, raise their eyebrows, purse their lips, then pointedly turn their backs. Ruth can feel her ears burning, both metaphorically and from the blush spreading across her cheeks.

Alex is now towering above her, the baby on his shoulder, craning his neck to watch an escaped balloon as it bounces along the corniced ceiling and reflects the light in its foil.

'G and T? Unlike you, darling. Was Charlie's vino not up to scratch?'

'Just fancied it.'

'Fair enough. Bit kinder to the waistline too, as long as it's slimline.'

Ruth doesn't respond, just sips the fizzy water, her stomach still churning.

Alex slides onto the sofa next to her and thrusts his son into her face. 'Look, Jakey, it's lovely Ruth.'

The little boy smiles gummily at Ruth. He smells faintly sweet, yet sour at the same time: a combination of milk and dribble with an undertone of urine.

'Hello, Jake.' She pretends to shake his hand. His wet fingers are curled into a little fist.

'Oh, stop flirting, Jakey! Who can blame him, though? You look gorgeous!'

With his free hand he pushes her still-damp hair behind her ear to expose her neck and kisses her above her collarbone. Her eyes dart to Sara: she is watching them from her vantage point by the fireplace. Uncomfortable, Ruth pulls away from him.

'Looks like our godson is enjoying his birthday party.' Ruth nods towards the increasingly frenzied chaos at the centre of the room.

The detritus of Alfie's present-opening session lies all over the cream carpet. By the bay window a child, sitting on his father's lap, sobs. The father is doing his best to soothe him, but the loss of a plastic motorbike to Alfie is too much to bear.

'Not putting you off, I hope?'

Alex smiles, nodding towards the distressed child. Ruth is taken aback: this is the first time he's mentioned children. Maybe it's him who has the sixth sense. 'You want more?'

Her throat feels sore suddenly, as though she's burnt it drinking something hot.

'I know it doesn't quite fit with my ideals – conservationists aren't known for being big breeders in general – but our child? Our child might be the one to save the world.'

'Neither of your other kids up for taking on that role?'

Her voice is sharp. She can hear it as it comes out. It is sharper than she intended. Alex's face falls. He's hurt. It's the first time she has seen that expression: he looks vulnerable. She quickly scrolls through her memory and is astonished as she realises this is the first time she has ever said anything less than kind, or even sarcastic, to him. Can that be true? In the corner of her eye she sees Sara moving in their direction, undoubtedly keen to remove her infant son from Ruth's proximity.

'I need the loo,' says Ruth.

The downstairs toilet is engaged. A small girl is emptying the contents of her stomach just as Ruth had done so recently.

Ruth climbs the stairs to the second floor and enters the large bathroom, locking the door behind her. She sits on the edge of the roll-top bath. For a few seconds she concentrates on her breathing: in through her nose and out through her mouth. The room smells of the candle that flickers in its frosted glass on the windowsill. 'Driftwood' the silver-edged label reads. Ruth shakes her head, wondering how much the perfuming of this largely uninhabited room sets Camille back per annum. Still feeling hot, she goes to the basin and runs the cold tap, placing her wrists under the stream of cold water. The noise makes her want to pee, so she sits on the toilet. When she wipes, she inspects the paper scrunched up in her hand: nothing.

She takes her phone from the back pocket of her jeans and opens her app.

Immediately she closes it and dials rapidly.

'Hey,' Fran's voice echoes on the line, 'can you escape? Or has Camille charged you with serving the babyccinos after dessert?'

'Fran, I'm late.'

Twenty-one

It's something to do with the sea, they decide.

Though they can reach no exact reason why, they have begun to think that their survival within the whale must have had something to do with it being a sea mammal. While all the living creatures of land and air seem to have been wiped out, just as with the biblical flood that Noah and his floating menagerie escaped, the populations of the sea seem to have survived unscathed. The fish and the mussels that provide the bulk of their sustenance stand testament to this. Perhaps, they surmise, it was because they were inside a sea creature that they escaped certain peril.

'Like Noah,' says Nik.

'Jonah was actually swallowed by a fish. People just think it was a whale because it was big. But that's different from Noah. Though they are both from the Old Testament.'

'Sweet Bible knowledge.'

'Well, I was named after one of the main characters.'

'True?'

'Sort of.'

They have to review their theory as, with the sun, birdsong returns and, shortly after, the evening canto of crickets in the long grass begins.

Is it all part of some Grand Plan? If not that of an interventionist deity, then maybe Mother Nature.

'Maybe we survived so we can repopulate the earth. Like Adam and Eve.'

They are lying in the dark of their bed, Nik's hand resting on Ruth's blooming belly.

'With Cain and Abel?'

'Maybe our survival was a mistake, eh? Mother Nature missed a bit.'

'Don't say it,' she warns.

'Human beings are the disease,' he intones.

Ruth rolls over and places her hand firmly over his mouth to stop him speaking. He tickles her under the arm and they dissolve into a tangle of laughter beneath their mismatched bedclothes.

They have days when it feels as though they are happy. But the second they recognise it, it comes crashing down. They feel guilty about everything. They wrestle with the fact that they are living when so many have perished, yes, but the guilt at bringing new life into such a world is worse.

What sort of life will this child have? Will it even be healthy enough to survive?

'How can we bring a child into this world?' Ruth has said this repeatedly over the last several months.

'How can we not?' It is the only reply he can give.

As far as Nik can see, there is no alternative other than to let nature take its course. That doesn't mean that whenever he is alone he doesn't curse himself for endangering Ruth by putting her in this situation.

For what?

A few seconds of pleasure?

Though he constantly longs to be close to her, he can't bring himself to touch her for guilt, and this only upsets her. His apparent lack of interest in sex makes her feel as though he judges her for the situation, as if she made it happen. But the truth is, they know they're both explicitly responsible for the most irresponsible act since, well, since Before.

As the days start to draw in, Ruth becomes frustrated by the growing weight of her baby. She is prevented from fishing, hunting. Her back curves to allow her pelvis to tip forward and accommodate her growing child. Her body is slow and heavy.

Unable to hunt, she turns to foraging. Methodically she picks the first of the berries from the overgrown brambles that line the roads and the apples from the trees that stand twisted in what were once gardens.

Nik jokes to Ruth that he has barely kept a houseplant alive before, but she has watched him since spring nurturing the seedlings he planted in eclectic containers. She has seen him hard at work on the land near the yacht club, the closest earth to the beach that can be farmed. He planted the seed potatoes they carefully stored over winter and the seeds from the pumpkins they found rotting in storage; he sowed the little grain that they stored, rather than ate, when their bellies groaned with hunger. She knows he has been ploughing his guilt and fear of impending fatherhood into hard, physical labour.

Soon he will start to harvest the fruits of his labour. She prays it will yield nourishment for their unexpected family.

One morning as Ruth gets out of bed she feels as though she can breathe again.

After weeks of the pressure of her full womb against her ribs, restricting the expansion of her lungs, there is space. She puts her hands to her expanded stomach and feels that the mound is lower than it was the day before.

'Nik,' she whispers, to his slowly waking form, 'the baby has moved down. I think we're getting close.'

That is the first time he leaves her overnight.

When Ruth wakes from her afternoon nap, she is horrified to find him with the tattered rucksack on his back.

'I need to walk into town.'

'I'll come with you.' She struggles to stand from the bed.

'No, not this town, the next one along.'

He is heading for the town where she had been kicked off the coach when she had been trying to get to Wellington. The closed-up, desolate, one-horse town where she had made the decision to head here, to the sea, the night before it had happened. It had taken her the best part of eight hours to walk to the beach, from dawn until the mid-afternoon.

'But you'll be gone hours.'

'Yes, but I have to go.'

'The baby might come.'

'Which is why I need to go now.'

Why would he leave her, vulnerable as she is and about to give birth any day?

She feels as if he is running away. What she would give to be able to do the same.

'We've got no medicine. Nothing if anything goes wrong. If something happens to you. If there's something wrong with the baby. We need drugs, antiseptic.'

It's true. The few antibiotics that she had had are long gone, and the only pain relief they have is a few half-empty blister packs of paracetamol.

Ruth is of the belief that if something goes wrong, there is little to be done. What will be will be. She has given up trying to control things.

'I'll be less than twenty-four hours. If I leave now, I'll be there by dusk. I'll sleep in the tent when it gets dark, get what I can from where the pharmacy used to be and be back as the sun sets.'

The hours of the silent day drag and the night is cold without him beside her.

She knows she must sleep, to preserve her energy for the birth, but without Nik, her ears are alert to every noise beyond the hut.

After a night of fitful rest, she stokes the fire, then paces around it, watching for his return.

The sun is high in the sky when she sees him on the horizon, moving towards her. The baby wriggles in her belly, responding to the elevated thud of her heart.

Ruth is woken before dawn by cramping in her thighs, which she puts down to a continual list of complaints since she ballooned at the later end of the pregnancy.

That afternoon, sitting with the sun on her face, on the crate Nik had found her to save her crouching to sit on the sand, she feels a trickle of warm liquid along her thigh. Touching it and bringing it to her face to smell, she realises it isn't urine but amniotic fluid. Soon after, her contractions start in earnest.

It is like nothing she has experienced, so muscular, yet involuntary.

She finds the pain makes it easier to turn in on herself, and for the first time in months she ceases to fear that she might die but becomes curious about the strength her body has.

After hours of kneeling, crouching and groaning, Nik says he can see what he thinks is a head. Lying on her back she reaches down and feels the matted hair on her baby's crown. But then time seems to stand still. As the sun begins to rise the next day, she becomes convinced that the baby is stuck and is filled with rage. Summoning a reserve she didn't know she had, she pushes herself back to kneeling and asks Nik to support her as she finds her way to standing.

Ruth bears down, yelling in fury. She feels an urge to relieve herself and then, with another rush of fluid, the baby makes its rapid appearance into the world, purple and silent.

Nik springs from behind Ruth and scoops up the still infant from where she lies, blood-streaked, on the carefully boiled cloths between Ruth's legs.

He sucks at the infant's mouth and nose, spitting the vernix and mucus out onto the floor of the hut, then breathes softly into her tiny lungs.

No sooner has the baby screamed in protest at being brought into this abandoned world than Ruth has a flash of clarity: now prone on her back, the energy of birth waning, she realises the wet between her legs is increasing.

She touches herself, where she is most tender, and when she brings her hand up from between her legs, she sees it is crimson. She is bleeding heavily.

Nik, still with the baby, cuts the cord using the stainless-steel scissors he has sterilised over a flame and uses a bulldog-clip to stem the flow of blood. Tentatively he examines each limb, counting the digits at the end of each, then turns the baby, looking for deformation. He can see none.

She is perfect.

He holds her to him and she pouts her lips slightly, looking for milk, her tiny eyes squinting but open, her black irises searching for a food source. He kisses the baby's damp forehead, then wraps her and lays her gently on the bed.

Turning to Ruth to share his awe, he sees her face grey in the morning light and quickly knows that something is wrong. Calmly he applies pressure to the tears, stemming the flow of blood before washing her gently with the sterilising solution he has prepared.

For all his care, it burns Ruth like acid and makes her scream, startling the child, who begins to wail, suddenly aware of her new-found hunger.

Cautiously, Nik tugs on the cord hoping to aid the birth of the placenta and with another grunt of discomfort Ruth delivers the huge, jellyfish-like mass. 'I need to sleep,' she says.

'Try to stay awake.' Nik moves Ruth's hips gently, removing the blood-soaked cloths from beneath her buttocks and replacing them with fresh.

The baby screams in hunger, the noise so alien to their ears, a noise other than either of their voices. They have been alone, with only the sound of the sea, for so long.

Nik gently inspects Ruth. Since the placenta has arrived the bleeding has stemmed significantly. Only a small stain spreads slowly on the fresh sheets on which she lies.

'Hold the baby. See if you can feed her.'

Nik hands her the raging bundle: their daughter.

'A girl?'

'A girl. *Taku tamāhine*. A daughter.'

'Frances. We'll call her Frances.' Ruth strokes the baby's soft downy cheek.

'Hello, little Frankie,' Nik coos, '*taku tamāhine*.'

Outside, in the light of an early spring day, Nik dices and shreds the placenta as the fire he has kept alive all night grows into tall flames. He takes one of their battered pans and cooks the diced placenta with a little seawater. The smell of the cooking meat reminds him of the liver and onions his mother would make when he was small, a dish he despised for its metallic animal tang. But now this food will be a feast that he hopes will nurse back to health the wan face that lies glistening with sweat on the pillow, in turn helping Ruth to feed their child.

As he stirs the browning meat, Nik feels unsteady on his feet, faint.

He puts out his hand to stop himself falling, then sits on the sand, leaving the food cooking over the glowing coals. His breathing is uneven and he makes a concerted effort to slow it down, taking even breaths as he was encouraging Ruth to do earlier.

Gradually, he manages to calm himself, then kneels and removes the meat from the heat to prevent it burning. 'Stupid.' Moments of stillness like this are dangerous, he knows. He tries to avoid thinking at all costs, keeping busy. When the thoughts come, so do the feelings. He can't afford to feel overwhelmed, not now; Ruth needs him.

Ruth and their child need him.

He needs them.

Nik steadies himself and scoops some of the cooked meat onto a metal plate with a spoon.

Outside the hut, he pauses. He can hear Ruth's voice. She is talking to the baby. Singing to her.

Twenty-two

Ruth took the Friday afternoon off work with very little difficulty. She let the head know she had a 'hospital appointment'. Flustered, he had granted her request – 'Of course, of course' – without enquiring any further, for fear of discovering anything more about the female body. Anyway, the summer holidays were imminent, and the structure of the school week was already somewhat lax, sports activities taking over more and more of the timetable. Not to mention that so many of the Ladywell parents seemed to find the eight weeks of holiday insufficient: many of her class had already been whisked away to their second homes.

Explaining her absence to Alex was trickier. She told him that Fran had surprised her with a train ticket to Edinburgh and she was going to freeload on the luxury of a work conference. 'Lucky lady,' he had replied, and left it at that. He had no reason to doubt her. As far as he knew she'd never had cause to lie to him.

Fran doesn't question for a second that Ruth's pregnancy has anything to do with anyone but Alex so she doesn't bring up Ben in conversation. Indeed, there's no way of knowing which of Ruth's unprotected trysts have resulted in her current situation and, besides, she's enjoying having the undivided attention of Fran's support. Why invoke her disappointment by letting her know that, once again, when she'd started having doubts about one relationship, she'd hedged her bets by trying to start another. She's embarrassed to admit that, despite her protestations that with Alex it was different, it's the same as all the others. She hates that she's so inconsistent in her affections. Is it an integral flaw in her personality? Maybe she isn't capable of loving someone long-term. In some respects she's okay with that – she imagines life as an Elizabeth Taylor type, dating handsome men well into her seventies – but ideally there wouldn't be quite so much collateral damage with every love affair.

She hasn't told Ben either. That was easy enough: he's done everything he can to avoid her since he left her flat that night, and on the one occasion they'd had no choice but to sit next to one another in the staffroom during morning notes, he assiduously avoided eye contact and practically sprinted from the room the second the meeting was over.

Before the procedure, Fran takes her to their favourite pizza place. It is almost noon as they sit down in the converted post office and order their pizzas.

'And a bottle of house red too, please.'

The waitress turns back and nods with a smile. 'Wine at lunch. Wish I could join you!' She bounces off to the counter to place their order.

Fran watches her go, appraising her as she types merrily at the till. 'She's sickeningly cheerful, isn't she? Is double denim back?'

'She's a ray of sunshine. Maybe she'd like to come with us to the clinic. Brighten things up.'

The girl returns, beaming, the bottle and two small glasses in her hands.

With Fran's encouragement, Ruth washes down, with a full

glass of wine, the two codeine and two paracetamol she had been advised to take, then tucks into her pizza.

'Feeling okay?' Fran talks as she's eating, her mouth full of semi-masticated crust.

'Yeah, fine.' Ruth reaches for the bottle and pours herself another glass.

'I think you're kick-ass, you know that?'

Ruth avoids Fran's steady gaze, pulling herself another slice off the pizza between them. 'I'm getting an abortion. It's hardly a triumph.'

'Ruth. I'm telling you I'm impressed with you. Can you hear me?'

Ruth doesn't respond, but continues to chew.

'You're my best friend and I love you. It drives me up the wall that you don't seem to like yourself as much as I do. But this? This is showing some real guts. Showing some real self-care. It's making a solid decision for a future you want. Not letting a bunch of unformed cells ruin either of your lives. Or, as importantly, ruin that unformed-bunch-of-cells's potential life. Kick-ass.'

Ruth nods but doesn't answer.

'Ruth? Can you hear me?'

'Yes. Okay. Thank you. Sure.'

But Ruth isn't sure that is how it is. She is definitely making a solid decision, but she isn't sure it's because she's fighting for some future she wants. Rather, it's preventing a future she's sure she doesn't want. A future that fills her with fear. She doesn't want a child right now. She isn't sure she wants kids at all. She knows at her age most women would be worrying that this might be their 'last chance' but she doesn't feel that way. It's not that she doesn't like kids, she just doesn't feel compelled to have one of her own. Not only does it feel like a giant responsibility that she isn't ready to take on, but bringing a child into this fucked-up world seems almost cruel. There are too many humans on the planet already.

'Finish it off?' Fran waves the almost empty bottle above the table, then splits the remainder between their glasses.

Looking at the people on the table next to them, Fran leans over the table and whispers. 'Is he that actor bloke? Always plays dickheads? Really short?'

It is indeed that actor bloke and he seems just as unpleasant in real life as his characters tend to be. He's giving the waitress a particularly hard time, requesting garlic oil then claiming he asked for chilli, could he have more pepper, on and on, with a hard edge to his voice that makes it seem he could start shouting at any moment. The girl in double denim looks close to tears. Fran, witnessing the girl's distress, winks at her to let her know they've noticed his unfair demands. The girl smiles back, appreciative.

'Yep, that's him all right. He's even shorter and nastier than his characters, it would seem.' Ruth is speaking loudly enough for him to hear, the mixture of codeine and alcohol working their way into her bloodstream, making her bold.

'My mum always told me never to trust anyone who isn't polite to waiters.' Fran addresses him directly and the actor checks over his shoulder, as if she must be talking to someone else. 'No, I'm talking to you,' Fran assures him.

The actor scowls and raises his newspaper in a vain attempt to hide his flaming cheeks.

When the waitress comes with the card machine, she quietly thanks Fran for speaking up on her behalf.

'"*Nolite te bastardes carborundorum*,"' Fran says, and hands her a folded tenner with the card receipt. 'For that drink after your shift.'

As they leave, the actor turns to watch them and Ruth feels a rush of pride. She links her arm with Fran's and is reminded of the number of occasions she has felt this: with Fran by her side, she is invincible.

She holds onto her friend and they walk up the hill.

They arrive at the clinic breathless and flushed with the exertion of the walk.

Fran flicks the bird at the middle-aged man standing outside. He thrusts a well-worn placard towards them. It is a large piece of cardboard with a grainy image of a foetus in the womb Sellotaped to it. Beneath the image he has scribbled 'MURDERER' in marker pen.

'You're a disgrace. Leave these poor women alone, go home and do something useful.'

Possibly due to her slight inebriation, Ruth finds the man's surprised response to Fran's confrontation inexplicably funny, and as they enter the waiting room they carry with them an air of levity that doesn't quite match their surroundings.

The baffled receptionist checks Ruth in and indicates that they should take a seat. The room's atmosphere is immediately sobering. They sit in the corner and, in a hushed voice, Fran offers to get Ruth some water from the dispenser in the hall.

'Two crimes in one. Unputdownable cone cups *and* made out of plastic.' She hands a full-to-the-brim cup to Ruth, who grimaces at the sacrifice of plastic for such a measly portion but downs the water in one go: her mouth is starting to feel dry.

They sit in silence, surreptitiously looking at the other people in the waiting room. There are several young women alone, each reading a magazine from the pile of dog-eared weeklies on the central table. A woman of a similar age to Ruth − in her thirties − with three children, the youngest no older than six months; the two kids are sitting quietly, the baby cooing in her pram. An older guy, shiftily looking towards the doors of the consulting rooms, twisting his rings around his fat fingers, his gold chain bashing against his chest as he rocks back and forth. Who is he waiting for? Next to him, a woman and her daughter, looking more like sisters: which is there for the abortion? Or is it both of them?

'Ruth Lancaster?' A nurse with cropped hair looks over the top of her glasses into the waiting room.

'Good luck.' Fran pats her thigh, Ruth rises, smiling at the nurse, and follows her through the door.

In the room the nurse has the ultrasound set up.

'Knickers off, please, and hop onto the bed.'

The wand covered in jelly is cold. The nurse studies the screen and nods. 'Would you like to see?'

Ruth shakes her head.

'No second thoughts? You're sure?'

Ruth nods. 'I took the morning-after pill.'

'It doesn't always work. But, then, you might have been pregnant already. Do you know your dates?'

'I'm decided.'

'Okay, then.'

Ruth feels a slight discomfort as the wand is removed. The nurse hands her a bunched-up wad of paper. 'Clean yourself up, pop your knickers on and we'll get started.'

Once Ruth is fully dressed again she sits opposite the nurse, who is typing furiously into the computer. Without changing her eyeline she slides a printed form across the table to Ruth and places a biro on top of it. After some time, she looks away from her screen, directly at Ruth.

'I need you to sign here.' She points at a box on the form. 'And here.' She indicates a dotted line. 'That's to say you're sure, and this is to say you're aware of the risks of medical termination.'

'Oh, okay. Sorry. Before I sign, do you mind – sorry – going over the risks again?'

The nurse reels them off by rote: haemorrhaging, pain, a small possibility of sepsis, the outside chance of the medication having no effect and the patient remaining pregnant, potential issues with future pregnancies.

'Right.' Ruth picks up the pen and signs the form.

'All very unlikely, though, love.' The nurse takes it from Ruth and signs it herself.

'Okay. I just need to get my colleague to sign this too. Back in a minute.' The woman exits the room, leaving the door ajar.

There are laminated posters on the wall. Images of foetuses, of wombs, of advice on how to wash your hands. There is a distinct tang of antiseptic in the air. The computer monitor on the table is massive, arcane-looking. Ruth can hear the computer itself whirring beneath the desk.

Outside the window it is turning into a beautiful sunny day. The leaves on the tree are like those near her flat: wide star-shaped hands. Sycamore? She should know: they do that stuff at school every autumn. The leaves are ageing now, as summer is rearing its head, turning from the fresh pale green that first unfurled in spring to a darker, lush green.

The nurse startles her as she re-enters the room. 'Right, that's all done.'

Businesslike, she hands Ruth one plastic cup with two pills in it and another with some water. 'So, swallow those with that and then that's you.'

The nurse smiles at her briefly, then returns her attention to her computer.

So, Ruth swallows them and that's her.

*　　*　　*

Back at Fran's they turn her big velvet sofa into a daybed with duvets and pillows. Fran makes them hot chocolate and they watch rom-com after rom-com, dozing as the sun sets.

Ruth wakes to a dark room. The television flashes colours into the empty space, lighting Fran's sleeping face at the other end of the sofa. It is playing a trashy film set at Christmas that the streaming service had queued up while they slept. Fran's cat sits on the back of the sofa, watching Ruth with her eyes narrowed. Ruth's known the cat since she was a kitten, but she can't fight the feeling that it doesn't like her. As if to confirm it, the cat bites Ruth's socked foot, then jumps down.

Feeling a slight ache in her back, Ruth makes her way across Fran's wooden floorboards, which she had helped her strip and polish when Fran had first bought the place. She walks along the tiled hall with its blue-black-painted walls hung with vintage mirrors, many of which they'd found together in the dust at the back of charity shops or haggled for at an early-morning antiques market. Ruth arrives at the toilet at the end of the hall. She pulls the string to turn on the light and sits on the toilet. She places her hand on her abdomen. It is not even tender. Inhaling deeply, she looks down and sees the faintest stain of pink on the preemptive sanitary towel.

'Sure,' she says aloud to herself.

Twenty-three

The baby sits on the sand, putting fat fistfuls of the black-flecked grains into her open mouth. She smiles an uneven-toothed smile at her mother, who sits just a short distance away, a bucket between her knees, slicing fish into long, thin fillets ready to be dried over the coals of the fire that evening.

It is the height of summer and the daily work has reduced for a peaceful few weeks. Soon the leaves on the trees will start to turn and they will begin to forage from dawn until dusk, taking turns to have the baby strapped to their chests. Then, when the days begin to shorten, they will harvest the fruits of their labours from six months earlier, the infant child sleeping beside them in the improvised crib as they work.

Ruth looks up from where her daughter plays towards the sun hanging low in the sky. She will need to build the fire soon, with Nik away.

Since the success of the trip to the chemist in those days before Frankie's birth, Nik has built up a small pharmacy in their stores. With a young child, he'd felt an overwhelming urge to stockpile things that might be required, should either mother or daughter cut themselves or drink some contaminated water or . . . or . . . or . . . His mind was constantly filled with the multiple horrors that might befall them and wrench away the two humans he loved. He was kept awake at night considering the fragility of their humanness. It was a daily

181

surprise to him that not only had he and Ruth survived but that they had created a child and, so far at least, managed to keep her alive.

Despite his constant vigilance for potential peril, Nik has been making more trips further afield.

He has become used to discovering the twisted, desiccated bodies of the dead – human and animal – who had avoided the atom-scattering initial blast but died for reasons that were no clearer to Nik and Ruth than the reason they had survived. He is now systematically emptying the contents of a supermarket, bringing home can after can of food for his young family.

He pulls the cart, its wheels oiled with the fluid from bottles found scattered by a crater he recognised was once a petrol station. It is heavy work and it takes him twice as long to walk dragging it as it does when he's unencumbered. Often he is away for two dark nights.

Ruth retreats to their hut early on these nights, stoking the flames of the fire before full darkness descends, nursing their child for as long as is required to keep her quiet, sleeping with the loaded shotgun they found in a farmhouse by her side.

She often scares herself awake, thinking she has heard a noise from outside, but always the sun rises and there is only them.

'Come on, Franks.' Ruth raises the baby to her hip, her small sandy thighs against her bare waist. 'Mummy needs her dinner.'

The child rests her mass of thick dark hair against her mother's chest and sighs. Ruth picks up the bucket of sliced fish with her other hand and turns towards the sea, away from the river, to walk back to their hut. As she does so, her eye is drawn far down the beach: on the other side of the river, something is catching the light of the afternoon sun.

A reflection?

She squints to see what it is, this dancing light that appears to be moving.

Could it be Nik? That doesn't make sense: the direction is off and it is too soon. He will just be leaving the town and, anyway, she knows pulling the cart on the sand is laborious work.

She puts down the bucket of fish and shifts the baby onto her other hip to free her right hand. She shields her eyes from the sun and looks again to the source of the light.

It is closer now, and all at once she can see exactly what is reflecting it. Her arms tighten around her soft, naked child as she takes it in: silhouettes, human silhouettes laden with bags, their shadows stretching long on the beach. The sun is reflecting on something they're carrying: rays of light dance around them as they move.

They're walking slowly down the beach towards her.

Ruth starts to back towards the hut, moving as fast as she can while keeping the approaching figures in her eyeline.

Frankie, desperate to return to the sand, begins to scream.

Hating herself, Ruth wraps her hand over the child's mouth to stifle her cries but she sees the figures stop. Then, as if in slow motion, one points towards her. Ruth's skin prickles as she feels their focus on her. She begins to run.

She races to the hut, flinging back the skins they have hung in the doorway and depositing the crying Frankie in the crib they had fashioned crudely with bars from fallen garden gates.

She exits the hut with the shotgun cocked.

Ruth has used the gun only a few times since they found it, and each time under Nik's instruction. She knows it is loaded, but if she has to shoot, she doesn't know what she'll do. She has never successfully reloaded it alone. Thinking quickly, she darts to where she dropped her bucket, the pieces of fish she was slicing spilling out of it. The white flesh is covered with sand, as if it has been battered and is awaiting deep-frying.

Sometimes her longings for things from Before come from left-field and knock her sideways. How inconvenient the human brain is to make her long for fish and chips when she's preparing to meet the first other humans she has seen in years. When she's preparing to discover whether they're friend or foe.

When she's preparing to fight to save her infant daughter's life and her own.

And all her brain can do is torture her with the thought of malt vinegar soaking through a greasy chip cone, with extra crispy bits and a tart, knobbly gherkin.

She shakes her head to knock the thought from her mind, then grabs the filleting knife from among the sandy fish.

She crouches, armed, ready.

But the figures seem no closer. Their position has barely altered from when they spotted her: they're moving so slowly.

Unable to run?

Or biding their time?

She stands, watching as they draw nearer, her gun ready.

Her breasts are leaking in response to Frankie's whining protestations at being left alone in the hut. The milk is wetting the front of her T-shirt in two noticeable dribbles. She spits on her top several times to try to disguise it: she wants to hide the fact she is lactating at all costs.

Why on earth did she agree to Nik leaving her? She's a sitting duck. Of course something was bound to happen when he was away. She's only lucky that he'll be on his way back now. He'll arrive within hours. If she's clever and they're unarmed maybe she can play for time, hold them off until Nik returns.

The slow-moving party is making little ground, but it is clearer now that they are three separate beings. The smallest is lending support to the skeletal frame of one of the others; the third is laden with bags, moving like a tortoise.

'Stop where you are!'

Ruth calls across the causeway where the river meets the sea, holding her gun high. 'I'm armed.'

'We don't have any weapons.' A woman's voice.

Ruth watches one of the figures stop, just skin and bones, draped in filthy rags.

'We have food.' The same voice again: she is bargaining with Ruth. There is an edge to her voice: desperation.

'Please. Can we crash here tonight? Set up camp? My husband needs to rest.'

Ruth pauses. She can see their faces now. She looks from grubby face to grubby face of the only humans other than Nik and Frankie she's seen in more than four years.

'Please.' The weak voice of the child, a girl, reaches out across the water to Ruth.

Twenty-four

London is strange in the summer. In the mornings it feels deserted without the usual congestion that the commute to schools creates, yet everyone she knows still has to go to work.

Ruth raised the possibility of a holiday in the sun with Alex back in May, but his work commitments meant it fell by the wayside and now she is looking at an entire summer stuck in the city. 'What's the point of so much time off if I can't find anyone to go on holiday with? I don't want to spend eight weeks in the flat on my own.'

It is late Sunday evening, the first weekend of the holiday, and Ruth has absolutely nothing planned for the week ahead.

'A "staycation" – trendy, and doing your bit for the environment.'

Alex doesn't look up from the paper as he answers her. His reading glasses are perched on the tip of his nose, making him look older than he is. His hair is in tight curls, still damp from the bath.

'I'd hoped you'd whisk me off somewhere hot and sunny.'

'Darling, I can't. It's just too busy at the moment. I'm sure it'll be sunny here. If the last month is anything to go by you'll need factor fifty just walking to the corner shop.'

'Hardly a romantic getaway, getting sunburnt on the pavement in Deptford.'

'I'll undoubtedly have to go to Norway at some point. If I do, I'll take you with me. A romantic couple of nights in Oslo?'

He looks over the rim of his glasses and kisses her before taking them off, rolling over and turning off the light, leaving Ruth awake, watching the lights of passing cars reflected on the ceiling.

So far there has been no call for Alex's expertise in Scandinavia, and each day Ruth is faced with finding ways to fill her time. The rhythm of her body clock means she still wakes early. Eagerly, Alex invites her into the shower; she acquiesces hoping that the athleticism of the sex will make her sleepy so she can go back to bed once he has gone. But, as the door slams behind him when he leaves for work, she finds herself sitting in the kitchen with wet hair and a cold slice of toast, the wide expanse of the day stretching out before her.

She reads a lot: the one benefit of so much time to herself. She steals *Moby-Dick* from her dad's shelf when she visits her parents.

'Isn't that mine?' Jim pulls it from her bag as she is unloading the boot, when he drops her at the station.

'Do you mind?'

'Not at all, but I'll have it back when you're done. I've got some new thrillers to take to the Costa with me. I'll leave Ishmael and Ahab to you.'

She waves as he drives off, slightly regretful that she turned down the opportunity to join her parents in Spain. But when they booked the tickets she was still hopeful that she would be going away with Alex. She wasn't to know that urgent aid issues would develop, putting the kibosh on Alex taking leave.

Alex was right, though: she doesn't need to go to Spain for the weather. London is gloriously sunny. She tries not to think of why the UK's temperature is akin to North Africa's and enjoys the sun.

She spends sweltering days in the over-chlorinated water of Brockwell Lido. She swims lengths but never sticks to one stroke, her breaststroke, crawl, backstroke punctuated by occasionally diving beneath the surface and holding her breath for as long as she can before bursting back into the warm summer air. She floats on her back and watches the planes leaving vapour trails in the sky over her head. Then she climbs the metal ladder and emerges from the pool, drying off in the sun, reading the thick paperback she has wrinkled with her damp fingertips, lying on a towel spread over concrete slabs. When she is tired of reading, she dozes, shifting in and out of consciousness as the children shriek joyously around her, plunging themselves into the water again and again.

On a particularly humid day, she takes up Fran's recommendation and hops on a train through the central artery of London to Hampstead Heath and dares the cold depths of the Ladies' Pond. Afterwards, on the grass, the green water having cooled her to the core, she feels completely at ease lying topless in the sun, surrounded by bodies showing just as much soft flesh. She dozes beneath the cadence of dozens of female voices before walking to the top of Parliament Hill and settling on a bench to read, taking breaks from imagining herself aboard *Pequod*, to survey the city below.

She finds herself eager for Alex's return from work in the evenings. She looks forward to having someone to converse with, to share a joke about something she saw during the day. She starts preparing dinner for him every night, opening a bottle of wine as she cooks. But often he is late and she finds she is annoyed and slightly drunk by the time he gets home.

'Sorry I'm late, my darling. What's for dinner? I'm starving.' He kisses the top of her head and she immediately smoothes her hair where the contact ruffled it.

'Lasagne.'

'Another feast of carbs?'

He pinches the flesh that protrudes above the waistband of her jeans. Ruth steps away from his hands and puts on the oven gloves. 'Well, it *was* lasagne, but I'm not sure how edible it'll be now.'

Alex cocks his head, looking at her. He reaches around to the nape of her neck and pulls at her hairband, freeing her hair. 'There,' he says, smoothing her hair behind her right ear. 'So much prettier.'

Towards the end of the holidays, they meet on a Friday night for ramen in New Cross. Since she has nothing to do all day, she gets there before him. She watches him arrive. He chains up his bike, checks his phone, then opens the swing door and looks around for her, cycle helmet in hand. He somehow achieves an appearance of both youth and middle age, looking like a boisterous child ruffled from outdoor play while simultaneously worn and old, like a ragged teddy bear.

'Hello, my beautiful girlfriend.' He kisses the top of her head, as always.

For a second Ruth thinks she is about to tell him how much she dislikes that, but she can't face the awkwardness that would undoubtedly ensue, so she fixes her hair where his lips have indented it and pushes the laminated menu across the table for him to peruse.

He sits and removes his cycling gloves. She watches him peel them off. He really does have beautiful hands. It was one of the first things she noticed about him.

'Great news.'

'Oslo?' Ruth's voice sounds embarrassingly eager. It is high-pitched with excitement even to her own ears.

'Oh, no, sorry, darling. Not Oslo, I'm afraid.'

'Oh.' Ruth feels as though he has handed her a big shiny balloon and immediately burst it in her face.

'No, the great news is that Sara is letting us have the kids this weekend!'

'Oh, right. Great.'

It is decidedly not great, in Ruth's opinion. Certainly nowhere near as great as a dirty weekend in Oslo.

'I thought we could go to the Natural History Museum. You love it there, don't you?'

'Oh, yes, great!'

That is great. She does love the Natural History Museum.

The waitress arrives with the beer Ruth ordered before he arrived and immediately gives it to Alex. Ruth could swear the girl almost curtsies as she hands it to him.

'Do you want the chilli ramen too? She's already ordered.' The waitress throws a dazzling smile in Alex's direction without giving Ruth a glance. It is as if she has disappeared.

'Has she now?' Alex raises his eyebrows at Ruth, who looks down at the table again. 'In that case, I'll have whatever she's having.'

Ruth looks up in time to see the waitress holding eye contact with Alex as she turns to go, her cheeks flushed pink. 'And I'll have the beer I ordered, too, please!' Ruth calls after her.

'Wow!'

Lily's eyes are wide with wonder. Her head is tilted right back, her Alice band dangerously close to falling off her head. Ruth pushes it carefully to a safe position just above her hairline.

'It's so big!' Lily's voice is breathy, filled with awe.

'What's happened to the dinosaur?' asks Alex.

'It's beautiful,' says Lily.

'Yes,' Ruth says, looking up at the bones splayed above her. 'Beautiful.'

In the pushchair the baby wriggles and moans.

'I know, buddy. I wanted to see the diplodocus too,' Alex says, to the writhing child.

A pungent smell wafts its way to Ruth. She looks down at Jake: he is obviously in discomfort.

'Pooh,' says Lily, holding her nose. 'Jake smells.'

'I'm not sure Jake is expressing his disappointment at a dinosaur skeleton being replaced by a whale, Alex. He needs his nappy changing.'

Alex sniffs the air. 'Pooh! So he does. Lily, you'll be okay with Auntie Ruth?'

Ruth cringes. There is something distinctly creepy about your boyfriend trying to make his kids call you 'Auntie'.

'Yes, Daddy.'

Lily's reply is distracted. She is concentrating on dragging Ruth by the hand towards the information board about the whale skeleton. 'Come on, Roof, I want you to tell me about the whale.'

Alex winks at Ruth, then turns the buggy towards the entrance, looking for a place to change the nappy.

'"Hope, the blue whale,"' Ruth reads aloud. '"The skeleton weighs four point five tonnes . . ."'

'When did the whale die?' Lily has her back to the board from which Ruth is reading, and is still staring at the bones of the creature that are suspended in the atrium of the main hall.

Ruth scans the dense information on the board. 'It died a long time ago. It says here that Hope, the blue whale, was found in Ireland on the twenty-fifth of March 1891. So that's over a hundred years ago.'

'The whale lived on an island? Whales live in the sea.' Lily's brow is furrowed.

'Yes, they do. That's right. But this one came out of the sea on the beach in a place called Ireland.'

'Oh, *Ireland*.'

Ruth tries to recollect whether her pronunciation has ever been corrected by a pre-schooler before and smiles down at the little girl. Lily's mouth is hanging open as she gazes up at the gigantic skeleton. 'You'll probably learn about whales when you start school, Lily. They were my favourite animal when I was your age.'

'What's your favourite animal now?'

Ruth opens her mouth but discovers she doesn't have an answer. Having a favourite of anything isn't something she's considered for a long time. Before Alex, on dating apps, there were often binary questions in an attempt to find something in common with other people who were just scrolling for a quick hook-up. As if answering 'Are you a dog or a cat person?' was a good way to predict that two people might establish a profound connection.

'I haven't thought about it for a long time, Lily. But, I guess, I still like whales the best.'

'Me too.'

Lily reaches up and takes Ruth's hand. Together they stand quietly looking up at the bones, which glow a soft white. In many ways the creature doesn't look very different from the dinosaur that Ruth remembers from her childhood visits to the museum. Without muscle, fat and skin suspended from the bones, it looks just as prehistoric. Without the knowledge she has, it could quite easily be mistaken for a creature from another time, a time that was lost when the earth reset itself. And yet there are echoes of the human form too, the interlocking bones of the spine, the fins on either side, so like fingers, five digits that, not encased in flesh, appear almost as human as the hand that is holding Lily's now. The ribs, too, a cage that once expanded and contracted, that housed lungs, which filled with air and expelled it, just as her ribs swing wide now as she breathes.

Ruth feels as though an electrical pulse crosses her brain as she makes the connection: the bones above her were a live animal; it was once alive just as she is now.

Did it have thoughts and dreams like her?

Did it have hopes?

Again a fleeting thought feels like a physical action as she recognises that one day she too will be nothing but bones.

The late-August sun streams through the long rows of windows above them; light pours through the tiny patterned panes and bounces off the bones.

Ruth feels Lily's hand tighten in hers. 'I like it, but it makes me feel sad.'

'Me too, Lily.'

'Why did it come out of the sea, Roof?'

'Good question. I don't think anyone knows why. They just sometimes do. Maybe Hope didn't know why either. She might have been following her instincts. She might have made a mistake. Or perhaps she was trying to get away from something.'

'She might've been looking for someone,' Lily suggests.

Ruth looks up at the beast's skeleton again, focusing now on the head, the two heavy bones of the bottom jaw, the solid plate above it. It is giant. Huge. A mouth easily big enough for a human to lie in, she thinks.

'Perhaps she was looking for something and got lost.' Lily's voice has a surety that stirs a feeling in Ruth's chest.

'Yes,' Ruth replies. 'Perhaps.'

Twenty-five

Nik feels as though he's been snatched out of sleep by the noise.

As soon as he is fully awake, he finds himself alone in Ruth's tiny tent.

The noise must have been a trick of his mind. He's been semi-woken by the light of the dawn and his subconscious has given him an additional prod, providing an imaginary soundtrack. Great. Now he's hearing things!

He groans as he stretches, and notes the deep ache in his back. He overdid it yesterday. These trips leave him feeling as if he's had a big one on the turps. Chance'd be a fine thing! He can't remember the last time he found any beer.

Sometimes he dreams of walking into a bottle shop and choosing a beer from the cabinet with condensation on the glass, or pulling a stubby from the chilly-bin at a barbie.

He sits up and tugs his jumper over his head.

No good torturing himself: best to focus on the now.

He unzips the tent and stands, stretching his arms above his head.

It's a clear dawn: if he gets going now, he'll be home before it's too hot. He can't wait to show Ruth the lollies he found. How rare it is that they indulge their cravings. Sugar: ordinarily they're united in missing it. This afternoon they'll be able to join together in relishing it.

He rolls up the tent and the sleeping bag, tying them into a bundle and wedging it into the loaded cart. The haul yesterday was pretty sweet. This supermarket has proved a treasure trove, and though the journey to get here means being away from the camp for two nights, he's got enough from one day's scavenging to supplement their diet for months.

Nik freezes as he hears it again. This time he's sure he hasn't imagined it. But he holds his breath, just in case.

He turns his head, looking in the direction it came from.

There it is again! The unmistakable call of a rooster welcoming the day.

The noise of the animals in the cart is pretty irritating. And his knee is smarting where he scraped it as he fell trying to catch the black wiry one. There had been so many, he didn't know where to start, but he went for the hens. They were easier to catch and, hopefully, they'd yield a fair few eggs. The rooster would mean more chooks, of course, but he'd looked pretty mean.

Oh, well, he knows where they are now.

He'll be back.

Despite his grotty knee, he's walked at quite a pace. It's a warm day but the excitement of getting the birds back and showing them to Ruth and the baby has been like having the wind behind him. He's even found himself humming as he walks, one of those tunes that Ruth is always singing as she works. He tries to conjure her voice, the pretty sound it makes floating on the wind.

Not far now, just the last bit – the worst bit: pulling the cart across the dunes.

He hadn't known how hard it was until he'd taken over from Ruth when she was pregnant. That woman was bloody strong.

When he'd first met her, he'd thought she was a spoilt little princess. And that accent. He'd always hated it. It reminded him of costume dramas his ma had watched on the telly, so stuck up. She seemed to be looking down her nose at him. And now he loves her voice, the accent even. To hear it feels like home.

He thinks of her, when he first saw her, running up and down the beach, tossing water at the whale, screaming at him. He understands now that all of that was grief: her every action was imbued with the trauma of everything she had ever known having been erased. He should have recognised it: her trying to save that whale was no different from him selling up and hitting the road, with only his camera for company, after Eva died.

Grief does funny things to a person.

Now he knows Ruth better than any other human ever, even his ma. Even Eva. Something he'd thought impossible.

Nik grunts as he pulls the cart over the hills, the chickens squawking in their crate, outraged at their imprisonment.

He looks towards the water and sees the silhouette of Ruth holding Frankie's hand. He stops for a second, his breath heaving, and watches as his naked daughter holds her mother's hand as she runs back and forth, escaping the lapping foam of the sea.

Something's off.

A metallic taste fills his mouth. The figure holding Frankie's hand is too short, her hair is longer, a different texture. The person holding his daughter's hand isn't Ruth.

He sees it then: two unfamiliar tents pegged in the sand beyond their hut.

Nik slides the harness from his shoulders and grips the handle of the knife in the belt at his waist.

*　　*　　*

197

'Here,' says the woman. She is pointing at a map with her cracked, dirty forefinger. It is carefully folded, but is worn and annotated with her scribbles all the way down the coast.

'We've kept records,' she says. 'Here, you can see we were tramping for two days – you see the "2" there? – to get to Cambridge. That was once we'd worked out that Matamata was buggered. But Cambridge was just as bad. Worse. Some dogs, though, and not gone as scodey as the ones we've met since, eh, Bill?'

'Yeah, nah,' croaks Bill.

Ruth nods, encouraging her to continue.

'Yeah, when they're feral, they're dangerous. But we caught and ate a few in Cambridge without too much trouble. Wish we'd had the forethought to dry out some of the meat to jerky. Clever as.'

'It was Ruth's idea.'

Nik has barely said a word the whole evening. He is just sitting and watching. Ruth can tell he doesn't trust the newcomers, even though they are his countrymen. She can feel the tension in him as he sits next to her. He is alert, primed like a coiled spring, ready to pounce.

The woman tears at the piece of dried fish using the teeth at the side of her mouth. She is missing one from the bottom row and there is a black incisor above it that looks like it's on the way out too. She is wearing some clothes Ruth has scavenged, a pair of tracksuit bottoms with a vest.

The woman has washed in the river with the soap Ruth offered them, but her hands are still filthy. They look almost dyed, so deeply ingrained is the dirt on the palms.

The girl sits next to her, her body touching her mother's. She is the image of her, hair unevenly cropped close to her head, her face pink from being scrubbed clean. She sips the broth

Ruth has warmed for them, watching warily over the rim of the tin, wrapped with a rag to prevent her hands burning.

'Then we got back on the highway – you can see here.' She points again at the map. 'It only took us a day's tramp, but that was where we first saw the cars. Some of them had stuff in them, more than we could carry. It was just getting used to the corpses. We hadn't seen any before then – they'd have been under rubble or . . . What's that you call it, Bill?'

'Their atoms would have been split,' Bill answers, then coughs violently.

'Blown to smithereens.' The woman returns to pointing at her map. 'Anyway, some of the cars had much better kit than we were carrying. Our tents, for example.' The woman indicates the piles of dirty bags and the two tents that are pitched just beyond the circle of the firelight. 'We had three, one to keep the bags in, but then Bill here started getting crook and, anyway, we haven't seen a soul since those bastards in Hamilton, until we came across you. So we figured, not worth lugging it.'

Ruth looks at Bill. His eyes, glazed white with cataracts, gaze pointlessly towards the light of the fire. His face is drawn, revealing his cheekbones and, above, the deep indents where his glassy white eyes sit unseeing in their sockets. His hair is lost in patches, the skin on his head showing sores, some open. He looks like a skull already.

With Frankie soundly asleep, Ruth leaves the hut to find the woman, Anna, sitting alone with Nik, illuminated by the glow of the fire.

'They've both turned in. Knackered,' Anna says.

'How long has Bill been . . .?' Ruth trails off. She hasn't dared ask until now.

'It's been mercifully quick.'

Ruth nods, hoping she'll elaborate.

'His eyes started to go first. Said he couldn't see clearly, then they started to cloud over, like a dead fish's. It was when we were near Hamilton. I know that because we tried the hospital. It'd been completely looted, of course, and I was certain we were being watched. We've not had much luck meeting other survivors you'd want to spend time with. Anyway, that's when I decided we ought to hit the coast and make our way down, see if we can get to South Island. Maybe it wasn't affected, or at least not affected so bad. Maybe there are more survivors. People who had shelters like us.'

'So it was an underground shelter?'

Nik seems so suspicious of their story. A bit rich, thinks Ruth, considering our own account of avoiding the blast.

'Yeah. Bill's dad dug it out in the early eighties. He was a bit of a character, you know. Everyone had a good chuckle at him in the town at the time. But I guess he had the last laugh: it's his genes that are living on!'

'Was it airtight? How long were you down there without any fresh air?'

'Nik.' Ruth places her hand softly on his to try to quell his questioning.

'We were down there for the best part of a month. Till the water ran out.'

'You had stores? You were ready?'

'Yeah, we'd stocked up. When Europe happened, Bill went to the supermarket and spent a fortune on tins and bottled water – filled the car. I have to admit at that point I thought he'd gone a bit nuts, like his dad. Turns out it was pretty smart. Just two days later – *kaboom*.'

'And it was airtight?' Nik is leaning forward, his eyes serious and concentrated.

'Nah. It had air vents to the surface,' Anna replies. 'We found some dust in the shelter, a few days after, so I guess it was coming straight through. I don't think Bill's pa had considered filtration. Who knows? Maybe that little bit of dust will do for us.'

'So, the last people you saw were in Hamilton?'

'Till you fellas, yeah. Plenty of dead folks along the way, though. Every building completely flattened. But then there was you. You and this whale.'

She points to their hut, then looks between Nik and Ruth. Her eyes are narrowed. She is still trying to work out the extent of their lies.

Nik hadn't wanted to tell these strangers the truth, but Ruth had let the cat out of the bag before he could advise caution. As it turned out, Anna obviously didn't believe them. But, then, Nik wasn't so sure about their story either.

'And you haven't heard of any other survivors? Heard anything on a radio?'

'Nah, we had a radio in the bunker but it was all just fuzz, after.'

'Yeah, we tried too. Nothing.'

Anna smiles at Ruth, her eyes creased at the corners.

'God bless Bill's pa for building it, the paranoid old git. Always said there was going to be a nuclear apocalypse. Turns out he was right – his dates were just off.'

'And Bill's cough?' Ruth is struggling to be polite and get to the information she is most interested in, but the woman doesn't seem too fazed by her being direct.

'Been a good while now. It's why we stopped so long up in New Plymouth. That and the scavenging.' Anna looks at Ruth shrewdly. 'I know what you're thinking. You're wondering how long till you, well, till all of us . . . You want to know how long we've got left.'

'I'm just trying to make sense of it.'

'Well, there's no telling why Bill is sick. He's been with me and Nina the whole time, from the shelter to now, and he's eaten all the same stuff. But maybe he was sick already. He was a smoker.' She pauses and picks up the stick by her booted foot, poking the fire. 'Maybe that's it. They always say when you give up the fags that's when it gets you.'

The sound of Bill coughing in the tent reaches them. Ruth feels compelled to change the subject. 'Did anyone you met in Hamilton know of others? Know anything more than you do?'

'Nah. A bunch of hoons they were. They were living like they were in *Mad Max* or something. It won't be long till they start eating each other, I reckon.'

Ruth shudders at the idea, suddenly feeling vulnerable sitting opposite this tough woman with her muscular forearms. 'That's why Nik thinks staying put is best.'

'You're a quiet one, eh, Nik?' She smiles, exposing her black rotting teeth.

'Just thinking, Anna. Listening.'

His voice is brittle, unfriendly. Ruth smiles weakly, trying to smooth over his hostility.

Ruth watches Nina playing with Frankie. It is the only time there is any light in her eyes. She is twelve, Ruth now knows. Tall for her age and mute, but for the mumbling she uses occasionally to communicate with her mother. When she is tasked with watching Frankie, making sure she doesn't put into her mouth anything she could choke on or crawl into the water where she could drown, she seems to have a purpose and, on occasion, the hint of a smile appears to play on her lips.

The past several days have been strange for Nik, spending time with his countrymen after four years with only Ruth to talk to. He has dropped much of the slang that used to pepper his language: it avoids the explanation required when Ruth crinkles her forehead and says, 'What?' in her most imperious British tone.

He has asked Anna non-stop questions about what they've seen on their travels.

Are the forests burnt?

Have you seen animals? Wild? Domestic turned wild?

He has a clear picture now, anyway.

The answers to his questions have satisfied what he felt in his gut to be true: New Zealand, at least the North Island, is as desolate and unpeopled as he feared. And those who have survived, four years on they're either dying or they've gone mad. He was right to persuade Ruth to stay put and build a life here. Who knows what would have happened if they had ventured further afield?

'We leave tomorrow,' Anna announces that evening, as they sit around the fire, a dinner of egg and sweet potato, *kumara*, lying warm in their bellies. She keeps her voice low, restricting the conversation to the adults. Across the fire her daughter is playing with Frankie, her face lit with a smile as the baby hides behind her hands, playing peekaboo.

'You could stay. Autumn is coming, then winter. It'll only be worse in the south.'

'Nik's right. Plus, there's safety in numbers. I think we could get on. It could work, all of us, together.' Ruth adds to Nik's plea.

It has been eye-opening having others around. A longing for community is awakening in her. She has been so busy surviving, so busy adapting to this new world, that she hadn't realised it was absent. But now, having spent time with other humans, even strange ones, it feels essential. It is something she wants her daughter to know, something she wants for herself.

'It's decided. We've got to keep moving. Stick to the plan.' Anna is resolute. 'It's good for you guys too. I know you don't want to be hitting the road with the nipper, but we can send back help if we find it. Look.' She holds up the map. There are new scribbles on the blue of the sea next to where they are located. A drawing of three stick figures, one male, two female – one smaller than the other – their names written under each: Ruth, Nik, Frankie. 'If there is anyone to find, we'll find them and send back for you.

'We're headed to Wellington. If it's anything like Hamilton, there'll be at least a few people there. People with mad ol' fathers-in-law who built shelters, or saw it out in basements – maybe we'll come across some others who are perfectly healthy cos they hid in a whale's mouth.' Anna smiles wryly at Ruth. She still doesn't believe their story. Her open disbelief has been making Ruth doubt its veracity herself.

'It doesn't feel safe, Anna. You said anyone still living in the cities had gone crazy. Think of Nina.'

'No offence, Ruth, but if I stay out here wondering whether normal life, or at least something like it, is going on just beyond that horizon, I'm likely to go crazy too.'

Ruth nods. She understands. Part of her feels the same.

'And as for Nina, if she's going to have any future . . .' Anna turns to watch Nina, who is bent over, animatedly examining a shell that baby Frankie is holding up to show her glinting in the light of the moon. 'Well, to have any chance of that, we'll need to see who else is out there.'

That night, Ruth is finding it hard to sleep. Though her body aches for rest, her mind is whirring like an engine.

'Nik?'

He stirs, groaning slightly as he quickly becomes alert. 'The baby?'

'She's fine.' Frankie is sleeping soundly by her side. Her snuffles are audible in the dark, as though a small piglet is wrapped up in a blanket between them.

'What's wrong?'

'Shouldn't we go too? Leave with them tomorrow?'

Nik rolls over. She can see his eyes shine in the low light, the curve of his jaw lit by the full moon shining through the tarpaulin above them. 'We've discussed this. I thought we'd agreed we're staying put.'

'Yes, we had. But now we know there are others, shouldn't we go?'

'Anna says, if they find others, they'll send them for us. It's better to stay here – there's much more chance of us being found. A moving target is harder to hit.'

He sounds so sure. It makes Ruth feel safe, protected. But still she can't shake the thought. It's like a thread of an idea has come loose from the spool and has started to unravel in her mind.

What about Frankie?

Who will she have if something were to happen to her and Nik? What sort of life can they give her without other humans to interact with?

Nik leans towards her and kisses her, then bows his head and kisses Frankie. 'Stay put, and eventually they'll find us. This is our home.'

Ruth listens to his breathing change as he falls back to sleep. Her eyes still open, she lies awake in the dark.

Shortly after dawn, they watch the family of three as they slowly walk down the beach, heading south.

'Fewer mouths to feed.' Nik puts his arm around Ruth's shoulders. She nods and turns away from the shrinking figures.

'Show me what else you found in town.' She walks over to the laden cart, the dirty blue tarpaulin pulled tight over its contents. The chickens cluck contentedly in their hastily built coop, pecking at the grain Nik has spread in the reeds. Ruth places Frankie on the sand where she can watch the chickens, then reaches over the bulk of the cart's load, pulling at the ropes to unload the rest of Nik's haul.

Twenty-six

The nights are long now and the clocks will soon be going back. Although she felt lonely and bored during the endless days of the summer, she now misses that freedom.

In the daily routine of school she feels trapped, and not just by her job. She feels restricted by the clothes the colder weather is forcing her into. She finds the bus, until now a space to think, claustrophobic. And the light is fading so quickly after school that it is often dark by the time she returns home, making her feel enclosed and restless.

She feels lonely, an isolation exacerbated by the continual movement of London around her. She misses her friends, but doesn't feel she has time to see them. Camille and Charlie seem to be booked up months in advance, and between Fran's work commitments, and her being loved up with Jenny, it has been difficult to find time when it's just the two of them, particularly since Ruth works to Alex's schedule too.

When she discovered Alex was going away this weekend, she decided, rather than facing Ben at drinks in the Monty, she'd do her best to lure Fran south of the river for an evening hanging out instead.

She is so excited about seeing her that she feels as if she's waiting for a date to ring the doorbell, rather than her oldest friend. She has stolen a bottle of good wine from Alex's rack and opened it to allow it to breathe, lit candles and made pasta sauce from scratch.

She needs to talk to Fran, but all week Ruth has been nursing a sense of looming déjà vu. She's not quite sure she's got the guts to talk about how she's truly feeling.

And what, exactly, is it that she's feeling?

That things with Alex aren't quite what she'd hoped they'd be?

That Alex isn't the man she thought he was or, rather, he's not the man she wants him to be?

Will she be able to admit to Fran that she has come to understand why she kept her affair with Alex secret for so long? That she didn't tell those who know her best because they would have told her what she can now see for herself: she and Alex aren't particularly well matched.

She doesn't want to taint the evening. But she does want to talk about an idea that has been percolating for a while. An idea that she thinks might save her relationship. But to do that, she'll need to admit that things aren't perfect, and she's not sure she can.

'Why has he suddenly plastered the place with pictures of his family?'

Fran is stalking the perimeter of the room while Ruth pours the wine. Watching her, Ruth realises just how long it is since Fran's been in her home. In fact, how long it's been since they spent any proper time together.

'They *are* his kids.'

She is all too aware, however, of the number of images of Alex's family now adorning her shelves and walls. Following Ben's uncomfortable observation that there wasn't much evidence of Alex living there, he had exploited her suggestion that he should feel free to have his possessions on show far more freely than Ruth had anticipated.

'Still weird,' Fran says, lifting the gilt-framed photograph from the shelf. 'This one's got his ex-wife in!'

Ruth tries changing the subject. 'How much pasta do you want?'

'Whatever you're having.' Fran continues to survey the shelves.

Ruth sits on the sofa, holding the bowl of pasta out to her. 'So, I'm thinking of jacking it all in and going travelling.'

Fran turns to Ruth, her eyes bright. 'Go on.'

'Calm down, it's only an idea. I'm just thinking about it.'

'Where? Where are you *just thinking about* going?'

'I'm not sure, but somewhere I've never been. Somewhere far away. New Zealand?'

'What does Mr Carbon Neutral think about you flying all the way to the other side of the world? He'll have to pay for a shit-load of trees to make up for your flights.'

Ruth chews a mouthful of pasta.

'You haven't told him yet?'

She doesn't look up for fear of seeing Fran's face. 'I'm waiting for the right moment.'

She feels a hand rest on her knee and looks up to see kindness in Fran's eyes. 'It sounds very exciting, Ruth.'

Fired up by Fran's response, and the wine, as soon as Ruth has watched her friend depart in a cab, she dials her parents' home number on her mobile. 'What would you say . . .'

Anne and Jim listen on speakerphone, having muted the TV to talk to her. She outlines the plans that have been forming and waits nervously when she's stopped rambling. The line is ominously silent for a few seconds.

'I reckon I can speak on behalf of your mum when I say we both think that sounds like a rather excellent idea, Ruth.'

'Sounds like a wonderful adventure, darling!'

Ruth is shocked to find her eyes unexpectedly filled with tears.

On Saturday she lies in bed, the duvet pulled up to her nose, racking her brain about when might be a good time to broach the subject with Alex. The autumn term is moving fast: it'll be half-term soon and then, before she knows it, it'll be Christmas and she'll have missed her chance. She should have handed in her notice already and flights are going to be ridiculously expensive as it is.

It'll be Sunday evening before they get any time alone. She should really seize the moment: Sara will drop the kids off soon. She is dreading another weekend playing stepmum.

Yes, she and Lily are now firm friends and Jake is as cute as they come, but she spends her entire week surrounded by small children. Ideally, as she's made the life choices she has, she'd like to spend her weekends doing grown-up things rather than having to appear endlessly cheery and constantly making compromises.

She can hear the rain outside, which means the plan of taking the kids to Crystal Palace to see the dinosaurs will be wet and miserable. Will she be able to convince Alex that another trip to the Horniman Museum would be preferable? Or could she strategically engineer an afternoon watching films she'd loved when she was Lily's age? She wonders how many of them have held up to the test of time.

Alex, already up and dressed, leans down and kisses her forehead, which is protruding from the covers. She holds her breath slightly, her eyes closed, lying stock-still so she appears to be dozing.

When she hears his retreat and pulls down the cover, opening her eyes just a slit, she sees his Lycra-clad form disappearing out of the front door.

Relief floods through her: he's going for a run, which gives her at least an hour alone.

Hearing the door to the street slam shut, she sits up in bed and reaches for her laptop. She opens the spreadsheet she's been working on and starts plugging in figures. It had started as a bit of a fantasy. During the long, empty summer, she'd done a bit of research, investigated where it might be possible. Then she'd looked at the cost of flights. The spreadsheet was the next step, an experiment, just to see how possible the idea might be.

Now the idea isn't such a fantasy any more, she has a plan and – she rationalises – if she has the plan completely worked out, it'll be much easier to present it to Alex as a fait accompli. With that thought, she opens a tab in her browser and copies the email address at the top. She pastes it into the address bar in a new email and starts to type.

It is chaos from the moment Lily and Jake arrive. The weekend passes in a blur of tantrums, which aren't restricted to the children.

Yet again Ruth finds the few minutes she and Alex have alone seem inappropriate to start the conversation.

Ruth is growing increasingly fond of Lily and Jake, but the flat is too small for them, really, even for a couple of days. They are more than ready to go back to their usual lives by the time Sara arrives to pick them up. When Ruth opens the door to her, she is glowing. At least someone's had a relaxing weekend, she thinks.

Once she and Alex have cleared up the peas that Lily had squashed all over the table, they collapse in front of the TV to watch a new Sunday-night drama. It is gentle fare, classic of the type of telly that appears on the nation's screens when the leaves start to turn. She isn't really concentrating but thinks that once the programme finishes she'll have an opportunity to make a cup of herbal tea and chat.

She becomes aware that Alex's hand is no longer resting on her thigh, but actively stroking her leg. She places her hand on top of his, to ask him to stop, but his fingers are insistent, moving higher and higher. So, she stands and says she has some prep to do for school.

He sighs and frowns at her, but lets her go.

Ruth sits in the bedroom for a while, listening to Alex as he heads to the fridge to pour himself another glass of wine, then changes the channel to the news.

She lies back on the bed and tunes out the noise from beyond the room, scrolling on her phone, glancing at friends' photos of holidays by the sea, funny pictures of people looking drunk over the weekend.

Irritated, she puts down her phone and picks up her book.

She must have fallen asleep while she was reading as the next thing she is aware of is fighting her way out of a dream: she is caught in a web of plastic, long tendrils wrapped around her waist dragging her deeper and deeper into the dark of the deep ocean.

'Off me, get off me!'

She tries to scream.

But her mouth is covered too.

Something is in her mouth.

Wet.

Warm.

Ruth wakes with a start.

In the dark of her bedroom, Alex is on top of her.

Kissing her.

His full weight pinning her to the bed.

Her jeans are undone, his hand has found his way up her

shirt and underneath her bra. She wrenches her head to the side and breaks away from his kiss. 'What the fuck?' Her breath is irregular, heavy. She pushes Alex off her and sits up. 'What are you doing? I was asleep!'

'You just looked so beautiful, lying there. I couldn't control myself.' He smiles up at her, reclining on the bed, his hands crossed behind his head.

'Couldn't control yourself?'

It is all she can do to repeat his words back at him. She watches Alex's smile turn to a frown of concern.

'Is something wrong?' He is propping himself up on his elbows. His shirt is open, revealing his chest, his face lit by the streetlight from beyond the window.

Ruth's brain is trying to work fast to keep up with the information it is receiving: he can't see anything wrong with his actions. How can this be?

'Are you okay, my darling?'

Alex reaches out to stroke her arm. Instinctively Ruth recoils. 'No. No, Alex. I'm not okay.'

He looks at her, confused.

'I was asleep and I woke up to you trying to have sex with me. While I was asleep.'

A look sweeps across Alex's face, as if a light has come on. 'Oh, for goodness' sake!' He throws himself back onto the bed, his head falling into the pillow.

'What do you mean, "for goodness' sake"?'

'Well, are you saying I have to ask your permission before I touch you?'

'Yes,' she replies. 'Yes, you do. And when I'm a-fucking-sleep, it's pretty hard for me to give permission.'

'Christ!' Alex closes his eyes and pulls his hands up his forehead, into his hair, exasperated. Ruth watches him, without saying anything, waiting for him to come to his senses and apologise. 'I don't know what is going on with you,' he says.

She sits still, stony-faced.

'I thought, well, I wanted a bit of comfort, okay? You've barely touched me for weeks.'

Ruth still doesn't respond.

'You can give me the silent treatment if you want. But, let me tell you, if you'd just watched the news as I have you'd be wanting a bit of a cuddle too.'

'What's happened?'

'What hasn't happened? There's the continued conflict—'

Ruth raises her hand to stop him. She doesn't want to hear any more detail, any more gloom.

Alex reaches for her hand but Ruth avoids him and stands, heading to the bathroom. She cleans her teeth and spits into the basin. She washes her hands and smoothes on a hand cream her mum had put into her stocking at Christmas. She sniffs her hand: it is too perfumed for her taste so she wipes it off on Alex's towel.

Re-entering the bedroom, she steels herself to continue the argument, but Alex is already asleep. He's under the covers, his clothes strewn on the floor beside the bed, the window next to him open, letting in the sounds of the street.

The curtain is open and the full moon is lighting the room as though it were a late afternoon in December rather than the middle of the night in early October.

Ruth presses firmly on Alex's left shoulder and he moves slightly. She gets into bed, managing to avoid waking him.

Sleep evades her.

She stares at the mould patch in the corner. It has got bigger, she thinks. It now nearly reaches the light.

How long ago was it that she had first noticed it? It's so obvious now, a testament to her laziness. It doesn't reflect well on

Alex either: he's mentioned it to her several times. But neither of them has done anything about it.

Lazy.

At least that is one thing they have in common, Ruth thinks.

She gets some pleasure from thinking how Alex would baulk at being called such: he prides himself on his athletic approach to life.

She can hear the vehicles passing in the street. Alex insists that they leave the window open a crack to 'let the air in'. Ruth breathes in now and considers how the constant flow of oxygen in their sleeping space might be somewhat compromised by the diesel fumes of the lorries making their early-morning trek towards Dover.

She feels as though she has been lying awake for hours.

Each time she is relaxing into sleep's embrace, she is hauled out again by one thought or another.

As the sun begins to rise, she listens as Alex's deep breathing progresses towards something more nasal. She turns towards him and tentatively places her hand on his skin. It is slightly damp to the touch: he is sweating. Her contact reaches through his dreams and he murmurs.

She wonders what he is dreaming about. Her? Their argument? Or the violent images he saw on the news.

Alex turns in his sleep and faces her. Instinctively he wraps his arm around her waist and pulls her towards him. Had he done this to Sara? Does he even distinguish between his ex and her while he is sleeping?

Ruth takes hold of Alex's arm and removes it from her waist, rolling further away onto her side. Her pyjama bottoms have ruched around her calves and she rubs her feet one against the other just as she always has since she was a little girl. Slowly, the soothing rhythm relaxes her. The noise of one foot rubbing against the other under the covers morphs into another sound: the rattle of pebbles rubbing together on a riverbed, the hollow echo of an endless sea.

Her body becomes light as sleep begins to take her, and she feels as though she is floating. The sound of the road outside is far, far away. Now all she can hear is the whooshing sound of the water she floats in and slowly she falls into a deep, deep sleep.

Twenty-seven

On first waking, Ruth often has the sensation of not knowing where she is.

It has been years now that she has woken in this place, but still she finds her mind trying to piece together the smells and sensations of her surroundings, trying to form a clear picture. Depending on the level of her exhaustion, it can take several minutes even once she has opened her eyes.

She looks down and sees the small dark-haired child with her nose pressed against her chest. Then she becomes aware of the warmth of the man who lies wrapped around her.

It all comes flooding back: this is her life now.

This happens as often as sleep transports her to her parents' kitchen or to a coffee shop, carefully balancing a full cup of milk – stained with streaks of coffee – making her way to an empty table through a jostling crowd. She often dreams of eating food she can no longer find. Whatever she has devoured in her dreams preoccupies her during the following day, until Nik notices she is withdrawn and asks: 'You okay?'

'Pasta,' she replies. 'Fresh spaghetti with dark red tomato sauce.'

Nik stops whatever task he is performing – sharpening blades, darning nets, slicing fruit to dry – and closes his eyes, allowing himself to remember too. 'And Parmesan,' he adds.

After a moment or two of reverential silence, they both recommence their tasks, and when they eat, they are grateful for the sustenance and let the memories of those long strips of egg and flour disappear over the horizon, just as the sun does every evening.

Once, on returning from his monthly scavenging trip, Nik pulls the cart across the sand towards the hut with a smile so wide that Ruth's heart leaps. 'Contact?' She feels almost breathless.

'Ah, yeah, no. Sorry,' replies Nik, 'but I've got something I know you're going to like.'

That night they eat pasta with tomato sauce, not the fresh kind that Ruth had loved in her former life but crushed parti-cles that were once dried spirals. They are still a delicacy: her mouth is filled with soft warm carbohydrate covered with sweet tinned tomatoes. If she closes her eyes, she can imagine the fruity tang of olive oil.

Nik puts some of the broken pasta corkscrews onto one of their dented metal plates in front of Frankie. She snatches it up with her strong fingers and brings the pasta to her open mouth, revealing uneven rows of teeth.

'Mmm!' She makes noises as she chews, wide-eyed, quickly grabbing another fistful of the foreign food.

'Yes, little one, fuckin' mmm!'

'Nik,' admonishes Ruth, 'I could really do without her first word being "fuck".'

'Ah, yeah, sorry, eh.' He points at his chest. 'Papa. Can you say that, Franks? Papa.' He winks at Ruth and grins, tomato sauce from the pasta colouring his lips with a hint of red.

Frankie's first word isn't 'fuck' or 'Papa', but 'Mama'. Just as it was the first word of most children who inhabited the world before her. Ruth witnesses all of Frankie's milestones as miraculous, from her learning to roll, to pointing to things she wants, to squatting by the riverside. Ruth could have wept with joy when this became a habit rather than a one-off: this new life they're building was not equipped for rag nappies being changed at the frequency a toddler with a foraged food diet requires. For each of these occasions, she has the urge to reach for her long-defunct mobile phone to call Anne to let her know that she, too, is succeeding as a mother. But on the day when Ruth is walking away as dawn is breaking – to check the traps they've set in the grassland – and hears her daughter's voice across the wind, 'Mama', she feels something within her shift. She runs back to the camp, and whisks her weeping daughter from her father's arms.

'Say it again, Franks!' she says. 'Say it again, my clever, clever girl!'

At moments like that her heart feels as though it might stop for how much she misses her family.

She has no photos of Anne or Jim, none of Fran or her cousin and his boys, none even of Camille and her children, whom she misses with an intensity that surprises her. All her photos were on her phone or the internet: she never imagined she wouldn't be able to access them, a fact that still seems impossible.

She wonders if Nik feels the same. If he wishes he had a photo of Eva. He must do. She has seen how he cherishes that single crumpled photo of his mum, the woman who looks so like him, sitting on the porch with her hair plaited, her eyes looking directly at you from the photo. The eyes she sees each day, looking at her from the face of her own daughter.

She sees little of herself in Frankie's physicality, but her temperament is so like hers: silently defiant, wilful, maybe – she blushes to acknowledge it – a little manipulative.

Watching her daughter, the way she copies Nik and herself so carefully, Ruth sees glimpses of her own parents. Frankie serves as a constant reminder. She regrets that she didn't let all those she's lost know more often how she felt about them; she never told them enough that she loved them.

She'd often sat and observed rather than contributed, so often avoided conflict with silence. How she wishes now that she'd spoken up more, defended herself and others. Fran had so often encouraged her to stop sitting on the fence and now she can see why: it was part of engaging with the world, being part of it. She wishes she had formed opinions more easily and been vocal about it, spoken up for what was right.

How ironic, she thinks. Now she is marooned in silence, and despite her efforts to avoid it, the conflict of mankind caught up with her in the end.

Throughout the winter, Ruth worries that the child will suffer from malnutrition. She perseveres with feeding her from the breast for as long as she can, fortifying her milk by eating parts of animals that make her heave: the red innards of the rabbits they have begun to catch, the bones of the smaller fish, the occasional egg from the chickens that Nik is so reluctant to kill despite their seeming disinclination to lay. She continues to feed Frankie, despite her small, sharp milk-teeth, and her deflated breasts.

Then, one day, for no discernible reason, Frankie just seems to have had enough. The child refuses her breast and Ruth discovers a new-found sense of freedom.

Rather than scavenge from the old world, as Nik does, she heads for the woods, the bush. There, she searches among the vegetation for mushrooms and berries. She becomes adept at climbing trees, finding among the branches the tender fronds of vines they can eat. She learns to steal the eggs from birds' nests to supplement those of their chickens and, once back at camp, hungrily sucks them dry. Sometimes she finds herself chewing the unripe bones of the chick that was growing within it: it makes her gag but she will not spit and waste the nutrition it offers.

Ruth watches as the animal life around them starts to multiply. Wild pigs squeal through the bush where she is harvesting delicious woody mushrooms. Wood pigeons coo in the trees. The buzz of bees leads her to honey: the sweetness is worth every sting she sustains in harvesting the dripping combs from their hives.

How have these animals survived? Had they burrowed? Hidden like her and Nik?

Their own attempts at farming might have proven only partially successful, but around them the land seems to be offering up a bounty. Passionfruit hang ripe and dripping from trees, watercress is knotted in the streams, vines and fruit trees that were once cultivated spring back to life, bowing heavy with peaches, plums, apples, grapes.

The water shares its bounty too: seaweed, samphire, fish, eels, oysters and various molluscs they pick off the rocks. They couldn't eat all she finds if they tried.

From each of her explorations, she brings home trophies for her family. They always save half, either by brining or drying, but the rest they eat fresh, enjoying the diversity Ruth's foraging brings to their diet.

Although spring is upon them, they are always looking forward: winter will soon come again and preserving is always on Nik's and Ruth's minds. They want never to be as hungry again as they were that first year. They want Frankie never to know hunger.

*   *   *

When the food stores are healthy, Nik focuses on scavenging for materials. He strengthens their hut, adding further layers over the original tent they had built, the bones of the whale as the frame. He adds ventilation so they can build a fire inside to warm them and cook when the weather turns.

He finds clothes, all shapes and sizes, some even suitable for Frankie. But it is only Nik who wears shoes. He needs them for the long treks he makes along the cracked tarmac of the roads, hunting out new places to scavenge. Frankie is barefoot at all times; Ruth, her old trainers now useless, wraps her feet in scavenged leather when she hunts. It makes it easier to move and, since she learnt that surprise is her best weapon in the hunt for wild creatures, feet that are almost bare make it easier to creep up on prey.

Their attire suits their roles: Ruth the hunter-gatherer, Nik the farmer, scavenger.

It is rare that they rest but sometimes, as the sun either sets or rises, Ruth sits on the beach and watches the horizon. She never sees any figures walking along the beach, as she had all those months ago. She never sees any boats, not a single ship.

Nik and Ruth avoid talking about Anna, Nina and Bill. They never discuss the possibility that they may return or that others may follow them. But Nik makes sure a fire is always smoking on the beach and they continue to maintain the 'SOS' that is marked out in the sand. There hasn't been a plane either, and they try not to hope that there might be, but now the skies are clear they wonder about satellites, which would require their message to be bold.

'That, moving.' Ruth points towards the dark expanse above them. A small speck of light is traversing the sky between the stars.

Nik moves his head next to hers. 'Where?'

Ruth takes his hand and follows the light with his forefinger as it moves across the black.

'There.'

'Oh, yeah,' he says, 'probably a shooting star.'

'Might be a shuttle.'

'Might be a satellite, with a sick-as camera. Better wave.'

He takes hold of her wrist and waves her hand towards the sky.

'*Kia ora*, spacemen!'

They laugh together, as he pulls her to roll on top of him. He touches her cheek, his face suddenly turning serious.

'*Ka nui te aroha.*'

'What does that mean?'

'It means I love you.' He closes his eyes, embarrassed.

She kisses him. 'You too, you dag.'

He laughs. It never fails to tickle him when she says something she's picked up from him in that accent of hers.

Moments of joy continue to punctuate the grind of their daily life. They are often not just comfortable but happy. They fight, of course, but their arguments are the short, sharp blazes of two people who know they can briefly let their anger fly yet there will still be laughter by the time the sun sets.

Ruth thinks of what her dad said to her once, when she was crying over some boyfriend or other, a man whose name she can't remember now: 'He wasn't for you, Ruthie. It's a quiet, surprising thing. Not a whirlwind and heartbreak. It's not *Anna Karenina* and *Wuthering Heights* – those relationships are fundamentally flawed. You'll just be going about your business and it slowly dawns on you that you couldn't do without that person.' She thinks of Jim often. She remembers him, puce, shouting at *Question Time*, or gently taking her mother's hand as they walked through the market square in town. She'd like him to know that she's finally discovered he was right.

She does miss books. There is little escape from her reality, other than in her dreams. It is the one thing Ruth always asks Nik for whenever he goes out scavenging. Books. In all of his trips, all he has ever found is mulched paper or water-stained tomes, the pages adhered to each other, making a solid mass.

When Frankie was just a few months old, Ruth had asked Nik to work through the rubble of the school she'd passed when she arrived in town. She described to him the location of the deserted classroom, where she'd pressed her nose against the window, hoping to find help. She told him of the shelves she'd seen full of books for the children. She was hopeful that there would be toys, paper, pencils, paint but he returned empty-handed.

'There were pencils,' he told her, showing her the few wooden blocks and a sealed box filled with broken chalk he had found 'but no paper. And what use is a pencil without that?'

She scolds herself for her lack of foresight, for not thinking in the early days before the rains came that the tins of food would last but the books would perish. All they were thinking about then was keeping their stomachs full, surviving from hour to hour. She watches Frankie exploring every stone and shell she comes across and feels a physical ache in her heart that she will never read a book: the words that constructed the worlds Ruth's imagination inhabited as a child.

Instead Ruth tells her those stories herself. She tells her of the Lion and the Witch that lived through the Wardrobe, and great adventures of princesses and princes. Without the books to restrict her, she often switches the genders of the protagonists, waking sleeping princes from their slumbers and sending young women on adventures in mythical lands.

Nik watches as Ruth talks softly to the child on her lap in the light of the fire, retelling the stories they know so well; he raises an eyebrow and forms his crooked smile as he hears her adaptations.

He tells stories too, stories Ruth has never heard, stories from New Zealand, tales that the Māori have been handing down to their children for centuries. He tells stories full of allegory. Folktales of curious animals, stupid humans, and gods of land and sea. Ruth revels in every word, knowing there won't be many new stories in her life.

But she is wrong.

Soon Ruth realises that, though books may no longer exist, they can all tell their own stories.

She can filter the world that was, mix it with the *once-upon-a-times* she remembers and instil hope for the future; while acknowledging the carelessness, selfishness and stupidity that have brought them to this point, she can suggest a life where it is better, where good choices will make it so.

So each night, as a prelude to her own dreams, she lies next to her daughter and strokes her thick, soft hair: 'In the Before . . .' she begins. Frankie and Nik lie still and listen to her weave words that paint a picture of another world in their minds.

Twenty-eight

She knows that nothing has really changed, but ever since that night in October when she woke up with his tongue halfway down her throat, Ruth can't help but feel that her relationship has fundamentally altered. She finds herself becoming more and more irritated with Alex. Rather than think it charming that he always orders her drink without asking what she wants, she now finds it obnoxious.

The way he raises his eyebrows at her when she slathers her toast with peanut butter has been irritating the shit out of her. She is livid when she returns to the sofa after nipping to the loo in the ad break of her favourite crime drama to find that he has switched the channel and once again has the news on full blast.

It is not just his behaviour that has come into focus. Ruth is finding that the magic of Alex's physical attraction has worn off, too. She still sees waitresses flush when he places an order and women of all ages glance at him surreptitiously as they pass him in the street. But more and more Ruth finds herself dreading the times he'll expect them to have sex. She's become an expert at faking sleep.

Why doesn't he have to go to Norway all the time now?

When he first moved in, it seemed as if he was away every other weekend. Now, he seems to be constantly in the flat, touching her. Whenever they are together, he always manages to have a part of his body attached to hers while she tries to remove it; it is as if they are doing some sort of weird contemporary dance. On several occasions she has felt so unencumbered on leaving the flat for work that she has sighed with relief.

To make matters worse, he is broaching the subject of their becoming parents more and more frequently. She feels like screaming, 'I don't want your bloody children! I'm not sure I even want you!' in his face. But, for some reason, she can't do it.

Is she scared of being alone? Is she a complete coward? She is disappointed to realise that, on some level, the answer to both of those questions is yes. She'd always thought she was brave at her core, even if she sometimes errs on the side of keeping the peace. But now there's an opportunity to prove her bravery and she is avoiding facing up to action.

She knows the conversation with Alex she's putting off isn't a proposal that they'll go travelling together but rather that she's going travelling without him. She doesn't know whether her going alone means their relationship is over, or whether she just needs to get something out of her system. Either way, with every day that passes she becomes more and more frustrated with herself for not telling him.

It is already dark when Ruth and Alex arrive at the park, though it is only late afternoon. As they approach, they can see Camille gripping the handlebar of the buggy with one cashmere-gloved hand, her frowning face lit by the blue glow of her phone.

'Milla!'

Camille looks up, squinting, a smile spreading as she makes out Ruth through the gloom.

'Hooray! You're here!' she says, her relief almost palpable. 'Alfie!' she calls towards the dimly lit climbing frame nearby. 'Look! It's Uncle Xander! He's going to hold your hand for the fireworks.' She turns back to Alex and smiles. 'Thanks, Xand. Alfie's been out of control this afternoon. Needs a bit of masculine authority to pull him into line. Charlie's been "held up" at the pub after the rugby. You're welcome to throttle him when he gets home, if I don't get there first.'

Alex groans, then heads over to the small child who is imploring him to 'Hurry up!'

'Good, now we can chat. We'll march up the hill, catch a quick catherine wheel, do a sparkler or two, then it's straight home for supper. If I'd known Charlie was going to be such an arse, I would never have suggested the bloody fireworks . . . but at least dinner's going to be scrummy. The nanny's doing a bourguignon. Absolutely yummo. Her mum's recipe apparently.'

'I thought she was German?'

'Oh, that one's long gone. Charlie doesn't even seem to notice this one and she's a much better cook.'

Ruth feels a surge of affection for her. As ever, she is baffled by the way her friend deals with Charlie's indiscretions but she can't fault her commitment to her marriage. Ruth links arms with Camille as she pushes the pram. 'There will be wine, though, yes?' she asks.

'Oh, darling, there are four bottles of stunning Kiwi Pinot pining for our return.'

Ruth sighs in relief. She isn't sure she can get through another Bonfire Night event without plenty of alcohol. Tonight is her second fireworks display of the week. On Thursday evening, she'd had to trek east after work to stand awkwardly next to Sara and her new boyfriend, James, in the cold, muddy park.

As Alex oohed and aahed with Lily, Jake screamed without pause, scared out of his tiny skin by the noise and being out way past his usual regimented bedtime.

'I hear you met Sara's James,' Camille whispers to Ruth conspiratorially, so that Alex can't overhear. 'Bit of a dish, isn't he?'

Ruth smiles to herself in the dark. Yes, she had noticed. She is just surprised to hear Camille voice it. 'He seems like a nice bloke.' Best to stay noncommittal.

'Don't go getting any ideas, Ruth. I don't think poor Sara could take it.'

'I'm quite happy with Alex, thanks!' Ruth answers too quickly, her voice over-bright and high-pitched.

'Are you, Ruthie?'

Back at Camille's, the mud and the cold of the fireworks display are soon forgotten. As is Charlie's earlier absence.

'He's such a naughty one!' Camille trills, leaning into Charlie's armpit. 'Booked it without me knowing. We've always wanted to see in the New Year in the Bahamas. Such a lovely surprise!'

'Sara and I went there when we were expecting Lily. We stayed in an extraordinary place. All inclusive, but not in a naff way. I'd go back in a flash if it weren't for the airmiles.'

'Oh, Xand, don't bore on about the bloody environment. Let us enjoy it. We'll deserve a few rums in the sun after Christmas with Camille's mother. Don't ruin it for us with all your doom and gloom.'

Charlie picks up the wine to refill the glasses. The conversation between him and Alex continues as he pours, their voices rising. He tips the violet-coloured wine into each long-stemmed glass, first Camille's, then Alex's. As he starts to tip the bottle towards Ruth's glass, Alex – mid-sentence – swiftly raises his hand and covers the top of it. Charlie, raising his eyebrow slightly, withdraws the bottle from Ruth's direction and proceeds to fill his own.

'What the fuck?'

The room falls silent, Ruth's profanity still ringing in the air.

'Darling?' Alex looks stunned.

'I can decide if I want more wine or not.'

Camille stares at Ruth, her eyes wide. Charlie bites his bottom lip awkwardly and surveys the tablecloth, scratching at an oily mark an errant pearl onion has left on the white linen.

'I was simply suggesting, with our plans, that you'd want to be reducing your alcohol intake.'

Alex is wide-eyed, his cheeks flushed, Ruth cannot tell whether with anger or embarrassment, but she is so angry herself she doesn't care. 'Our plans?'

Ruth can feel her cheeks burning. She avoids Camille's eye and stands up, pulling her phone from her back pocket. 'Thanks for a lovely evening, guys. But I think it's time we called it a night. I'm going to order a cab.'

After a silent taxi ride from north to south London they arrive home. Ruth darts out of the cab and charges up the stairs. Entering the dark flat alone, she hears Alex call after her from downstairs.

She needs space to think. She runs into the bathroom and turns the lock. She turns around several times, then catches sight of herself in the mirror, spinning in an empty room. She laughs at herself, then sits on the side of the bath. Turning the hot tap, she watches the water splutter out. Steam fills the room as the water in the tub rises.

Alex taps on the door to tell her he's going for a run. She ignores him and pours her indulgently expensive bath foam under the running water.

Once in the bath, she submerges her head completely; she can hear only the muffled thud of her heart under the water. She holds her breath for as long as she can and emerges feeling calmer. Slowly Ruth lathers her hair, washing the smoke of the bonfire out of it. Then, while the conditioner soaks in, she reaches for her razor.

Looking down, she surveys the stubble between her legs. Ever since she started seeing Alex, she's been shaving her pubic hair, legs and armpits almost daily, as is his preference – 'I like you smooth, it feels so much cleaner.' Not only is hair removal a chore, she's constantly itchy and fighting ingrown hairs. Ruth looks at the angry skin on her pubis: it is red in patches where exhausted hairs are fighting to grow back. She wonders why she is putting herself through it and decisively places her unused razor back on the side of the bath.

She emerges from the bathroom into the semi-light of the lounge.

Alex is still out.

In the bedroom, sitting on the duvet, wrapped in a towel, Ruth opens her laptop to a bookmarked page. A series of destinations, creating a loop around the world, sits in the basket on the screen waiting for her confirmation. Ruth takes a deep breath, types in the digits of her credit card and presses enter.

She exits the bedroom to find Alex, in his running gear, sprawled across the sofa; his face, lit by the television screen, is red and sweaty from the exertion of his run. He is still avoiding her eye, so she places the full length of her body and her towel-wrapped hair directly in front of the screen. Alex has no choice but to look at her. He picks up the remote and mutes the sound. 'Forgiven me my foibles?'

The gold in his eyes suddenly seems very prominent and she feels her stomach flip. Momentarily, she is wrong-footed by this biological reflex. But it isn't enough. She's bored with herself. It's time she and Alex had a proper conversation.

Twenty-nine

Ruth evens out the surface of the sand with her feet, erasing the letters engraved there. She uses a stick to mark the fresh canvas from her standing position. Her blossoming belly makes it hard to sit for long on the sand next to Frankie.

'F,' she says aloud. 'Now your turn.'

Frankie takes up the smaller stick and grips it as she has been taught. She looks up to check with Ruth that she has got it right; Ruth nods encouragingly. Concentrating, her tongue pressed between her front teeth, she approximates the markings her mother has made.

'F,' she states. Looking at her mother, awaiting further instructions.

'You don't need me to show you,' Ruth replies. 'Write the rest of it. You know the letters.'

Creases form in the little girl's forehead as she takes the stick to mark them in the sand. She sounds out each one. 'R-A-N-C-E-S.' She looks up to her mother for confirmation.

'Well done, that's perfect.' Ruth smiles. 'Now, let's do all of your letters. Write out the alphabet, please, Frances.'

'I'm tired, Mama.'

The little girl sighs, as Ruth uses her foot to erase her daughter's letters, leaving the sand a blank canvas once more.

'We'll rest when Papa returns. Write your alphabet, please.'

Frankie groans.

*   *   *

Frankie hates lesson days. She likes to be active. Her favourite days are when she can help with the fishing, when she can sit with her mama in the boat and watch the thin wires, looking out for even a slight vibration. Then she taps her mama, who slowly brings the fish, flashing silver in the sun, to the surface of the dark blue-green sea, pulling it slowly along the surface towards them and whipping it from the water into the boat. Then it will thrash until her mother hits it with the big stone. She loves sitting in the hull of the boat while her mother rows back to shore, singing. Sometimes she joins in, her voice dancing with her mama's, the splashing waves the background to their song.

She likes to help her mama pick the berries. She is allowed to eat as she picks, though not too many or she will need to squat in the scratchy bushes while her tummy makes noises that sound like tarpaulin flapping in the wind.

Sometimes, when the leaves are brown and gold, her mama will take her to the traps and she can help her hunt for mushrooms. She must never put any into her mouth or even touch one. Once, when she was little, she tried to eat a red mushroom when her mama wasn't looking and then she was very, very sick and her mama says they are lucky she is still alive.

She wishes she was big enough to go scavenging with her papa. Sometimes he is away for nights, coming home with things they use to make their camp strong. Most are from Before and they are strange and confusing. Last time her papa returned, he handed her mama several brightly coloured plastic bottles and she had danced with delight. 'Come on, Frankie, we're going to wash our hair!'

Her mama's voice was strange and high-pitched.

The liquid in the bottles smelt strong, like the berries that sometimes fermented in their jars and made them explode, but with something harsh about it too, like when they burnt something that wasn't wood on the fire and the smoke made her throat hurt. She had cried as her mama pulled the liquid through her hair with the detested comb, protesting that it hurt. But her mama ignored her and continued to sing a song about washing a man out of their hair. Once it was dry, her hair still smelt so strongly it made her feel a bit sick. That night in bed, the smell pervaded the hut. After storytime, her mama kissed her head and said, 'Mmm, squeaky clean,' and Frankie vowed never to allow any of that foul-smelling liquid near her head ever again.

As much as she longs to go with her papa, she knows that for now, at least until the baby arrives, she must stay with her mama. Her papa has told her that it is her job to look out for her, so if that means doing her alphabet, then she supposes she must.

With a deep breath, Frankie takes up the stick and starts to mark the sand with the letters, speaking them aloud to Ruth as she does so.

Ruth watches as Frankie slowly carries the dry wood from under the truck over to the lightly smoking fire-pit, piece by piece, piling it up. Her little girl is not yet five years old, yet she knows how to build a fire.

She feels a repeated thud from within her belly: the baby is awake. Kicking. Ruth puts her hand to the bump and feels the unborn child move again. It will not be long now, weeks, days even. Her pelvis aches with expansion; her body is preparing for birth.

She looks at her daughter struggling to open a jar of berries. What will happen to Frankie if she doesn't survive? It was close last time and then she was five years younger.

Ruth still cannot fathom how they were so careless a second time. She thought that her time for babies had passed: menstruation was irregular and her hair was flecked with more and more grey. She is in her forties now, and she knows Anne had her menopause young, as she never tired of telling her: 'We always thought we'd have more than you, Ruthie, but I was too busy being a feminist to realise my biological clock had other ideas.' A bit of an un-feminist statement, Ruth always thought. This time, when the sickness hit her, Ruth's mind turned to Bill, his clouded eyes, his skeletal frame, rather than the fact that four years earlier she had experienced exactly the same symptoms. Then her stomach had begun to swell and she understood.

Another autumn when she won't be able to hunt and forage lies ahead. Nik will take over, as he did before, but things are different. They rely so much more now on what she catches and gathers rather than on what he can scavenge. He keeps having to travel further and further, finding less and less that is worthwhile. They will have something to harvest again soon, though not as much as before. Most of the precious seed they tried to cultivate this year failed due to the heavy rainfall just after they had sown it in the spring.

'Come, Mama.'

Frankie sits cross-legged on the sand by the fire. The flames are jumping high, eating up the brittle wood.

'Let's cook.' Ruth makes a porridge of mushroom, seaweed and slices of eel cooked on a flat hot stone in the coals. They eat in silence, the wet slap of Frankie's chewing the only sound other than the crackle of the fire. 'Close your mouth when you're chewing, please, Frankie.' She knows it is perverse to try to instil table manners while they sit with their dirty calloused feet in the sand. Yes, they are eating from old tin cans with bent spoons, but Ruth always worries. What if that ship does sail past the shore? What if that satellite does transmit a picture to a far-off computer and a chain of command is set off to send out that plane? What if, even, that young girl, Nina, now a woman, returns from the South Island, bringing word of civilisation? She can't let her daughter be a freak who will struggle to fit in. So Ruth continues to mother Frankie in the same way Anne did her. It is one of the strongest vestiges of hope she nurtures.

'And that was how it was, in the Before.' Ruth concludes their nightly story, pulling the blankets over Frankie's sleeping form. She stands and stretches.

Her hips ache.

She pulls up her ragged clothes and places her hands on her belly, gently scratching the surface of her bump: the stretching of her skin makes it itch like crazy. She longs for some cream or oil to soothe it, something like the softly scented cocoa butter that sat on the shelf in Fran's bathroom – Ruth used to steal a dollop whenever she used the loo. But there is nothing like that here, just melted fat, when she manages to catch the game that renders it.

A noise.

Outside the hut.

Ruth turns towards the door. It can't be Nik. He never travels at night. Even under a full moon the cracked road is treacherous and increasingly overgrown with hazards. The smallest of cuts sustained in a fall could easily become infected, and they need to reserve all the antiseptic and antibiotics they have with a new baby on the way, even if the expiry date on most has long passed.

There it is again.

Scuffling.

Ruth is convinced there is something outside the hut. She holds her breath, listening closely. There is noise a little further away, too. The sound of bottles falling and crashing against each other, plastic ripping.

Someone is in their food store.

Quietly as she can, she moves towards the shotgun beside their bed. It is hard to see. The fire is almost out, only minimal light cast by the glowing coals. Ruth misreaches and the gun falls to the floor with a crash. The child in the bed stirs. 'Mama?' Frankie's voice is tremulous.

'Sssh.'

Ruth gets to her hands and knees with difficulty. Her belly hangs heavily, pulling her spine downwards towards the earth. She trails her fingers across the floor, searching. Finally she makes contact, feels the cold metal of the gun's barrel where it lies on the mismatched matting of their floor, against her fingertips.

Another noise.

She turns, still on her knees, to face the entrance of the hut. Growling.

Next to her, Frankie is whimpering quietly. She has heard noises, too, and is sitting wide-eyed, looking towards the door, with the covers pulled up under her chin. 'Mama,' she whispers, 'is it the Big Bad Wolf?'

'Sssh, darling. Cover your ears.'

Frankie obeys. She clamps her small hands tight over them, her eyes shining wide and alert in the semi-dark.

Ruth's heart is hammering and her breathing is even more laboured than pregnancy has made it thus far. She brings the gun up, pointing towards the roof of the shelter and cocks it. Then, taking a deep breath, she fires once through the tarpaulin: a warning shot.

She reloads and points the gun towards the door before she pulls the trigger three more times.

Nik feels pretty downbeat as he pulls the cart past the rubble of the dairy. He is nearly home and he is dreading seeing Ruth's face as she tries to downplay her disappointment with what he is bringing home after so long away.

He should have tried somewhere new.

He'd told himself yesterday that returning to the old supermarket was the best plan: he didn't want to go too far afield with the baby on its way. But, after nearly two days' running around like a blue-arsed fly trying to catch that bloody rooster, and only a few dented cans and a scraped-up arm to show for it, he has to admit that he's managed to waste yet another trip. He'd had visions of returning to camp victorious. He'd imagined how Ruth's face would light up on hearing the bird's strangled crowing as he rolled up with the cage strapped on top of the cart. He knew she was worried about not being able to hunt and a rooster – even a scrawny old bastard like that one – would mean they could get some of the chooks' eggs fertilised. If one or two of the eggs gave them another rooster they'd be set: chooks on tap! But yet again, he's returning empty-handed.

He'll get that cock-a-doodle-dooing bastard yet.

He pulls the cart off the tarmac and into the sand. His thighs burn from the exertion. He looks towards the hut. No smoke. Odd. They always leave the fire alight: it's one of their pacts.

Getting closer now, he looks at the food store and sees that one of the corrugated metal sheets has been pulled away, exposing the rows of jars and tins, the sacks of food stored under tarpaulin. Berry juice and broken glass spread from the ripped plastic sheeting and leak into the sand, staining it like blood.

Something is very wrong.

Nik struggles to release himself from the cart's harness and reaches for his knife. Holding it in front of him, he stalks towards the hut.

He looks at the fire again. The coals are not even glowing – it's been out for hours.

Moving towards the tent, he sees dark patches on the sand here too, but unlike the berry colour by the store, the staining is so dark, such deep red, it looks almost black where it is smeared, dragged along the sand. Something or – Nik's heart stops – someone has died here.

He keeps his eyes trained on the hut, the knife gripped in his hand, ready to strike.

'Hello?'

He holds his breath, listening for a response.

There is silence.

His heart gallops in his chest.

Then he hears the sound of tarpaulin being moved at speed.

'Papa!'

His daughter runs towards him smiling. The front of her roughly fashioned dress is stained dark red with blood. Nik uncocks the gun, slings it over his shoulder and runs towards her. 'Baby!' He grabs the child, swinging her up into his arms.

'We were awake all night!' Frankie's voice is muffled where she is nuzzled into his neck.

Nik, his heart still hammering, carries the child towards the hut but stops on seeing the bloody mess by the door. It is like a scene from one of the gory films he used to enjoy scaring himself with at the cinema: a jumbled mess of limbs and snouts, piled up, golden fur stained with blood.

'Mama shot 'em, Papa, killed 'em dead, she did. They were

big mean dogs, trying to eat our food. So now we are going to eat them.'

Nik is struggling to take it all in, piecing together marks in the sand where the bloody animals have been dragged with the multiple shot-holes he can see in the front of the tent.

'Mama's gonna show me how to skin 'em, like she does the pigs,' says the child, proudly. 'She'll do it, because the knife is sharp. But she's gonna let me help, eh.' Frankie licks her lips and smiles at her shocked father. 'Yum, yum.' She points at the dog corpses piled upon the grubby plastic sheeting at his feet.

Nik slowly kneels so his eyes are level with Frankie's and takes her gently by the shoulders. 'Where is Mama, Frankie?'

'In the tent.'

Frankie puts her finger to her lips. 'Sssh! Mama and the baby are sleeping.'

There is no fire in the tent either. It is cold and Nik can't see far in the gloom.

'Ruth?' The air smells sweet as he approaches the bed. In the dim light he can see the mound of Ruth's form beneath the covers. 'Ruth?'

There is a noise then. A cooing from beneath the sheets. It sounds like a trapped dove.

The bundle of covers heaves to life. An inhalation, a groan. 'Ruth!'

Nik sits on the bed and pulls back the covers. Ruth is lying on her side, her hair loose, tendrils stuck to her forehead with perspiration. The clothes she wears are stained where she holds a bundle of cloths to her chest.

'Māia,' says Ruth, positing the name. She hands the child, wrapped in rags, to Nik. She is so tiny. They were not expecting her arrival for a few weeks yet. The infant's lashless eyes look at him myopically, her face still squashed and red from the pressure of birth, white vernix in the crevices around her mouth and in her ears.

Nik's eyes fill with tears. He holds the baby to him and she wriggles slightly: she is strong despite her untimely arrival. 'Māia?' He is smiling at Ruth, tears falling down his face.

'Yes, Māia. After your mother.'

'I thought you wanted Anne, after yours.'

'I got to choose Frances and, anyway, she's more of a Māia, I think.' Ruth raises herself slightly on her elbow to look at the child cradled in the nook of Nik's arm.

He leans in to kiss the top of Ruth's head. 'Brave. Courage. Māia.'

Nik sits quietly next to Ruth. She turns her gaze from the baby and meets his.

His heart feels so full it is almost painful. 'Māia,' he says.

Thirty

'It wasn't a sudden decision. I didn't wake up and think, I need to go. It's something that's happened gradually.'

Alex looks up for the first time in twenty minutes. The gold in his eyes has dissipated, giving way to something harder. 'You gradually booked flights to the other side of the world?'

'No. I mean the process of deciding to go away.'

'So you haven't booked flights?' The lines at the corner of each of Alex's eyes seem to smooth as hope spreads across his face.

'Sorry, yes. I have booked flights. I didn't book them gradually.'

Alex looks back at the floor. He now has his hands either side of his head, his elbows on his knees, as if he is cradling the weight of his skull. 'And you're going on your own?'

'Yes.'

She hears herself say it and it's true. She has made a decision and stuck to it. Warmth spreads across her chest. She's done it! She pressed the button her finger has been hovering over for months. For years she'd carried a nagging doubt that somewhere along the line she'd chosen the wrong fork in the road, the safe path, the easy street. She's finally done something about how unhappy she felt, and she's done it all on her own.

Her attention is caught by a strange sound coming from Alex. His head is bowed and he is snorting, his back shaking as he snatches at short breaths.

Is he crying?

Ruth sits next to him on the sofa ready to console him, but she sees he isn't crying at all: he's laughing.

'What a joke. You won't last a week!'

'Excuse me?' Ruth feels slightly light-headed.

'It just strikes me as rather hilarious that you think you'll be able to navigate a trip to New Zealand all alone, without me or Fran there to hold your hand. I mean, how on earth will you cope being so far away from your bloody parents? Who'll be on call pandering to your every need?'

'I . . .' Ruth is lost for words. This certainly isn't the response she was expecting.

'I? I?' He is imitating her. 'You, you, what?'

Ruth closes her mouth and looks down at her hands in her lap.

'You are such a mess, Ruth. What do you think you're going to find on the other side of the world that you haven't found here? Some sort of salvation? You're so desperate for someone to save you, aren't you? But have you ever stopped for a moment to question what you need saving from, what you're running away from?'

She's finding it difficult to keep up with what he's saying. It feels like she's being pelted with ideas she hadn't even considered.

Running away? She isn't doing that. Is she?

No, she's going towards something, not away from it.

'I'm not running away.'

'You think someone out there is up to the job of saving you? You thought I was that bloke and now you're dropping me like a hot stone because you're disappointed that, while I do everything I can to look after you, I don't quite cut the mustard. I'm not like one of those blokes in the novels you're constantly mooning over.'

Alex stands and walks over to the kitchen. Pulling a bottle of wine from the fridge, he pours some into a mug from the draining board. 'Real life is boring, Ruth. It can't all be romantic getaways and grand gestures.'

'Really? That's what you reeled me in with.' Finally she has found her voice.

'Reeled you in? Listen to yourself! You think I caught you? Trapped you somehow? You bloody seduced me. You wrecked my marriage.'

Here's the anger, Ruth thinks.

'You wrecked my marriage because you were bored. You were a bored little girl in desperate need of someone to look after you, to protect you from all the things you find frightening about the world. And let's face it, love, that's everything. You couldn't hide in your books any more so you selected me as your knight in shining armour. You wanted me to look after you. But whenever I try, you push me away.'

He's angry now, pacing the kitchen. His anger emboldens Ruth, his words making her feel righteous. 'You think you're some sort of saviour? You don't look after me, you control me. There's a difference. You make every decision for me. I can't have my own opinion about anything.'

'Ha!'

He stops pacing by the wine bottle and refills the mug, then turns to her. There is a faint smile at the corners of his mouth that is so repellent it cancels the effect of every handsome feature on his face. He is shaking his head slightly as he stares at Ruth, his eyes hard, penetrating.

'What?' She is screaming. Her mum has always told her not to raise her voice in conflict as it undermines her argument.

'I'm just wondering, dearest Ruth, whether you've ever truly had your own opinion about anything.'

Ruth's hands are shaking. It feels as though energy in her body is longing to escape. It is coursing along her arms to her fingertips, making them vibrate. She opens her mouth to speak. Carefully she modulates her tone, as her mum has always advised, but she can hear that energy in her voice too, a tremor that shakes her words. 'You know, Sara warned me about you. I didn't know what she meant when she said it. I thought she was just jealous. But I get it now. You're a control freak. I can't breathe. You're suffocating me.'

'I'm evil, am I? That's what you are saying? I'm abusive somehow?'

He looks more than angry now: he looks hurt too, confused.

'I'm not saying . . . You're not evil. You just aren't for me. I thought you were, but you're not. And from what you're saying, it sounds like I'm not for you either.'

Ruth holds up her shaking hands in surrender. 'We don't love each other.'

Alex doesn't respond.

'Can you tell me it's different for you?'

They stand in silence. For the first time in months they know they have something in common. Two people who have made a mistake. People who mistook physical chemistry for something so much more.

Ruth catches Alex's eye. She feels sad suddenly for what they're losing.

'You know, Ruth,' his voice is much more measured now, 'and I can tell you this because it's something I've learnt myself, it doesn't matter how far you run, you're never going to be able to escape yourself.'

Alex closes his eyes and rubs the bridge of his nose, as if he has just removed his glasses. Ruth can see that he is consciously trying to calm himself.

'I'm going to pack a bag.' He puts down his empty mug and walks towards the bedroom. He pauses, his back still to her.

'Can I just ask why? Why New Zealand? Why not just break up with me? Ask me to move out?'

She opens her mouth, but her mind is whirring, struggling to process everything he's said.

'Ruth?' He sounds exasperated. 'Do you even know?'

Thirty-one

Māia is six now. Six is older than Frankie was when Māia was born. Six is quite grown-up.

She is allowed to do a lot of grown-up things, like build the fire, help with making the food, feeding the chickens and doing jobs around the camp.

The problem with being six is that there are still things she isn't allowed to do. She isn't allowed to use the knives without her parents or sister watching; she isn't allowed to go in the boat on her own; and she isn't allowed to wander any further than the crops. More than anything, Māia wishes she could leave the camp. She is so envious of her sister's trips with one or other of her parents to hunt and forage.

Learning almost makes up for it, though. She loves her lessons. Unlike her sister, Māia loves to carve out the letters in the sand. Not only is it interesting and exciting to discover new things, it is also the only time that she has Mama's undivided attention. Like her mother, Māia loves words, ideas. She loves to carve the symbols of the English language into the sand, but also to learn the words of *te reo Māori*. She likes that everything has more than one name, that the same thing means different things to different people. It fascinates her to think that something can exist beyond what it is called.

She is hungry to learn.

Her father calls her a 'bloody *nohi*' but she doesn't mind, as long as she gets some answers to the questions she asks incessantly.

'Mama, tell me again. How did you cook *kumara*? Before.'

Māia listens as her mama tells her about the oven in her parents' house. About the oven that rotated its contents, that pinged when the food was done, that made a potato, which is like *kumara*, go from hard to soft in under seven minutes. She laughs and calls her mama a liar for her tall tales, just as she has ever since she could talk.

It just seems so ridiculous to Māia, as far-fetched as any story.

People kept dogs in their houses?

Cars were used for moving about?

There were machines that flew in the sky?

Her mama tells her now of tinfoil, of wrapping food in metal to cook it, like they wrap their fish in leaves to put it in the coals. Yes, the same metal cars were made from, but thin. Māia laughs and shakes her head. Why would they go to the bother of making such a thing? There are plenty of leaves on the trees.

She would have liked to meet her grandparents, but she is glad she lives now, not then: it all sounds so complicated.

Since she was an infant, she has listened carefully to the stories her parents tell around the fire each night. Now she tells them too. She knows she mixes it all up, but she's not entirely sure what her parents exaggerate anyway. In her tales, the stories of Before get tangled up with her mother's fairytales and Māori legends of *taniwha*. Sometimes she gets it wrong intentionally so her parents shriek with laughter; it's easy if she puts two stories together that she knows will seem fantastical when intertwined.

She loves to hear laughter. For Māia, laughter is the sound of love.

If only it were easier to make her sister laugh.

Māia loves Frankie as much as her sister finds her irritating. Māia's favourite time is when she is in bed next to Frankie at night. Her sister will rarely let her touch her when she is awake. She is constantly shrugging off her embraces or batting her away as she tries to hold her hand. So Māia takes the opportunity on the occasions that Frankie wakes from her dreams with a start, to wrap her ever-lengthening arms around her sister. Māia snuggles her small form against her older sister's back and strokes her hair, whispering a story into her ear to soothe her. She pieces together tales just as they sew together worn-through sheets and clothes; stitching together the memories and myths her parents have fed to her. She knows she must be careful at night only to tell stories that soothe. Stories with monsters and daring are for around the fire, when she holds the whole family captive.

When Frankie returns from wherever she has been adventuring with Mama, Māia quizzes her on what she has seen. How many steps away were they? Did they stop and eat? Which plants did she see? Were there any other people?

Both of the girls ask this question of their parents regularly. 'Are there others like us?'

'There were,' is their parents' tired reply. 'There were.'

Before she was born, all the food didn't have to be caught, collected and grown. Papa tells her that they used to be able to scavenge more too.

She has to be careful not to annoy Frankie too much – not to follow her or accidentally touch her when they are swimming or bathing – for then Frankie will torture her with stories of the meals they used to eat before Māia can recall eating.

'There was food sweeter than berries, so soft in our mouths it would melt on your tongue.'

'Stop it, Frances.'

'It was soft and smooth and not like anything we eat now. How sad you will never try it.'

'Enough.' Her father always protects Māia against the cruelty he sees her sister deploy, but she would never tell him the things Frankie does to her that he doesn't see. She never speaks of the sand Frankie sprinkles into her food. Or how she sometimes leaves her alone by the river as the light fades after they have emptied their bladders; then she has to find her way back to the camp, carefully placing her feet so as not to fall into one of the rabbit holes punctuating the dunes. She adores her big sister and never wants to see her punished.

Unlike Frankie, Māia has the patience to stand in the shallows of the creek until the baby eels dart around her feet. She grips the sharpened stick, as her mama taught her, before letting the growing strength of her shoulder thrust it through the unwitting fish, staining the water crimson.

When she grows just a little taller, she will be allowed to do the same in the sea, where the bigger fish swim. But for now she can only watch her mother from the shore, or join her in the boat, alerting her to any moving lines. She sits cross-legged in the dirty hull, surrounded by the catch as they return to the shore. The silvery scales of fish stick to the skin of her bare legs.

'My little mermaid,' her mama says, as she lifts her from the boat onto the sand.

Māia loves, particularly, stories of the sea. Stories of mermaids, whales and sea monsters, of Paikea and Māngōroa.

'Can we have a mermaid story tonight, Mama?'

'Yes, when Frankie and Papa return.'

'And the story of the whale?'

The story of how her parents met and the beast that saved them obsesses her. She asks questions about it all the time.

'How did you breathe inside the whale, Mama?'

'I don't know, Māia.'

'Did the whale have any babies, Mama?'

'I don't know, Māia,' Ruth answers. 'I hope not. It would have been sad for the babies to lose their mama.'

'Why did the whale die, Papa?'

'I don't know.'

'Did you eat the whale's meat, Papa?'

'Yes, Māia. We ate the meat.'

'We live inside the whale's bones,' Frankie whispers in her ear, lightly tugging at her hair; they are supposed to be sleeping.

'I know,' says Māia, wiggling away from her sister's grasping hands. 'It doesn't scare me.'

It is because of the child's obsession that at first Ruth doesn't believe her.

Ruth watches as a haze of dust rises behind Māia where she kicks up the sand as she runs. She is knee-deep in the creek, washing clothes. Her daughter arrives breathless. 'Mama! It's back!'

'What is, baby?' Ruth continues scrubbing. Always, she is at work. In this new world, where so little is clean, it seems pointless, but she cannot shake the desire to feel washed sheets against her skin at night, threadbare as they are.

'The whale!'

'Yes, baby.'

'Mama! Mama! Come! It's swimming in the ocean.'

Ruth looks at the child: her cheeks are flushed, her hair, flecked with sand, long and wild around her shoulders. 'Remember the story about the little girl who cried, "Wolf"?'

Ruth has found the fairytales and fables of her childhood so helpful in teaching her children right from wrong. Though she wonders if she shouldn't just let them run free, become truly wild. She can't help but feel that that might be their best chance of survival, whether people exist beyond or not.

'But, Mama, I'm not crying, "Wolf." I'm crying, "Whale"!'

Ruth feels a laugh escape her: what a marvel this small child is. She is surprised daily by her easy grasp of language and concepts in spite of all the odds.

'Come, Mama!'

'I can't leave the washing, Māia. It will float away. Leave the stories for night time and help me here.'

'But, Mama!'

Her voice is becoming high-pitched. Her little hands are formed in fists by her sides, her face growing pinched with frustration.

'The whale will float away too! Please!'

Ruth ceases her toil. Her daughter is pointing towards the sea. 'Tell me, what does it look like?'

The little girl sighs in frustration. 'It looks like a big camp on the horizon of the ocean. It's moving along the line where the sky meets the sea. It's like when you and Frankie are in the boat out on the ocean, far away. But the whale is like a much, much bigger boat.'

Ruth starts at the word.

Boat.

Could it be? After all this time?

The sound of her mother's voice calling to her is suddenly in her ears, an image of her father – blue light reflected in his glasses – flashing across her mind's eye.

She pulls the sheet, heavy in her hands, from the water and throws it, with a slap, among the other clean sheets on the tarp. Ruth extends her hand to her daughter. 'Show me, Māia.'

The two of them pick their way across the dunes towards the camp.

Did I leave the fire burning? Ruth questions herself. They don't always now: it has been too many years to set hope every day. The SOS they drew in the sand isn't always visible either: the wind blows and covers with sand the stones that spell out their message. Occasionally they uncover it, but it seems point-less. After such a long time Ruth and Nik are convinced that no help is coming. What if now, on this one day, a ship is on the horizon and there is no way to let it know they are here? Ruth's heart rate elevates and she starts to walk as fast as holding the child's hand will allow her. As they approach the beach, she strains her eyes towards the horizon.

Her sight is not what it was – though when she looks in the stained wing mirrors of the truck she can see that they haven't started to cloud yet, like the eyes of the man who sat around the fire with them so many years ago. She tries to comfort herself that her mum always needed glasses, and her dad needed them for reading and driving as he got older. Maybe the deter-ioration of her vision is genetic, not a sign of encroaching illness.

'Where, Māia? Can you point?'

The little girl stands with her hand above her eyes, surveying the horizon. 'I can't see it, Mama.' Māia shakes her head sadly. 'You took too long, eh?'

They stare at the horizon, silently. Māia's small hand gripped in her mother's. Time passes as they stand still together. Stillness is not something Ruth indulges in often: there is always some-thing to do. She closes her eyes for a second, listening to the waves softly beating the shore, hearing her own breath along-side her daughter's. Her shoulders ache, and so do her fore-arms. They ache to the bone. Recently the pain has become more and more noticeable.

She feels her daughter's hand squeeze her own.

'Mama.' Māia's voice is sotto in reverence.

Ruth opens her eyes. Before her, a little closer than the horizon, she sees the white flank of a blue whale breach the waves. The creature arches and, for a second, it hovers above the water, as though it were in flight. 'Māia!'

Ruth's voice catches in her throat as she pulls her daughter close to her.

Thirty-two

'To life without Alex!' Anne raises her glass to the suggested toast.

'See ya, Alex, wouldn't wanna be ya!' Jim responds, clinking his glass against Anne's.

'I thought you both liked him.'

'We put up with him.'

Ruth watches her parents exchange a look. 'What?'

'He is a very handsome chap, darling, but he was rather . . . full of himself.'

'I couldn't fault him on his politics, but your mum and I weren't too keen on the way he talked to you, Ruthie.'

All weekend Ruth has been struggling not to let Alex's angry words echo inside her head.

She came to her parents, vacating the flat so he could clear out his things without further conflict, but being around her mum and dad, she can't help but hear his accusations at every turn. Her dad picks her up at the station: is that her being mollycoddled? Her mum tells her she's proud of her: is that her being spoilt? Is it such a crime to have parents who love you?

'You didn't seem yourself around him at all, and at Easter, well, at Easter you were just so sad.' Anne takes Ruth's hand. 'Anyway, that's done with now. What's next?'

'What about this trip of yours? Have you got any further with that?' Jim asks.

'Yes, forget about that man. Tell us about these whales,' Anne says, pouring more wine into Ruth's glass.

Alex's voice rings loudly in her ears. But she pushes it to the side. She won't let him completely ruin the trip for her, even if he's dampened her initial excitement.

After dinner Jim turns on his desktop and the three of them crowd around the computer to look at the organisation Ruth has contacted.

'Ruth is going Down Under to save the whales!' Jim's voice is raised jubilantly as he relays the news to her aunt on speaker-phone.

'Well, it's a holiday. I'm just trying to tie in something worth-while,' she says faintly, under the hubbub of conversation her dad's announcement has created.

'It's not going to be all work, is it, Ruthie? You'll make time for a bit of fun too?' Anne is dropping her off at the railway station.

'It's summer over there. I'm sure there'll be a bit of time for lounging on the beach and reading.'

Anne winks at her, and that evening Ruth receives credit for her e-reader account with a message: 'For when you're not saving the whales, Mum xx'.

That is not the last gift Ruth receives from Anne. She seems to be dealing with her only daughter's imminent departure by indulging in the mollycoddling she'd been inclined to all Ruth's life. Ruth imagines what Alex's response would have been to the daily missed-delivery card from the postman. Before work, she collects packages containing variously: a water canteen, a first-aid kit, a Swiss Army knife, walking socks, a stick of char-coal that can purify 'even stagnant water', a postcard-sized book on survival in the bush.

'There *are* shops in New Zealand, you know, Mum.'

She is grateful for the kit, but her mum is under some rather false impressions about how adventurous Ruth is planning to be. She's planning on hotels and cute B-and-Bs rather than hostels and bivouacs.

'Always be prepared, my darling. Your dad and I once had to make a camp on Snowdon when the weather came in. The Girl Guides really came in handy then, let me tell you.'

As the end of term inches closer, Ruth wonders if Fran feels the same mild anxiety about her impending departure as she does. It will be the longest time they have spent apart since they met at primary school. Even when they went to different universities, they still saw each other almost every fortnight.

Is this what Alex meant about her being unable to function without Fran to hold her hand? Isn't she allowed to be worried about missing her best friend?

Ruth is angry that the time she ought to be enjoying with her friends and family is infected with doubt. She hasn't had any contact with Alex since he moved out, but each evening she has taken to putting her phone in another room to stop herself calling or texting to scream at him for making her feel so shitty.

Ruth does her best to push him out of her mind when she's with Fran. They spend weekends together, visiting their favourite parts of London. They venture out to galleries and museums. On the floor of the turbine hall of Tate Modern, waiting for timed entry into the Hokusai exhibition, they lie under a big moon, reminding each other of how they sat under a big sun a few years ago. They howl with laughter recalling who they had been sleeping with at the time, and how obvious it is now that their paramours had been so horribly unsuitable.

Without Alex dominating Ruth's time, they can let their friendship fold into their everyday life as it did before: talking on the phone, meeting after work, watching TV at each other's flats with a bowl of fresh spaghetti smothered in a whole jar of tomato sauce from their favourite deli.

'I'm so glad you threw up on me all those years ago,' Ruth says, licking the spoon clean of the ice-cream they're sharing directly from the container.

'Imagine if I hadn't. You'd never have noticed me. And instead of being the interesting, world-adventuring human you are now, you'd still be hanging about in Suffolk harping on to everyone about Greenpeace.'

They are sitting on the sofa at Fran's, doing little other than existing. Days like this are when Ruth wonders if she's doing the right thing. But every night, after packing her possessions into cardboard boxes to get the flat ready for its new tenants, she dreams.

She dreams of water, a recurring dream which visits her most nights.

She is deep below the surface, in the darkest-blue water, where the shafts of light barely break through from the clear turquoise above.

She is swimming, slowly traversing the watery expanse, and feels a longing so intense that she wakes with tears streaming down her face.

Then, in the dark of one night, she thinks of Alex, of the things he said that have made her doubt herself, and she feels a sense of calm.

She knows she is doing the right thing.

She isn't running away: she is running towards something. She can't quite articulate what it is, but she just knows that, for once, she is choosing the right path.

*　　*　　*

Ruth is increasingly excited by what she will be doing once she arrives in New Zealand. She has been planning it all carefully, without help from anyone, and feels a disproportionate sense of pride about this, considering she has officially been an adult for nearly twenty years. Her visa will allow her to stay in New Zealand for a year, so she doesn't have to rush anything. She'll start with a month or so, enjoying the summer on North Island, then head down south, to the marine project she's been in contact with, to train as a volunteer. There are no guarantees, of course, but she hopes this means she'll learn something, be useful and, best of all, it will give her the chance of seeing a whale up close. By working alongside conservation professionals, a sighting is at least a possibility, more so than if she'd signed up for a whale-watching trip. Ruth can't believe it's been so easy to organise – never has something she wanted come to her with so little friction.

'When it's right, things just flow!' Camille is stirring a sweetener into her black coffee. 'I'm not sure your heart was ever really in teaching little kids. That's probably why it was so hard to find a job.'

'Maybe, but it's been creepily smooth. I'm starting to worry something awful is going to happen to make up for my good luck.'

'Nonsense, darling. You deserve it.' Camille sips her coffee, the clear gloss on her lips leaving a shiny crescent on the rim of the cup. 'I'd say you're set for a run of good luck after escaping from bloody Xander.'

'He's your son's godfather!'

'Not my choice. Charlie insisted – must recognise his old chum from that dreadful school of his. Personally, I've always thought him rather ghastly. Thankfully, now he's not with either you or Sara, I don't have to be nice to him any more. Bliss! He can be relegated to one of Charlie's pub friends.'

'You could have told me!'

'Ruth, by the time I knew you were messing around with him, it would have been awful of me to say that I thought you'd made a terrible choice. Besides, at the time I was more worried about poor Sara. But it turns out you've actually done her a favour and now she's shacked up with James – Dish of the Year. Another example of something rubbish turning out to be what was destined to happen all along.'

'Honestly! You and destiny! Next thing I know you'll be reading tarot.'

Ruth laughs but Camille smiles and places her incredibly soft hand on top of her own.

'What I'm talking about is good old-fashioned energy, Ruth. "What's for you won't go by you" and all that. Commit to something and enjoy things unfurling for you in just the way they should.'

Despite Ruth's protestations, Fran throws her a leaving party. When she arrives at the 'Pre-Christmas Drinks' at Fran's Walthamstow flat, she is greeted by a Bacchanalian gathering of her closest friends and some she wouldn't even class as acquaintances. Fran had cobbled together the guest list by mining her social-media 'friends' and going through her phone while she was in the loo.

'I knew there'd be some ringers in there.' Fran laughs into her vodka-tonic. The two of them are leaning on the fridge, surveying the crowd.

'Everyone seems to be getting on surprisingly well, though.'

Fran nods towards the patio table where a rather inebriated Camille is in deep conversation with two of Ruth's friends from her book group. 'God! I hope they stay away from politics or this little party might end in a bloodbath.'

Ruth grimaces.

'Well, I think I've done rather well. I've managed to bring all sectors of society together, in what is currently a fairly cordial affair. Plus, I even kissed Camille on the cheek when she arrived.'

'You've excelled yourself, Fran. Thank you. And thank you for being nice to Camille.'

'Just don't ask me to be nice to Charlie.' Fran shudders.

Ruth raises her glass to her. 'Cheers!'

She looks around the room at her friends, people she has known since school, several from uni and her PGCE, colleagues and friends, with the odd dating-app mistake thrown in. Though the party is in her honour, Ruth can't help but feel it has taken on a life of its own.

Of course, neither Alex nor Sara is in attendance, but Ben has somehow made the invitation list. There is no reason he wouldn't – she hadn't divulged, even to Fran, the possibility of his being the cause of their trip to the abortion clinic. More surprising is that he accepted the invitation. He is sitting in the garden under the festoons, smoking and flirting with a loud woman she doesn't recognise. She can hear their conversation from where she stands in the kitchen. She has to admit, he is quite funny.

The night ends with just five of them: Ruth, Fran and Jenny, Camille and, unexpectedly, Charlie. They all sit on the floor around the low table in Fran's lounge in various stages of inebriation. Completely unburdened of the children, thanks to Camille's mother being in town to watch the nanny watching them, Camille and Charlie refuse to let the party end. The light is starting to creep along the rooftops of the houses opposite as Charlie pulls out another gram of cocaine and starts to cut it into perfect lines with his bank card. Camille rests her head on Ruth's shoulder – she can feel the vibrations of her voice through her bones. Opposite her, Fran leans against the sofa, absentmindedly stroking Jenny's hair, her head resting in her lap. They're a good match: Jenny will have moved into Fran's by the time Ruth's back – she'd put money on it.

The conversation started as gossip: a delightful rundown of who partnered whom over the course of the evening. It has descended into something nonsensical and repetitive, thanks to the drug. Even so, Ruth is enjoying feeling so close to her friends, this unlikely collection of humans she's collected as her nearest and dearest. Sometimes, when she's at her lowest, she feels as though she doesn't have many friends. She wonders if Fran would give her the time of day if they'd met as adults, and questions what on earth she has in common with Camille. But tonight, sitting on a ridiculous velvet cushion she had egged Fran on to buy, she feels warm and connected and in love with all of them, even Charlie.

It is Sunday afternoon, following a few hours' broken sleep on the sofa, and the moment Ruth has been dreading arrives. The sun is high in the sky as she sneaks out of Fran's front door into the fresh December day. She can't face a long farewell: she'll make a run for it now and call them all tonight to say goodbye – less chance of tears that way. She pulls her gloves from her bag and puts them on, then wraps her scarf around her neck.

When she turns to close the door, she finds Fran lingering on the step. 'Sneaking off?' She kisses Ruth quickly on the lips and pulls her in for a brief hug. 'Have a ball. Call me. Don't be a dick. See you in a few months.'

'See you in a year,' Ruth reminds her.

'Sure, if you can stand to be away from me for that long.' Fran winks at her and closes the door.

The bar in the terminal isn't the most picturesque spot for a farewell meal. Anne stacks the ketchup-encrusted plates that the previous occupants had left, then uses some hand-sanitising gel and a napkin to wipe off the sticky rings of multiple pints. Clearly waiters are in short supply.

'Feeling excited, darling?' Anne is scraping with her thumbnail at a piece of fried egg that has adhered itself to the table.

'Yes, a bit nervous about the flight. I've never been on a plane for such a long time. And the stopover in LA is bound to be a pain in the arse with the extra security.'

'Just smile and be polite.' Anne looks tired around her eyes: it was an early start. 'You must wear sun cream, darling. That hole in the ozone layer is no joke – melanoma are rife in that part of the world.'

'Yes, Mum.' Ruth reaches out and takes Anne's hand. She can't remember the last time she'd done so and it feels odd – her mother's skin is so soft and thin. It feels so different from holding Alex's hand. She shakes her head to dispel the thought of him and smiles at her mum.

'Oh, my darling,' says Anne, her eyes welling with tears. 'We'll miss you so.'

Jim approaches the table with their drinks. 'I had to wrestle a tray out of them,' he grumbles.

They talk as they eat their tepid meals, guessing what films might be showing on the plane, getting Ruth to double-check that the plastic Ziploc folder in her rucksack definitely contains her passport, visas and currency. Anne insisted that Ruth take two hundred pounds in New Zealand dollars in a money-belt in case her luggage gets lost or there is an issue with her bank card. Though Ruth knows this to be unnecessary, she acquiesced to keep her mum happy.

Jim gets up to check the departures screen three times during consumption of his lacklustre chilli con carne. 'It says there's a twenty-minute wait for Security, so better not be too long, Ruthie.'

Once they've finished their meal, they walk towards the barriers where Ruth will scan her boarding card and pass to where her parents can no longer accompany her.

'Right, then, kid.'

Jim smiles, slipping off the backpack he'd insisted on carrying the few metres from the bar to the gates. He holds out the straps for Ruth to thread her arms through.

With her parents smiling at her, she suddenly feels very small. She is whisked back to that September day, thirty-odd years ago, when she had allowed them to kiss her goodbye at the gates of All Saints Primary School. She'd impatiently made her way towards the front door, her brand new patent-leather shoes almost skipping to join the other girls, their white socks pulled high, and the boys trying to loosen the tight shirt collars around their necks.

As Ruth's eyes start to glisten, Anne reaches out and wraps her arms around her daughter's shoulders.

'It's not so long until Easter, darling!'

Anne is speaking softly into her hair, a simple action so loaded with nostalgia it makes Ruth inhale sharply.

'You'll be slinging another shrimp on the barbie for us before you know it, Ruthie.' Jim joins them in their embrace.

'It's Australia where they say that, Dad.'

'Oh, well, "sling another pot of manuka honey on the barbie", then!'

They all giggle at Jim's terrible approximation of an Antipodean accent and hold each other close.

Through the gates, before she turns behind the frosted-glass panels that lead to Passport Control, Ruth looks back again. There they stand, her mum and dad, looking greyer and smaller than they ordinarily seem, smiling at her. Ruth can see they are putting on a brave face. She feels rather foolish for being so emotional – it will only be a few months until she sees them again. Alex is wrong: she can survive without them. And, anyway, it's only a year until she comes home. A year is nothing in the grand scheme of things.

'I love you.' She mouths the words carefully as she looks back at the waving figures.

Then she takes a deep breath and walks down the corridor towards the queue for Security.

Thirty-three

As Ruth tells her daughters about her family, about her friends, she realises so many of her memories are anchored around celebrations. Birthdays, Easter, Christmas, New Year, the annual parties that brought people together over food and drink.

She misses those celebrations.

'You want us to resurrect the Christian Church?'

They are digging. The winter rains have just about passed and it will be time to plant again soon: the signs of spring are already showing.

'No, that isn't what I'm suggesting at all. I'm just saying I miss holidays. So much of our life is working, Nik. Even the girls work every day and Māia is still so little.'

'So you want to throw a party?'

'I suppose so, yes.'

'At Easter? You want me to dress up as the Easter Bunny and hide fuckin' eggs? Oh, cool, no problem, Ruth. I'll just nip down to PAK'nSAVE and grab a bunch of chocolate eggs and lollies.'

Nik's tone is distinctly sarcastic.

'Look, I haven't thought it through. It's just an idea. Easter, Christmas, they were pagan festivals originally. About celebrating the seasons. I think we should too. For our daughters.' Ruth feels disappointed at Nik's response – she had anticipated something rather different. 'But if you think it's a stupid idea, I'll shut up.' She turns her back on him and continues to dig.

She wakes a few days later to find the camp decorated with spring flowers and numerous different-coloured birds' eggs in a bowl at the door of the hut. She is as delighted as her daughters when Nik interrupts them in dressing for a day of hunting.

'No work today, girls. Today we're just gonna chill and celebrate spring. Who's for an egg?'

From then on, those days when they down tools and do nothing but swim, laugh and eat, mark out time. They are the occasions that observe the passing of the seasons, the years.

The autumn slips into the cooler air of winter and the days are at their shortest.

They cook together: a whole pig buried in a pit – a *hāngi*. Then, with full bellies, they lie on their backs and watch the stars. Nik is chewing a bone, sucking the last of the delicious roast meat from the gristle. He pulls it from his mouth with a smacking sound and uses it to point to the sky. He gestures towards a constellation. 'You see that, girls? Those stars, the seven stars? That's Matariki. That's why we're celebrating. It's a new year.'

The girls look up to where their father indicates.

'Yes, Papa.'

Their voices chime together. These occasions have a way of unifying them, but not in the way their parents might hope. Rather than enjoying the ceremony of remembering, they find their parents' nostalgia embarrassing. They listen dutifully to the story Nik tells them. It's about family, about loyalty, about fighting siblings, and they cannot help but feel that he is being rather pointed in his telling of it this year.

'And look there, girls.' Now their mother is pointing to a series of pinpricks in the sky. 'Those are how we know we're facing west. It's called the Southern Cross. It's how hunters and sailors could tell their way until we had machines, Before.'

'Yes, Mama,' Frankie responds fondly, while retrieving a bone shard from between her front teeth.

'Where I'm from, that cross, it can't be seen. There is another set of stars to find the way. And they form a shape that looks like this.' She holds aloft the dented, battered pan that Frankie cooked the mushrooms in. 'Can you guess what they called it? The people where I'm from?'

'The Pan?' suggests Māia.

'We called it the Plough.'

They talk about their family then, about Māia, their grandmother, after whom Māia is named, and their father's father Nikau, who died when he was only a little boy. They talk about their mother's parents, Anne and Jim, who lived on the other side of the world.

Matariki is about remembering the family who have gone, but it is impossible to remember people you have never met. To Frankie and Māia it's as if their parents are telling folktales, just as they used to every night when they were little.

'Just wait,' Māia whispers in Frankie's ear, 'they'll start on the bloody whale in a second.'

Frankie guffaws and Māia cackles to hear her sister enjoy her joke.

'What's so funny, little chooks?'

'Ah, nothing, eh. Go on, Papa.'

Each bump in the road sends a vibration through the cart, every jolt a pulse of pain through his thigh. Nik bites his lip, trying to breathe through it. He pushes his face into the old duvet that Ruth has bundled up beneath his head. He bites it, screams into it, anything to try to release the clean-hot pain that is throughout his body, making even his fingers fizz in agony.

'It's just a tiny bump.'

Ruth is breathless. He can tell she is pulling the cart as fast as she can. At points when the road is smooth she is practically running. She's like bloody Superwoman when she needs to be.

And she does need to be: his only hope is to get back to the camp. Where they keep things clean. Where they have the last of the medicine. Where their daughters are.

Nik howls in pain as the cart shudders over a raised seam in the road.

'You're like the Princess and the Pea! I don't believe you even felt that,' Ruth shouts, over her shoulder, her eyes trained on the road ahead.

They aren't far now: he can see the shells of the rusting caravans ahead.

'Yeah, except the princess didn't have a shard of bloody metal sticking through her thigh.'

Nik grimaces and turns his head back into the duvet howling like a wounded animal. What an idiot he is. Why couldn't he have just let it go?

That bloody rooster.

Logically, he knew it wasn't the same bird. He'd first found those wild chooks when Frankie was still barely able to walk and now, though it blew his mind to admit it, his daughter is a woman.

It might not have been the same rooster. But it was a rooster.

And he'd got the bastard.

Yeah, he'd been showing off, up on that wall. He'd so enjoyed the hunt with Ruth, how they'd cornered the bird together.

And he was jubilant. Finally he had the rooster under his arm. It was a glorious moment: Ruth below, on the flat, beaming up at him as the bird squawked and struggled against him, shedding the few feathers it had.

Then it had gone for him, pecked right at his face. He'd leant back to avoid the creature's beak – protecting his eyes – and lost his footing. He'd fallen.

He thought he'd wet himself when he felt the warmth of liquid on his leg.

Then he looked down and saw the blood, the metal protruding from his flesh. That was when he became aware of the pain and passed out.

But now he is awake. Awake and in bloody agony. He lets out another howl.

'We're here, Nik. We're almost home.'

'What a muppet, eh?'

He sees his daughters' eyes widen as they take in the extent of his injury. His wounded leg.

Ruth removes the binding from around the protruding metal. Dried blood pulls out his hair, adding stinging insult to injury.

His daughters are rapt. They watch their mother's every movement, fascinated. He hasn't looked at it himself. He can't or he'll think about what this might mean.

His leg is raised on the plastic chair, the one he'd found within the whale. Māia is holding his ankle, Frankie his shoulders.

'Right,' says Ruth, gathering herself. 'You need to hold him. Tight.'

He feels his daughters restraining him, feels the pressure of Ruth's hands around the wound.

He looks up at Ruth's face. At first he thinks she's angry but then he knows it's worse: she's frightened.

The sun hangs low in the sky, casting a long orange shaft from the horizon to where the sea meets the shore. The warmth of the day has already departed, the breeze from across the water making itself known around Ruth's ankles, the nape of her neck. She pulls the salt-stiffened collar of the fleece towards her ears and bends down to push a log into the flames that have begun to lick the kindling.

Hearing distant voices, she stands alert and peers towards the long grass, into the thickening gloom.

'If you'd held still, I'd have got him.'

'Yeah, right, it's your aim that was off. It had nothing to do with me moving.'

She can see their heads now, moving through the grass as she hears it rustle with the agile movements of their legs, the smaller trailing the larger, their wild hair and the sway of their gait as recognisable to her as her own reflection in still water. Their voices lift towards her on the wind: she hears every syllable now, though they consider themselves out of earshot.

'You watch it, eh. You spooked him and now we're empty-handed. You explain it.'

'You aren't my first choice of hunting partner either, you know.'

Māia's voice rings out like a bell across the reeds. Her baby is not such a baby now.

'You egg.'

As they reach the edge of the grass both girls fall quiet. They have seen the silhouette of their mother against the glow of the sun. Māia steps forward, her hard-soled feet wrapped in skins indenting the pebbled sand. 'Mama, I scared the deer. We didn't catch anything.'

'She's not hunting with me again.'

'I'm not hunting with *her* again.' Māia jabs Frankie with her elbow.

Frankie responds by grabbing a handful of her sister's hair.

'Enough!' Ruth puts the fight to bed with two syllables even before it has begun. 'Will you feed us with your bickering?'

Frankie releases Māia's hair from her fist. Māia takes her hand from the punctured skin of her sister's arm and they stand, empty-bellied and heavy-hearted, behind their mother, heads hung in shame.

Māia looks at their home and drops her voice to ask her mother: 'How is Papa?'

'Sleeping,' Ruth responds.

'Does he seem any better?'

'He seems asleep.'

'I'm sorry we didn't catch anything, Mama. I'll cook some roots.'

They eat in silence, around the crackling fire. The waves wash on the sand, punctuated only by an occasional cluck emanating from the coop where the chickens are settling in to roost.

Thirty-four

Ruth has a stopover in LA. She makes it through Security and Immigration and, with relief, ascertains that her flight is not the one to Auckland which departed forty-five minutes ago. She takes a seat in the departure lounge and dials her parents' home number.

'Hello, Lancaster residence.'

'Hi, Mum.'

'Hello, darling! Happy Christmas! Your dad's here, darling – putting you on speaker.'

Ruth rolls her eyes: it's always harder to steer a conversation when her parents use the speakerphone, though they do it every time. 'Thanks for the disclosure, Mum, I was about to bad-mouth him.'

'Happy Christmas, Ruthie!'

'Not Christmas here yet, Dad.'

'Oh, yes, of course. What time is it there in *Hollywood*?'

Jim's attempt at an American accent is as bad as all his others.

'Have you two been at the sherry?'

'Just a drop or two to drown our sorrows! We're all alone this Christmas. A couple of old drunks, stuck in deepest, darkest Suffolk, while our daughter lives it up in the sunshine on the other side of the world,' Anne says.

'And no Auntie Sue and the kids this year, either.'

'Wish them season's greetings from me when you call them. It'll be Boxing Day for you when I arrive in New Zealand.'

'Are you calling on your mobile, Ruth? Won't you be charged through the roof?'

'It's just a quick one to let you know everything's going smoothly. I'll get a SIM card when I arrive.'

'You're at the airport, darling?'

'Yes, in LA. Through Security and Immigration, but only just. It was a bloody nightmare. The woman checking my bag had a machine-gun strapped to her back. I felt like I was in a war zone.'

'Well, with that president of theirs, you aren't far off.'

'Anyway,' Ruth says, moving the conversation on – she hasn't called for one of her dad's political debates, 'the gate should be announced soon. I can't wait to get on a plane so I can go back to sleep.'

'Make sure you buy a big bottle of water.'

Anne's mothering instinct doesn't see five thousand miles as a boundary.

'Yes, Mum.'

The Tannoy interrupts their conversation: Ruth's flight is boarding shortly – the gate has been announced.

'Oh, that's me, I'd better go. Not sure how far the walk is to the gate.'

'Have a good flight, Ruthie.'

She can hear that her dad's attention is now elsewhere.

'Call us when you land, darling.'

'Yes, of course. Call you when I get there,' Ruth responds and hangs up.

Ruth is shaken awake by a sudden jolt, followed swiftly by another. For a second she struggles to recognise her surroundings.

She is sitting upright. The light is harsh. She squints.

Another jolt, a judder of mechanical parts.

She pieces it together from the corners of her frazzled memory.

She is on a plane.

The Tannoy fuzzes for a second before the captain's voice booms out. It seems unconscionably loud, but Ruth is aware that might be sensitivity on her part.

Her mouth is dry and her shoulders ache. She wipes dribble from the side of her mouth and gives the steward an embarrassed smile as she hands him several empty miniature bottles. Intense alcohol consumption helped to block out the images of the heavily armed officials at Immigration in LA but she was paying for it now. Ruth had been concerned that she would be put on the next plane home but, following a brusque search of her bag and a thorough inspection of her paperwork, she had been allowed to pass through to her connecting flight.

The plane lurches slightly and the 'fasten seat belt' lights come on. The descent into Auckland International Airport has begun. The captain advises that the toilets are now out of use and that the cabin crew should prepare for landing in twenty minutes.

Ruth looks out of the window. She sees nothing but sea, glinting in the sun.

Her stomach turns over with a sudden pang of nerves. Maybe I'll see a whale from here and then I can just get on the next flight home, she thinks.

From here the ocean is vast and looks almost green under the light of the morning sun; the sky is clear.

Ruth reaches in the pocket of the seat in front of her for the bottle of water she purchased in LA, cursing herself for the expense. Her new metal water canteen is in the hold somewhere beneath her, packed with the multiple other travel accoutrements Anne had foisted on her. She opens the flip-lid on the plastic bottle. It crackles as air enters. It has been compressed as the pressure increased during the flight. Her insides are probably like that too. The thought makes her feel nauseous.

She puts the water back into the elastic net attached to the seat in front of her and closes her eyes, feeling the downward motion of the plane. She listens to the mechanical gear changes of the wings as they are controlled by the pilots.

It is all so perilous, she thinks. One wrong move and all these people will be dead.

The plane's wheels make contact once, twice, and finally a third time before the engines roar into reverse. It seems to take a long time for the vehicle to slow, but once it does, the more enthusiastic or nervous passengers break into applause.

Ruth rolls her neck and looks out of the window. The sunny day outside does not match her interior landscape. She needs a coffee.

The Tannoy scratches to life again: the pilot tells them they have been instructed that the airport is in special measures. Anyone with a connecting flight is to stay on the plane and await further instruction.

'Jeez,' says the woman in the seat next to her. 'My flight to Dunedin is in fifty minutes. They'd better not leave us hanging around too long. When's your flight, lovey?'

'Oh, I'm getting off here, I'm afraid!'

Ruth's not sure why she's being apologetic to a stranger but she's relieved that she's not getting caught up in anything that will delay her stretching her legs and having a wee.

* * *

Once she is off the plane, she turns on her phone.

No signal.

She hears other passengers grunt in irritation as they, too, struggle to connect to a new carrier. Ruth shrugs, and pockets her mobile. She'll call her mum once she's through Immigration. They tend to get weird about you using it in Passport Control, anyway.

As in every other airport, the walk seems interminable. First down nylon-carpeted hallways and then through the departure lounges. People with their hand luggage in the seated areas at each gate wait patiently to board.

Ruth stands on the moving walkway and glances at the large departure screen. A lot of the flight statuses are flashing from green to red. 'Boarding' is changing to 'Delayed'. She looks closer. There's a lot of cancelled flights too. Paris CDG: Cancelled. Schiphol: Cancelled. London Heathrow: Cancelled. Strange.

Ruth gets off at the end of the metal walkway and heads slowly to the next. Her legs are aching and she needs the loo. She sees a yellow-lit sign with a silhouette of a woman wearing a pronounced skirt and makes her way to the toilets. The starkly lit room smells strongly of cleaning fluid, a mixture of lemon and pine, with an undertone of something more human. On her left there are multiple doors, on her right a wall of mirrors with washbasins before them. There are two women by the hand-dryer, embracing. They are both red-faced from crying and are heaving to catch their breath. Ruth averts her gaze and heads into a cubicle.

She hangs her backpack on the back of the door and wipes the seat with a handful of bunched-up toilet roll, a perfunctory step enforced by Anne when she was a child, which is now second nature. Then, at the basins, Ruth washes her hands thoroughly but dries them on her hoodie to avoid interrupting the weeping couple.

Ruth steps onto the next conveyor belt and starts to walk.

The airport is remarkably empty.

It's probably just her perspective: the population of London is almost twice that of the entire country of New Zealand. After living in London, it's likely that everywhere in this country is going to seem deserted.

She feels a wave of relief when she passes a crowded departure gate: she'd begun to wonder if there'd been a crash or something, she'd seen so few people.

At the gate a group is surrounding an official standing on a chair so she can be seen.

Why isn't she using the Tannoy?

A couple is sitting on the floor, pale-faced, and by the bin, a man is vomiting into the clear plastic bag suspended from the hoop attaching it to the wall.

Ruth reaches into the front pocket of her backpack and takes out the antibacterial gel Anne forced upon her when she was packing. She smears it liberally onto her hands. Just in case. All these people being sick around her, she certainly doesn't want to catch a lurgy.

The Immigration hall is creepily quiet, everyone waiting silently and patiently. Airports always have a bit of a weird vibe – a slightly charged quality to the air – and Immigration here has nowhere near the aggressive quality she'd felt in LA. But there is a distinctly strange atmosphere in the queue. Everyone seems unnaturally quiet and still.

Ruth reaches for her water bottle and takes a big slug.

She really does feel pretty hung-over, which probably accounts for her sensing a weird atmosphere: nine times out of ten, when she has creeping feelings of paranoia, there is a direct correlation to how much alcohol she consumed the previous night.

Finally she reaches the front of the slow snake queuing for Passport Control.

Ruth shoulders her backpack and approaches the desk, smiling at the official behind the Perspex screen who greets her with a glower. She passes him her passport, the page open to her photograph.

He holds it up to compare it with her face. Ruth adjusts her smile to the neutral face she knows is a good likeness of the photograph. Ordinarily this routine raises a smile from even the most stoic Immigration official, but not on this occasion.

The man raises his eyebrows and turns the passport over to inspect the cover.

She sees something pass over his face, something she can't identify.

'My visa is at the back, stuck in.'

The man avoids her gaze and nods, turning the pages of the small burgundy booklet until he finds the page with the document stuck to it. It stands out, light reflecting from its foil, a blue watermark of a large fern leaf beneath the printed text. He inspects it and nods, reaching for his stamp. He depresses it twice on an empty page and signs his initials within one of the stamps. 'Welcome to New Zealand.' He hands Ruth's passport back to her.

'Thank you!' Ruth feels a wash of relief and reaches out to take it from him.

But he doesn't release it. She looks up to his face and he makes eye contact with her for the first time. 'I'm so sorry,' he says. 'You're in our thoughts and prayers.'

Thirty-five

'But, Ma, please! Let me go with you, it wasn't my fault.'

Māia scrapes the spilt meal from the dirty tarp back into the burnt pot, while watching her sister. She is following their mother around the camp, pleading with her, as she angrily wraps her kit to take to the forest with her.

'You waste food and you both pay. You aren't little kids any more. If you don't want me to treat you like babies, don't act like them.'

There was no moving her ma when she had made a decision, so Māia doesn't bother to try any more. It doesn't seem to deter Frankie, though.

'Ma, please don't leave me with her. She's a fuckin' snake.'

'Frankie!' Their mother's voice is brittle with warning.

Frankie finds it difficult to remember to curb her language around her mother. Her pa's language is peppered with expletives, which means that the odd swear word goes unnoticed in his presence. She has only ever heard her mother swear twice that she can remember and on neither occasion was it appropriate to point out her hypocrisy.

'Sorry, Ma.'

'You say you are a woman now, Frances. Why I still have to tell you to mind your language is beyond me.'

Frankie nods, contrite, and hangs her head. She exhales as Ruth returns to packing her hunting tools and walks towards the tent, her feet padding on the compacted sand of their camp.

'Not like anyone'll ever fuckin' hear me swear, anyway,' she mumbles, under her breath.

'Hey!'

Her father, exiting the hut.

His matted grey-flecked hair is pulled back and tied with a piece of cord. He is thinner, his clothes hanging from him, but the colour has returned to his cheeks. He can walk now, but there is a hobble that will likely mark his gait for the rest of his life. During his time recovering in the hut, his temper seems to have altered irreversibly too.

'You don't disrespect your mother like that. If you've got something to say, say it to her face.'

Frankie feels the flush creeping up her back. Then her cheeks sting, displaying her shame.

'Turn around and tell your mother what you were saying.'

Slowly she turns back to see her mother's creased eyes trained on her. 'Tell me, Frances.'

She summons her courage to speak. After all, she was only telling the truth. 'I said I don't know why I have to mind my language. It's not like there will ever be anyone to hear me.'

Silence hangs over them as they stand around the lightly smoking coals of the fire. The sun is almost a full orb over the horizon now: morning has broken. The gulls over the sea caw to each other, unaware of the tension beneath them on shore.

Ruth rubs a hand over her tired eyes. It is a movement that has become habitual to her. Fatigue and the constant ache of her failing vision have made it so. But at this moment it is the pure exhaustion of trying to instil hope in these two young women. Hope that she has been struggling to conjure for some time now, but conjure it she does. For her daughters. What can she give them but hope?

'Frankie, there are others. You know there are. You saw them.'

In truth, Frankie can barely remember the occasion her mother is referring to. She has been told so many times of the people who came to the camp, then left to voyage to the south where there might be others, that she feels as though her memories are nothing more than the stories she has been told. Sometimes she dreams of a sick man whose skull you can almost see through his skin, like when they boil a deer head whole to make stock and free the bone of any remnant of meat. She wonders if the man she dreams of is one of those visitors who came to stay. He is the only human in her dreams other than her family. It is no wonder that is the case: she has only ever seen her family to dream of. She has dreams about things other than people, about animals that talk, about far-off places her mother describes, though she knows the pictures her sleeping mind draws will never match what her mother saw. She wishes she could see an image of the things and people her mother describes. She has seen her grandma, her papa's ma, because her father used to capture pictures with his camera. But she will never see the land on the other side of the planet that her mother so vividly tells them of each night. It makes her heart hurt and that hurt quickly turns to anger. She is so angry these days, it frightens her.

'Frankie,' her father is trying to catch her eye, 'what have we told you?'

She nods to stop him: she has heard it all before.

'If your mother and I survived, there is no way that there aren't many other families out there like us. We said it even before we had our visitors and we still say it now: stay put and, eventually, they'll find us.'

'Yes, Pa.'

Ruth continues to bind her pack, pursing her lips to stop herself saying anything that might contradict Nik. Another family squabble will only curtail her day's hunting further. Increasingly, she feels they should be emboldening their daughters to move, to discover what is over the horizon, not impressing on them that 'staying put' is the answer.

But this is not the time for that debate: the sun is too high already and they need to get going. Nik's limp makes progress slow as it is. It would be so much quicker to go alone. But she has spent enough time alone over the last few months, when she feared Nik might leave her for good. Now he is well, she is determined they should be separated as rarely as possible.

Secretly she's pleased that Frankie's behaviour means she can orchestrate a day alone with him.

Māia has scraped the meal back into the tin and is eating it carefully off her spoon, watching her sister's interaction with their parents. She can see Frankie doesn't believe what she is being told. She isn't sure that her parents are convinced.

'Stop staring at me!'

Māia raises her eyebrows and continues to eat. She doesn't know what she has done to deserve her sister's scorn, particularly this morning. They were friends just yesterday when they shared the last of the honeycomb they'd found when they ventured to the forest.

'You girls, you need to get on. One day, you'll need each other. See if you can make up while Papa and I are away. We should be back by sundown, but if not, eat without us. I want those skins cleaned. Make sure you do it, or they'll be ruined by maggots.'

Cleaning skins is dirty, laborious work. They both hate it. Legs knee-deep in the creek's slow-running water, they sit with their rag-covered buttocks on the sandy banks, scraping the meat from the hides. The sisters have not spoken to each other since their dispute at breakfast earned them this, their most loathed job. That was hours ago. Now the sun is high in the sky. Not a single word has passed between them since they watched their parents disappear along the beach to the north and, automatically, went about their chores. The industrious scene might have been perceived as companionable but for the morning's events.

Māia is getting bored of the monotonous work. Her forearms are flecked with fat and gore. With difficulty, she pulls the hide she is working on onto the bank to stop it floating away. She takes a deep breath as she stands and stretches, then wades waist-deep into the water and allows herself to fall back until she is completely submerged. She can hear the small stones moving along the riverbed.

Peaceful.

She holds her breath and opens her eyes. She cannot see very far in front of her. It's just like life, she thinks. You can't see what's coming.

Her lungs protest, they need air.

She pushes herself up through the water's surface, back into the hot afternoon air. She flicks her long hair over her head, spattering Frankie with water. She watches her sister wipe it from her eyes and carry on working: there'll be no messing about today.

She lies back in the water and floats, watching Frankie work. Her movements are methodical as she picks at the hide.

Once they have removed every scrap of flesh and fat, they will scrub the hides in the water. Then they will stretch them on the racks, and when they are completely dry and leather-like, they will become clothing or bedding or be cut into small sections to wrap things in. A good hide will last years and is worth every moment of labour, boring as it is.

Her eyes move to her sister's legs, the red smudges on her thighs. 'Franks,' she says.

Frankie ignores her, as though the picking of flesh is as absorbing as watching a family of rabbits before throwing the first spear.

'Fine, be like that. Just thought you'd like to know that even if you'd been allowed to go you couldn't have, eh?'

Frankie feels her blood rise. She couldn't have gone? It was always the plan for her to go with her mother to the forest. It had been weeks since she had been alone with her and, though she was ashamed to admit it, she'd wanted to have her ma to herself for a few hours. To stalk through the trees in silence together and, on the long walk home, to talk to her, to ask her what was wrong.

Frankie knows something is bothering her mother: she can see it in the tightness around her jaw, in the way she is so quick to snap at her.

She wants to ask her if she can help. If it was something she had done. If there was something wrong with her father. But those precious moments had been lost. Scuppered because Māia's childish behaviour had made Frankie lose her temper and lash out, spilling the breakfast. And as there was no crime greater than wasting food, she had been replaced by her father on the forest run, likely the last this side of winter.

'You made me lose my temper, playing silly beggars.'

'I was just trying to have a bit of fun with you, you looked so serious. Anyway, like I say, it doesn't matter. Your blood is here.'

Māia disappears back under the water.

Frankie moves aside the skin she's working on and looks between her thighs. Sure enough they are stained bright red with blood. She puts her hand to the cloth at her crotch and it comes away red. 'Fuck.'

Her sister is right: she wouldn't have made it as far as the forest without being turned back, and the delay would only have irritated her mother. Frankie still hasn't got used to the signs that her blood is coming. Will she ever?

Her mother tells her that, Before, even with computers and reminders that beeped at her from the phones everyone kept with them constantly, she often couldn't place why she was angry and sad until she found her underwear stained with blood. She tries to make Frankie, and now Māia, count their days, but they're so often tied up with the work of the camp that they miss a day and give up.

Māia seems to have a sixth sense for the approach of hers. 'How do you know?' Frankie had asked her sister, in a moment of weakness during her last cycle. Her cramps were keeping her awake in bed and Māia soothed her by rubbing her lower back. Māia told her that it's mostly the moon, but she feels it in her breasts, in her increased thirst, and finds their mother's humming even more irritating than usual.

This helped Frankie very little, for she was always aware of her breasts, how they swung when she walked, so much heavier and larger upon her chest than either her mother's or her sister's. And there was never a day when it didn't cheer her to hear her mama sing.

Māia rises from the water now, her skin glistening. She takes her cupped hand and brings water up to her lips and drinks it, then heaves herself onto the bank next to Frankie. She stands, still dripping from the stream, and lifts both of the heavy hides over her shoulder. 'Come on,' she says, extending a hand to her sister.

Frankie takes the offered hand grudgingly and allows herself to be helped to her feet.

'We'll get you some rags and then you can rest while I make you something to eat. You must be hungry – you didn't have a scrap of breakfast.'

Another cycle of seasons passes. It is not long since they watched the sun burn a deep red and slip over the horizon, but they are all awake after just a few hours' sleep, standing on the beach, observing its arrival, the yellow morning rays reflecting on the sea.

It is the longest day of the year. Summer Solstice. The twenty-first day of December, or thereabouts – they haven't used a calendar in years. But they know, by marking this day, so close to the day that everything changed, that it has been eighteen years.

Ruth stands with her hand in Nik's. The air is already warm. She looks at her daughters by her side, their eyes watching the ocean, the early sun's rays reflecting on their bare shoulders. She reaches out and takes Frankie's hand too.

'Hold your sister's hand.'

Frankie sighs, then reaches out and takes it.

Māia smiles at her mother, thanking her for encouraging her sister's kindness.

They all close their eyes, standing silent until the sun is high.

Afterwards, they eat. Fruit that is in abundance at this time of year but is a feast nevertheless. It makes their mouths and hands sticky, so after they have eaten they wash together in the creek. They play, shrieking as they splash one another.

Tonight, they will eat together as the sun sets.

They will drink the wine they have made in an old wooden barrel from a glut of grapes. None of them understood why it made Ruth laugh so hard when she tasted it. 'Now *this* tastes like manure.'

Tonight, when they are a little drunk, Ruth will sing and they will dance with the sand between their toes.

But while the sun is high and hot, Māia and Frankie want to swim in the sea, to row to the old wreck of a lighthouse and jump from the rocks, an activity they love. It is frowned upon when they ought to be fishing but today they are free to indulge for hours on end.

For Nik and Ruth, though, there is only one place they want to spend a day together.

They emerge through the trees to the summit.

The sun is at full height and the emerald lake glints invitingly.

Nik catches Ruth's eye mischievously. 'You should give me a head start, you know, on account of my hobble.' Nik indicates the scar on his leg where the metal ripped through his flesh.

Already, Ruth has dumped her bag and is tearing at the straps she wears around her feet to protect them as she walks.

Nik joins her in the race to undress, but she is swifter.

He pauses to watch her as she walks away from him, carefully stepping across the rocks towards the clear water. Her body has not changed much since he first saw her undress out of the corner of his eye. Her ribs are more prominent, her skin darker, her hair wilder, hanging, covering more of the expanse of her back. Though he can see her only from behind now, he knows the changes that have occurred to the front of her body: her breasts are lower, the nipples bigger after years of nourishing their daughters, her stomach rounder where she carried them in her womb.

He notices something new about her body, though, looking at her now as she slips into the water. Her long legs and broad hips are covered with bruises, some dark and angry, the colour of storm clouds, others yellow, the colour of leaves in autumn.

'Come on, slowcoach!' Ruth calls, as she rises from the water, her long hair wet across her shoulders as if she were a siren.

He throws his threadbare shorts over his shoulders with a comedic flourish and joins her in the water.

Afterwards, they lie on their backs on the rocks, allowing their skin to dry in a patch of sun. They are clean and warmed by their unusually uninhibited love-making: it is rare that their daughters are not within earshot. Although it has been years since they first had sex, Ruth continues to be surprised at the power of her desire for Nik. His body. She runs her hand across his chest, his belly.

She traces the green-blue marks of his tattoos: she knows the story behind every one.

His skin feels thinner than it did; the hair on his legs is grey, white at his groin.

So is hers; the mass of it. How she fretted about it. She'd spent so much time and money on removing it and now it barely crosses her mind.

There is so much from her old life that she doesn't miss.

'Tell me something you miss, from Before.' she says.

'Footie,' Nik says longingly.

'Earphones,' Ruth adds. 'The radio.'

'TV.'

'I miss dinner parties,' she says. 'I always thought I hated them, the nerves getting ready, everyone talking over each other, showing off. But I miss them. And family meals. Any meal at a table, really.'

They hold each other's hands, listening to the sounds of the bush that surrounds them.

Slowly Ruth takes Nik's hand and moves it to the side of her neck behind her ear. Then she reaches for his other hand and moves it to the same place on the other side. 'Swollen,' she says matter-of-factly. Nik turns to see her face. She keeps hold of his hands and moves them down: there is inflammation at the top of each of her thighs. 'And here,' she says.

Nik nods.

'The night sweats, the bruises, and I'm so tired, Nik. I'm bone-tired.'

'Yes,' he says.

'We need to get the girls ready, Nik.'

'Yes.'

'Are they ready, do you think? For life without us?'

'Frankie is already a better hunter than me.'

'Doesn't take much . . .' Ruth says, smiling slyly.

'True.' He smiles back.

'Should we have tried to look for others? To have moved further than we have?' Ruth's breath is short between each question.

'Sssh,' Nik soothes.

'I can't help but think we've done wrong by them, staying still.'

'We've kept them safe.'

'There could be civilisation just over the horizon.'

'Maybe. But there's probably danger too.'

'Humans!' she says, shaking her head. 'Have humans always been scared of what might be around the corner, do you think? Of the unknown, difference. Our species, with so many possibilities at our fingertips. We drew imaginary lines on the earth and told each other we shouldn't cross them. Thinking we'd be safe if we stayed still, in our own little square of marked-out land. That didn't work out very well in the end, did it? Animals do it too, I suppose, have territories. But the survivors, they roam, migrate. Elephants do, big cats do, birds do, fish do. Whales do! They move between the warm waters and the cold, feeding and breeding. I want our daughters to be like that, to be free, to look for a new life. A life as good as mine has been with you.'

She rolls onto her side now, resting her head on her hand, her elbow propping her up on the rock so she can look at him squarely. 'I only found you because I moved,' she says, her eyes burning fiercely as she gazes into his.

'Yes,' he says.

He has no doubt the girls will survive. They are ready to hunt and cook and build and fight. But him?

A world without Ruth. It is not something he can countenance. He brushes his hand through her damp hair.

A memory: his hand on Eva's forehead. Her hair spread across the stiff, starched hospital pillowcase. She'd told him. She'd said there was so much more love in store for him, that the end of her life wasn't the end of his.

Eva.

He would like to be able to tell her just how right she was.

He gently pulls Ruth towards him. His lips meet hers.

They kiss.

And, for a while longer, they lie on the dusty rocks, looking at the patterns the wispy clouds make in the sky, talking of the things they miss from when they were younger.

'Birthday cards,' he says. 'Balloons!'

She laughs her throaty laugh, which echoes through the surrounding trees.

'Croissants!' she calls up to the sky.

Thirty-six

'Fraid this is the end of the line, folks.'

The driver stands in the aisle at the front of the bus raising his voice, trying to wake the few passengers who have managed to sleep through the vehicle's abrupt halt.

'I've been ordered back to Auckland. Seems Wellington's a no-go. They've had to block off the port.'

Those passengers who are awake groan collectively, waking those still lucky enough to be lost to sleep.

'How the hell are we supposed to get home?'

'Thanks heaps, bro.'

'What are we supposed to do? We've got kids to get home.'

The driver holds his hands up while abuse and questions are thrown at him. 'I'm sorry, all. I can only do what I'm told. It's not worth my job to keep going.'

Ruth takes out her phone to check the map she'd down-loaded in Auckland to see where they are. Their location means nothing to her: as far as she can tell they are in the middle of nowhere. She closes the map and automatically tries to open one of the social-media apps, but fails. She tries one of the others: it crashes and returns to her home screen. Ruth's face suddenly feels very hot. Her hands tremble and feel too big as she scrabbles to open the news app on her phone. Nothing has changed from when she last looked. The page isn't updating.

She breathes deeply. Panicking isn't going to help anyone.

She tunes back into the heated discussion at the front of the coach.

'I don't know, I said. All I know is that I've been told to get home and—'

A hubbub of voices interrupts the driver and whatever he is about to say.

Ruth's stomach churns.

'Jeez, I'm sorry I can't tell you more – I don't bloody know!' The driver raises his voice now to a shout. 'Anyone who wants to come back with me, wait on. Anyone who's gonna make their own way, grab your bags. Bus is leaving in five.'

The passengers are hushed. Everyone is looking at their phones, trying to refresh the screens to no avail.

Ruth watches the rear lights of the coach as it heads back down the road it came along, her oversized rucksack at her feet. She feels unsteady. Those fitful few hours on the bus were the closest she's come to sleep in the last three days. Her entire body feels empty and tender, as if someone has shaken every thought and feeling out of her, then stamped all over her, pummelling every muscle.

She unties her hair and runs her fingers through it, untangling it, then scrapes it back and reties it. She rubs her hands across her face, trying to massage away the exhaustion. Her skin feels oily, dirty, though she only showered yesterday. Or was it the day before? It was when she got back to the hostel after the second day at the embassy, wasn't it? She raises her arm and sniffs. Maybe it wasn't yesterday. What does it matter?

She looks again at the map on her phone, thankful she can use it without the internet. There is a town, just over four hours' walk from here, by the sea of the South Taranaki Bight. The name immediately rings a bell: one of the conservation-project centres is along that coast somewhere. She can't remember the town exactly, but surely someone will be able to point her in the right direction if she asks around. How many whale-conservation centres can there be? Then, maybe, from there she can organise passage to Golden Bay, once she's found out what's going on.

Ruth hitches her rucksack onto her shoulders, strapping it around her waist and bearing the brunt of its weight on her hips. She wobbles, a wave of nausea crashing over her. For a second she thinks she's going to faint, to fall asleep there and then. Her body is crying out for rest. But she holds on to the strap around her waist and puts one foot in front of the other.

The sun is starting to lighten the sky behind her. It seems as though she is trying to walk away from it as it slips over the horizon. As if she were walking towards the night.

The surface of the road changes beneath her trainers: the asphalt is looser, almost gravel-like. She is no longer on the tarmac of a state highway. There are still evenly spaced white lines marking two lanes, but now, rather than streetlights lining the road and a metal-fenced walkway to protect pedestrians from speeding vehicles, each side is bordered by wooden fencing. In time the fencing gives way to bushes interspersed with clumps of pampas grass.

Fran used to tell her that the residents of any house with pampas grass in the front garden were swingers. 'It's a well-known fact that wife-swappers signal to each other with the jauntily feathered reeds.'

Ruth closes her eyes. She can smell the smoke of Fran's cigarette.

She can hear Fran, as if she were next to her, punctuating her revelation with the full stop of a deep drag on the final stub of her cigarette.

Ruth shortens her stride to fall into step with Fran.

She smiles, knowing that Fran would have pointed it out in the garden of every home they passed as they varied their walk home from school, trying to delay separation from each other by taking more and more circuitous routes, dragging their feet and scuffing the toes of their new shoes.

A bird screeches.

Ruth loses her footing, skidding on the gravel. Her ankle turns painfully beneath her. She rights herself. It seems to her that there is still a hint of tobacco on the air.

Pain slides across her chest, and she flattens her palm over where her heart is pounding. Then she puts down her head and continues to walk.

Beyond the fences to her right lies a sea of farmland, a gently undulating patchwork of tilled brown earth, waving green grasses and waist-deep wheat that is starting to tinge golden as the sun creeps further up the sky.

Ruth's stomach starts to rumble. She hasn't felt compelled to eat for days. In fact, the thought of food is repellent, but her body is still demanding sustenance. She tries to remember when she last had a meal. There were some chips, when she was sitting on the wall outside the hostel next to that crying Danish girl. The dried-out sandwich she had in the embassy. But that wasn't recent. No, the last thing was that tasteless energy bar in the bus station.

In the absence of food, she drinks deeply from her water canteen, grateful that she was alert enough at least to fill it at the tap on the forecourt of one of the petrol stations she passed. She hopes it's potable: there was no sign saying, 'Drinking

Water', but at least there wasn't a sign saying it shouldn't be consumed.

Her stomach gurgles, but if anything she feels hungrier still.

The temperature is still that of the night. Ruth shivers at the chill in the air, though she can already feel moisture gathering on her shoulders under her hoodie. Her small backpack is on her front, protruding like a pregnant belly. Its weight helps to counterbalance the giant rucksack on her back and prevents her toppling over.

A soft wind catches the loose strands of her hair and blows them across her face.

She can smell algae.

The river.

It must be running alongside the road, close enough to smell, but not to hear. It will be travelling out to the sea, just like her.

The first rays of sun project her long silhouette onto the road ahead of her. She doesn't recognise herself, her shape distorted by her bags, her limbs lengthened by the angle of the sun.

The tread of her feet seems to echo back from the silence. A rhythmic call and response.

Ruth is reminded of a song Anne used to sing to her when she was little. A song about a shadow, call and response: 'Little Sir Echo, how do you do?'

Ruth can hear Anne's voice raised in song. She closes her eyes. She is sitting on a stool too high for her age, her legs dangling as she eats her breakfast.

Ruth's feet crunch on the gravel.

Anne sings to her again, encouraging her:

'Little Sir Echo, how do you do? Hello?'
'Hello!'
'Hello?'
'Hello!'

Ruth stops walking and stands, feet apart. She is swaying slightly as if she were drunk. She can't remember the next line. She can see Anne, with her back to her, singing it as she wraps the sandwiches for Ruth's packed lunch in tinfoil, then places them carefully in her treasured lunchbox with the matching flask.

At the corners of her closed lids, Ruth feels moisture gathering. She opens her eyes and pulls up the hem of her vest to wipe them.

She sets her jaw and ups her pace until she is challenged enough to be slightly out of breath. It brings her back to the moment, stills any thoughts of home, of what has happened or is about to happen.

It is just her and her body, working to move her forward.

Ahead on her left she sees an opening in the road.

Getting closer she sees that it leads to a shingle drive and a farmhouse. It is a small white clapboard bungalow, the curtains drawn at each of its five visible windows. The gate is closed with a heavy chain and padlock. She hears a dog barking and picks up her pace.

She passes a barn: door-less, it exposes the neatly stacked walls of hay bales within.

Her body is wilting now, the exertion of her hike using the last of her reserves. She weighs up the possibility of its being a warm and safe space to sleep, then hears the dog barking again and decides to stick to her plan of heading for the town, the beach.

She'll find someone to help her contact the project, and somewhere to stay, or at least buy some food.

The sun is getting high now. The fields that surround her have transitioned from an expanse of crops to grazing land for livestock. Sheep with almost full-grown lambs cluster at metal troughs. Horses graze in open fields, looking up to take her in as she marches past them. Somewhere, in a coop beyond her field of sight, a cockerel calls, welcoming the day.

A group of sullen-looking black and white cows gather closer to the fence as she walks past their enclosure. Their brown eyes, rimmed with long lashes, gaze at her as she approaches.

'What?'

She hears her voice lost in the breeze: it sounds small, hollow.

Ruth riffles in the pocket of the bag on her chest and tries to focus her eyes to see the time on her phone. She has been walking for just over three hours; the air around her is warming as the sun gets higher in the sky.

She unlocks her phone and tries once again to access the news app. Nothing. She refreshes her emails.

Nothing.

She tries to search the internet.

Nothing.

Her legs scream in complaint as she picks up the pace once more. The straps of her bag are rubbing her shoulders.

To her right, she notices a small metal postbox on a pole at the side of the road. There's a drive that leads beyond, through some trees, presumably to one of the farmhouses that are becoming increasingly frequent the further she walks along the road. The little metal flag is raised: they've got mail. It soothes her somehow. Surely if things were as bad as all that, the postal service wouldn't be running.

A wave of exhaustion hits her and her thirst is overwhelming. Ruth stops and unloads the bags, first the little backpack on her front, then the rucksack, unclipping it cautiously from her waist and feeling the weight transfer from her hips to her shoulders. She heaves it off, grunting audibly, and lets it fall with a thud into the dust by the side of the road. Her clothes are stuck to her body with sweat. She unzips her hoodie and removes it. The soft breeze starts to cool her skin. She sits on her rucksack and stretches her feet in front of her, legs aching.

Looking along the road, she squints, trying to make out any landmarks in the distance, hoping for a glimpse of the blue expanse of sea on the horizon.

She can see nothing but more road, more fence, more farmland.

Ruth raises her arms above her head to release her shoulders and recoils: she stinks. She considers the river as a place to wash but decides against it: God knows what's in the water.

The sun is rising steadily. Surely soon she'll arrive at the town.

She closes her eyes and listens.

There is the sound of the breeze gently rustling the grass and distant birds singing. Birds whose song she doesn't recognise: it is as if they are singing in a foreign language. There is not a single sound that betrays human life, no voices, no machinery whirring, no vehicles purring, not a plane in the sky above. Not a single car has passed her.

She feels her stomach clench.

Her brain feels out of step with her body, as if one part comes to terms with the reality she is living, then forgets, only to be reminded with a jolt moments later.

It's like sustaining multiple electric shocks of grief.

She sighs, shuddering, exhausted, and unclips her water canteen from her rucksack, drinking deeply before reattaching it. She closes her eyes briefly, the sun shining pink through her eyelids. No, she can't fall asleep here on the side of the road, so exposed. She'd promised her dad she'd look after herself.

Her dad.

Again, her stomach contracts.

She exhales, then braces her hands against the gravel pushing herself up to standing.

Thirty-seven

Ruth looks out in the direction of the sea. She can perceive nothing more than the change in the light; her eyes are the colour of stone.

'The sun is setting, Ma.' Frankie holds her mother's arm to steady her. Ruth leans on her daughter a little more to allow herself to turn. Slowly they pick their way back to the fire.

'Can you smell the food, Ma? Māia's cooked for us. Pumpkin and seaweed with mussels.' Frankie carefully guides her towards the fire. 'We dived for them, Ma, like you showed us. It'll be the last we eat for a while, the rocks are covered with them – it's time for them to spawn.'

They talk to her like this now: a constant narration. Just as she did with them when they were babies. They started to do it to fill the increased silence. Then, as it became clear Ruth could not see, to try to keep her with them, stop her descending any further into a sightless world.

These days, they can count the words she utters to them daily on the digits they possess between them. Too much talking makes her tire quickly: she conserves her energy to say only the things that truly matter, such as she loves them, before she sleeps each night.

Their father died three seasons ago.

Though their mother's sickness had developed first, as winter came their father became ill again, just as he had when he'd fallen. His descent was so much faster than the slow development they had observed in their mother; it was almost as if he had wished for it.

They had realised very early during their parents' illness that their unity was the only option for survival. As their mother had warned them so often, they need each other.

'Māia is spooning it onto the plate now, Ma. The pumpkin is so orange it looks as though it came from the glowing coals.'

Frankie lets go of her mother's hand to accept the plate from Māia. 'Would you like me to shell them, Ma? So you can feed yourself? Or would you like me to feed you?'

Ruth nods and holds out her open palm.

Frankie proceeds to shell the mussels and hands them to Ruth, alternating with a piece of hot pumpkin, flecks of seaweed across it.

Ruth brings each morsel to her mouth, chewing carefully. After only a few mouthfuls, she raises her hand to indicate she has eaten all she can. Frankie looks at the plate of food on Ruth's lap: she has barely touched it. She frowns across the fire at her sister, who shakes her head. What can they do? Force-feed her?

As Frankie takes her turn to eat, Māia rises and places her hand on her mother's alarmingly bony shoulder. 'Do you need to go, Mama?'

Ruth nods and allows Māia to lead her to the creek. What she passes these days is liquid, but thick like tar, not unlike the infant meconium that she wiped from the bottoms of the two girls who now wipe hers. Second childhood, she thinks. Though, of course, few who used that turn of phrase Before expected such decrepitude to hit them in their fifties.

She is now useless in the camp. The few tasks she can do without sight, the girls can achieve in a fraction of the time, and even those chores she can fulfil with any competence, she tires of quickly. Shelling just a few nuts is followed by another long sleep. There is no frustration in this now, just peaceful resignation. On the days the girls leave camp together, she stays in bed, a flask of water infused with berries within reach. She sleeps while they hunt, waking to the hum of their voices when they return.

Without her eyes, she can hear things more acutely. It is obvious to her that the way her daughters communicate with each other has changed. Yes, when she is present they keep the constant soundtrack of their dialogue going, as if to describe all that surrounds them, but when they are alone and don't know they are overheard, their conversation is much changed too. She notes that the slew of expletives, with which Nik endowed them, has decreased markedly. They know she hates it.

Her father had told her off for it too: 'Effin' and jeffin'', he'd called it.

She misses her dad, even now.

Maybe the girls are just growing out of swearing, like she did, finding clearer ways to give voice to their frustrations.

They seem less combative too. Sorority has blossomed in the absence of their needing to compete for attention. But, also, she has noticed that their language is starker, more efficient. When they talk to her they use more words than she has heard since she was in a crowded bar in London; when it is just the two of them, they use enough to get a point across. They are as good shots with their words as they are with their spears. And if she and Nik raised one thing, it was excellent hunters.

It's a relief to know that they will be able to fend for themselves when she is gone.

In her dark, silent days, Ruth has found more time to think than she's ever had. She gets lost in memory. Her days seem like lucid dreams, a waking sleep.

She has lived in fear of death for as long as she has been aware of being alive. When she was younger, it was a feeling that she would miss out, make the wrong choice. Then it was pure animal survival, until her daughters, since when, every day she was afraid of leaving them without the tools they needed to survive – no, to thrive.

But something has shifted: she is no longer afraid.

Nik is gone.

Gone, like her parents, Fran, all her friends.

Every day is like sitting in a waiting room for Death to release her.

And, more importantly, free her daughters.

It is their time now. She has done her job.

She has lived so much longer than she ever expected to. It has been two winters since her symptoms became unavoidable but now her body is heavy with its desire to return to the earth.

Each day she wakes, it is a surprise, and she finds she is turned inwards for the majority of her waking hours, considering the length and breadth of her life, reviewing each of her million choices, feeling gratitude for what she has seen, done, survived.

For the most part, she is happy with the life she has lived. Yes, it has been hard work and relentless. And there has been pain. Her life has been shorter than she might have expected, but it has been longer than those of many she loved. It has been lucky in so many ways. She has few regrets.

She is surprised to discover that she rather likes herself. It certainly wasn't the way she felt for much of her life. There were times, Before, when she wasn't sure she was worth liking.

That *is* a regret: how much energy she put into trying to make people like her. She laments the time she wasted on worrying that she wasn't nice or good, so much focus on intangible concepts, when other people's opinions of her were none of her business. She had been selfish occasionally and made stupid mistakes, but the time she'd squandered on self-evaluating and criticising herself was her biggest crime.

Someone once warned her that no matter how far she ran, she'd never be able to escape herself. That had scared her, the idea of being stuck with herself. And she had run, despite the warning, she had run hard, desperately trying to shed her own skin, to shed the parts of herself she was ashamed of. But now, as she stares Death directly in the eye, she could laugh with glee: she's glad she didn't manage it. It was accepting all the parts of herself, even the shameful bits, that meant she could love and be loved.

And how she had loved!

Her parents, her friends: she had carried her love for them with her all her life. Though they would never know it, they had taught her how to love her daughters, taught her how to love Nik.

Nik.

It was love that had made her life worth living.

'Shall we have a story, Mama? Or are you too tired?'

The stories had left the camp for a while, when Nik died. Their hearts were all too heavy to imagine the spun threads of other realities when it was all they could do to comprehend that this one would be without him for ever. But slowly they returned, a favourite part of the day for all three of the women Nik left behind.

'Yes, Māia. Tell us a story.' Ruth's voice is hoarse.

Carefully, Māia and Frankie help Ruth sit by the fire and wrap frayed blankets around her shoulders to keep her warm.

'What sort of story shall I tell?' Māia asks.

'Tell me how you and your sister will leave this place. Tell me the story of your adventure to find the others. Tell me where you will go when I'm gone.'

Māia looks across to her sister.

Frankie draws in a breath. Give her what she wants, her shrug implies.

Māia knows that her sister hates these stories, that they go against everything she believes in, everything their father has told them about staying where they are and waiting for others to come. Māia knows that Frankie is not even sure that others exist.

'Māia?' Ruth's voice is searching for her daughter in the dark.

'Yes, Mama.' She settles herself. 'As the first rays of sun creep over the horizon . . .'

Ruth's cloudy eyes reflect the orange light of the fire, glistening. Then she closes them, listening to her daughter's voice describing a future full of hope.

For so long, she thinks, I thought I was at the centre of the story. She understands now that she was just a part of it: the world will get on without her very well.

'She's sleeping.'

Frankie tucks the blankets around their mother. She rises, walks to the side of the hut, takes a piece of driftwood from the store and throws it onto the glowing coals. It quickly catches flame. 'In case we sleep too.'

This is one of the rules, the first rule, that Nik made them promise to abide by as they sat beside his sickbed in his final days: 'Never let the fire go out to less than smoke. It is how we keep warm and cook but also how we can be seen, when the others come.'

The sisters lie side by side on the rug that Frankie laid out by the fire. They ache from the day's travails and are happy to lie in companionable silence, watching the stars. The noise of their mother's heavy breathing reaches them, then begins to morph into a fierce snoring.

'Ah, peace and quiet!' Frankie raises her voice to be heard over the cacophony of her ma's nasal grunts.

Beside her, she can feel her sister shake with silent giggles. It is infectious and soon Frankie is laughing too. Their laughter is so wild now, they can no longer contain it, their voices peel in the night air and a harmony is formed with their mother's roaring snores.

The young women laugh until they are breathless, then fall silent again, holding each other's hands against the rug, watching the stars above them.

Though neither of them knows it, they are thinking of how their mother told them that those stars may no longer exist and trying to wrap their heads around the concept of the triviality of their own existence.

They ought to be sleeping. But, in this moment of peace between them, accompanied by their mother's heavy breathing, they are happy just being.

Thirty-eight

Ruth can feel the seams of her sports socks rubbing on the outer edge of each little toe.

There'll be blisters.

She mentally runs through the contents of her first-aid kit: plasters, small, twenty-four; thermometer, one . . . Slowly, calmly, she counts through the items she can remember just as she used to when she played Kim's Game with her mum so many times, so long ago. As she runs through the list, her internal voice keeps time with her footsteps. Step, antiseptic wipes, four; step, latex gloves, four . . .

Her eyes are focused on the road ahead. She read once that successful runners swear by keeping a focus point on the road before them, not looking too far ahead or to the side, never looking behind to see what competitors are up to. She employs that strategy now, and feels invigorated for it. The time is passing more quickly, the focus on the weight of her luggage less intense.

In the periphery of her vision, she sees something white in the field to her right. It isn't like the others she has been passing all morning. It is a carefully manicured sward with white markings painted on the grass: a playing field with a football pitch, rugby goals and a cricket ground marked out. Beyond that, further down the road, uniform single-storey brick buildings: a school.

Ruth picks up her pace.

It is a Monday just before 9 a.m. Surely she can find someone there who can help her.

The gates are open but as she turns into the car park she sees only two cars. It must still be the Christmas holidays, or do they have their long summer break now?

'Hello?'

Her voice rebounds off the building, echoing.

'Can anyone hear me?'

She waits but the only response is her own voice.

At the front door she tries the handle, just in case. It is locked. She shakes it with frustration.

Walking around the perimeter of the first building, she comes to a classroom. Inside, rows of knee-high tables with small wooden chairs neatly spaced behind them.

A primary school.

It's not so different from her own classroom back in Ladywell: the whiteboard surrounded by paper-chains made unevenly by tiny hands, the carpeted area in the corner with a larger seat for the teacher, the shelves behind it crammed with books for storytime. The set-up is just the same as where she would read the books the children had so carefully chosen: Arthur handing her the same book for the third time that week; Rosie Archer, her fine blonde hair pulled tight into a French plait by her monosyllabic au pair, sitting as close to Ruth's feet as possible without actually touching; Sammie, his big eyes turned up to her, drinking in every word, like a parched houseplant.

A sudden wave of nausea tugs at Ruth's stomach.

Her cousin's boys, shouting over one another as the Jenga blocks crash down and tumble across the rug in her parents' lounge.

She can feel her mouth filling with bitter liquid.

Lily, one little hand holding her own, the other clutching the toy whale Ruth had bought her in the Natural History Museum's gift shop.

She bends over and vomits onto the earth beneath her.

She narrowly avoids the bag that protrudes from her chest, the sour liquid cascading from her mouth and hitting the parched ground, spattering her trainers and shins.

The sensation makes her heave once more.

Where is all this liquid coming from? She's barely consumed any water.

Once the nausea has passed, she stands and wipes her mouth.

She rights herself and is pulled slightly off balance by read-justment to the weight on her back. The overloaded bag pulls her against the brick wall of the school building.

She can feel her chest tightening. She is struggling to catch her breath.

Her hands trembling, she undoes the rucksack's clips and lets the bag fall heavily to the ground. She finds herself on her knees, her hands in the mud. Her breath is staccato, she feels light-headed, and her skin is wet with sweat.

Trying to control the shaking in her hands, she fishes her phone from the front pocket of her bag and tries futilely to open her social-media apps once more.

Nothing.

A noise involuntarily escapes her mouth, a noise she doesn't recognise as her own voice.

Although it is difficult to do so with her hands shaking so violently, she navigates to her photo album. She swipes left, going back in time. A picture of her with her mum and dad at the airport. A selfie with Camille in the early hours at the party.

Fran, half cut, the angry cat on the sofa behind her. Her and Fran, their make-up perfect as the party begins. Her mum, having coffee. Mum and Dad. Fran. Camille and the kids. Fran. Her and Fran. Mum and Dad. Fran. Mum. She swipes more and more frantically, looking at the pictures of the people she loves.

The next photo is of her and Fran standing at the top of the hill in Greenwich Park. Alex took that picture last New Year's Day, a year ago, almost exactly. She can hear Fran's voice in her memory: 'You idiot.'

A drop of water falls onto the screen of the phone.

A tear.

She is crying uncontrollably now, making it difficult to see the images.

She snatches for breath, short, sharp inhalations; her lungs don't seem to be following her command. Although she is struggling to see, she manages to dial her parents' number. Once again she is greeted by the high-pitched tone that tells her she can't be connected. She holds the phone to her ear, her face wet against the screen, the sound of her unconnected call ringing in her ear.

'Mum?' She sobs.

The sound from the phone cuts out.

Ruth pulls the phone away from her ear and looks at the device. She squints to see clearly, her eyes swollen now from the tears. The screen is blank. Black. Dead. Frantically, she presses the button on the top of the phone to try to switch it on.

Nothing. The battery is flat.

For a second Ruth holds her breath, staring at the blank screen in front of her. Then she feels as though she is slowly deflating. At her core something is crumbling, folding into itself, as if the weight of the realisation is pushing her towards the ground.

Still on her knees Ruth leans forward, her tear-streaked face planted in the dry mud of the flowerbed, and a guttural scream emanates from her crumpled form.

Thirty-nine

The light on the beach begins to turn grey and thicken. The two women stand side by side, a slight sheen of sweat across their bare shoulders. Each of them holds a shovel. Their waists are wrapped in what amounts to little more than rags, but they both stand strong, muscles taut, barefoot in the sand as the air cools around them.

They look down at the fruit of their labours: a freshly turned mound of black earth and sand among the reeds and grasses. Next to it is a mound of similar proportions, but it has been undisturbed for some time now. New shoots of life are beginning to struggle through.

'And then there were two.'

'I wish you'd stop saying that.'

'Just saying what I see.'

Māia sinks to her knees and places a hand on the recently disturbed sand. She pauses, and then, after a moment of reverence, starts to pat down the sand to make it firm. Frankie walks around the mound to the other side and follows her sister's lead, mimicking the action they had watched their mother perform around their father's grave so recently.

They work in silence, just the thud, thud of their palms against the sand beating a rhythm to the ever-present music of the sea against the shore.

Once all the sand is firm, they look at their palms. They are remembering how, when they had done the same for their father, they had held hands, the three of them, and said nothing to one another until the sky turned black.

On that night, they had gone to bed with empty stomachs, the two girls beside each other in the dark listening to the absence of their father's struggling breath.

'Papa always said, "There must be others." He said, "Just wait. Just stay put and they'll come here."'

Frankie squeezes Māia's hand, her head bowed. 'That was just for Mama, Māia. He was saying it for her cos he was dying. There are no others. We're the only ones.'

The blunt force of Frankie's language lands like blows. Māia loosens her hand from her sister's grip and wipes the grains of sand from her palm against the hide of her skirt. She stands. 'I think we should leave.'

'We will stay.' Frankie stands now too. She picks up the rusted shovels beside her sister and slings them over her shoulder. She turns away from Māia and walks towards their camp.

Māia steps back to look at the two hillocks they have made: her parents side by side.

She listens. All is quiet but for the sound of the sea at a distance.

Still she is aware of the absence of her mother's constant humming. It has irritated Māia her entire life but now she would give anything to hear it again.

'Goodnight,' she whispers, and turns to join her sister.

Now they are used to the rhythm of their new life.

'Frankie, let's leave. Explore. See beyond. There might be a future.'

Each night it is the same. Māia suggests departure, Frankie tells her they will stay.

'There is no future. There is nothing beyond here. You've seen. Just ash and new green through the ash.' Frankie turns the fish she has impaled upon a stick in the fire. The flames lick at the silver scales, turning them black.

'We could go across the sea. Sail to England. We could use our boat.'

'Māia, stop!' She takes the fish from the flames, its scales charred, and places it on the leaves before her sister.

'It is just you and me. And that's okay. We are the last. And that's okay. Everything needs an ending. We are the end.'

Māia takes the fish her sister hands to her and breaks the white flesh beneath the black skin into flakes, then brings it in her forefingers to her mouth. She chews and looks out towards the horizon, the sun burning the last of the day's light in an angry orange that illuminates the water.

Her eye is drawn by a movement in the water.

There is motion in the waves, between them and the horizon. The water cleaves and a dark bulk rises above the level skin of the brine, shimmering in the final rays of the sun, then disappears. Then, just metres from the first, a second appears, splitting the waves, then a third.

Māia feels her heart beating in her throat. She puts her hand on her sister's forearm and directs her gaze towards the water.

Frankie sucks in the air, filling her lungs. 'They've come back!' she whispers, her voice full of awe.

The sisters watch in silence, their breath quickening.

The sea parts, revealing the undulating spines of three animals, one large, two half the size of the first.

'One . . . two . . . three. Franks, there's three!' Māia stands, breathless, pointing towards the whales.

Beside her, her sister comes to her feet and takes her hand.

'She's spawned. Mama said . . .'

Frankie squeezes her sister's hand to stop her. She can feel her eyes moistening. She cannot dare to hope or the tears will start and never stop.

Māia looks towards her sister and nods. She understands.

A tail rises above the water, and falls with a violent splash.

They draw breath sharply, laughing with surprise: the whales are dancing in the water. It is an action that has such freedom, such play. Their hands are now on their brows to help them focus on the huge creatures cavorting in the waves. They watch them shoot air from their blowholes, creating great arcs of water in the air. As the spray falls back to the sea, it catches the light, forming a great arc of colour, a rainbow.

'She came back to say goodbye to Mama.' Frankie is whispering. She doesn't want to disturb this magical moment with noise.

The fire behind them crackles.

'Two little ones. With the whole ocean to roam without fear.'

'They won't get sick like Mama and Papa?'

Frankie is suddenly fearful of this unaccustomed joy. 'No, they'll be strong like us. They are the new world. The next world.'

They watch the whales until the light fades and all they can see is their own shadows cast on the sand by the fire.

Māia feels her sister's grip loosen. 'Maybe we'll see more than whales soon. Maybe we'll see a boat. The people coming from South Island, coming back to find us,' she says hopefully.

But she is speaking to her sister's back: Frankie is walking to the fire.

'Frankie?'

Frankie turns. She sees her younger sister's tear-streaked face. She cannot resist her any more tonight. 'Maybe. Shall we go to bed?'

'I'll have dreams if I go to sleep now. Will you stay with me a bit? Watch the stars before bed, remember Mama?'

'Sure. Maybe you can tell me a story too, eh?'

'Yes, sis.'

For weeks when Ruth had been ill inside the tent, they had guiltily chosen to sleep outside, under the stars, rather than in the stench of impending death. Now that she is gone, the home they have known since their birth is empty.

The girls lie on the sand by the dying embers, wrapped in blankets, beside each other. Their faces are turned up to the heavens.

'The whale had babies,' Māia says.

Frankie grunts in response.

'If the whale had babies, that means there must be a papa whale, right?'

'Of course.'

Though, in truth, Frankie is unsure that that is unquestionably the case. Her mother had never avoided the subject of reproduction. Ruth used the animals around them as examples – the bird lays an egg once she is fertilised; the fawn comes some weeks after the mating call of the buck can be heard in the forest – but the details were hazy and Frankie failed to see how it impacted on her. As long as reproduction kept happening, there would be enough food and that was all she was worried about.

'Do you think we'll ever have babies, Frankie?'

Māia's question hangs in the air between them. Frankie has felt her sister circling it all night and feared her asking. 'Go to sleep, Māia.'

Behind her, she feels her sister nuzzle her face into her neck. On her skin there is moisture: Māia is crying again.

'Tomorrow let's hunt. We can dry the meat and gather berries, start to store for winter.'

Māia inhales sharply with delight. She longs for the shared chase. While they have been nursing their mother, they have not roamed further than the grasses. 'True?'

'Sure. Just, on the way, do me a favour and keep the fuckin' noise down. I could've got that bloody wood pigeon the other day if you weren't thumping around like a great oaf digging the grave.'

'Go easy, Franks. I was digging our mother's grave!'

'Well, move a bit lighter on your feet and I won't need to mention it.'

The girls' voices rise and fall as they snipe at each other, lilting above the sound of the waves until they roll towards each other and finally fall asleep.

Forty

Ruth wakes. She takes in her surroundings: she is lying in mud, a bush to her right, a wall to her left. It is light, daytime. She is warm, but there is dirt on her face, on her arm where she is lying on the ground. She feels rested, though.

How long has she been asleep?

Where is she?

Her face feels tight, her eyes puffy from tears she's shed.

Why has she been crying?

She becomes aware that she is gripping something in her right hand. She unfurls her fingers and looks at the dead phone. Then she remembers.

Ruth pushes herself to be seated. She catches her breath and leans against her rucksack on the ground behind her. Her thirst is unbearable. She licks her dry lips and a rancid taste fills her mouth. Oh, yes, she was sick, wasn't she?

Still fuzzy with sleep, she fumbles to unclip her canteen. She shakes it: there is barely anything left in it. Unscrewing the lid, she tips it and pours the final drops into her open mouth, careful not to touch her lips and transfer the residue of vomit around her mouth to the vessel. She leans forward and spits the swilled water onto the grass. She clips the bottle back onto her bag, hitches her rucksack onto her back. She takes her weight back fully onto her feet and walks away from the school, continuing her journey towards the coast.

She must have been asleep for hours: the sun is hanging low.

The houses are more frequent now, surrounded by less land. They are homes with gardens rather than farmland. Still the windows of all the properties she passes are obscured by blinds, curtains or shutters.

Where is everybody?

Each house is set back slightly from the road, the gate to each driveway either chained or bolted, the metal postbox at the entrances punctuating the verge. Between the houses there are clumps of trees, some evergreen, some deciduous. Ruth recognises a small copse of birch, but there are other species she can't name, trees that are native to this land. Birds sing merrily in their branches, the long grass in the shade of their leaves rustling slightly. The breeze is stronger now and its scent has changed. A sign of the ocean?

A white bridge appears on the road before her. As she reaches it, Ruth can see a slow-running brook weaving below the road. She stops and leans over the bridge: the water looks crystal clear. Could she drink it?

A noise in the distance catches her ear: an engine.

She takes her eyes away from the light dancing on the water and looks towards the sound.

There is a vehicle on the road in the distance, coming from the direction she is heading. Instinctively, she steps out into the road and waves her arms: if the occupant is heading back where she came from, maybe she should too.

The vehicle gets closer. She can see that it is a car, its roof heavily loaded with suitcases.

It doesn't seem to be slowing as it approaches her − if anything it is driving faster.

Ruth catches the eye of the woman in the passenger seat; the man driving doesn't even glance in her direction, his eyes firmly fixed on the road. The woman is holding a small bundle – a baby? – to her chest. Her face looks tired.

She has to step back quickly as the car speeds up, swerving only slightly to avoid her.

'Please!'

Her plaintive call is lost in the exhaust fumes as the car speeds away from her.

The back seat is full of stuff, the back window blocked with bags and random items stuffed haphazardly into the boot.

She watches helplessly as the car gets smaller and smaller. When she can no longer see it, she turns resolutely and starts to walk at pace in the opposite direction.

Surely there are more people where they came from.

Soon she is striding next to what seems to be a campsite. Behind a fence, mobile homes stand in regimented rows, some with washing hanging before them.

A sign of life!

She can see a burst of colour ahead: a building with a red sign on the roof. The entrance? A shop? Her thirst drives her quickly towards it. The shop has a large oval sign on the roof proclaiming 'Lucy's Dairy' in red enamel lettering. Along the faded canopy that protrudes above the door, more signage, hand-painted this time: 'newspapers', 'takeaway', 'sundries', 'post', 'fishing supplies'. Ruth's heart beats faster as the door reflects the sun. It opens and someone emerges: a woman, her grey hair cropped short, the spectacles on the end of her nose attached to a chain that snakes round her neck, glinting in the light. She is wearing a checked shirt, which is rolled up at the sleeves. She takes a cigarette out of a packet and lights it swiftly, inhaling deeply.

'Oh, thank God!' Ruth exclaims, then runs, as well as she can with her bags, towards the shop.

'What a greeting!' The woman smiles, exhaling white curls of smoke from her nostrils.

'The shop's open?'

'Course! I don't shut even for the Queen's birthday.'

'Oh, thank God!'

'You go on. I'll be in when I'm done with this.'

'Thank you!' Ruth exhales. 'Thank you!'

Inside a radio burbles in the background, a male talking in a deep, smooth voice. Ruth can't make out what he is saying.

The shop is hardly an embarrassment of riches. The shelves are sparsely stocked and everything looks a bit sun-faded and dusty but there is a little of most things and a smell of cooked food. Somewhere in here she'll find something she'll be able to eat immediately.

'Mornin'.'

The woman re-enters the shop, greeting her as if the exchange they'd had seconds before hadn't taken place. She moves behind the counter and takes a seat next to the cash register, becoming immediately engrossed with multiple chits of paper that are laid out in piles on the worn wooden surface.

Ruth watches as the woman picks each receipt off the wad in her hand, studies it closely, then adds it to the pile that sits beside her on the countertop. Then she takes a pen from behind her ear and marks something in an exercise book that lies open at her elbow.

'Let me know if you need help finding something. I won't stop or I'll lose where I am.'

'Thank you.'

Ruth unclasps the straps on her shoulders, unloading her bags by the door.

The noise prompts the woman to look up from her task. 'Did you pack the kitchen sink as well?'

Ruth smiles politely.

'Yell if you need me.' The woman returns to her work, carefully moving each receipt from one pile to another.

Ruth rubs her shoulders: they ache from the weight of the bag. Her arm aches a little where her weight must have been pressed as she slept on the ground.

A rack of newspapers catches her eye and she makes her way over to it. The front pages are plastered with the few images anyone has managed to get, the same ones she has seen repeatedly over the last three days: dark, grainy satellite images of, well, nothing, just flattened earth. Words jump out at her: 'Devastation', 'End of Days', 'Dead'.

It is too overwhelming to read another article full of conjecture about what has happened but she picks up one of the papers to look at the date on the top right-hand corner. Is it worth reading for any new information?

'Ah, sorry. Those are yesterday's. Not had a delivery today. I tried to call but the lines are a mess. I'm hopeful the van just got delayed, happens sometimes. It's normally when the weather's shocker that they're late, but today's sweet as, so who knows? Maybe you can come back this arvo, see if they've sorted themselves out.'

'I just wanted to see if there was any news. My phone's stopped working.'

'Oh, it's all doom and gloom. I'm half listening to the radio. They're saying we should all take cover, run for the hills. Seems a bit sus to me. Been through all this before. When I was a girl it was the Americans and the Cubans that had my parents petrified, and then in the eighties, the Americans and the Russians showing off to each other: "My weapon's bigger than your weapon." Men! Anyway, it's probably just a load of noise but if I am going to cark it, I'll bloody well do it in me own home, thank you very much!'

Ruth smiles, then makes her way to the produce.

There isn't any fresh bread but there is a pack of anaemic vacuum-packed rolls. She picks them up and grabs a bag of oranges, three cans of beans, a large bar of chocolate and a packet of pretzels, placing it all by the till. On the counter, there is a small heated glass box with two sad-looking pasties inside it: that must be the smell that is making her stomach scream in hunger.

'I'll take those too, please.' She points to the pasties. Then she swings round to the cold cabinet and picks up a large bottle of isotonic fizzy drink. She opens the lid and drinks a third of the bottle's fluorescent orange contents, burping immediately. 'Sorry, I've been walking all morning.'

The woman nods in terse forgiveness. She is concentrating on typing the cost of Ruth's shopping into the till with a fore-finger, carefully reading the price of each labelled item. Ruth is becoming increasingly aware that she not only needs to drink and eat, but also to empty her bladder, have a good wash and find somewhere to charge her phone. 'Do you have a bathroom I can use, by any chance?'

'Sorry, love, we don't have one fit for human use here. It's just a long drop out the back. Can't let the customers see that!' The woman laughs to herself. She types the final item into the till.

'That'll be eighteen dollars, ninety-one.'

Ruth opens the money-belt at her waist, peels off a twenty-dollar bill and hands it to the woman.

'Ta, I'm just kidding about the dunny, love – can see you're hopping. There's public facilities at the beach.' She lowers her spectacles to inspect the note then starts to type the number into the till. ''Fraid they can be a bit of a mess in the summer. That said, don't think there's many on the beach today – the

336

circus packed up and shipped out pretty sharpish when the news came in. Must be the first time a stranding like that hasn't got a load of punters in. Like a ghost town out there – no wildlife services, no do-gooders, no hippies. When I saw it, thought I'd get a few caravans rented at least, but only that photographer fella took one. Yeah, think that's all that's left at the beach now too, that fella and his camera. And the whale, of course, poor beast. So, if you've tramped all this way for a look, you're in luck.'

For a moment, it seems to Ruth that everything is still.

There is no sound.

No movement.

Just that word: whale.

'Whale?'

The woman is counting out Ruth's change, copper and silver coins, one by one onto the counter.

'Yeah, poor beast washed up Christmas Day. It's on its last legs, eh, so you'll have to gap it down there if you want to get a look. Not long for the old thing now. But, then, if you believe all this, we're all up the creek. So it's probably as good out the water as in it.'

Ruth is fumbling, dropping the food as she shoves it into the top of her rucksack. She feels as if her hands are made of cloth: she can't seem to use them properly.

She is shaking, energy coursing through her body like electricity.

She can hear the radio clearly now. The voice is recorded. It is a statement on repeat: 'The Prime Minister instructs all citizens to stay indoors and shelter in place. Store fresh water, if possible, and stay in an internal room with no windows. If you must be in a room with windows, it is recommended . . .'

Ruth is grappling with the straps of her rucksack.

She pulls the heavy bags onto her shoulders as if they had no weight at all. She clicks the buckle at her waist shut and charges for the door, the smaller bag still in her hands.

'Have a nice day!' She hears the woman cry, as she exits the shop.

The bell jangles as the door crashes shut behind her.

Forty-one

As the first rays of sun creep over the horizon, it lights the beach: the camp is unrecognisable, the pieces of their home reconfigured, awaiting their next function.

The hut, Ruth and Nik's home for so many years, is stripped of its layers. Nothing remains but a cage of bound bones. The tarpaulins lie in a pile next to the heavily loaded boat. They have been taken down and washed, then carefully mended and folded. The centre of the boat is piled high, its contents tied down with ropes, which have been replaited to repair any fraying.

A foul smell hangs in the air: they burnt the mouldy hides from the dismantled beds that have served them for so long.

Māia returns from washing in the creek, a threadbare towel wrapped around her head. She approaches her sister. Frankie is sitting on a skin to protect her recently cleaned clothes, sharpening her knives while she waits. 'Okay,' Māia says, 'you can do it now.' She pulls at the towel and her hair tumbles around her shoulders.

'Sure?'

'Yes. We made a deal.'

Frankie selects a knife from the collection on the skin and motions for Māia to sit. There is a slight hesitation, but then she follows the instruction. Frankie gathers her sister's hair together. Then, holding it with one fist, she slices through it with the knife. The gold-flecked strands fall to the ground in a heap.

'There,' says Frankie, 'that's the worst bit done. Now I'll cut it real short, like mine.'

With their heads shorn, the girls are less dissimilar, though their heights still differentiate them. They look more like sisters. It is practical too: their movement will be unimpeded and from now on, at sea, any fresh water they have will be used for drinking: Frankie isn't going to waste such a precious resource on something as trivial as washing.

As Frankie packs the last of the items they have selected to take with them, Māia studies the faded map. Now they are about to depart, she is questioning herself. They have planned carefully how far they will be able to travel on the boat each day. It will be possible to cover much more distance in it than they ever could by walking, and she has promised Frankie that they can make it to South Island in just a few days. She has charted a route that sticks to the coast, so they can go ashore if required, but she is worried that if their progress is too slow, Frankie will abandon the idea and make them come back.

It has taken Māia months to convince Frankie. But as the first signs of spring began to show she noticed that Frankie was thawing. She was listening for longer before cutting her off and more than once she caught her looking at the ratty old plastic-covered map of New Zealand that they had found among their pa's things. When Māia had asked her what she was doing with the map, Frankie bristled, saying she was just looking at it, as they both did at their father's broken camera, the phone and the few bits of jewellery that had belonged to their mother. But Māia could sense a change stirring in her sister.

Māia longs to see others. She still loves Frankie with a force that sometimes overwhelms her but there is a constant feeling that something is missing. Just as she knows when she is hungry she must eat, or when she needs to pee she must squat, she feels an urge to find other humans for a reason she cannot fully define. She knows she misses conversation that involves more than two, particularly as her sister can be so monosyllabic, but she also wonders how it would be to meet new people and, though she feels shy to admit it to Frankie, she would like to have adventures too, adventures like the princesses in the stories her mama used to tell them.

'Pull it real tight, Māia.'

They are covering what remains of Nik's truck, their store, with tarpaulin that they are pegging deep into the sand. Although Frankie has agreed to this exploratory trip, she wants to make sure their things are well preserved, should they return. Knowing that what they could carry with them on the boat was limited, she has spent the last week dividing and sorting their possessions, building a travel camp and kit for their voyage and packing what they will need to eat. Everything else, she has carefully stored. She has made every effort to ensure that what they are leaving behind is water- and dog-proof.

'Is it clear? Do you think?'

The two young women stand back and look at their handiwork. The final tarpaulin, now fixed tight over the covered store, is like a patchwork: on the surface they have sewn the outline of a huge whale, and within it, as if they are floating in the great expanse of its belly, are two figures of roughly the same size: their mother and father.

'I think it's clear. Might even be visible from above.'

'For the satellite?'

'*If* there's a satellite. Mama only said there *might* be one.'

'Yes, I know. Just like there only *might* be others.'

'Exactly.'

With that Frankie picks up the bag with the few things of her own that she is taking with them. Under all the mending, the bag is the one that Ruth brought to this beach more than two decades ago.

'Come on, then,' she says. 'We should get going if we're going to go.'

'I just want to say goodbye.'

'Be quick.'

Frankie turns and strides towards the boat.

Māia picks up the two jaw bones she had removed from the door-frame when they dismantled the hut and sets off at a jog towards the dunes.

It is still very early and the air is cool. It feels strange as the breeze slides over her newly shorn head.

She arrives at her parents' graves. They have a covering of reeds now, but Māia could find them with her eyes closed, such is the frequency of her visits.

She can see her parents, laughing, their faces illuminated by the fire. Her face lights with a smile now too, a smile that echoes both of theirs.

Carefully she places one bone on either side of the two mounds, like brackets, containing them.

She steps back.

From here she can read the words she has carved into the grubby bones; the letters shine bright white where they are engraved. Her parents' names.

Now if anyone comes they will know they are here.

'We're going, Mama. Going to find others.'

'Come the fuck on, Māia!'

Frankie's voice reaches her over the sound of the rustling grasses.

Gently she places her hands on the sand, closing her eyes.

Then she is on her feet, running towards the sea at a pace. 'Give me a break! I'm running, aren't I?' she yells to her sister, as she races across the dunes towards her, weaving swiftly through the reeds.

Frankie has pulled the boat to the very edge of the surf, her bare legs in the water.

Māia joins her in seconds.

Silently they launch it, just as they have done hundreds of times before to fish. This time, once the boat is in the water, they don't head out to sea but turn it with the oars, then raise the sail, a new one, a big one they have fashioned to catch the wind and move the boat faster. After several failed attempts, this design is effective: the wind catches it almost immediately and they are swiftly moved in the direction they want to go, south, in line with the land.

The sand draws backwards and forwards as the waves lap the shore.

As the water stretches out into the bay it holds a slight vibration.

It is not audible from where the two women sit on the surface, steering their boat. But if they were to cease rowing and jump into the waves, just as their mother did so many times before them, if then they should submerge their heads beneath the soft foam and let themselves float in that turquoise brine and close their eyes, then, listening beyond the wash of the stones against the ocean floor, they would hear three whales: a mother and her two calves, singing.

Thank You

Claire Wilson, my agent. Whether it was serendipity, reading between the lines or simply my reading too fast; whatever it was that forged our alliance, I am very grateful. Also, to all at RCW, particularly Miriam Tobin and Safae El-Ouahabi.

Melissa Cox, my editor. Every suggested edit, tweak, design idea has aligned perfectly with my vision for this book. I am so very lucky to be the recipient of your creative, thoughtful editorial talent. To the team at Coronet. Particularly, Lily Cooper for guiding me through the early publishing journey with a smile, even during a global pandemic. Vero Norton, Helen Flood and Alice Morley who started championing this book even before the ink on the first proof was dry. Morgan Springett. Hazel Orme for her carefully considered copy edits and Alasdair Oliver, for the stunning cover design.

The team at 28 Plays Later, particularly Sebastian Rex, its founder. It was in my response to the prompt for Day 9 of the playwriting challenge in 2018 that the seed of this novel germinated. Benedict Hudson and Suzanne Goldberg, my writing mates/accountability partners during that month's challenge.

David Warwick, Anna Templeton and Lesley Ferris, for vouching that I was a suitable candidate for a creative writing MA. Although life took a turn that meant I didn't take it up, the offer of a place on the course gave me the confidence to write the rest of this novel. I wouldn't have written this book without your kind references.

Mono in Camberwell. Your one shot flat whites and pear and chocolate cake fuelled the first draft of this book.

Nicola Barr, for your suggestions in India and the drink and generous advice at the Sun of Camberwell a year later. There was definitely something in the green juice!

Of course the biggest thanks go to those that I ought to tell I love more regularly;

James Ronan, for listening to me wang on about this idea for ages before gently suggesting that talking wasn't enough and I ought to get on with writing it down.

Jessica Preston, my first early reader. Your consistent championing, friendship and support are a treasure and entirely disprove the theory you don't make any more true friends once you're over thirty.

Claire Dewar, Alison Wren and Joanna Elphick, my oldest and bestest friends. For hours of laughing until we ache, for the many times I've cried on the shoulders of each of you and the innumerable adventures and glasses of wine that have gifted me a vault of epic stories; most of which remain untold and some that are more unbelievable than avoiding the apocalypse inside a whale.

My family: Zoe Sawyer, Gregory Sawyer and Alexia Sawyer for informing my writing about sibling relationships, your careful reading and feedback on the text and being such good friends to me, and Ruby. Thanks also to the more recent additions to our gang: Jack O'Carroll and Simon Boase. Thanks to my Nana, Dolly Gordon Shaw – hopefully not long before you can see it in the bookshop in Bury St Edmunds now! – and though he won't get to see this, my grandad, Frank Shaw; the original story-tellers. It's definitely in the genes. My dad, Graham Sawyer, for walking the baby round and round the village in that rickety old buggy whilst I wrote, for reading a book that didn't have a single detective but did have multiple sex scenes written by your daughter (sorry!) and for your unreserved support.

My mum, Valerie Sawyer, who taught me to love words, and continues to help me learn how best to use them. For the mornings looking after the baby whilst I wrote, and the late nights spent casting a careful eye over my work. For understanding the story I was trying to tell, without judgement. For your guidance, your support, your love and the million other things you do for us all. Thank you. Without you this book simply wouldn't exist.

And finally, my daughter, Ruby. I said at the beginning that this book was for you, so it seems apt that the last words in it should repeat that sentiment.

The Stranding
Reading Group Questions

1) Now that you have read *The Stranding*, go back and re-visit the Prologue. How do you think the author used this to pull readers in and set their expectations?

2) When we first meet Ruth in the Before she is beginning a relationship with a married father of two – why do you think Ruth is making these choices at this point in her life?

3) Whales and the images of whales are scattered throughout the book – why do you think Ruth feels such a connection with these creatures and what do you think they symbolise for the reader?

4) The book depicts many relationships between friends and between families. Which of these did you find to be most interesting?

5) The characters discuss what they miss most from the Before – what would you miss most in their situation?

6) What do you think went on elsewhere in the world while Ruth and Nik were re-building? Did you think there were other survivors?

7) What do you think happens to Māia and Frankie when they depart on their boat?

8) The author deliberately keeps the 'end of the world' event ambiguous to reflect Ruth's head-in-the-sand attitude to the news and everything going on around her – could you understand this and find it relatable, or would you want to know everything you could?

9) The book takes place in London, the south-east of England and New Zealand – all distinct landscapes. If you have been to any of these places, did you feel any sense of recognition, and if not, did it make you want to visit them?

10) What do you think would be the biggest challenges for survival in a situation like the one Ruth and Nik end up in?

11) Do you think that Ruth and Nik's relationship would have happened if they had met under different circumstances? How much do you think Ruth finding herself on the beach with Nik and the whale had to do with the choices she made, or do you think it was always meant to be? How much of what happens to Ruth is fate vs. circumstance?

12) What do you think the insides of a dead whale smell like, and would you be able to stand it if it meant surviving?

Kate Sawyer
Author Q&A

1) *The Stranding* is your debut novel. Where did the idea come from, and was it the first idea for a book you had ever had?

The seed of the idea from which *The Stranding* grew actually came from a playwriting challenge. A few times now I have participated in The Literary Challenge's '28 Plays Later', a challenge to write twenty-eight plays, one each day for the twenty-eight days of February. Each day you get a prompt and then you have 24 hours to write a play. The prompt that inspired this novel was 'Blue Whale'. I immediately had the idea of a family living inside the bones of a dead whale post-apocalypse and wrote a short play with Ruth, Nik and their two daughters. For the next year the characters kept playing on my mind, I found myself questioning how they found themselves there, what had happened, who they were, and then around two years after I'd written that first scene, I sat down and wrote Ruth's story.

I have had ideas for stories that I thought might work as novels before, but I never got any further than writing a scene or a short outline of a story. Who knows, those ideas that continue to pop up in my thoughts may still find themselves as a novel one day!

2) **How long did it take you to write the book and did you find the structure of going backwards and forwards in time confusing?**

I wrote the first draft of *The Stranding* in eight and a half months. At the drafting stage I didn't find writing out of sequence confusing at all – in fact, it helped me not to get bogged down, to find moments that reflected each other and to work out who Ruth was in different situations. During editing it became a little more confusing! Moving scenes or rewriting things when you have dual timelines to consider can be a bit like unpicking a mistake in a tapestry – pull the wrong thread and it could be a disaster! I enjoyed it though, it was a big puzzle I had to solve. As part of the final edit I took it apart, checked it chronologically and then put it all back together again. It was very satisfying.

3) **The central theme of the book seems to be about connectedness rather than a typically dystopian survival story – why did you choose to explore your character and her relationship with the world through a post-apocalyptic lens?**

As I say, the initial idea was of a family living on a beach post-apocalypse – and who knows how the subconscious joins the dots to bring about those flashes of inspiration. However, to write a book as I did, moving back and forth between pre- and post-apocalypse was a very conscious decision. I knew there were certain things I wanted to write about the way we are living now; I wanted to write about the privileges, the joys and the struggles of daily life for a sort of 'everywoman' character, and it occurred to me that an apocalypse was the most stark device to allow for contrast and comparison. It seems to be an unfortunate aspect of the human condition that, to quote Joni Mitchell, you don't know what you've got till it's gone, and complete annihilation of the world as we know it seemed like a dramatic opportunity to explore that, both for the character of Ruth and, I hope, for readers to reflect on their own situations. As a writer it was an exciting opportunity for a leap of imagination too, an opportunity to explore the questions I was posing. What would I miss? What would I need? What could I do without? What is absolutely essential, not just for survival, but for living a happy, fulfilled life? For me, I realised that a lot of the answers to those questions were to do with people and relationships and so that is why they sit at the centre of the story, alongside the nuts and bolts of survival.

4) Why did you choose to set half of the book in New Zealand and what kind of research did you do to bring authenticity to your depiction?

It came from that initial idea of a family living inside the bones of a dead whale. When it came to me, I immediately searched where you might be able to see a blue whale; there are actually quite a lot of places depending on the time of year, due to whales' migration patterns – however, New Zealand just felt right. As I got further into writing the novel, I realised locating half of the story in New Zealand was very useful in more ways than I had originally considered. The distance from the UK meant that post-disaster, Ruth had little possibility of making contact or travelling home, it was helpful too that the landscape and weather systems of that part of New Zealand are relatively habitable and that there is an abundance of flora and fauna. It was also fun for me as a writer that, though they spoke the same language, Ruth and Nik were from places on different sides of the world; it gave opportunities for both friction and accord between them, but also gave scope to the stories and the culture that they decide to bring into their changed world and pass on to their children.

As the story in New Zealand is set primarily on the same few square metres of beach in a post-apocalyptic landscape, even if I had been able to visit the west coast of the North Island on a research trip, I'm not sure it would have been massively inform-ative to the particular story I was telling. I did, however, chart the walk Ruth does from the bus to the beach pre-apocalypse and 'walked' it on Google Street View! I changed it so that it wasn't set in a specific place, but it was good to know I was describing the right landscape and buildings of the area. I did a lot of research on foraging, plants, weather and wildlife in the area too. The most important research, though, was to help inform my writing of Nik. I lived with New Zealanders in both Australia and London all through my twenties and so I had a good idea about little cultural and language differences, but I found watching some of the brilliant film and television that has come out of New Zealand over the last twenty years very help-ful. I also read a lot about Māori culture and mythology and watched a lot of great videos about Te Reo Māori; as it's a spoken language it was so useful to hear it used rather than just read it.

5) What has been the thing that has surprised you most about being published and readers discovering your book?

Almost everything about being published has surprised me, but the thing that has been the hardest to get my head around is that people are actually reading the book! Although it is an unmitigated delight to see *The Stranding* on the shelves of bookshops and to meet the brilliant booksellers who are pressing it into readers' hands, I have still found it hard to truly believe that people are at home, at the beach or on the daily commute opening the pages, reading the words that I wrote! So when I've met readers at events or they've contacted me by email or social media, it's been a surprise and delight to find that they think of these characters I created as real people. They care about them and want to know what is next for them and even say things like: 'Oh no, Fran would never do that!'. It's truly wonderful!

6) What is your favourite moment in the book? And was it your favourite to write?

Any of the family moments, both in the Before when Ruth is with her parents and in the After with Nik and Frankie and Māia. I love writing the dialogue between family members and in this, particularly, the sibling relationship between Frankie and Māia. If I were to pick one scene between them, it would probably be when they are by the fire and they hear Ruth snoring in the tent – a little moment of joy and silliness that they share.

In general, it's fun to write the friction and sniping and in-jokes between friends, siblings, lovers and family members. It's so interesting to me that real dislike often manifests as politeness or disinterest. There's something beautiful about layers of discord only being able to sit on a solid foundation of love.

7) **You read the audiobook edition (Kate is an experienced actress) which is very unusual for a fiction writer – did you discover anything about the book when you went to record it?**

Well, my first discovery is that reading audiobooks is very hard! Haha! No, it was actually a very enjoyable experience. But, unlike stage performance, reading an audiobook is a very intimate and technical thing. You have to imagine that the microphone is the listener's ear and that you are telling them the story clearly and calmly. Prose is much harder to read than dialogue; written sentences tend to be longer and so you need more breath and when your voice is being recorded you suddenly become much more aware of the little speech impediments that make your voice individual, and you have to quickly make your peace with them!

It was a real privilege to record the audiobook so close to publication. It gave me the opportunity to revisit the text really closely, it was great preparation for events, but, I admit, I also found myself moved at times. There was an embarrassing moment when my producer had to come into the recording booth to bring me a box of tissues and give me a hug! I think it was the combination of being swept up in the story, but also the realisation that I'd soon be sharing it with the world. I always find that happy, hopeful things make me cry more than truly sad things!

8) Which things would you miss most in Ruth and Nik's situation?

People. There's no two ways about it: the thing I would miss the most would be my family and my friends. But, having thought about this a lot over the last few years, I've realised that aside from missing my loved ones, much of what I miss could be divided into three categories:

- Basics

    Safe water, food, central heating, a good mattress, soap, medications, clean clothes: the everyday things that we all take for granted.

- Art

    Books, film and television particularly – I just love stories.

- Frivolities

    I'm not sure what this says about me, but I've identified that there are quite a few things that really aren't fundamental to survival or emotional wellbeing that I would miss terribly. Croissants, avocadoes, glitter, a nice massage, great coffee, balloons, lipstick. Silly things that really don't matter, but that bring texture and moments of joy and pleasure into our lives.

9) Can you tell us about what you are writing next?

Yes! My second novel is on its way. It's about a family and their relationships. It's set over the course of one day, but also the past forty years and it is told from ten different perspectives. At first glance, it is quite different from *The Stranding*: there is no obvious world-changing event and not a single whale. But I think readers will find there are threads that connect the two books in themes of relationships, responsibility and perspective on our own actions and those of others. At its heart it is the exploration of how relationships can be complicated and how we can love one another, even if we don't always agree.

THIS FAMILY

THE NEW NOVEL BY KATE SAWYER

COMING SUMMER 2023